RIDERS BY NIGHT AND GUNFIGHT AT THE O.K. CORRAL

A WESTERN DOUBLE

NELSON C. NYE

WOLFPACK
PUBLISHING

Riders By Night and Gunfight at the O.K. Corral: A Western Double
Paperback Edition
© Copyright 2022 (As Revised) Nelson C. Nye

Wolfpack Publishing
5130 S. Fort Apache Rd. 215-380
Las Vegas, NV 89148

wolfpackpublishing.com

eBook ISBN 978-1-63977-948-2
Paperback ISBN 978-1-63977-949-9

RIDERS BY NIGHT AND
GUNFIGHT AT THE O.K. CORRAL

RIDERS BY NIGHT

ONE
ITCH FOR A WOMAN

KURT CARDIGAN, big and riled and intolerant of obstacles, shifted his weight from one boot to the other and wished the goddam stage would get a rattle on. He had wasted two hours in this furnace already and not a dust on the whole damned horizon! Nothing but desert, sky and mountains seen through a shimmering film of heat that curled and crawled off the rough plank walks and broiled above the hoof-tracked street in the blistering glare of the noonday sun.

Tucson!

You could have it!

He was a yellow-haired man in trail grimed clothing with a spatter of dust streaked across granite features. A steel-gray glance that was like chilled lightning snapped from under his sun-bleached brows and considered the view with no leavening of charity. His long solid lips pinched in at the corners and impatience lifted his burly shoulders and swung him about in the stage office doorway. Irritation danced from each clank of his spurs and the high-heeled boots took him back to the counter.

"Butterfield'll have to do better than this or the Goverment'll take the damned mails away from him!"

The agent looked up with tired apology. He brushed damp hair back away from his forehead with fingers that left a smudge of ink in their wake.

"We're not often this late—"

"By God, you're plenty late now!"

"That's a pretty rough stretch between here and El Paso—lot of up-an'-down country around Dragoon Springs. ... A terrible lot of them Indians—"

"He knew all that when he bid in the contract!"

The agent's cheeks flushed but his eyes fell away from the big man's look and he picked up his pen with a shrug of the shoulders. "I'd hurry it for you if I could, Mister Cardigan."

Cardigan's answer to that was a snort.

He wheeled, turned away, clanking back to the door and again, with his legs firmly planted under him, sent his testy stare over the empty miles that spread, dun and tawny, to the faraway pass that cut through the mountains. That way the stage must come if it *did* come. If it didn't come soon, he'd go out there and hunt it—or would he?

He didn't know, by God, whether he would or not! There were times when he thought it couldn't get here quick enough; there were others when he'd get to mullin round in his mind and call himself forty kinds of a fool and wish he could send that damn woman back.

He didn't know, by grab, whether he wanted her or not!

He reckoned a man didn't know his luck when he had it.

Take himself, Kurt Cardigan, a man used to

baching it— everything going along fine as silk till he'd got that goddam itching for a woman. He could easy of got him any number of squaws but he just couldn't stomach the stink and the grease of them. He wasn't no durned Mexican! What he wanted was a white woman —and none of your goddam floozies, either!

It was the sight of that nester Rickven's daughter that had got it all started and choused him up this way. He'd been doing all right till he had run into *her*.

He'd been passing their shack a mite early one morning— the old man was away, gone to town or some- thing. He'd been following the creek, it being shorter that way, and had come onto her without a rag on her. She'd been poised on that ledge at the pool by the waterfall. The noisy rush of the water, the pine needles or something ... he guessed his horse hadn't made much sound. He had sat there, struck dumb, scared to open his mouth even. Plump, she was, and redheaded, with the skin of her body looking white as fresh milk.

When he'd finally woke up, he had got the hell out of there.

But he hadn't forgot her. Nor the look of her body with her hands trying to cover it. Nor the man-fear staring at him out of her eyes.

You'd kind of think the thought of her having that body... Well, it wasn't anything that should of made a man hate her—but it made Cardigan hate her. It had filled his head with an unreasoning anger and still could do it every time he thought of her. While he'd been riding and sweating and risking everything, he ever had hoped for in the choking dust and heat of this hellhole luckier guys had got them women like that—double-breasted doo-dads with creamy smooth bodies that washed themselves and smelled sweet and purty.

Every time he thought of it, it made him curse. He'd been ripe for trouble—for almost any fool thing, when that daffy Jupe Krailor had shown him the paper with the Heart and Hand column, he had got off the Tombstone stage.

Cardigan hadn't hardly dared believe his own eyes. All them women wanting to come out here? Why the hell would a stall-fed Eastern filly—with every last thing you'd expect 'em to howl for—want to come out into this godforsaken country? It didn't make sense—but they did. There'd been three of 'em in that column alone fairly frothin at the mouth to get themselves out here! Seemed like all they wanted was a man to take care of them. Some of them even offered to send on their tintypes and two of them had claimed to have "character references"—like as if he cared about their goddam characters!

He'd come near to tearing that damned paper up, he'd been that disgusted to come on it so late. A St. Louis paper nearly six weeks old! Any fool could have told you any woman in her senses wouldn't of passed up her chances for six whole weeks—not without, by grab, there was something ailin her!

But the thought of those women wouldn't let him alone. Three of 'em eating their hearts out to get here and him, Kurt Cardigan, feeling so horny he was just about ready to climb on a squaw!

He'd waited till the rest had rolled up for the night, till he couldn't hear another dang thing but their snoring; then he'd crept from his blankets and hunted that paper. Had found it, too, and had tucked it away where he'd have it handy to study it over when he got off alone.

He could still remember how his hands had shook smoothing out that paper when he'd found the right page again. It was just like he'd been in a shakin fever, and he'd thought he'd never hold it still enough to read it. One of them women didn't want to leave town. Three or four wanted local sports, gents with property, fellers with a business. A couple of more which had wanted to come West didn't sound like nothing he would want no truck with.

But the other one— Damn! He could still quote her words, every dadburned one of them:

REFINED YOUNG LADY, vivacious, 23, despising cold toast, coo-coo clocks, and close relatives, desires correspondence with brown-eyed rancher, preferably one living west of the Pecos. Object, matrimony. Address: Miss Docie Balinett, 5486 Rimboldt Street, St. Louis, Mo.

* * *

DOCIE.

Docie Balinett! Just like docie-do in a brush-popper's hoe-down. Docie. ... By God, it even *sounded* like class!

He had given himself all the arguments, but he'd known all the time he was going to write—and why not? Sure, some guy had likely landed her already, but it didn't cost no fortune for a man to find out, and what gent ever really and truly hit his stride till he got hitched up to a female woman? Hell's hinges! This here was a damn tough country, and it took a pretty salty feller to lick it. There'd been times he'd been so hungry his belly had thought his throat had been cut, but he'd have the laugh on these bastards yet. He'd come into this country to make his mark and, by God, he'd sure as hell make it!

That was the Irish in him; the Cardigan heritage, the red blood of his forebears than ran hotly through him, as ready to welcome a fight as a frolic. Pride—that was it! Well, he knew what pride was. Pride was something his kind had to have. Deep inside him, a man might not care for all the things he did—might be downright sorry for some of them, but he'd keep it inside him. There was no good looking back and no good in excuses; excuses was for guys that couldn't tough a thing out. Well, they'd get no excuses from Cardigan. When he shoved his chips out, they were out there to stay.

And there was no damn pride in drifting. You had to make a stand someplace. It was all in finding out what you could do, where your natural bent lay, and in sinking your roots down. That was another good reason for having a woman; it gave a man something to tie to.

Well, he'd tried about everything the West had to offer from chasing cows' tails to mule skinning. He had driven a stage. He had been a freighter. He'd gone down in the ground like a goddam worm but what had it got him? He'd thought to cut the mustard that time he'd tried ranching ... on the level, that is; but you could have it, and the drought and the maverickers and the whoopin redskins—you could have the whole push, and welcome.

There was easier ways than playing nursemaid to a bunch of dumb horn-clacking crazy damn cattle. You might as well prospect to be a real sucker. Work your damn tail off for some rich banker. No banker owned *him.—not* Kurt Cardigan, damn their eyes! When Cardigan opened his mouth men listened. They didn't give him no back talk. Kurt Cardigan had things; he had a damn nice spread tucked away in the mountains and cattle and horses in uncounted numbers. And he had, moreover, a way with a pistol that men considered before they opened their jaws to do any yappin.

He slapped the big pistol that swung at his hip and twisted his head and threw a wink at the agent: "I'm goin' to drift over yonder an' feed my face. If that stage gets in ... if somebody comes here askin' for me just remember you never heard tell of me—savvy?"

* * *

THAT WAS how he figured to take care of Docie.

Without she was a heap bigger fool than he thought, she damn sure wouldn't be expecting no different. She was probably all right. She hadn't made no offer to pass on her tintype which he figured she would if she had been at all worried.

She'd be a looker all right. He didn't doubt that. Five foot seven she had said in her letter. That would be about right-make her have to look up to him. It gave her plenty of frame to hang her meat on; he reckoned she'd be built like a tin-roofed smokehouse. That's what he wanted, a good, rugged woman. A man couldn't spend all his time in a bed. By God, in this country, you had to be practical.

He guessed she could handle the yard chores all right. Once he'd shown her how she could probably string fence. He kind of smiled a little thinking what a help she'd be around there. He'd let her spade up that patch northeast of the house... She'd probably want to put in a truck garden for them; a woman, he reckoned, might get tired of boiled beans. He could damn well do with a little change himself.

Yep! A woman had her place, no getting around it; a man didn't rightly do no living till he had himself a woman around. He expected she could cook like nobody's business and just the thought of that bare white skin she'd have under her bustle was enough to get a guy hot all over.

He sucked in his breath with an impatient curse and glared out over the sunbaked miles like he'd fetch that stage by sheer force of willpower. If she stacked up right and took to the country, he would tog her out like a million dollars. He'd get her a rig with big red wheels and drive her down the main drag of Tucson and give all them bastards something to goggle at. "By cripes," they'd say, "there goes Kurt Cardigan! I kin remember that bird when he didn't hev a pot—an' lookit the lucky bastard now!"

By God, he'd make their eyes bug out.

Maybe he had ought to get slicked up a little. Maybe he ought to buy him a new shirt or something. He threw a considering look at the Mercantile and laughed a little and kept on up the street toward the hash house. Time enough for that when he'd filled his belly. Hell, maybe she wouldn't be on this stage, maybe she wouldn't get in till tomorrow. Time enough to doll up after he'd looked her over.

It wasn't that he really doubted she'd suit him. But this country had long since taught him it was smarter to play your cards close to your chest than to wish you had later when you didn't have no choice. He had done his part: he had sent her the money to get herself out here. If she didn't fill the bill, she had nothing on him. She wouldn't know Cardigan from Adam's off ox.

This was what had finally decided him to write her. It didn't cost such a pile to get her out here and if she measured up, he'd have something well worth it. And if she didn't measure up, he could damn well saddle up his horse and hit out of here. He hadn't promised her nothing. He'd said straight out he'd have to look at her first, that he wasn't buying nothing—hogs or women —unseen.

But he'd told her he would pay the price of getting her out here—it was worth that much to get an armful of woman. Women was goddam scarce in this desert.

* * *

HE WENT into the hash house and ordered his meal. He slanched a cursory glance at the other two -eaters and promptly dismissed them as of no consequence. The farthest was a Mexican teamster slumped over his chili at the counter's other end. The other was a skinny dried-up old wart you didn't have to see but once to know was a desert rat.

A drummer came in with a fat cigar and flopped himself down on the stool next to Cardigan. He got out a white handkerchief and mopped his face. "Don't it ever cool off in this goddam country?"

The stove-up range cook that ran the place came up with Cardigan's grub and said sourly, "Them as don't like it ain't obliged t' stick around."

The drummer grunted. Then he gave him his order and mopped his face again. As he was putting the handkerchief back in his pocket he looked over at Cardigan and abruptly said heartily, "How they goin,' pal? Been a long time since I seen you last..."

Cardigan eyed him and reached for the butter. "Reckon you got me mixed up with somebody else."

"Oh, no—not me," the drummer said, grinning. "I never forget a face. You're a horse trader, pal. Lemme see ... it was over around—"

"You never seen me before in your life," Cardigan said, and the drummer stopped chewing and stared at him, startled. He stared like that for five or six seconds and then he took off his hat and peered inside it and ran pudgy fingers around the moist band. He looked at Cardigan again and then hastily away and covered his balding head with the derby and scratched three matches trying to kindle a cigar that was already lighted.

Cardigan ignored him and put away his plateful with a noisy relish. He got a second cup of coffee and another slab of pie.

The drummer didn't look to have much appetite. He got up pretty soon and took himself off. The prospector finished and shambled out also and the Mexican presently wiped a sleeve across his mouth and went over to the door where he dug out the makings and rolled himself a smoke.

Another man came in. He had a star on his shirt-front. He looked disinterestedly at Cardigan and took the stool recently warmed by the drummer. The cook came up wiping his hands on his apron.

"What'll it be this noon, Frank?"

By the cook's few words, and by that star he was sporting, Cardigan knew this man for the town's new marshal, Frank Esparza. He had never before met Esparza face to face and he eyed him covertly, thinking about him. He was a tired looking gent with a wrinkled face who told the cook he'd take the same as usual. This man had the rep, Kurt knew, of being honest and he had a known reluctance toward resorting to gunplay which had brought him the support of the town's big moguls who were against gunplay on general principles. Studying him now Cardigan dismissed most of the rumors he had heard. This fellow wasn't the kind to be afraid or bluffed either.

Cardigan paid for his meal and got up and went out.

In the shade of the building, the Mex teamster sat snoring.

Cardigan stepped into the smash of the sun and scowlingly observed the stage hadn't come in yet. Then his glance, traveling farther, went still, bright, and narrow.

A man by the hitchrack was eyeing his horse.

The cigar-smoking drummer. The dude in the derby.

TWO

COMPLICATIONS

WHEN HE SAW that dude looking over his horse Cardigan knew straight off, he had made a mistake. His fine run of luck had gone and rung in a joker, and it made no difference that he didn't want trouble. Trouble was out there piling up fast, curling up with the heat off that limonite dust. It was in the sly eyes of that meddlesome drummer squinting this way and that as he sized up the points of Cardigan's dun.

That drummer was a kid with a match around powder.

If that feller had known him, he'd of had better sense. But the guy was a dude, a damned puking tenderfoot who hadn't no knowledge of the customs of the country. A man who had known him would have thought a long while before poking his nose into Cardigan's business.

Cardigan knew he had better do something before that damned marshal put his face out the door. With that dude, anything would be likely to happen. It was a cinch the guy's jaw would start swinging in a minute. He wouldn't have to say much...

If it had been any horse but old Snuffy, Cardigan reckoned he'd been tempted to walk off and leave him. Not that that would solve anything in the long run, but it might stave trouble off a little bit longer, long enough anyway to let him get clear of town.

Cardigan scowled, shook his head. This was one of those things you couldn't walk off from. There'd be plenty to remember he had ridden that horse.

Damn the dude anyway!

Two men were talking on the porch of a saloon that was twenty-five feet from the drummer's placement. A third gent was standing in the stage office doorway where a short time before the whole street had been empty; and worse—a lot worse—Frank Esparza was sitting dead in line with a window.

At the first sign of trouble, he would jump for the door. That was what he got paid for.

"Damn!" Cardigan growled. He'd have to play this thing careful.

There was just one chance and, abruptly, he took it. He moved forward through the dust, feeling the burn of it through his boot soles and feeling the burn of his anger, too.

He stopped by the man who stood eyeing the dun.

The drummer heard him. You could tell by the jump and swell of his shoulders, by the way, he half turned with his guts all up where his swallower should have been.

"You're a-leavin' all right, but not on that horse, pard."

The words were pitched low but there was a throttled fierceness in Cardigan's voice that blanched the red look of the man's sunburned features. He opened his mouth, but no sound came out. Cardigan saw the scared eyes jerk a look at his pistol and he laughed, short and harsh.

"Some guys," he drawled, "don't know when they're well off. Start shiftin' along towards that stable, mister."

The drummer's face glistened. "You got me wrong—"

"I got you all right. You got that part straight."

The drummer's parched tongue scraped across his dry lips. Then he stiffened, went still, glaring back at Cardigan, outrage tautening the coat about his shoulders.

"You look kinda young to cash in," murmured Cardigan.

A hot wind flew off the roadway, bringing its smell of scorched dust and fluttering the scarf ends at Cardigan's throat.

"You—you wouldn't dare..." the man muttered, and again that short laugh came out of Cardigan.

"Git movin,' mister."

The sound of the hash house's screen door banging made a sharp report in the street's hot quiet, and Cardigan said with a plainer impatience: "Git goin'...git goin,'" and started forward.

The drummer fell back. He flung a trapped look out over the roadway, but Cardigan's own look never wavered. It stayed hard on the drummer, and he put out a hand and touched him lightly, and the man whirled away from that touch with a snarl.

Their steps sounded loud on the rough board planking and Cardigan's neck felt cold where the whipped—up wind flung grit across it. But he did not look around.

They came to the stable yard. The man, with a half-defiant glance, turned around.

"Right on into the stable," directed Cardigan, and a sullen growl came out of the drummer. "Stableman's a friend of mine," Cardigan said. "If I was you, I'd keep my trap shut."

The drummer kept going but there was nothing reassuring in the set of his shoulders.

Cardigan's lips tightened. Deep in the marrow of his bones, he didn't like this. If ever a damn fool was perched on a powder keg that guy was Cardigan and Cardigan knew it.

There was just a bare chance his lie about the stableman would keep the dude's mouth shut. Cardigan had no friends and was well aware of it. Friendship was built on respect and affection and the working arrangements he'd flung up in this country had little in common with such sterling virtues.

Which was plenty all right so long as things ran smooth. But he had a black hunch all the smoothness was over, that the smoothness had ended when this bird in the derby had planked down his fanny on that stool in Jelks' hash house.

Who'd have thought a damn dude with a couple dumb questions could be threatening to wreck in a handful of moments what had taken long years of mighty close figuring to bring to the point where...

A red fog of anger surged over Kurt Cardigan when he heard voices sound rumbling out from behind where a pile of stacked barrels cut off all view of the stalls in the rear.

It was cool in here after the glare outside, but Cardigan never noticed. A wicked impulse leaped through him and sent a hand to his gun butt, and he stood that way, rocked and quivering and glaring, while he fought to put down the wild roar of his blood.

Gunplay wouldn't buy him nothing but trouble. Killing this dude would take a heap of explaining and there was a damn good chance his tongue wouldn't be up to it.

With a bitter reluctance, he took his hand from the pistol. Anger still rowelled him. He took the dude by the throat. "Listen," he grated. "I've took off you about all that I aim to. Just keep that damn mouth shut. You're gettin' out of this country—just be thankful an' *git* out 'cause there's other ways of goin' than on the back of a horse!"

He didn't half know his own strength it looked like. Alls he'd done had been to shake the guy a little, yet when he let him go the dude's knees wabbled and he staggered in a circle like a chicken with its head off, finally bringing up gasping against a stack of sacked feed.

Cardigan gave him about ten seconds then he hauled him up and scooped up the derby and clapped it on his head. "If you open your face, it will be the last time."

He gave the guy a shove toward the squabble of voices.

The livery keeper and another old codger were insulting each other over a game of seven up.

"Ed," Cardigan said, "this gent wants a horse. He's in a hell of a hurry. Had bad news—he's got to get outa here. Mebbe you better let him have that dun."

The stableman laid his cards down carefully. He looked at the dude and rasped his jaw. "Where's he got t' go?"

Cardigan scowled. "El Paso," he said. "Can you shake it up a little?"

"We-ell, I tell you, Kurt. I ain't got that dun. I sold-"

"You got that apron-faced roan?"

"Yeah, I got that roan, but he's lamed up a little—"

"What about that buttermilk filly?"

"He could hev her, I guess. But she'll come a little high. You recollect I—"

Sweat crept out across Cardigan's cheekbones. "How much?" he said blackly.

"Well, that filly ort t' bring about eighty-five dollars."

"He'll pay it. You'll have to throw in some gear."

"That'll be extry—another twenty-five dollars. I can't rightly spare—"

"Where's she at?"

"I'll fetch her." The stableman picked up a rope. "I got her outside... she might be jest a little bit high—kin this feller ride?"

The possibility that he couldn't hadn't occurred to Cardigan. He scowled and said, "Sure. Shake it up. Which saddle?"

"Expect he'll hev to take that McClellan."

Cardigan got it and picked up a bridle, motioned the drummer ahead of him. The man's look turned ugly. So did Cardigan's. The dude got to moving.

They watched the old man put his rope on the filly. With her taffy-colored hide and white mane and tail she looked so set up Cardigan came near to wishing he hadn't never sold her. Another thought came and he knew he'd been right. These flashy-colored hides were too easy to remember.

He sleeved the sweat off his cheeks and gave the old man the saddle, adjusting the bridle while the stableman cinched up.

"That'll be a hundred an' ten," the stableman said, and Cardigan looked at the drummer.

The dude put a hand inside his coat and the bones shaping Cardigan's face showed plainer; but the dude brought his hand out carefully, empty.

"Must've left my wallet at the hotel," he mumbled, and Cardigan nodded.

He pulled out a roll and peeled off the money.

"The hoss-breedin' business must be doin' all right," grinned the stableman jocularly, winking at the drummer. But the dude didn't smile. The old man sighed. "Some of yore folks sick or somethin'?"

The dude looked at Cardigan and didn't say anything.

"Well, you wanta watch out," the stableman said. "Keep yore eyes wide open goin' through that pass. Them redskins is riled. Ain't a one been in town here for more'n two weeks— they been brewin' up somethin,' you kin bet on that."

Some thought palely twisted the drummer's features.

Cardigan snorted.

He bent over the makings and shaped up a smoke. When he tongued the paper, his teeth threw a shine against the tan of bronzed features. "He'll git by all right —I'll see to that."

He cursed under his breath when the stableman's

eyes touched him, curious, considering. "Goin' through with him, eh?"

The drummer looked like he would lose his dinner.

The stableman said in a tone tinged with envy, "Sure wisht I could sell some stuff to the Cavalry. I'd make 'em come after 'em—you wouldn't ketch me pushin' no stock through that pass. Not with the way them Injuns been actin'."

Cardigan said, "I ain't pushin' no stock. I'm goin' to hunt for that stage."

"What good'll that do? Ain't nothin' but redskins—"

"My God!" the dude cried. "Are you kiddin'?"

The stableman looked at him. "A man don't kid about Injuns, son."

Conflicting emotions were tugging at Cardigan. The whereabouts of that woman, the need he felt of finding her were companion worries that, combined with inclination, were pulling him one way while the even greater need concerned with this dude was ever more strongly urging him another. He knew he ought to get out and hunt that stage— he'd money tied up in that goddam woman and he sure didn't want no redskins scalping her. But he'd money tied up in other things, too, and this puking dude could lose it for him if he got to swinging his jaw around. And the guy held the cards to make him lose more than money.

Once loose on a horse there was no telling what he'd do. He might run to the marshal. He might hit for Camp Grant...

If only, thought Cardigan, *I'd kept my damn mouth shut!*

That was where he'd slipped, back there in Jelks' hash house. Instead of laughing it off, he'd played tough with the feller. The guy would not be forgetting Kurt Cardigan now. He would not be forgetting that dun horse either.

He'd be swinging his jaw the first chance he got.

There was one thing Cardigan would sure have to do. He would have to stick with him. He'd have to stick with him anyways till he got beyond where his damn talking would matter. And that meant for sure at least to Dragoon Springs.

Under his breath Kurt Cardigan cursed.

There had ought to be a law against dudes, goddam it!

And the worst of it was he had to pick up that horse, that dun he had hitched to the stage office tierack.

He thought too much of that dun to leave him— Why, old Snuffy and him was pardners almost! He'd as soon cut off his right arm as leave Snuffy.

Yet he knew that was what a smart man would do.

He sleeved the sweat off his face again and scowled. A man was a fool to let feeling for a horse ever get in the way of good sense that way. He always had been a fool about Snuffy.

He sure hated to haul that dude back uptown. But he couldn't afford to leave the guy here—he'd run off at the mouth till hell wouldn't have it. Like to run off uptown if he saw that marshal—the guy was scared enough to. That Injun talk had turned him plumb green.

Cardigan's scowl grew blacker.

There was no use blinking it. He couldn't leave the horse. All feelin aside, that dun had the best set of heels in the country. Speed might count before he got done with this.

He had sure got himself into one fine mess! If he hadn't sent for that woman—but wishes wouldn't butter no parsnips. He had to get this crazy dude out of here and he sure couldn't leave him while he went after Snuffy. He'd just have to take the guy with him.

The time for thinking, he reckoned, was a considerable while past.

"George," he said, breaking into the stableman's rambling discourse, "we better git over an' fetch your wallet an' we better start humpin' or you won't never make it."

"I'll go fix you a bill o' sale—"

"You do that," Cardigan told him. "I'll drop by for it next time I'm through town." He looked at the dude. "Let's git goin.' You can lead that filly till we git to the hotel."

He took the dude by the arm and urged him streetward.

Soon as they got well away from the stable Kurt stopped. "I'll take that hundred an' ten now," he said, and the dude passed it over without any argument. He was too plain scared to even open his mouth.

Cardigan looked at him. The guy was scared plenty, no doubt about that. There didn't look to be any more fight in that feller than a man would expect to get from a field mouse.

Cardigan peered up the street. He didn't have many choices. He had to get the horse. He had to keep hold of this guy, but it would be doubling the risk to tote him back uptown. And he sure couldn't tie him, not unless he gagged him, and to leave him like that would just be asking for trouble.

He guessed he'd better chance his luck and leave

the guy loose.

"George," he said, soft and careful, "I've got to go fetch my horse. You kin slope if you want to but you'd better wait here. There ain't nothin' in this world that's any quicker than a bullet."

THREE
GUN TOWN MARSHAL

CARDIGAN, whistling a bawdy tune, struck off up the street at a saddle-cramped swagger. You would never have guessed by his cocky look that inside his pants his knees were shaking, or that his heart was banging around in his gullet like a shut-in bird trying to fly through a window. He would not have been one bit surprised to have heard the departing clatter of that filly. If the guy had any sense at all he would know damn well no feller would be fool enough to shoot him in a town. If he had any sense he'd jump onto that mare and take off through the greasewood like a bat out of Carlsbad.

But if the dude was doing it, he was being mighty quiet. Cardigan could catch not the faintest sound of hoofbeats. He heard the drone of a fly, a restless horse stamping, but no commotion of any sort broke the drowsy hush of the noontime quiet. He could only hope the damn lunkhead would stay there.

With that blasted stage better than three hours late

and him eating his heart out about that woman you would think he had enough on his mind!

He tried to figure where that dude could have seen him. "You're a horse trader, pal," the damn fool had chortled.

There was only one way he could have gotten that notion; the dude must have seen him with a bunch of horses.

And it must have been around a town. And Kurt hadn't been near a town in six months, or he never would have got so het up for a woman.

That thought pulled his mind back around to Docie and the goddam stage that was three hours late. Them redskins *had* been acting queer lately. Used to be you could see a bunch any time squatting with their prats hunkered down by a porch edge and no more look on their fat lumpy faces than a guy could twist from the flat of a skillet. But this morning there hadn't been one stinking Injun...

"Your name Cardigan?"

Cardigan stopped with his throat dry as cotton. He was almost even with the saloon's warped porch and the men who'd been on it weren't there anymore. Asleep on his feet the dun dozed thirty feet away and it might just as well have been a full thirty miles for it was Frank Esparza who'd stepped into the sunlight, Frank Esparza who now stood watching Kurt across five yards of questioning silence. Frank Esparza, the town's new marshal.

"I said is your name Cardigan?"

"That's right," Cardigan said.

"Understand you raise horses."

There was in Cardigan then a sudden urge to violence. It was a thing built up of all the years he had been here, of all the things he had done and all the things he had tried to do; an urge compounded of the plain expectations those things had engendered.

But none of this thinking touched the surface of his features. By a tremendous effort, he held himself still. *Was this it?* he wondered. *Was this how it was to be?*

He met the marshal's stare and nodded.

"That's right," he said again.

A kind of stillness settled round them, a charged sort of quiet that might, it seemed to Cardigan, erupt at any moment. It had never occurred to him before that this street could be so wide or so completely without sound.

A small wind whipped up and ran through the fronds of the scaly-barked pepper trees while Esparza continued without movement to watch him.

The marshal lifted a hand then and scratched at his chest and the stretch of the faded cotton shirt showed how well good living had padded his belly. His eyes ran the loops of Cardigan's gun belt and considered the pistol that weighted his holster. Then they swiveled away and went across to the horse, to that dozing dun Kurt had come here to fetch.

"Is that a horse of your raising?"

Cardigan stood very still and very softly sighed. He settled his weight and tipped his head a little forward and he watched the marshal's eyes and said: "Sure."

* * *

THE MAN SHOULD HAVE GONE for his gun. It was the natural thing for a marshal to do when a gent laid claim to a stolen horse. It was the thing Kurt Cardigan had looked for, the obvious answer to the cards turned up. When, instead, the marshal merely smiled it threw Kurt Cardigan completely off balance. All his forces had been marshaled to meet and beat gunplay; he could not adjust himself that swiftly to such a sudden shift.

It left him weak in the knees and a sudden wild anger began churning his bowels, leaving the length of him drenched in cold sweat.

He looked at the man through a glaze of bright fury, at his white grinning teeth and the pink flabby jowls that hung down like old wattles. His hands itched to feel themselves around that fat throat.

The old fool was talking and the fostered care of six years in this country was a habit even stronger than Cardigan's anger. He forced himself to listen. "What was that again?"

"Understand you raise stock for the Cavalry."

For the Cavalry... Christ!

"I've sold 'em a few," Cardigan finally growled gruffly.

He was still mad and scared and he still didn't get it. This old gander talked like he held all the cards but he sure as hell wasn't playing it that way. If he knew so damned much why keep beating the bushes?

The marshal scratched himself again. "Is that stallion for sale?"

"Old Snuffy? Hell, no!"

Esparza nodded. "That's a mighty fine horse, Mister Cardigan. If he's a sample of the kind you're raisin' out there I expect I can throw some business your way. Tell you what—I'll ride out there..."

"Not right now—not with me you won't. I've got to git out an' hunt that stage."

"Hunt the stage?" The marshal's eyes showed surprise. "What would *you* be figurin' to hunt that stage for?"

"Well, by God! Ain't it late? Don't you know—"

"I can't see that it's any of your concern."

"It's about time *someone* was gittin' concerned!"

Cardigan brushed the marshal aside and went by him, un-looped the dun's reins, and climbed into the saddle. With the muscles of his back, all scringed up and cringing he wheeled the horse round and, without another look at the roan-cheeked lawman, put him down the road at a businesslike canter.

FOUR
"THAT GODDAM STINKIN' DUDE!"

THERE ARE times when a man doesn't feel like thinking when thoughts and the things conjured by them are matters best left entirely alone. This was one of those times, but the knowledge did not tend to cool Cardigan or lessen the savage turmoil inside him. Had his thoughts been broncs he could have penned them up, but who could put his rope on worry?

It sure burned him up to think of the way that old coot had talked to him, leading him on like a snake-hipped hooker and never even putting a hand near his smokepole.

Just the same, in a way, he was glad Esparza hadn't. Shooting was the last thing he wanted right now. Right now, all he wanted was to find that woman and he couldn't do that till he got rid of this dude.

To hell with Esparza! Let him run his bluffs if it made him feel good. If he had known anything he would of played it different, he never would have let Cardigan get away from him. And that was for sure!

He gave a sudden reckless laugh. It wasn't likely the

marshal was even suspicious. And what if he was? Let him go to the ranch and look around for himself. A fat lot of good that would do him. He could look till hell froze for all of Kurt Cardigan. There was no fancy artwork on Cardigan's acres.

It was the horse right under him now that was dangerous. This red-maned buckskin with the flashing heels, this whirlwind, this hellcat, this crazy-headed outlaw that, despite every urge of common sense and good judgment, Kurt Cardigan could never quite bring himself to kill.

Oh, he'd meant to, all right; he had sure aimed to do it. When the boys fetched him in with the fat mares that night, he had cursed them out proper. "Why you goddam fools," he'd said, "*Look* at him! A give-away horse if I ever seen one!" Danger was bred in his very bones—in those cat-quick feet and rolling eyes, in the taffy-colored hide and that lean jagged blaze on his face like white lightning. "A picture horse!" Kurt had lashed at them, furious. "God damn it to hell! What you apes tryin' to do—get my neck stretched for me?"

He'd been plumb against the red dun till he'd learned every man of them shared his feelings. They had grabbed him by mistake, caught him up with a band of foaling mares. A range stallion. A wild, untamed devil who never had known the feel of a saddle, they had fetched him along to see which could break him. They had fetched him down from Wyoming some place. "Hell, there ain't no Wyomin' waddies round here," Curly Lahr had scoffed. "What the Christ are you scairt of?"

Knowing better, knowing well what a threat that yellow stud represented, he had let the horse stay. If the boys wanted to ride him let them have their fun. If they didn't plumb kill him, he could shoot the horse later.

That was the way he had looked at it then.

So, they'd all tried their hands. They were a tough lot, too, but that damned dun was tougher. He was the orneriest horse they had ever encountered—a biting, kicking, sun fishing fool. He had killed one bungler. He had crippled another.

The crippled guy, Hennessy, like to lost his damn mind. "Rope me that sonuvabitch! Tie up the bastard!" he had sobbed through the bloody froth on his lips. "I'll fix that devil—ear 'im down!" he'd raged. And he'd have done it, too, if Kurt had stayed out of it. With his broken leg dragging he had crawled through the dust with a knife in his hand. Oblivious to the pain of his hoof-caved ribs he'd have cut the horse to ribbons in his fury if Cardigan had not stopped him.

Kurt had never been able to figure out why he'd bothered to step in and save that horse. It was against all reason. He had rightly recognized the horse as a menace, but he hadn't let them kill him and he wouldn't let them geld him. As a matter of fact, after that first day, he wouldn't let the men touch him.

They hadn't liked it a little bit. They'd eyed him like he'd taken leave of his senses. "You'd better kill that bayo coyote," Lahr said, "before he puts another notch in his tail."

That was mighty sound reasoning, best advice in the world and Cardigan knew it, yet he'd made no effort to get rid of the horse. And he wasn't a man to be swayed by sentiment, cynically rejecting all sentiment as weakness—which it was.

He regarded the horse as a constant hazard yet

continued to work with him, knowing a tremendous elation at each small sign of progress. That dun was smarter than a heap of humans, but a wild streak in him made him savagely distrustful of anything smelling like a man-critter to him. Yet he came to whinny at Cardigan's approach and in the end suffered Cardigan to ride him.

It was the proudest day in Cardigan's life.

The men did not share his enthusiasm. They profanely predicted he would rue the day he had knocked the knife out of Hennessy's hand. "Sure, you're ridin' him, but that don't prove a goddam thing! That bastard'll kick you hell west an' crooked!"

Cardigan laughed at them.

Lahr had pinned the name of Jubal Jo on the horse but most of the time Cardigan called him Snuffy— which he sure as hell had been till Cardigan tamed him.

With Kurt, the big stallion was wonderfully gentle. You'd have thought Kurt had brought him up on a bottle if you hadn't known how he had come to get hold of him. But the men shook their heads. "That goddam hoss'll kill him' yet!"

They'd become inseparable. For a man who considered sentiment a weakness that horse took up an awful lot of Kurt's time. For weeks at a stretch, he would seldom be seen on any other horse. "This goddam dun can do anything,"

he told them. When Lahr heard about it, he twisted his face up and spat, disgusted. "It's a wonder he don't take the damn bronc t' bed with 'im!"

Cardigan wasn't by nature an introspective man, being mostly given over to taking things as he found them, but there were times when he wondered himself about that horse, about the feeling that seemed to have sprung up between them. It was a damned funny thing when you stopped to consider it.

He knew well enough the risk he was taking, pirootin' around on a stolen horse. In this kind of country where a horse was a man's only means of transportation—where, indeed, his very life might depend on whether he had a horse available—the end of a gent accused of horse-thievery was apt to be sudden and frequently uncomfortable.

He had never, he thought, tried to fool himself. The danger in having this horse around lay not in the animal's own proclivities but in the chance of his being recognized. It made no difference that Kurt himself hadn't stolen him. Snuffy did not belong to him—that was the wedge any lawman would work on. Cardigan had no intention of returning him and had announced this decision when he'd answered "Sure" to the marshal's question.

Wyoming was a long ways off. Who around here could dispute his right to this blaze-faced dun once he'd gotten that drummer out of the country?

Remembrance of the dude put an end to his thinking, and he leaned forward in the saddle, abruptly going still, staring.

With a smothered oath he pulled the horse to a stop.

The dude was gone.

He wasn't even in sight!

With a curse, Cardigan kneed the dun forward. The blabber-mouthed bastard was probably back in the stable spilling his guts to that nosey liveryman!

But one glance up the lane that led to the stable disclosed no sign of the buttermilk filly.

He looked at the hoof-tracked dust where he'd left them

and there, sure enough, was the crazy nump's shoe prints. There was where he had climbed up onto the horse. And there was the filly's sign, off at a walk, curling round behind the buildings, making for that pile of old crates behind the Mercantile. Yes... and there, by God, was where he'd poured on the leather—straight out into the goddam desert!

The crazy tenderfoot fool!

How long did he think he would last out in that stuff? He would get himself lost before he sweated a blister—was probably lost right now. He'd go tearing around in a thirst-frantic circle and play out his horse within ten minutes of town. It was the way of his kind: it was what they all did when they got off alone into the quiet of the wastelands. Never used no sense, just kept running in circles like a bunch of fool chickens with their heads cut off. The buzzards would. be picking his bones by tomorrow.

Unless Kurt went after him.

He sat there a moment and thought about that.

Why the hell should he?

Hadn't the dadburned peckerneck been enough trouble? The guy had asked for this! He wasn't nothing to Kurt but a threat and a menace.

The smart thing to do was to ride off and forget him. Without that dude, Frank Esparza could whistle. There wasn't one chance in ten the guy would ever make it back.

Cardigan squinched up his eyes and looked off into

the glare. A hot wind was blowing off those sun-blasted ridges, a wind that would fry a man's skin like a stove top. Nothing could live out there that didn't know it— nothing but the hoot owls, the gophers, and the goddam snakes. In the blinding glare of that brassy heat, that damn fool drummer couldn't last two hours.

And besides, by God, he'd got to hunt for that woman!

Christ! To think of her alone on that stage—and on account of Kurt Cardigan! You couldn't get around it. He had sent her the money to get herself out here. And she'd said she would come; said he didn't have to take her if she didn't suit his fancy. By God, it took real guts to do a thing like that to come half across the country on the chance of a guy you hadn't never seen liking you!

What happened to that dude wasn't no skin off *his* nose. If that dude had got his rights, he'd be damn dead anyway for stickin his mug into someone else's business. Most of these birds would of bashed his damn head in.

Cardigan knuckled the sweat from his eyes and scowled blackly.

Mostly Butterfield's stages ran right on the dot. His drivers didn't lallygag around picking daisies. A busted axle or a wheel off couldn't account for them being this late. They were used to such things and could makeshift in spite of them. That stage was bogged deep down in trouble, and it was dollars to doughnuts the trouble wore feathers.

With a growl, he fed old Snuffy the steel, whirled him suddenly round, and pulled him up with an oath. "That goddam stinkin' dude!" he cursed and bitterly took up the drummer's trail.

FIVE
STAGE FROM EL PASO

THE HEAT BOILED down like the wrath of God. You could see its filmy shimmer curling off the rocks, you could feel it in your nostrils like a searing flame. In all that waste nothing moved in Kurt's vision save the blue-gray peaks that smoked in the sun dance.

He had thought to find the dude fairly quick, had been sure of it, but already he'd ridden for one solid hour, and the damned fool's tracks still unreeled before him. It was against all the logic of Cardigan's experience that a man as unused to the desert as that dude looked would have stayed on his horse and kept going this long.

One thing surprised him even more than that. The guy hadn't chased himself round in circles. He hadn't foundered the filly in a panic for haste. The tracks led straight southeast as an arrow, as straight toward St. David as though he were heading there. Yet how could he be? The guy was an outlander knowing nothing of this country, knowing nothing but he needs to get away from Kurt Cardigan.

Cardigan sleeved his face and cursed.

He still hadn't figured what to do with the guy. He sure couldn't waste much more time on him, not nearly enough now to see him to the Springs—not, anyways, if he would find that woman. What a man ought to do was to put a bullet through him. That's what you'd do with a snake that attacked you—that's what you'd damn quick do with a Injun! Why should a man treat a dude any different? Only a dimwit would turn a snake loose to come back and maybe do a good job next time.

That was sound thinking. It was mighty good thinking Cardigan told himself, but he knew all-fired well it jus' wasn't in him to do it. He was tough all right, but not that tough. There was a soft streak in him that was more damn dangerous to his health than that stallion. He could knock down a man in a fight and forget it. But he never had been able to bring himself to up and shoot another feller down in cold blood.

If the stinker would just cooperate a little... maybe fall off his horse and bash his damn head in or kick off from the heat or get snake-bit or something. You sure wouldn't catch him crying about it.

But until that happened, he felt bound to hunt him, even though he might begrudge every minute of the time.

He would a whole heap liefer be out hunting Docie. He *ought* to be hunting her, he told himself scowling. Just the thought of her out there alone, by God, was enough to make a guy throw up his breakfast.

* * *

THE SUN COMMENCED SLANTING toward the Tucson Mountains and for the hundredth time, Kurt stood up in his stirrups and sent a black glance over the desolate surroundings before sinking back with a frustrated curse. Nothing but cactus, desert growth, and dust. Nowhere did anything move but the greasewoods. Nothing but heat and the white glare of emptiness curling away into lost horizons.

He knuckled the sweat from his burning eyes and pressed on again with his gaze on the tracks in the dry parched dust, convinced when he topped each yonder rise, he would finally come up with the fleeing drummer. It was sheer damned hope for there was no truth in it.

It just didn't make sense that that yellow-shoed dude could keep ahead of him this way. It was surprising enough the guy stayed in the saddle. It strained belief that he should keep going this way mile after mile, maintaining his lead, without killing the filly.

But the filly was still going strong by the sign. Of course, Cardigan wasn't really pushing his own horse—a man would be a fool to in this kind of heat, but that was just what you'd look for a damn dude to do. And the guy had been plenty scared to start with.

He wondered if the fellow had water if the garrulous stableman had thought to provide him. He'd ought to have done it as a matter of course because Cardigan had said the dude was quitting the country, but he was damned if he could remember seeing any canteen.

That tenderfoot fool had ought to caved long ago. It just wasn't reasonable he should keep on going. Yet there were the filly's tracks.

There wasn't no chance the guy had fell off. Cardigan would have noticed; there would have been the changed gait of the filly besides. No horse without guidance would have gone this straight, nor this steady.

He threw a look at the sun. It was getting late. He looked again at the tracks. They'd been walking here, taking it easy just as if the guy was an old-timer at it. "Savin' his horse!" Cardigan told himself bitterly. He'd misjudged this guy plenty. By all the signs and signal smokes the guy wasn't going to cash in at all.

He scowled again at the sun that was barely an hour from the jagged crests of the western crags. He'd got to find him 'quick or yell calf rope. He sure couldn't trail no dude in the dark.

They mustn't be, he judged, much more than twenty miles from the town of St. David. It wasn't a town, really, but a settlement of Mormon farmers hubbed about a cross-trails store that among the country's cowhands was mainly known for its whisky. North by east of this place, about an easy day's ride lay Camp Grant and the U. S. Cavalry.

Roughly calculating his position Cardigan figured he was not more than five or six miles to the south of the stage road; a couple miles farther east it would swing directly north to skin through the Pass and whipsaw its way through the Dragoon Mountains. They were getting right into the Apache country and if a man set any value on his hair, he had damn well better be keeping his eyes peeled.

Still more than half convinced he must sight the dude soon, Cardigan pressed on. But at dark, he had not caught him. The guy was still driving straight as a string for St. David. He might or he might not yap when he got there but one thing you sure had to hand to them Mormons—they were almighty good at minding their own business.

"'T' hell with 'im!" Cardigan said, pulling up. The moon wouldn't rise for another three hours, and he was damned if he was going to hang around here waiting on the extremely off chance, he might still catch that dude. Any guy with the wit to get himself this far would sure have the sense to keep on going. It was a heap more important that he locate Docie, which was what he had wanted to do in the first place. He'd given them Injuns too much time already.

He cast about in his mind for the likeliest place where whatever had happened to the stage might have happened. There were too many choices. That Dragoon country was an ambusher's paradise, a mighty rough country, crossed and crisscrossed with ridges and arroyos, a land of mesquite and yucca where ambush was possible at every turn. The nearer he got to that slot of a Pass the rougher the country was going to become; but the chances were—if Apaches were responsible for the stage's non-appearance—he would find the stage, or what was left of it, someplace in the canyon. The stage road through this dusty hell was strewn with the wrecks of abandoned wagons sticking their gaunt ribs out of the sands among the bleached-white bones of mules and horses.

He was glad he hadn't touched his water: he'd prob-ably need it all before he got done with this. One good thing about redskins—most of their devilment that was sprung in the dark was generally geared to those hours that were closest to dawn. This gave him a leeway of about six hours before he would have to start watching for them. He wished he could say as much for the whites who made this region their stamping ground, but he knew their kind for a chancy lot and there was no predicting their actions.

He pushed steadily on through the deepening night, conserving his horse but determined, if he could, to make the west end of the Pass by dawn.

He kept away from the stage road. Proximity to that would be a heap too likely to decrease a man's chances. There was a pile of riffraff in this country, men run out of more settled regions, and he'd troubles enough without inviting their attention. Several times he detoured to avoid darkened camps, warned off by the smell of woodsmoke, by the snores of stertorous sleepers, or by the sounds of horses rattling their hobbles. And always, through the slow-passing night, he kept thinking of Docie till he couldn't hardly stand it.

He saw her in a thousand guises and none of them calculated to cheer a man up. While before he had pictured how she'd look in a bed, he saw her now through a film of horror. If those damned red bastards had taken her...

Such thoughts set him wild, left him filmed with sweat; but he wasn't a man to fool himself. He knew mighty well what her chances were, what likelihood there was of him finding her unharmed.

He got jumpier than ever as the hours drew closer to the crack of dawn. What if his horse stepped into a dog hole or slipped in the rocks and broke a leg? What if he couldn't locate the stage? Suppose he'd guessed wrong and overshot it?

He commenced hearing things that had no existence outside of his head and once he'd have sworn, he was followed. Dawn was less than half an hour away when he broke through a thicket of chaparral and came onto the rutted stage road.

The Pass lay just yonder. Through the damp gray gloom, he could see the dark sides of the canyon, and his hair started crawling as he caught the dark bulk of a twisted mass not hardly a hundred yards ahead. Something nauseous gripped the cold void of his belly as he rummaged the shadows about that thing and could find no movement, no life about it.

He sat stiffly unmoving for five long minutes while his bitter eyes raked the shadows round it, probing each bush, each rock, and each hollow. He almost flung himself out of the saddle when a cactus wren flitted out of a nearby cholla. With a harsh curse, then, he started forward and cursed again when he came to the thing at the edge of the road.

It was nothing but the wreck of an abandoned wagon.

Yet the scare stayed with him. He had been too long in this harsh land to pass up the value of sudden hunches. He had stayed too long on the trail of that dude and fear lay cold as frog legs in him.

He walked the dun into the canyon, rifle across his pommel, eyes narrowed, searching the rimrock with all the care in him. Fear and hate clenched his jaws till his back teeth ached and his muscles were tight as drawn bowstrings. He tried to shut thoughts of Docie out of his mind, yet it almost seemed he could hear her screams and his back and belly were cold with sweat.

It was much lighter now, day was almost at hand,

but no sound of twittering birds came to ease him. The canyon was choked with a breathless hush. Each fall of the stallion's hoofs seemed loud as a gunshot in that quiet. Cardigan knew what those devils could do to a woman they didn't want to keep for squaw's work.

The thought of it almost made him retch.

He watched how the sun suddenly brightened the east, flinging its thin clear fight on the rimrocks, noticing how the advent of it seemed to deepen the canyon's solitude, making the shadowed sides more dark, more suggestive of ambush, of hidden eyes watching; and he pictured the stage toiling up the grade with the grunting horses digging into their collars, great muscles bulging, harness creaking with the awful strain as the iron-rimmed wheels ground against the shale and went noisily jolting over the outcrops—the sudden stop, the driver's oath, the shearing scream of a woman as the hideous painted faces ringed them and the ululating cries of the shrieking Apaches rose and lifted into a paean of hate.

He cursed himself for a daunsy fool and touched his heels to the dun's wet flanks, only to grunt and pull up sharply as they topped a rise of hard-baked ground and saw the abandoned stage before them half capsized in the dusty road.

It was appalling the way that Abbott-Downing looked with its elegance rent and slashed to ribbons, the splintered boards of its seats all over, its stout leather braces scarred with axe bites, its storm curtains hanging in dismal tatters.

The bloating shapes of two dead horses grotesquely lay amid the tangle of harness and a man was sprawled near the first on his face and it was plenty plain he would never get up.

Cardigan stared, too sick to curse. He wanted to retch but he couldn't do it. His stomach was tied in a rigid knot, and he thought for a minute he would go clean crazy as he thought of the woman who had been on this stage.

A merciful numbness seized his mind holding back the grisly thoughts that clawed it and the reins groaned in the clutch of his hand as he kneed Jubal Jo toward that carnage.

Another man lay in the dust of the road with both hands grabbed to his blackened chest where the shaft of an arrow showed between them while the skin of his face hung down like gristle.

There were no more corpses.

Three times, very watchful, he rounded the stage, but he had seen them all. Arrows pin-cushioned its sides and there were more arrows sticking from the two dead horses.

He sat the big dun looking down at them sickly, seeing where the others had been hacked from the harness and driven off when the marauders left. He saw the slashed mail sacks laying in the road and the litter of torn-up letters around them, fluttering now in the early breeze; the scattered bags and luggage with the knife scars on them. But always his eyes kept returning to the horses, to the boot tracks that showed around the tangle of harness.

He turned the dun finally and rode nearer to the stage, then around to the boot and to the sprung-open door on the stage's other side. And at each pause, he nodded with his heart beating wilder.

Boot tracks everywhere, not a mark of a moccasin.

How long he sat there staring down at them he had no idea but his face, when at last he lifted it, had the look of something pounded from metal. His hands were cramped from their grip of the reins.

It was not Apaches he had to reckon with. This was the work of renegade whites.

SIX
MAN TRACKS

TO A MAN as familiar with sign as Cardigan, it was no trick at all to pick up their trail. There'd been five in the party, and they'd struck off north quick as ever they'd gotten outside the canyon, driving the stolen stage stock with them. One of them had the girl up in front of him, the marks of that horse showing deeper, more sharp lines; it was a pretty safe guess that guy was the leader.

It would be hard to say which bunch this was. There was a pile of tough outfits roving the country preying on prospectors and any small fry that looked worth the trouble. Men without code, these were, without scruple, wolves of the chaparral, savage and deadly.

This was their stamping ground, a land with blood spilled across every foot of it, a range sliced up into draws and gullies, split and quartered till at times you'd have thought there could be no crossing it; but always the outlaws found a way and, although sometimes they left no trail at all, Cardigan managed to hang and rattle.

It was not easy. It took a heap more time than he

cared to give it and was a task at once calculated to wear a man down and try the most dogged tenacity, beset as it was every stride of the way by the ever-present threat of ambush.

These border ruffians were a wily breed, much practiced in the art of eluding pursuit and fully aware of the fate they courted. They overlooked no bets save the one he had constantly to guard against—ambush, and he was amazed they did not try that as well. They might try it yet. They probably never dreamed they would be followed so soon—all this ducking and dodging was a natural routine with their kind of gentry.

Not for a moment dared Kurt let down his vigilance. One moment could be an eternity sometimes. The time required for a finger to squeeze a trigger could be infinitesimal and one bullet could finish him, could stop him forever. Until his burning eyes went blind from the glare, he was bound to keep them prowling the slopes, scanning each thicket, each shade patch, and pocket. It was the price he must pay for continued living.

This was a canny breed, cunning as foxes to throw off the hunter. Doubling and twisting they antigodled continually, employing every guile in their feral natures that might tend to confuse any following party.

The ledges drove Cardigan to most of his cursing and the renegades seemed to be always finding them, great barren outcrops of rock long winnowed of soil by gale and cloudburst, rust-red, blue-green, sometimes black with mineral. Many of these he was forced to circle several times before he could pick up their sign again, and, such times, he acted like a man possessed.

Heat lay over these barrens like smoke and a

scorched smell came off this bone-dry land that was like the stench of a burned out kettle. Lifeless it stretched like a faded blanket, monotonous, immeasurable, to the desolate peaks that, like drunken sentries, tottered and danced on the brassy horizons.

The rock points of the Dragoon Mountains fell behind and gradually turned blue in the shimmering heat and, by noon, the sign of the quarry had grown noticeably fresher. Patience, Kurt felt, was nearing its reward. He could no longer doubt he was overtaking them. Though his bloodshot eyes could not yet pick them up he was convinced they were not now far ahead of him. He wet his mouth with the lowering contents of his government-issue canteen and gave half a hatful of the tepid water to the horse that had fetched him all this way and again pressed forward.

Shortly after one, following the sign up out of a wash, he came onto a yucca-studded bench of sand and reined Jubal in with a bitter curse. Less than two hours ago this bench, by the sign, had been the scene of a running fight. The ground was crossed and recrossed with tracks in a way that left small doubt of what had happened. To Cardigan, the evidence was completely convincing. Coming out of that wash the renegade crew had run head-on into a file of cavalrymen. Panic had routed the stage-robbing crew, sent them ducking and dodging, every man for himself. There had been no pause, no chance for palavering. They had whirled for the brush going hellity-larrup and it was useless, in that scuffed-up sand, to attempt to track down individual sign.

Cardigan had neither the time nor the patience. He put the dun into an immediate circle, scanning for sign of that heavy horse's hoofs. It was the only sign Kurt gave a damn about, the double-burdened horse that was carrying Docie.

He rode twenty yards in the start of his circle, changed his mind, reined the dun to the left to cut it larger, to commence where the trail was less tangled by churning. He had to go clear into the greasewood before he found tracks that were sufficiently separate to read without getting out of the saddle. Speed right now was all that counted. He was hunting for sign he could read at a run, and he found it before a scraggly mesquite thicket.

A trail of broken branches led through it and, riding his stirrups, Kurt Cardigan followed. The trail came out on the farther side in a welter of converging tracks and there stopped, forever, beneath the still-warm body of the man's dead horse.

Cardigan felt as though fate had double crossed him. His hands got to shaking. All the strength fell out of him, and his weight dropped into the saddle heavily. He sat there like a man gone blind.

"God damn it!" he said savagely and stared at the dead black horse in a fury. But he was too used up to swear anymore. He felt spent as a wrung-out dishrag.

He looked at that dead black horse without words and at the green-backed flies that droned off it angrily as he kneed the blowing dun in closer to have a try at the brand on its topside shoulder, but the mark wasn't any iron he recognized.

"Hell!" he said then. "What difference does the goddam brand make!"

Then his mind commenced working, began sorting things out again. This was the horse, and it was plenty dead. Where was the man—and where was Docie?

Being careful to avoid disturbing the tracks immediately around it, he skirted the horse and commenced a painstaking combing of the brush all around, but he wound up with no further sign of either. Baffled he came back to the black but the tracks there didn't tell him much. There were too many of them superimposed on each other. What Cardigan wanted was to find that man in the hope he might learn what had happened to the girl, and he sure couldn't do it from that maze of trompings.

He went back to the thicket but there was nothing in there.

There were no dead men anyplace around here. Then he remembered. There wouldn't be, of course—not without they were buried, and he saw no sign that would indicate that.

By the way, all those tracks went flying around it was a cinch there had been some powder burned. Nor did Cardigan consider it the least bit likely that this black horse had been the only casualty. Any unhorsed jaspers would have been picked up—probably by the soldiers. Men of the stripe these renegades had sprung from would be too intent on saving their own hides to waste any time on the wounded.

Of course, he could always go to the post. If the soldiers had taken any prisoners, they were bound to have removed them to Camp Grant for trial. It might be quicker, in the long run, to go there and question them. It might. But in the meantime, Docie. . .

He wouldn't think about that.

He got back on the dun and rode due west a while.

The black horse had been heading that way when they'd dropped him. When he reckoned, he'd got far enough out to get something Cardigan started another circle, watching particularly for any set of tracks that would seem to be carrying more than the weight of an average rider.

But there weren't any single sets of tracks, none whatever. He made a full circle before he would believe it. The frantic renegades had all spurred west with two or three cavalrymen after each one of them—and they hadn't done any loitering. You could tell by the tracks those cavalrymen were riled.

A guy might as well hunt a needle in a haystack as to try in all that welter of tracks to pick out a set that were toting double weight.

Cardigan's mood wouldn't stand frittering round. With an oath, he took after the nearest bunch of tracks.

Three soldiers had spurred after one renegade. The fear had sure been in that feller. He hadn't thought once about hiding his trail. Those cavalry sports must have been too close for the damn scared fool to do any more than spur and sling leather —and he hadn't done that any great while, either.

Half a mile from the scene of the original encounter a carbine bullet had put an end to the chase. You could see where the horse had gone down like a rocket, carried end over end by its own momentum. And there the horse lay, in that cat-claw tangle, head twisted under it, too dead to skin.

And there was where the rider had landed, hard, on a shoulder, just beyond that pear clump. here was where he'd clawed to his feet. There was where he'd gone down again, headlong. You could see where the bastard had tried to get up... the print of his scuffed left boot toe beside the mark of his bent right knee. Forward of that and deeper, much deeper, was the smooth rounded hollow where his left knee had rested, and just to the right of it, complete and sharply defined, was the full spread print of the guy's left hand. You could see where his weight had pressed it deep, the left hand's fingers and that right braced forearm, just before he'd give out and flopped forward on his face.

There was where the soldiers had come up. There was where they'd got off their horses. Here was where they'd stood a bit, watchful, wondering probably if there was any more fight in him, perhaps calling orders, maybe waiting for his answer. One of them had gone forward then. Then the rest had come on and picked the guy up.

Taking him back to the camp, Cardigan thought. Back to stand trial or to be turned over to the civil authorities. Or, maybe, to be buried.

To be buried, he hoped.

With a disgusted grunt, he turned the big dun figuring to try his luck on another set; it was all he could do, keep running them down. Then the idea struck him that it might be better to swing north from here in a kind of half circle on the off chance of picking some more up that way. It would save a lot of time if he could do it, he thought.

So, he turned the dun north and wheeled away at a canter, dividing his attention between the ground before him and the surrounding brush. For only a fool would ignore that brush. A wounded sidewinder could be just as deadly as one that hadn't ever shaken his rattles.

The country looked empty as a flung-away hat, but he had lived with danger too long a while to put any trust in the look of appearances. Looks were for suckers like that fool of a marshal.

The next tracks he crossed showed but three in the party. The man being chased appeared to have the better horse. He must have had quite a lead and been steadily stretching it because the other gents' tracks frequently swerved far aside in what could only have been hopeful tries to shortcut him. They hadn't been very successful, it looked like, because the chased man's tracks finally straightened into plain departure and, a short distance later, Cardigan came to the place where the soldiers had quit.

There went their tracks angling back toward the bench. One of their horses had been limping badly.

Cardigan's lips showed a grim satisfaction. With that same set look, he inspected his rifle, thrust it back in its boot, and had a look at his six-gun. These chores attended to; he took up the trail.

* * *

AT FOUR BY HIS SHADOW, Cardigan came to the boulder-strewn course of the dry San Pedro. Here the fugitive's tracks turned into a rutted freight road that came up from the south and probably went to Camp Grant, which lay about thirty miles to the east and north.

Cardigan briefly grinned. It was a cinch the guy wouldn't stay with that road long; Camp Grant would be the last place he'd head for. He'd swung into that road to hide his tracks and he'd done a damn good job of it.

The guy had got hold of his head again and the knowledge turned Cardigan thoughtful. It was time to look spry and he slowed his horse, glad of a chance to breathe the stallion though he knew Jubal was good for many a mile yet; the big dun had once taken him one hundred miles without stopping and done it in twelve hours.

He sent swift looks up and down the road. The brush was thin along here, yet he scanned it carefully, having no desire to fall into an ambush. Satisfied, he gave his attention to the ground along the west edge of the road, pretty well convinced the man would leave from that side—and he did.

Where water, below a ridge, had gullied that edge during some long-forgotten cloudburst the fugitive, making out to be a casual traveler heading south, had eased his horse down into it. Cardigan eased Jubal into it also. Those tracks had been left less than an hour ago.

It was a cinch the guy's horse was about washed up. That wild flight from the troopers hadn't helped it any. By the sign, it looked to be going lame.

This could help. It was also bound to increase immeasurably the chance of ambush for the guy, slowed down, might get plenty cute. He was going to be watching his backtrail plenty.

Cardigan stopped the dun and sat turning it over. You could think all you wanted but the facts stayed the same. If he didn't come up with that fellow by dark, there was a mighty good chance he wouldn't ever come up with him. The guy knew the country and Cardigan didn't. He would have to chance ambush. He would have to press on, cut down the man's lead, and someway close with him before dark fell or he might just as well call it quits right here.

As long as the way remained open Cardigan pushed Jubal Jo along at a lope, but when the chased man's trail began to twist through the brush he was forced to slow down.

Palo Verde grew here and the tall-stalked pitahaya thrust up its bloom like a hat on a rifle. The footing became broken and rocky, and the dun's shod hoofs made a too-loud clatter as they scrambled up the slope of a shaly ridge. The greasewood here was far apart, puny. Wolf's candle lifted its gray spiked branches and the renegade's tracks went over the crest and showed as a series of pale contusions dropping down the dusted shelving of the ridge's north flank.

The fugitive's earlier headlong pace had dwindled now to a slow limping shuffle. His horse couldn't last much longer. That crazed panic flight from the men in blue had squandered its strength, poured it out like gold from a drunkard's purse.

Cardigan pulled the dun up with his head cocked, listening, gathering, and sifting all the stray vibrations; but nowhere in all that brush-choked yonder could he catch any sound of man or horse. With his bold-featured face still tipped to that listening he considered the buff-colored ground where the slope leveled off down there to the left of him, the fugitive's tracks, and the direction they pointed through that yonder tangle of chaparral and pear and the knife-thin gash of a canyon beyond.

It seemed all too empty, too deceptively silent.

There should anyway be a few birds twittering down there.

He raked the brush with his eyes and canted his shoulders. If that fellow was down there, what was he waiting for—wasn't a rifle shot good enough for him? Had he lost his rifle? Had he run out of cartridges?

There was a way to find out and Cardigan took it.

This was going to be risky but anything he tried was apt to be risky and time was dangerously near to running out. With his face tight and tough Kurt Cardigan nodded and kneed Jubal Jo into motion. As though he were walking on eggs the big dun moved down the slope with his ears cocked. Cardigan's rifle lay across the pommel, but he came onto the flat without anything happening.

He said, "Mebbe he ain't here after all," and studied the tracks with a sharpening attention that extended itself to the roundabout brush.

Except over that ridge he had just negotiated there was no other way off this flat but the canyon whose gash showed dead ahead. The ridge and the rising ground that flanked it made of this flat a kind of pocket. The tracks, looking more and more ready to stop, led off toward the canyon by the shortest cut, and they looked to have been made during the last ten minutes.

Was the man still here or had he gone through that canyon?

SEVEN
DEAD POSSUM

HE GLARED AT THE TRACKS: half minded to quit them.

Chasing after this guy had been a damn fool business. It had looked good at the start because he'd wanted to save time and catching any of the renegades had looked like the answer. Now he wasn't so sure.

He'd been doing all right till he'd found that dead horse; right then was when his thinkbox had jammed. He should have kept on circling till he'd come onto the tracks of another horse packing double— *those* were the tracks he should have found and followed. Even if he ran this guy down it might do him no good so far as Docie was concerned. The guy might not have any idea where the girl was.

But if he quit this guy now and went back to the bench and then didn't find nothing, he'd have to chase down every last track that led out of there. The girl could be a damned grand-maw by that time!

He guessed he had better forget that bench. A bird in the hand was better than no bird. He could at least squeeze the gizzard out of *this* one. It might not get him back that woman, but it would sure put the fear into the rest of them buzzards.

That goddam brush didn't look very good.

He'd been shot at plenty, and he knew the way lead could sing whizzing past you. It wasn't no sound to stamp and yell boo at.

That guy was probably holed up in this brush right now, setting there grinning with a gun in his hand, just waiting for Cardigan to make a right target.

And all the while time was getting shorter. And time, every tick, was working for the other guy; it wasn't doing anything for Cardigan at all. He had just two choices. He could bust on in and maybe get himself shot or he could turn his horse around and get the hell out of here.

There wasn't nothing complex about it. It was just as damn simple as rolling off a log. It was just a question of which he valued most, the girl—who probably wasn't anywhere around here—or his hide.

He was turning his horse when he suddenly stiffened with his eyes looking like they would roll off his cheekbones.

There, in the brush not ten feet to the right of him, was another set of tracks. Like the ones he had followed they were heading toward the canyon—fresh tracks, too, and heavy looking, like the goddam horse might be packing double.

Cardigan's eyes turned bright and narrow. They raked the brush with a keener interest. His shoulders lifted and a deepened breathing was reflected in the tightness of the shirt across his chest. "I guess," he said to the dun, "we'll go in there," and sent the horse forward without further dalliance.

Midway through the brush of this flat a low wind, wheeling out of the canyon, ran across the tops of the greasewood, waving them, touching his face with the remembered coolness of higher altitudes.

There were a number of second-growth pines up ahead, stunted, and stubbly, along the trail just before it turned into the canyon. Pausing again before he reached these, Cardigan, easing around in the saddle, carefully considered the surrounding brush before his glance dropped once more to the deeper indentations left in the dust by the second horse. This horse had gone into the canyon. He was not so sure about the first man's mount—the one he had followed into this country till he came to where its sign crossed and mingled with the hoofmarks left by the heavy-burdened one.

Cardigan quit stalling then. He rode straight toward the jaws of the canyon. There was nothing in sight from the entrance to where, a couple of hundred yards up ahead, a bulge in the righthand wall cut off all view of what lay beyond it. At that point, the sides of the canyon pinched in till the passage looked barely the width of a wagon. It was not much more, he found when he got there, with weathered rock walls rising sheer above him for hundreds of feet to a bright crack of sky that looked miles away.

He could still vaguely pick out the tracks of the horses where they made disturbed areas in the talus that littered the passage floor. He wished he knew the length of this canyon and where this hidden trail would take him.

He rode more slowly now with his rifle booted and a hand near his gun.

The walls, after a while, began to fall back a little. The talus gave way to patches of soil that, as he progressed, became more frequent and of larger extent, muting the dun's footfalls and cooled with the tender green of wild ferns.

A feeling took hold of Cardigan that before the evening advanced much further he might come up with those fellows and be seeing them through gun smoke.

He watched Jubal's ears with a cold vibration in the pit of his belly. Far as he could tell there was nobody near him, but the cold feeling grew, and, of a sudden, on an upswing of breeze flowing through the canyon he caught the sharp smell of woodsmoke.

The dun's ears shot forward, and he grabbed for its nostrils and had it wheeled clear around before it knew what was happening.

He rode almost back to where the walls narrowed before he took his hand from Jubal's muzzle. He swung quickly down then and stripped off saddle and blanket, bridle and all the rest of his gear, and turned the dun loose on a lass rope. "You stay right here an' no nickerin,' you savvy?"

The big dun softly snorted, and Cardigan picked up his rifle and started forward on foot, being careful to walk where he'd give the least warning.

It was coolly damp between the high walls and pungent with the aroma of ferns. Berry vines and creepers matted the floor and all the time the smell of woodsmoke got plainer.

Cardigan's face turned tight with the strain of this business and all his nerves were set on hair triggers.

When a group of quail drummed from under foot he came within an ace of letting off his rifle.

He stood frozen, glaring, heart hammering madly for a good twenty seconds after the quail were gone. He reckoned he'd better be getting hold of himself.

He made himself stand there till his heart quit pounding, till his breath came natural and the sweat went off him. But he couldn't get the cold feeling out of his belly.

* * *

ROUNDING a bend in the canyon passage he saw a side canyon opening to the left. There was considerable dropped rock about the entrance to it and it looked a choice spot for an ambush.

He approached it gingerly, rifle ready.

Them goddam quail had scared him stiff, and he didn't want no more surprises like that.

He took a grip on himself and kept his rifle at the cock in both hands while the woodsmoke smell got stronger and stronger. There was no doubt about it— they were in that side canyon, but he still hadn't heard one dadburned sound.

He reached the first of the rocks and crouched there without hearing anything but the pounding of his heart and that made enough noise to drown out a pump-jack.

He tried to think what he'd better do next. He wanted to get him a look down into that gulch, but he was scared to move till he got some sign. Those guys might be a heap closer than you'd think for. They might be no farther than the other side of these rocks and he would be a gone goose if they saw him first.

He wished the hell he'd kept his eyes on those tracks; he'd forgot all about them in the smell of that woodsmoke. He couldn't see any from where he was now—not without getting up. And getting up, by grab, might be mighty unhealthy. It wasn't that he was afraid of them bastards, but a mistake right now could be almighty permanent.

Blocks of rock, like young houses, lay scattered all about him, broken by their fall from the cliffs above. He crouched there and sweated, trying to talk himself into boldly sticking his neck out and not managing to move his neck one damn inch. He had the feeling, if he did, he might find himself looking into somebody's pistol.

While he hunkered there trying to screw himself into doing it, he suddenly stiffened to the mutter of voices. They were held down and muted, but they were voices all right and they were almighty close.

Should he make his play now? They were argufying now, probably engrossed in their business, and this might be a good time to do it if only he was sure just where they were at.

He gripped his rifle tighter. He guessed he'd better do it now. His patience wouldn't stand much more of this fiddling. And there was the light to be thought of— it wasn't getting no better. If he waited till dark, they might get clear away from him. The tempting smells drifting in with that woodsmoke reminded him his gut was getting powerful puny.

He started forward at a crawl, wriggling toward the next boulder.

Crawling, he decided, was for centipedes and Injuns. All the goddam sandburs and gravel in the country seemed to have shacked up in the lee of that boulder and it felt like his hands and his knees had found most of them. It was a nerve-twisting business what with having all the time to watch out for his rifle, not to stub it full of dirt and not to bank the damn barrel. It didn't leave him much time for any fancy listening and it come over him sudden, them galoots had quit talking.

When he reached the damn boulder, he didn't know whether to stick his nose out or not.

It could be just a little unhandy for a feller if some other gun-lugger happened to be doing the same thing.

He crouched there listening but all he could hear was the wind groaning around him.

What the hell were they doing?

Far as he could tell he was the only guy around there and he got to darkly wondering if them birds had pulled out. It made him feel like a sucker and the thought turned him reckless.

There was a way to find out and, scowling blackly, he took it. He grabbed off his hat and stuck his head around the boulder.

The view wasn't improved any great amount to speak of. He found himself staring at a dust-whitened bush that grew up beside the rock a couple feet in front of him. The only way he could look past it was to wriggle on out there.

It wasn't what you'd call a right attractive idea.

The more he thought about it the less he liked it. This rock would stop bullets but the goddam bush wouldn't even stop a fly.

Belly in the dirt, hands, and knees sore with burr points, Cardigan knew a sudden sense of bitter outrage. He would sure make them sweat if he ever got hold of them! He'd make them bastards wish they'd never been born! Steal his woman, would they? Drag her around like a blanket squaw! By God, if they'd touched one hair of her—

He pulled up in cold panic.

What if she was ugly! What if she was one of them, big raw-boned wallopers, with shovel teeth and a blacksmith's muscle like that long-haired partner old Bill Huxley had drawn that time, he'd got high on Merit's Patent Elixir!

God almighty.

Just the thought of such a turn put the cold sweat all over him.

"Jesis!" he said.

He would sure be hooked if he went storming out there to save the old bag and she got her peepers on him. Hell's gilded hinges! It would sure be rough to go to all this trouble and then wind up with some warhorse like that!

Maybe he had better slow down here a little. Maybe he had better go at this thing cautious and get him a look at her before he leaped.

Yeah. That was the ticket. Play it close to the chest. Not do nothing rash till he had got him a look at her. Then, if she didn't suit him, he could let those bucks have her.

But while he was cheering himself up with that another thought struck him. If she'd been ugly them bastards wouldn't never of run off with her.

He rubbed the palms of his hands on his pants legs. He put his hat back on and picked up his rifle.

He wriggled on around the rock and inched himself forward till he got his sweating face within a whisper of the bush. He still couldn't see much. The bush grew flat against the ground. Nothing less than a buzzard could see anything through it.

He chewed on his lip and finally stuck his damn head out.

At first, all he saw was that wreck of a cabin with the whop-pyjawed door hanging wedged on one hinge strap. It was sagged back against the gulch's rocky left shoulder about a hundred yards off like the first good wind would send it kiting into kindling. Then a movement snapped his glance a little farther to the right.

Above a tiny fire, a man was crouched facing him. There was a skillet in his hand. A blackened pot was in the embers and beyond, down the gulch a ways, were a couple grazing horses turned loose on hobbles. He didn't see the girl and the second man wasn't in sight.

They were probably in that cabin.

Thought of it made him grind his teeth and his eyes took on a shine that was wicked as he hitched himself around a little and cuddled the rifle snug to his shoulder and drew a bead on the guy by the fire. It was all he could do to keep his squeeze off the trigger.

It wasn't any scruple that stayed his hand. It was the thought of that other guy—the one in the cabin—that kept Kurt Cardigan from pulling that trigger. He meant to get them both and he didn't want to have to camp a week here to do it.

He would wait till that other guy stuck his face out, till he got them both away from that cabin, then he'd cut them down like a couple of snakes.

It made him boil to think of them here with that girl. She was probably scared half out of her wits. Only one thought kept him from going hog wild; they'd been running too fast to work her any mischief—but any fool could tell you what them fellers was after.

The thought did not tend to cool him off any.

Consumed with impatience he lifted the rifle, but he lowered it reluctantly without doing anything. The guy with the skillet was only part of this business; there was another guy with him, and he aimed to get both of them. It sure burned him up to watch that guy cooking and him starved enough to eat a dog with the hide on.

Then a guy came out of the cabin and Cardigan almost jumped to his feet.

Grave Creek Clanton, the old wrinkle-faced whelp!

Grave Creek Clanton that he'd picked from the gutter and set up in business with a stable at Payson—there was gratitude for you! Taking Cardigan's money and making off with his woman!

When he was able to see straight again and to think straight, Cardigan knew there was no time for foolishness. That Clanton could shoot the buttons off your shirt. He had jumped more claims and slit more throats than any other bastard in the country, and Cardigan was taking no chances.

He waited till Grave Creek got to the fire. Then he peeled his lips back and let him have it. He flung the barrel over quick and snapped a shot at the other guy.

The bird with the skillet went ass over elbow but Grave Creek Clanton never even staggered. He spun like a cat and started heating his axles. Straight down the gulch, he streaked with both legs flying.

Cardigan jumped to his feet and ran out in the open. Grave Creek was dashing down the gulch full tilt, doing his damnedest to get into the trees. Cardigan dropped to a knee and crashed a couple slugs after him.

The second one got him, and he went down like a duck. He flopped around on the ground like a wolf with its throat cut.

Cardigan got up and worked the lever of his rifle.

With a fresh shell under the hammer, he felt better. He even felt a little sorry for the bastard now. That had always been his trouble, too much pity, too much softness.

He was halfway down to where he'd seen Clanton flopping when the sidewinder reared right up on his hunkers with a gun in each fist and both of them spitting.

Something belted the brim of Cardigan's bonnet. Something jerked at his vest, cut his holster plumb off. Then he went down on his belly and never quit firing till his rifle was empty.

When the smoke cleared away Grave Creek Clanton wasn't moving. He was flat on his back, and he wasn't playing possum.

EIGHT
AN OLD THIEF GOES HOME

BUT CARDIGAN WAS all through playing Good Samaritan.

He guessed he would go on up to the cabin and get that girl cut loose of her ropes and maybe after that, if he got to feeling like it, he would come back down here and plant these jaspers.

He started for the shack, but his knees got to shaking so bad he couldn't make it. He got down on the ground and shook and sweat till his stomach muscles came out of their tangle and he was able to draw a full breath without retching.

Evening's lonesome light was filling this gulch and he looked at the shack but didn't put any strain on himself getting over there.

He had to get a couple things straightened out in his mind first. Like whether he had ought to fetch the girl or not. Of course, if they'd left her tied up—and he reckoned they had, or she'd been out before this—he guessed he would have to; but right now, the idea of having him a woman lacked considerable of being as attractive as it had. He didn't know what the hell had come over him, but he couldn't get worked up over that woman for sour apples. Not even the idea of crawling in bed with her seemed worth a second thought the way he felt right now.

He reckoned maybe he'd feel different after he got some grub in him. Been a powerful long while since he'd sunk his molars in a good piece of cow flesh and, one thought naturally leading to another, it came to him one of them guys had been cooking.

He got up with a groan and moseyed over to the fire.

As a matter of precaution, he looked the cooker over first. But there was no need to worry about that guy. A little wrinkled-up wart with a face like a bullfinch, he had caught Kurt's slug square between the eyes.

Cardigan looked at him and grunted. Then his glance found the skillet. A piece of burned sow bosom was stuck to its bottom. He cut it loose with his knife and bit him off a sample. He picked up the smoke-sooted pot from the ashes and found it half full of good black Java which slid down mighty easy.

He finished the pork and poked around some more but, except for the frijoles strewed all over the ground, there were no further eatables anyplace in sight. Looked like these cabrones had been living off cut straw and molasses. Guessed the road agent business wasn't paying off no better these days than raising cattle.

With a disgusted grunt, he finally headed for the cabin. Might as well see what kind of a card he'd been drawing to, but he sure wished again he'd never written that letter.

Time, he reached the sagged door he was sweating like a nigger. He was shaking in his boots like a boghole rider after tailing twenty steers. He had to get behind and shove himself to get him to the door and he damn near bolted when he heard a stifled groan.

"Jesis!" he said and couldn't turn a finger.

If that had come from a woman, he didn't want any part of her.

Like a wolf in a trap, he stood there with his hackles up, scarcely even breathing so intently was he listening. Gray gloom crept through the gulch and thickened and all he could hear was the bumping of his heart.

He finally lifted a hand and found it frozen to his rifle. He wanted to laugh but his mouth wouldn't shape it.

What the hell was in that cabin?

With an almighty care, he set his rifle against the wall. With an equal stealth, he eased the pistol from his trousers where he was being forced to pack it on account of Grave Creek Clan-ton.

The inside of that cabin was black as a stack of stove lids.

He looked a long while before he decided to go in there. He felt prominent as a new saloon in a church district, and it took all the strength of his entire body to lift one foot and put it down across that doorstep. The floor gave out a banshee wail and his eyes plunged into the blackness wildly. He damn near choked the grip off his pistol but nothing happened.

He took a ragged breath.

He gnawed at his lip and felt sweat collect in the palms of his hands and then, off in a corner, there was a kind of hoarse breathing; and he tipped up his gun and said: "Strike a light!"

He half expected the blackness to explode in a gun flash but nothing at all happened. No one moved. No sound came out of that tight black silence and Cardigan snarled: "Strike a light, by God, or I'll let you have it!"

The only answer he got was a faint repetition of that labored breathing. Then a tired sigh came from the corner. "You'd ... be wastin' your lead," a man's voice said faintly. "I ain't got much more than ... a couple breaths left."

Cardigan's eyes raked the gloom suspiciously.

"Where you at?"

"Over here."

"I could figure out that much."

"I'm...in the bunk," the man said, so low Kurt had to lean forward to hear him.

He was thinking to himself he'd better watch this fellow. He might of lost his gun and this could all be a trick to get Kurt over there. He might be crouched with a club. He might have hold of a knife.

Cardigan licked his lips. "What's the matter with you?"

"Hell... I'm all shot t' pieces." The labored gasp of his breathing became suddenly frantic, and he cried in a half-strangled voice: "It's so goddam black!" And then, weakly: "Are you there, Art?"

"I'm right here," Cardigan said. He moved forward a little, all his senses alert for the first sign of treachery. "Where's the girl?"

The guy didn't answer. There wasn't any sound but the man's terrible breathing. Cardigan, listening into that blackness, heard the slats of the bunk creak. "Mother!" the man cried brokenly, but Cardigan kept a tight hold on his pistol.

"Where's the girl?" he repeated, but all the breath seemed to be running out of the man.

With a smothered curse Cardigan plowed through the dark till his knees brought up against the side of the bunk.

He drew back the hammer of his gun and struck a match. The light raveled down across the man on the bunk. He'd been shot all right —he was a hell of a sight. His beard-stub-bled cheeks were the color of chalk.

His eyes fluttered open. "You...you still there, pard?"

Cardigan, scowling, put the pistol away. He reached down a hand to the man's bony shoulder. "What'd you do with the girl?"

The man didn't answer. He seemed too far gone even to notice the light and it was obviously only a matter of moments now.

"The girl!" Cardigan said. "What'd you do with the girl?"

"Girl...Oh! Soldiers got her—got Benny an' Snell. Clanton turned her...loose when they dropped his horse. Figured that might stop 'em, but...Pull my boots off, will you?"

The match burned out and Cardigan dropped it. He bent over, hating it, and pulled the guy's boots off.

"Don't," the man pleaded, "tell Mother I...died like this."

"Hell," Cardigan said, "what you need's a drink—"

"Hold...hold my hand will you, pardner?"

Cardigan took the cold hand.

It seemed to please the guy someway. Another of those terrible sighs welled out of him. "Could"—the cracked voice took on a wistful note— "Could you sing me a...hymn?"

"Well, Jesis Christ!" Cardigan said and stopped. After all, the poor bastard was just about done for. It was little enough anyone could do for him. "What about—" He scowled a moment, trying to think of one.

"Somethin' with Mother..." The man muttered faintly.

Cardigan swallowed a couple of times to get the sow belly out of his gullet. He could damn well do with a drink himself. He cleared his throat self-consciously and sang in a husky baritone:

"After the roundup is over
after the shippin' is done I'm going to
    see my mother
before my money's all gone. My moth-
    er's heart is breakin',
breakin' for me that is all; An' with
    God's help I'll see her
when the work is done this fall.
" 'Twas along in the shank of the
    evenin'
this boy went out to stand guard, The
    wind was blowin' fiercely
an' the rain was fallin' hard.
The cattle they got frightened
an' ran in mad stampede; Poor boy, he
    tried to head them—"

The man's cold hand squeezed Cardigan's fingers. "Tell her that," he whispered, and his grip fell away.

Kurt Cardigan reached up and pulled off his hat. "God damn it," he said and got out of there.

NINE
SUNDRY MATTERS OF MOMENT

WHEN THINGS GOT TOO tough in Nogales, Stella Mae Larpin, who had once been a stockbroker's darling, threw her clothes in a bag and took the next stage for Tucson. There was nothing for her in Nogales anyway; all the loose jack had gone to Cananea arid, a girl in her business had things tough enough without competition from Mexican chippies. All her favorite Johns had run out on her, and she was tired of the same old sevens and eights.

Tucson, she'd found, was a big improvement. Things really hummed on Meyer Street and the sports who patronized Long Tooth Emma's were strictly on the up and up and never tried to hand you any crap about charging it.

Long Tooth Emma kept the squirreliest place. You never would have guessed the old bag was a madam. She dressed like something out of Godey's Lady Book and used the most refined language Stella Mae had ever heard. She had real class and no mistake about it.

Her place was right in the heart of town, a big old

adobe smack up against the bank. It was the flossiest joint outside of Dodge City, and its Sunday Chicken Dinners were the talk of the town. It had been a hotel and a lot of folks still thought it one—a thought Miss Emma was happy to cultivate. The old lobby was used as a sitting room with a bar at one end and a melodeon at the other and almost any evening you could find six or eight of the town's solid citizens taking their rest there and auguring politics, the price of beef or which horse was going to win the race next Sunday. Most of the horses around Tucson were "short" horses—Doc Gallaway called them "gamblers' horses" and he sure had the right of it, considering the betting.

After scratching for a living like she had in Nogales, Stella Mae found life at Miss Emma's like a dream. It was the softest berth she had ever got into but there was times when all the quiet and refinement made her want to jerk her hair out and tear around screaming. Navajo rugs on the polished floors, serapes on the walls, and framed oil paintings of range life and horses and pine-covered hills. That kind of stuff could get on your nerves and make you wish, by God, you hadn't ever been born—particular when Charlie sat down at the melodeon and played that piece about the tender apple blossom.

Top Hat Charlie was an English remittance man who'd been shipped to Arizona to die with TB. He didn't work for Emma but ran a faro bank at the Gold Plate Saloon and had the reputation of being the fastest dealer in the West. He had the airs and appearance of a Princeton man and was one of the few high rollers who had the good sense to stay away from booze. And was damned good-looking in a cold, reserved way, but the craziest guy she had ever run into. Every time he sat himself down at the melodeon it was to play some dirge like that tender apple blossom and his taste in women was confined to Mexicana's.

The guy Stella Mae could really have gone for was a yellow-haired rancher by the name of Kurt Cardigan. The guy really got you. He wasn't a regular and most of the time he would just drop around and wag his jaw with Miss Emma or listen to the gab of the Johns at the bar. Sometimes you wouldn't see him for months at a whack, but he sure was a sport and when he went on a tear, he would throw his jack around just like it was washers sawed off a lead pipe.

Would she ever forget the time he'd dragged her off shopping? Been figuring to fix up his house, he'd said, and wanted her opinion on what junk to get and how to arrange it. He'd drawn her some diagrams and talked the thing over till she could just about see the place with her eyes shut. It had been fun at first picking out that stuff and seeing the looks on the shopkeepers' faces; it had been a peck of fun till it had suddenly come over her what her kind of woman had on tap to look forward to. Ever since that time she'd had just one ambition: to get herself a stake while the getting was good.

That Kurt was a card and no getting around it, but anyone could see he'd never fall for a woman. He would kid with them all and make a pass when it pleased him, but you just couldn't picture the guy in double harness. She remembered that time they'd gone swimming in the Santa Cruz...

Thoughts of Kurt Cardigan always made her restless, but she wasn't the kind to beat her head against a wall. Some things you could get and some you couldn't. The smart thing to do was to get what you could and the John she was putting her best foot forward for was Cardigan's range boss, Curly Lahr. With his mop of red hair and his saturnine eyes, he wasn't a man to whom laughter came easy and he wasn't any favorite with the girls at Miss Emma's. But Stella Mae reckoned she had got Lahr figured and always made out like she was glad to see him. He wasn't free and easy like his boss and sometimes, in a clinch, he would get pretty rough. But Stella Mae could make out to put up with a powerful lot if it looked like getting her what she was after.

She was after security, but not that alone.

She had no intention of selling herself short and reaching out for a meal ticket when more could be had by playing her cards right. A rolling stone, to be sure, might gather no moss but it was bound to acquire a certain amount of polish, and if her three years of rolling around with men had left her few illusions there had been compensations of more practical value.

She wasn't thinking of the experience those years had given her but rather of the insight that had come as result of it, Stella Mae had always figured she could add two and two; she could add three and two now and make it come out five.

She knew men and, in the aggregate, precious little good of them. Some were worse than others but at the bottom of them all, there was a hard core of selfishness that influenced all their actions.

This was knowledge and an asset, all you had to do was use it.

Thinking of the two men, Cardigan, and his range boss, she had analyzed the things she saw and settled on the latter. Cardigan was fun to be with. He possessed a certain attraction and a considerable reputation; he had land and cows and horses, a standing in the community not enjoyed by Curly Lahr. But she had watched him with that yellow horse and, tough as big Kurt Cardigan was, she sensed in him a soft streak. It took a man as hard as nails to get anyplace in this country. Any softness was a weakness and someday that weakness would catch him out.

In the taciturn Curly Lahr, she saw a means of reaching her goal. In the redheaded, green-eyed ranch boss Stella Mae recognized, beneath his dour exterior, a burning ambition that would never let the man rest as the hired hand of another.

Here was a man to be reckoned with.

Bone and brawn might tame this country, but bone and brawn would be little likely to lay at her feet those things that Stella Mae secretly craved. Outwardly Cardigan was plenty tough, but Lahr was tough inside and out. Right away she had sensed the guile in his nature, the hidden craft, the drive of the man. It seemed strange he had managed to fool Kurt so long; she had guessed what he was up to within a week of meeting him. Cardigan's ambition was tempered with caution; Lahr didn't know the meaning of the word. It wasn't caution that was holding Lahr back but only plain horse sense—good judgment: he was biding his time; merely waiting for the break.

She didn't know his background or need to. She saw all she needed in the man himself. His driving hunger was fused with subtlety and a sharp and corrosive discernment. He knew what he wanted, and she'd have bet every stitch she had on her that he saw how to go about getting it.

Curly Lahr wanted power and when he ruled this country, she aimed to have a share in the spoils he'd come into.

* * *

ED REAGAN, proprietor of the Lone Star Livery, couldn't get his mind properly fixed on his card game after that dude had gone off with Kurt Cardigan. There was something about that business that was fishy, and his thoughts kept trying to turn up what it was.

In the first place, the danged dude hadn't talked enough. Even counting the bad news, he was supposed to have received it still wasn't natural he should be so close-mouthed. Most of the dudes Ed had ever met up with had been as long on talk as they were short on savvy.

Ed was glad when his friend said he guessed he'd have to go.

Afterwards, when Reagan had the place to himself, he didn't clean the stalls as he'd intended doing; instead, he tipped back his chair in the shade of the entrance and tried to figure out what had stirred this unrest that was jumping around in him.

Perhaps the feeling he had was compounded of several things.

He considered that a while and after a bit, he nodded. Why, for instance, had Cardigan been in such a sweat?

What was it he'd said now? That the dude needn't worry about Injuns, that Cardigan himself would be going through with him. That he wasn't delivering no horses—that he was riding up there to look for the stage.

And why should Kurt Cardigan care about the stage?

That was queer in itself when you stopped to consider it— almost as queer as him offering explanations. It wasn't like Cardigan to ever explain anything.

Yet Cardigan had told him the dude was in a hurry, that he'd had bad news and had to get to El Paso. The dude had looked, right enough, like he'd had bad news, but he hadn't looked to Ed to be in much of a hurry. It was Kurt all the time that had been trying to rush things, Kurt who'd suggested his speediest horses, Kurt who had helped him to get the mare ready and had paid the whole cost right out of his own pocket.

It had looked uncommon, strange to Ed Reagan.

He had known Kurt Cardigan for upwards of five years and never before had he observed the big rancher to show as much lather over anybody else.

"By crackey," Ed said, getting out of his chair, "I believe I'll jest take me a little walk uptown."

He stopped by the barber shop and stuck his head in the door. "Seen Cardigan around?"

"Yeah," the barber said, "but he ain't here now. Had some words with Esparza an' rode off towards the Pass."

So, he'd had words with Esparza.

Reagan turned that over and went across to the stage office. "Joe," he said, with his elbows on the counter, "was Cardigan expectin' anything on that stage?"

The agent glanced up and considered him briefly. He brushed the damp hair back away from his forehead. "He didn't say, Ed."

Reagan rasped his gray jowls. "Did he...did he seem a-tall put out account it hadn't got in?"

The stage agent looked a long while at his desktop. He puffed out his cheeks and finally picked up his pen again. "Afraid I can't answer that question, Ed."

"But he musta said somethin'!"

"You didn't hear it from me."

Reagan stared and then snorted.

Outside in the burning glare of the sun, his glance swung over the drowsing town and picked up the dust-yellow ribbon of road where it crawled through the heat on its climb toward the Pass. No stage and no riders anywhere on it. The desert lay blistering in its infinite hush and a spiraling dust devil tossed its brown breath across the shimmering blue of the faraway mountains. Somewhere out there that dude and Cardigan were riding...

With a grunt, Ed Reagan bent his steps past the bank and past the entrance to Miss Emma's and turned into the Oasis House. At the desk, Frank Esparza stood beside the stooped clerk. They both looked at Reagan and neither man spoke.

Reagan vaguely felt a little uncomfortable and wondered if the pair had been talking about him. He said, "Looks like them 'Paches musta grabbed that stage," and the clerk gloomily nodded.

"Does sorta look that way," the marshal said and, with a thoughtful tug at his mustache, walked out.

Reagan peered after him. Then he turned to the clerk. "You got a dude stayin' here?"

"Funny you should ask that. Frank just asked me the same damn thing."

"Well," Reagan said, "I was just kinda curious."

"So was Frank. The guy's been here three days an' no one said a word about him. Now?—"

"What sort of lookin' feller is he?"

"Kinda short an' fat. Wears a stiff hat an' smokes black cigars. Sunburnt—"

"That's the guy," Reagan said. "What name does he go by?"

"Accordin' to the book his name is Sam Sollantsy. What's he done—stuck up the bank?"

"S'far as I know he ain't done nothin.' I was—"

"Yeah. Just curious. You an' the marshal. I'm gettin' curious myself. In fact, I'm gettin' *damn* curious. Somebody shoot him?"

"No," Reagan said. "It's just that... Well, I'll tell you. He come into my place a while ago an' bought a horse."

"Lots of— Oh. Yeah," the clerk said, looking carefully at Reagan. "What'd he want a horse for?"

"There was some talk of El Paso. Seems he'd had some bad news an' had to hit out—"

"Must of been damn sudden," the clerk said, scowling.

"What I thought," declared Reagan, nodding. "Takin' off across the desert in all this heat. Of course —" Reagan had a sudden hunch not to bring Cardigan into this, and he let the rest trail off, spreading his hands with a shrug. "Didn't hop his bill, did he?"

"I'll take care of that," the clerk told him, frowning.

Reagan dragged his spurs back out onto the porch. The trapped heat off the street was like a breath from a furnace.

A man moved from the wall and went down the steps with him.

"Happened to hear your remarks about that drummer," Esparza said. "Did he tell you himself he had to go to El Paso?"

"Well, not in so many words, but—" Reagan began to wish suddenly he had kept his nose out of this. "That seemed to be the idea," he said lamely.

"Where'd he get this bad news you mentioned?"

"He didn't say."

"What *did* he say?"

"Well, to tell you the truth he didn't say much of anythin'."

"Did he give you the notion he might be runnin' from something?"

Reagan wiped his forehead. "I can't say that he did."

"Looks damn peculiar. What did Cardigan want?"

Reagan stopped stalk still. "Cardigan?" He had to moisten his lips twice to get the one word out.

"He was down to your place, wasn't he?"

"Sure, he was down to my place," Reagan said, not liking the way Frank Esparza was eyeing him.

"Well?" Esparza said.

"I don't get the connection. He drops in at my place whenever it suits him—"

"He dropped in with the dude."

"Now you mention it," Reagan said carefully, "I guess he did. What about it?"

"How long you known Cardigan?"

Reagan wished more than ever he had kept his nose out of this. He didn't know where this talk was being herded but he had a strong hunch that being a party to any talk inimical to Cardigan could be mighty unpleasant if the matter ever happened to be brought to Kurt's attention.

There'd been occasions in the past to amply justify this feeling. Take the case of Val Jones that had packed the star at Paradise. Been pretty well liked when he'd been cowboying for the Cherrycows, a little wild maybe, perhaps a little too ready to reach for his shooting-iron. In a puncher, those penchants had aroused no great amount of animus, but he had fetched both failings to his job as town marshal and a lot of people up there thought him prone to exceed his duty. Cardigan had breezed into town with Curly Lahr one day and inside of ten minutes, Marshal Jones had jumped him. Nobody ever had quite got the straight of it, but Val was said to have used some rough language and wound up his insults by demanding Kurt's gun. Lahr had afterwards said he was afraid there'd be gunplay. He had rushed up behind Kurt and clapped both arms around him just as Cardigan had slid his gun from leather. There had been some confusion, probably mostly in the minds of those who had seen it, but the gun had been discharged and when the smoke cleared away Val Jones had been dead with a hole blown plumb through him.

The coroner's jury had turned Kurt loose, and no one had called it a miscarriage of justice, but there you were. Val Jones was plenty *corpus* and no two ways about it.

Reagan took off his hat and mopped his bald head industriously. "What was that you was sayin'?"

"I said how long you known Cardigan?"

"Well, let's see... four-five years."

"Bought any of his horses?"

"I've bought a few off an' on."

"Suit you all right, did they?"

"They was worth what he charged me if that's what you're gettin' at."

The marshal pushed out his lips. "You ever been out there?"

"Can't say that I hev."

"Well, these horses you've bought—come pretty cheap, did they?"

Reagan turned it over.

"In my line of business, you got to watch all the angles. Most of the time I buy from fellers that ain't got no reg'lar market for their stuff, fellers in the sticks, guys that ain't got no reason to look fer fancy prices. When I wanta git good ones I buy 'em from Cardigan."

"Think he raises pretty good stuff, do you?"

"When you git a hoss from Cardigan you know it'll git the job done."

"When he came into your place with that dude," Esparza said, "what were they talkin' about?"

"Since you ask me, I didn't hear 'em talk about anythin'."

"When they headed for your place," Esparza said, "they were together."

"Look—" Reagan grumbled, "it's too damn hot to stand out here chinnin'. Let's go down to the stable— time I was gettin' back anyway."

They turned toward the livery without further talk, the marshal appearing thoughtful, Reagan thinking, too.

Reagan dropped into a chair at his desk and got out his handkerchief and mopped his face again. "If we don't git rain soon, we'll forgit what water looks like outside of a pail or dipper."

The marshal said bluntly, "When Cardigan and

this drummer headed for your place, they were together."

"All right," Reagan said. "I ain't arguin' about it. So, what if they was? I can't see where all this gabbin' is gettin' us."

"When two gents walk together, they most generally talk some. You say they didn't talk much after they got here. Now it caught at my attention they didn't do much talkin' on the way down here, either."

"Well," Reagan said, squirming around in his chair, "you an' me didn't f that matter. Mebbe they jest happened to meet up with each other. The dude had got bad news—he was in a big hurry t' git to El Paso. He sees Kurt Cardigan, goes dashin' up to him. 'Where kin I git a hoss?' he says. Prob'ly Cardigan says, 'Why'n't you try the livery?' an' brings the guy down here."

"It could've happened that way," the marshal conceded, but not as though he put any stock in it. "Suppose you tell me what happened when they got there."

"I already told you. Nothin' happened. I sold the guy a hoss."

Esparza looked at him.

Reagan mopped his face. His hand got to fiddling with the papers on his desk and he picked one up and dropped it into the drawer.

The silence piled up. So did the film of sweat that beaded Reagan's forehead.

The marshal considered him. When he finally spoke, it was in the measured language of Ed Reagan's generation. There was a broad streak of tolerance running through the casual words; there was a sadness in them too and, underlying all, there was a hard core of pressure that was not to be ignored.

"This town is changin', Ed. Different crowd taking over. Used to be when a gun went off no one paid much notice. If a man was dead, they buried him. Now they want to know all about it, all the little whys and where-fors. You might say I'm a sign of the changin' times. I'm the watchdog they've hired to make sure their notions are properly respected, I'm the bloodhound they feed to find out the answers. Kind of lonesome job, all things considered. But they don't care about that—they don't care about me or about town limits or any other thing. When you sum it up all they want is protection.

"That's all *you* want. The right to eat an' live and run your life as best suits you. You're a part of this, Ed. You pay part of the taxes. You want to share in the things my job makes practical. But it doesn't end there. The knife cuts both ways. When I took this job, I told you, boys, that. I can handle my end. I can keep the wolves down, but I can't give you protection if I don't have your confidence."

Reagan stirred in his chair, scrubbed a hand across his jowls. "Well," he said testily, "what're you gettin' at?"

"Just this. When I go to a taxpayer for information, I like to feel I'm getting it."

Color touched the stableman's cheeks, and then anger. "I told you!—"

"It's the part you ain't told me that I'm waitin' to hear. Somethin' happened in this stable, somethin' connected with that dude, or you wouldn't of gone up there askin' about him."

"I thought the guy was loco goin' off in this heat!"

"Suppose you told him about those Injuns—"

"Course I told him about 'em!"

"It takes a mighty brash dude to thumb his nose at Apaches."

Reagan shut his mouth.

"You're holdin' something back, Ed. There's doubt workin' through you and a lot of suspicion. A marshal generally knows when a man is feelin' jumpy."

He stopped long enough to get out his pipe and he sat a moment holding it, then put it away.

He looked at Reagan steadily. "It takes a mighty brave man or a mighty anxious one to get on a horse an' cross that desert right now. You say it was bad news that made him clear out of here but where would he get it?"

He got up and put his hat on. "It sticks out a mile, Ed."

"What does?"

"The part you ain't mentioned. The part about Cardigan."

TEN
HIDDEN MANEUVERS

COMING out of the shack Cardigan clapped on his hat and his narrowing glance, intensely aware of that shape by the fire, turned edgy and angrily filled with resentment.

Death was so goddam final!

He raked a bitter glance through the roundabout shadows.

It was almost full dark and the wind tumbling down off the rimrocks was as cold to the touch as a bartender's heart. It was generally that way out here on the desert; when the sun went down the air cooled quickly, but never had its cold so got into him before. He pulled the scarf closer about his neck and didn't much like the feel of that either.

He didn't know what the hell ailed him. He tried to pull himself together. He was hungry, that was all. Dog tired and bone weary. He couldn't understand such weariness; he'd been tired before, but his knees hadn't shook.

He swore in a disturbed uneasy fashion and caught

up his rifle and set off up the canyon. Then he slowed down and stopped while he rolled up a smoke. But the thing had no taste, and he threw it away, entirely dissatisfied. Unrest churned through him like wind through a hayfield and he clenched his jaws like he would grind off the cups of every tooth in his head.

If only he never had written that woman!

There was the start of this, the black root of everything. No use to blame Krailor or Rickven's daughter—with his own damn hand, he had written that letter.

No harm, he had thought, in just writing a letter...

He cursed, scowling blackly.

The cards were dealt now, and he would have to play the handout, like it or not. But he couldn't help thinking what a nizzy he had been. Kid stuff, by grab—and him a growed man!

"Love 'em all you feel like but never lug 'em home." That was what he'd told the boys, and he had made it stick. It was just plain hoss sense and had worked out well for them. And here he was now all set to break his own commandments.

But he couldn't back out now; by this time Docie would be waiting at the fort—probably swinging her jaw in forty directions. Telling that nizzy old gaffer of a post commander all about how she had come here to marry Cardigan. A fine kettle of fish. He had always made out to be a man of his word and if he turned her down now every tongue in that goddam fort would start wagging!

Pride aside, he couldn't afford it. He was selling the cavalry a heap too many horses to get the colonel riled up over any play like that. Let that dimwit ever get it into his head that Cardigan's word wasn't something you could bank on, there wasn't no telling where this deal might wind up. Maybe he had ought to pull out of this business. No matter how well a man covered his tracks there was always the chance of a slip-up; and the way things were going of late, by godfreys, it behooved a man to figure mighty careful.

There were currents in Cardigan, wheels within wheels. He'd come into this country to make his stake and had got a pretty fair start on it; not so good a start, however, that he could relish any thought of pulling out now. What he was doing, he told himself, was not a bit worse than plenty of other guys—some of whom were right important gents in this country, and respected.

There was a wild streak in him and a soft streak, too, and these were compounded by the stubbornness bequeathed him by a long line of forebears who'd gone after what they wanted. What, for instance, was the difference between a banker foreclosing on some poor bastard's outfit and a guy who merely lifted three or four of his horses? To Cardigan it seemed a simple matter of degree and, in this light, all the odds were with the latter. There were unwritten rules in this country and so long as you played by these rules it was nobody's business but your own how you lived.

The rules were flexible enough to suit Cardigan's purpose. Gamblers, for example, were expected to try and fleece you; if you fleeced them instead, folks laughed and slapped your back. When they fleeced you, you were considered a sucker. If you caught a gambler cheating, you were privileged to shoot him, and no one thought the worse of either of you for it. If you got shot yourself that was all right too unless your friends cared to make something of it.

Rumor might paint a man black as forty stove lids—might call him a bandit, a rustler, or stage-robber, but he was seldom accused or treated as one until he grew so bold or so careless that somebody got the deadwood on him. When that happened, if the guy had any wheels in his think-box, he cut his stick in a hurry and removed to calmer parts.

If he was able.

Cardigan grunted.

Most of them were. As a matter of insurance, most of those operating outside of the law had friends scattered around in likely places who would give them the word before anything happened.

Cardigan hadn't bothered to make friends. Why split the profit? he had asked himself; it assayed low enough after splitting with your men. He never went out of his way to hunt trouble, but he never had tried to make folks beholden to him. He had preferred, instead, to keep his trap shut and play his hand as he found it.

He was beginning to realize the shortcomings of this method.

Too many things were piling up on him. Self-sufficiency was fine if a man could afford it, but how many could?

It was a startling thought which had never before occurred to him. He was a man who had learned to live by his wits, to absorb impressions as a sponge sucks up water, to make his decisions on stray words and gestures, on the shades of expression flitting through a man's eyes, on marks in the dust and inexplicable feelings. And the whole feeling of this country in the last few hours was bothering him.

He paused to shape a smoke, still thinking about it.

The paper tore in his fingers and he flung it away while his thoughts got blacker and blacker.

It was writing that letter that had got it all started. If he hadn't written that St. Louis woman, he would never have gone to meet that stage. If he hadn't been stewin about the damn stage he'd of taken a smoother line with that drummer. If he hadn't got tangled up with the dude, he'd of hunted the stage right after he'd eaten and would have had no call to swap words with the marshal. Or to of done all that jawin in front of Ed Reagan. Or to have found himself needing to go on to Camp Grant when all of his druthers would have turned him straight home.

Though a horse thief could swing just as high as trees grew, there was one thing from which Kurt could still take comfort. He might look no better in the eyes of the law, but it could not be said that his depredations had ever worked a real hardship on anyone. He didn't stick up banks, rob stages, or roll drunks; he confined his thievery strictly to horses and the men he stole from could afford it.

* * *

AT RANCH HEADQUARTERS, the crippled cook, Hennessy, looked up from the bench where he'd been cutting up spuds and watched Curly Lahr get off a lathered horse. It was three o'clock in the afternoon, a peculiar time for a range boss to be showing up at headquarters.

Lahr tossed his reins and clanked into the shade with his sun-ruddied cheeks about as genial as a bulldog's. "Kurt back yet?"

"Ain't seen 'im."

Lahr scowled a while, silent. "You can slack off on that grub," he said then, taking off his hat and thumbing the sweat from his eyes. "Crew won't be in fer a long time yet —they're bringin' in a bunch we picked up around Florence."

"Ain't that gettin' a little mite close?" the cook said.

The range boss' eyes slammed into him—hard. "This cookin' job suit you?"

Hennessy sat there a moment. "I've done things I like better," he said finally, and got up and dippered water into the kettle of spuds. He poured a slug into himself and limped back.

"Kurt's been gone quite a spell. Three days," Lahr said, "an' not a word outa him."

Hennessy wiped off his knife on a pants leg. "He coulda gone on a bender—"

"He ain't doin' no bendin' in Tucson—I looked."

The cook said worriedly, "You don't reckon that damn yeller stud—"

Lahr made a noise with his mouth and sat down. "You tell me. Here's what he done, near as I can make out. He rode that dun into town an' hitched across from the stage office, hangin' round there all mornin'. Fed his face at Jelks' hash house an' then him an' some coffee drummer went down t' Reagan's stable. The drummer got a horse an' took the road fer El Paso.

"Comin back from the livery Cardigan stopped in front of Warner's an' Esparza come off the porch an' swapped talk with him. Then Kurt climbs on to that yeller stud-hoss an' hits off across that blisterin' desert. That make any sense t' you?"

Hennessy imbedded his knife in the bench. "What the hell would he talk about with Frank Esparza?"

"That," Lahr said, "is what *I* want to know."

"By cripes," Hennessy said, "I don't like it! That marshal was out here this mornin' nosin' round..."

"Three days ago, Kurt talks to him; today he comes out here—"

"To look at some horses!"

They considered each other across a lengthening silence.

Lahr's narrowed eyes watched the corrosive of his thought darkly spread through the crippled cook. He said at last, very softly, "Which ones did you show him?"

"Didn't show 'im any—wasn't nothin' up but them gelding's in the corral there. I told him t' come back when the boss was t' home."

"An he rode off then?"

"Not right then. Wanted t' know 'f it would be all right fer him t' go out an' look around. I told him he could look if he wanted but he wouldn't see much outside of some young stuff that wasn't quite ready t' be put t' work yet."

Hennessy scrubbed the back of a hand across his whiskered cheeks and, above that hand, his questioning eyes quartered Lahr's face with a need for knowledge. He said: "Esparza asked a funny thing then. Wanted t' know if we been losin' much stock. Now, why would he be askin' a thing like that?"

Lahr's laugh was short. "Didn't you jest say yourself you thought Florence was close? Hell! We been nickin' outfits a heap closer than that; an' it ain't been Kurt—it's been me that's had t' take these damn close-in bunches."

It looked for a bit as though the bait would go untasted; then the cook got up and said dustily: "Why?"

Lahr knew mighty well what the man was asking but he chose to misread the cook's plain question.

"Hell's fire!" he scowled. "Why's a man do anything round this spread? You ought t' know by now who gives out the orders. Alls I do is pass 'em along—an' ramrod 'em through!" he added bitterly.

They were silent then with the cook plainly thinking and making hard work of it. But Lahr, knowing through long study when to keep his mouth shut, stared glumly down at his boots, and said nothing. He had cast his seed on fertile ground and was satisfied to let it grow without prodding.

Hennessy said at last, darkly. "Mebbe I better cut loose of this outfit."

"The rats," Lahr murmured, "are always first t' quit ship."

The cook wheeled his head with a sullen stare. "You hankerin' t' hev your neck stretched?"

Lahr shrugged.

Hennessy snorted. "When a man starts stealin' from his neighbors he's jest out-an' out askin' t' git his neck stretched. I'm gittin' out! Any time you find me dancin' on air it'll be fer a heap better reason than helpin' t' stuff dollars into someone else's pockets!"

Lahr said contemptuously, "You churn air like a windmill but what does it amount to? Blowin' off steam don't profit a man nothin'. Your guts is like quicksand —'f you had any bottom you'd do somethin' about it."

The cook came off the bench with his teeth bared

but Lahr didn't even turn his head to look at him. He said, "It's mostly like that with these guys that talk big. You don't hear me soundin' off, do you? I don't like to be suckered no better'n the next, but you don't hear me runnin' off at the mouth about it. An' you won't. I leave all the runnin' fer fellers like you."

It was almost more than Hennessy could take. Anger had chased all the fright from his features and outrage was painting brash pictures in his head, but some vestige of caution still was in him, and it finally set him back down on the bench.

Lahr let him glower for a while and then said, "I had this thing pegged the day he rode out of here. Findin' out he had that talk with the marshal an' now hearin' from you that Esparza's been out here only shows me the proof of what I'd already figured."

"Well?" Hennessy growled.

"We piled up this dough on a kind of pardnership basis, Kurt t' take the bigger share for the plannin' an' bossin', but with each of us due for a good-sized cut. We been free to draw on ours anytime but, mostly, we've just let it pile up with his. We—"

"Hell, I know all that!"

"Know how much you got comin'?"

"I kin figger it out—I know I got plenty," the cook said irascibly.

"We all have," Lahr nodded, "an there's men been double-crossed for a considerable sight less. An' on top of that—if he could get shucked of us—Kurt would have this whole spread plumb free an' beyond touchin'. It kinda makes a man think," the range boss said, slow and thoughtful. "There's a pile of good graze bein' held by this outfit. If he could cut loose of us—"

"But that's where we got him," Hennessy grinned, feeling better. "He can't chuck us out if we don't want t' go."

"Oh, can't he?" Lahr said and spat contemptuously.

The cook sat still for a couple of heartbeats and then dark color moved into his cheeks. "All right—all right...I ain't *gone* yet! He might scare some of the dubs on this payroll, but he sure couldn't bank on scarin' us *all* out."

"You talk like a fool! He could *sell* us out, couldn't he?"

The cook started swearing in a tight, bitter way.

Lahr lifted a knee, hooked a spur on the bench, and sat there impassive with his green-eyed gaze still roving the hills. He waited till the cook had run through his rage, till the breath ran out of his wicked talk and his shoulders sagged back against the bunkhouse wall. Then he put his plan before Hennessy.

As he let it unfold the cook's mouth fell open and fear grew bright in his eyes for a moment and then faded away before the creep of desire. Lahr knew then he had this man and could use him, and he rammed home his points soft and swift and sat back.

"But what about the others? What about Krailor an' Shiloh Frayne?"

"Do you feel like you got to look out for them?"

"Well, no ... I guess not," Hennessy said, with his thoughts still pawing it. "But will it work?" he asked worriedly, still a little afraid.

"It'll work if you remember what I said an' keep your mouth shut. I don't think you'll spill nothing. You an' me is the only ones in on this deal an' if anythin' leaks out, I'll know what to do about it."

* * *

THE CIGAR-SMOKING DRUMMER in the yellow shoes and derby rode into St. David at ten o'clock of a star-sprinkled evening on a buttermilk filly that still looked to have a deal of miles left in her.

There was nothing spectacular about his arrival.

He passed up the first two or three darkened farms, turning finally down a lane to where a two-storied house still showed a lighted window. He hitched the filly to a post, brushed his clothes off a little, stepped up onto the veranda, and put his knuckles to the door.

After a while, he rapped again, and presently a man with his hair every which way and a pair of rough pants pulled on over his nightshirt came to the door with his galluses dangling.

He had a lamp in one hand and a pistol in the other.

"Yeah?" he said.

"Your name Scowsen?"

The lamp holder nodded.

"I'd like to have a fresh horse. My name's Sollantsy."

One further moment the man looked him over. "Barn's around to the back. I'll fetch out a lantern," he said and closed the door.

Unhitching the filly, the man who called himself Sollantsy led her on around back. Directly the man came out with his lantern, and they crossed the yard to where a large red barn comfortably squatted in the shadows. The man hung his lantern on a peg inside the door and several horses nickered softly from a long row of stalls. There were six horses stabled there and none of them was work stock.

"That roan geldin' suit you?"

Sollantsy nodded and the man led him out. The derby-hatted drummer then walked over to the kak-pole and lifted down a forty-pound stock saddle, got himself a dry blanket and bridle, and proceeded to get the roan ready for travel. He looked around at the man once. "I want that filly given extra good care."

The man had already taken the saddle and pad off. "Will you be wantin' any grub?" he grunted.

"No. But I'll be glad of fresh water."

"There's a spring-fed pipe just outside the door yonder."

"Which way to Benson?"

"About a half mile east you'll strike a north-south road. Turn left an' stay with it."

"How far?"

"Seven mile, more or less."

Sollantsy nodded. With an economy of movement, he went up to the roan, pulled the slack from the latigo, and swung up into the saddle. No money changed hands. "Take care of that filly," he said and rode out.

An hour later he was dismounting at the Benson Livery.

Leaving his horse there he stepped up to an all-night lunch wagon, downed a couple sandwiches and a mug of hot Java, scouted out a hotel, and signed for a room. "Like some writin' materials," he told the yawning baldhead. "One envelope'll do."

The frowsty old clerk rummaged around and came up with the requested articles. "Hell of a time to be writin' a letter."

"You know how it is with a woman." Sollantsy winked.

The bald clerk grunted. "Only kinda woman I ever felt the need of is the kind that's near enough t' crawl into bed with. You don't hev t' write them no letters."

Sollantsy chuckled, picked up his things, and went down a dim-lit hall hunting numbers.

Inside his room, he turned the key in the lock, scratched a match and lit the lamp, and set his writing things down on the washstand. He tossed his coat on the bed. He set pitcher and washbasin carefully on the floor. He got a cigar from his vest and lighted it over the chimney of the lamp and pulled up a chair and sat down by the washstand.

He remained there a while, silently smoking and thinking. Then he yawned, squeezed the sweat off his forehead, and let his breath go in a prolonged sigh. He got up again then, slipped his shoulder harness off, and hung it on the back of his chair. Resuming his seat once more he picked up the pen and dipped it into the inkpot.

He wrote for an hour, filling four pages with cramped lines of words. Then he folded them into the envelope, sealed and addressed it and put on his coat, and took it down to the clerk.

After which he went to bed.

ELEVEN
MELODY IN LEAD

THE STAGE STATION at Bisbee was no better and no worse than those she had found at half a hundred other towns, decided the girl now seated on the dusty and knife-scarred waiters' bench in the trapped heat beneath its sun-warped wooden awning. Dingy, faded, and paintless, it looked to have plumped itself down against the face of a cliff in much the same fashion as some careless roustabout had plumped down the twelve sacks of grain that took up one end of the dust-windrowed planks beneath the bench on which she was seated.

The girl was dressed in dove-gray, tight-waisted taffeta with a ruffle of lace and black ribbon at her throat, the whole buffly powdered—like her hat and her gloves—with the dust from the road.

In the opinion of the man lounged against the sacked feed she was quite a looker. He'd been covertly observing her ever since he had stepped up here, though she hadn't thus far appeared to notice his presence.

Now he looked at her boldly. "Kinda tiresome wait-in'," he offered conversationally. "Stage won't git in fer a hour yet."

"Thank you," she said, without turning her head.

"No trouble a-tall. Goin' t' Tucson?" he asked.

Again, she nodded, still without turning.

Snooty, he decided.

But she sure was a looker. And the way that dress fit from the hips on up was enough to stop the U. S. Cavalry. If a feller could shine up to something like that, getting hitched wouldn't be half bad, he decided and went over to the horse ne had left at the porch edge.

Three riders on slow-moving horses were coming up the dusty road. Punchers, it looked like. He gave them no attention. Rummaging in the slicker lashed behind his cantle he dug out an apple. Been figuring to eat it himself but he reckoned he could get along without it. Polishing it briskly on a leg of his pants he moved back to the girl and held it out. "Mebbe you'd be likin' t' sink yer teeth in this?"

She looked at him then, and at the apple, also. "No, thank you." But she smiled the smallest bit and, encouraged, he said, "Long ride t' Tucson—be a good while 'fore you git there."

"Yes," she said and looked away again.

He scowled at the apple, abruptly tossed it up, and caught it. Then he wiped it again on his pants leg and bit it. "Hev many hosses back East where you come from?"

"Quite a few."

"Good as this 'un?" He waved the apple he was chewing toward the horse he had left at the porch edge.

The three horsemen had come abreast of them and turned in at a hitchrack directly across from them. The three riders swung down and went into the building. Still chewing, Jupe Krailor said, "Good as him?"

"I'm afraid I don't know enough about horses to say."

"Don't, eh?" He dragged a calloused hand across his scraggle of whiskers. "What you figgerin' t' go t' Tucson fer?"

"Well... really!" she said, and then suddenly she was smiling. "How many children do you have?"

"Huh! Who—me?" His cheeks took fire and he backed off a little. "Hell, I ain't even married—or about t' be!"

"That *is* queer, isn't it? You were taking such a fatherly interest—"

But the man was moving off. Catching up the grounded reins of his horse, with his neck still red he set off across the road.

That building over there was the Copper State Bank, easily the most pretentious looking edifice in town. The evening shadows, she noticed, were lengthening, that from the bank reaching almost to her feet. The long dusty street with its clutter of wagons and hitched horses showed but very few people; probably most of them were home getting their faces washed for supper.

A scurry of wind picked up dust from the roadway and, three doors down, a dog came off a porch and commenced to root beneath it. She could hear the hard beat of a blacksmith's hammer and a man's head and shoulders pushed through the batwings of the saloon next door and sent a speculative look in her direction, afterward withdrawing.

She looked for the man who had thought to be a lady-killer and found him over against the hitchrack where the three men had left their horses. Her glance considered him, idly noting his worn and grimed clothing, the battered hat which he wore, and she remembered the long uncombed hair curling down around his collar. Some range rider, probably, though he had more the look of a grub line rider, she thought, recalling his run-over boots and discolored spurs. She thought it odd how his appearance was so little in keeping with that of his horse, which was a good one suggesting plenty of bottom—like the horses beside which he stood now and whittled.

He seemed absorbed in his task, yet she had the impression that his sharp little eyes were on her still, and she felt vaguely uncomfortable.

The sunlight was bright and golden where the blue-black shadows hadn't rubbed it out. Heat still clung to the underside of the station's warped wooden awning, and she looked again at the horses, wondering about the three men in the bank, oddly surprised that they should have such good mounts. A roan, a bay, and a white-stockinged sorrel. They looked a deal more like race-horses than cowponies.

The station agent came with his slow limp to the doorway and poked his head out, giving her an encouraging smile. "It'll git here finally—always does," he said. "Why don't you go over to the Rimrock House—that's the hotel yonder—where you'll be more comfortable. I'll see that you don't miss it—"

"If you don't mind, I'd rather wait here," she said.

"Lord, *I* don't mind!" He laughed a little at the

vehemence of his words. And to make sure she properly understood him, he said, "We put that bench there for the convenience of our customers."

He couldn't figure her out. She'd come in with an escort of troopers from Camp Grant; the sergeant had confided that she'd had a bad scare. She didn't look scared; she was the coolest looking woman he had seen in a long while, and the most strikingly unusual. Blackest hair, whitest teeth, and reddest lips he'd ever seen. But it was her eyes, he reckoned, that really got hold of you. Hazel. Clear and deep as mountain water. Honest. The most honest eyes he had ever encountered. He had never seen a woman quite like her, and the thought made him wish that he were twenty years younger and not chained down with a job at a stage depot.

He sighed and went back to his cluttered desk.

The girl turned her face and looked off down the road again. With its tortuous trails and cliff-flanked street, she thought this was one of the ugliest towns she had ever been in. The raw red earth of the hillsides was the depressing color of rusted iron, and the houses she saw on the yonder slopes were little, better, or bigger than packing crates. How in the world did folks live in a place like this?

She pondered the question but what she had seen of it gave her no answer. She did not have to wonder what they did for amusement. The mines had fetched them here in the first place, of course, and what wealth they wrenched from the stubborn earth went mostly into the saloons and brothels, of which there were plenty.

The old, old story of the wild frontier.

She frowned a little, considering it. How could better things come where men lived hardly more civilized than animals, where toil and greed and savagery were the common order of the day? Was all life harsh? Was there nowhere anything better than this? What of love and warmth and graciousness—were these nothing but words on a printed page?

She shook loose of her thoughts with an impatient lift of her shoulders. Love and graciousness, like freedom, were all very well, but the first need in life was security. She was not a bargaining woman, but security was something she never had known. It was the most desirable thing she could think of.

* * *

THE MOOD WAS ABRUPTLY SHATTERED, her eyes drawn sharply across the street by the sound of a muffled explosion. Over there, by the hitch rack, the would-be lady-killer had dropped his whittling, and now, to her surprise, he had a rifle cradled in his arms and the reins of four horses were in his left hand.

Two men with heavy sacks were backing out of the bank; a third, back toward her, still stood in the doorway with a gun in his fist, his face obscured behind the folds of a pulled-up neckerchief. And the two with the sacks were masked likewise, she saw, as they coolly turned and stepped across to their horses.

She heard boots sound behind her and the agent's grim voice. "Inside, miss—quick!" And then he was brushing past her, a determined man with a shotgun. Crouching low, he dived for the pile of sacked feed but, just short of it, he stopped and straightened. With a tight, choked cry he suddenly buckled in his tracks, his dropped gun clattering across the warped planks.

Smoke drifted whitely from the lady-killer's rifle. Gun sound clouted the fronts of the buildings and, even as she watched, the man whirled and with another burst of firing drove three punchers behind the Lone Star Cafe.

The men with the sacks were mounted now, fighting their rearing horses. And then they were gone, dust billowing behind them as they cut for the open range.

The man in the Copper State's doorway chose that moment to whirl and come pelting toward the hitchrack where the other man waited with the two remaining horses. The lady-killer tossed him the reins of one of them, swung onto his own, and drove a final shot toward the Lone Star Cafe. He was wheeling his horse to take after the others when a man came onto a porch two doors down. The slanting shafts of the sun kicked light from his lifting rifle, from the bit of metal that was pinned to his vest.

Flame knifed brightly from the crouched-forward shape of the man still afoot, and the girl saw the lawman stagger back against the wall. But the man who had shot him wasn't satisfied. Again, flame spurted from the muzzle of his gun, and the lawman folded across the porch rail.

He sheathed his pistol then and jerked his horse's head around and hauled himself into the saddle. "Come on—come on!" his companion shouted; and they churned up the dust in a great wide circle. As they swept past the stage office the man who had shot the badge-toter suddenly lifted a hand as though to clutch at his hat. If that was his intention it got there too late, for the hat sailed off and he did not stop for it but spurred after his companion with his red hair flying wild in the wind.

TWELVE
AN OLD TROLLOP EXPLODES

THE COLONEL WAS VERY sorry Kurt had had this trip for nothing but Miss Balinett, he said, was no longer around. Yes, the troopers had intercepted the stage robbers and had fetched her in unharmed, but she'd been in a swivel to get to Tucson and had gone with an escort to catch the stage at Bisbee.

The nizzy old gaffer had wanted to discuss horses but Kurt had cut the talk short, bribed a tarp from the sutler's wife, and, sprawled still dressed across it, had slept the clock very nearly around.

That had been three days ago. Refreshed, shaved, and washed in the creek, he had quit Camp Grant early yesterday morning and had made good time, considering the amount of traveling Snuffy had done in the past five days.

He knew there'd be no use in him going to Bisbee; long before he could get there the girl would be gone. So, he'd struck straight for Tucson, cutting across the country by the shortest means available; and now he could see it, just yonder—a scattering of light beneath the black shadows of the Santa Catalinas.

He held the big dun to a leisurely lope despite the impatience that prodded him. This conservation of horseflesh was an old thing with Cardigan who never knew when he might really need every ounce of speed he could get. Sometimes he would ride for hours at a walk and had done so on this trip, for in a country life this—and in his kind of business —another ten yards of travel might spell all the difference between continued living and an unmarked grave.

Sometimes, like now, when his mind got to thinking of the risks he ran and the mighty little pleasure he got out of the business, he wondered if horse stealing ever really paid. He knew, of course, it was the soft streak in him that turned his mind along such daunsy trails. But a man couldn't keep from thinking.

It was numbskulls, mostly, that played the outlaw game; puny little bastards, too weak for honest living, and the lazy lads that would go to any length to keep from turning their hands at any regular job. These, and the natural born bullies and chiselers, made up the bulk of the owlhoot legions. The exceptions were plain damn fools like himself who had a craving for excitement and didn't have the gumption to keep a rein on it.

Sometimes, he thought, he'd give anything, to be honest, to get his damn feet back on the straight and narrow. But the same old thought always struck him each time he figured to sponge the slate clean and start over. Just one more haul... just one more haul and he'd quit the damn game. But it was ever and always the same old story. Like drinking hard likker, riding the owlhoot got to be a habit; and he knew in his bones there was just one end to it.

But one of these days he *would* quit—he *really* would. Maybe if this girl was his kind, if she was something to be proud of, he might even start over for her sake.

He laughed a little, wryly, at the foolishness of any such notion as that. He might quit, but it wouldn't be on account of no skirt.

The game wasn't what it had used to be. Times were changing. The country was getting too damned settled up. The risks were greater and the profits much leaner—it was a dog's life at best and, with the cattlemen organizing like they was all over, it was getting, by cripes, so you couldn't turn around without ramming into some kind of star-packer.

He thought about that for the next couple miles. And he thought of the dude and Frank Esparza and the loose-jawed way of that liveryman, Reagan. He kept seeing the dude and Esparza eyeing Snuffy...

The writing was on the wall, all right. It might be a good thing for him to quit right now—to get out of this business and live like a Christian. The boys might not much cotton to it, but a bigger share in the pot they'd built up ought to wipe the scowls off their faces. Last winter had sweetened the kitty plenty—they must have pretty near twenty thousand right now. Split five ways that wouldn't be too bad. If he were to add from his own another five hundred to each man's share ...

It was sure as hell worth considering, he thought; and then he called himself seven kinds of a fool for even dreaming up such a cockeyed notion. He must, by Gawd, be going soft in the head!

But the notion stayed with him all the way down the slope to the Santa Cruz Valley.

He'd been lucky, up to now; but no man's luck continued good forever, and all the signs and signal smokes gave urgent warning his was headed for the rocks. There was that dude and Esparza and what this chase had shown him about that bastard Grave Creek Clanton! That was gratitude for you!

They were all alike, this ragtag breed of the chaparral. All cut from the same rotten cloth! Shifty, greedy, an untrustworthy lot whose allegiance was worth no more than the size of the cut it got them. And when that cut seemed no longer sufficient—or other interests provided a chance that looked better—they would sell you out to the quickest bidder.

It was a time to be thinking, to be adding the score up. And he did so.

Something was plain enough to Cardigan then. He'd better pay off his crew and get them out of the country—give 'em the whole damn pot if he had to. But get rid of them. Now. Before it was too late.

* * *

HE CAME into Tucson by a woodchopper's trail, still moodily thinking as he followed it through the squalid Mexican quarter, and so into the brighter lights of Meyer Street. There was a stage pulled up before the Overland office and the sight pulled his mind back around to Docie.

He ground-tied the dun and stepped into the office. A Mexican at the counter was buying a ticket for Yuma. Kurt looked at the clerk; this wasn't the fellow he had accosted when he'd come here to meet the woman from St. Louis— Cripes, but that seemed a long time ago! This was a bull-necked guy with pink sleeve garters. A pair of iron-rimmed spectacles sat on his nose, and he gave Kurt a look over the tops of them. Counting out the Mexican's change he said: "Well?"

"Was you round when today's stage got in from Bisbee?"

"Yup."

Kurt was having a little trouble with his swallower. "I was supposed t' meet a woman—"

"Wasn't no woman on it."

Kurt frowned. "I don't reckon you could be mistaken?"

"I don't make mistakes," the agent said testily. "There was jest three people got offa that stage. Breckenridge, Fowler an' a lady—there wasn't no woman on it."

One of Cardigan's big fingers traced a brand some puncher had carved in the counter. "Lady, eh? What kinda lookin' lady?"

"Best damn looker that ever hit *this* burg. Class— real class. You ever see Lizette? That one they called the 'Flying Nymph' that was here with the Monarch crowd last year? She couldn't hold a candle to this one."

"Pretty well stacked up, eh?"

"Like a basket of chips."

"You didn't catch her name?"

"Come off it, pal. She didn't look like nothin' you'd be figurin' to meet."

Outside, with Snuffy's reins in his hand, Cardigan stood a while, thoughtful. He guessed it probably wasn't her, but it could be. That bull-necked ox in the stage office might call any skirt a lady that wasn't over forty and his ideas of feminine pulchritude might not gee at all with the facts of the business. Still, he ought to make sure. If it happened to be Docie and she really was a looker, he'd be a fool to go off and...

With a curse, he swung into the saddle. How the hell did you go about finding a woman when you didn't even know what she looked like?

He didn't realize he'd spoken the thought aloud till a kid, peering up at him, said with a grin, "You might try the hotels."

Of course! That was it! The hotels, if she'd put up at one of them, would have her name on the register.

He tossed the kid a cartwheel and turned Snuffy's head toward the Empire House which was not over six doors away up the street.

But she wasn't there, and she wasn't at any other of the places he tried. There was no Balinett on their books that he could find.

To hell with her then. He had spent enough time traipsin round on her account. He'd step into Long Tooth Emma's here and scour the trail dust from his gullet. If Docie wanted to find him, she could come out to the ranch.

Long Tooth Emma's was the same inside as he'd remembered it. Biggers, the banker, was over at the bar shooting the breeze with three or four ranchers, and Emma, togged out in her silks and satins, was fanning herself in the horsehair rocker.

"Well!" she said with a grin when she saw him and bounced up out of her chair and came over. "You've certainly set *this* town on its ear!"

"Me?" Kurt looked at her blankly.

"You!" She grinned and gave him a playful push with her hand. "Stella Mae'll have something to say to you—cryin' her eyes out ever since she heard it. Putting on the dog, aren't you, Cardigan?"

He looked at her, frowning. Under this banter there was a hard core of something he couldn't quite nail; and he didn't get that stuff about Stella Mae, either. What the hell did *she* have to cry about?

He cuffed back his hat. "Come off it," he said. "I come in for a drink—"

"You mean you're not serving liquor?"

Cardigan wheeled his shoulders half around and stopped. "I don't get it."

Miss Emma bared her golden fangs. "Now listen, dearie. I always say, 'live and let live.' How you latch onto your money ain't nobody's business but your own, I say. But after all"— the coy smile showed a tight streak of malice— "you don't find me antigodlin around trying to get myself in the horse business, do you?"

She was riled, all right, no doubt about that. But he still couldn't think why she'd be on the prod with him. And he was too damn tired to care one way or the other. She was right about one thing. How he got his money was no business of hers.

He said: "If I ain't welcome in this dive—"

But she cut him off with a wave of her hands. "I got competition enough in this town without you importin' anything from outside—"

"What the hell are you talkin' about?"

"That stylish bitch you shipped in from Bisbee!"

A great light broke over Kurt. His eyes opened wide and then closed to slits. "Where'd you get that stuff?"

"Don't give me that. It's all over town how she went into that stage office askin' for you!"

Beads of sweat stood out on Cardigan's forehead. "Why, you lyin' old—"

"It's you and this Balinett baggage we're discussing. Top Hat Charlie was right there when the stage come. He knew her, too. 'Docie Balinett!' he says." With a simpering smile, she mimicked the Englishman's old-world preciseness.

Her green eyes spat flame.

Black rage looked out of Cardigan's stare. One big hand reached out and took her by the throat. The old harridan's voice flew into high C. Cardigan said with an oath: "She's not what you 'think—"

"D'you think I'm a *fool*! He knew her, I tell you— what's more, he hired a rig to drive her out to your place! You can't do this to me, Kurt Cardigan! You stick to your horses or I'll—"

* * *

NIGHT'S SHADOWS, huge and monstrous, lay across the land. Smell of dust and sun-parched vegetation came windborne off the desert which stretched to the south like a dead dun sea. That wind waved the dry browning fronds of the pepper tree whose filmy branches laced the deeper dark piled up at the left of Miss Emma's parlor house, hiding the hitchracks and the customers' horses.

The stores and shops had closed long since so that most of this section of the street lay dark, though a thousand lights winked and gleamed and fluttered in the next block north where Honkytonk Row set the pace by which men lived and died, by which they fought and had their hopes and guarded secrets—Honkytonk Row with its raucous many-tongued voice ever calling the unwary with its siren song and tawdry show of a joy it never fulfilled.

Flinging out of the harlots' house, Cardigan half turned that way in the natural impulse of a man hard used. But the clank of his spurs suddenly stilled, and he stood there, caught in the churn of his tumultuous thoughts. Drink might warm the cold pit of his belly, but it would not mend the mistakes he had made or make black, white no matter how much of the stuff he poured down.

For man cannot alter the things he has done. He may hide them away, but their taste remains with him. Smart though he be, and wondrous conniving, he cannot turn back the cold hands of time. The finger writes, but neither piety nor wit can lure it back to cancel half a line.

Who first put that truth on paper was possessed of a wisdom dearly learned, Kurt thought with a bitter scowl. For he had found it true, and that knowledge was a fire burning through him now—a lifted axe about to sever the stay ropes of his life.

He had played the fool and here, too late, he knew it.

He must get to the ranch and get shed of his crew, get them off the place and out of the country. It did not occur to him they might demur at any such precipitate departure, or that it might be more practical to depart himself. They were men with a price, every one of them; pay that price and they did your bidding—the belief was founded on past experience. And he was not himself concerned with flight, but only with covering the tracks of past errors.

A more discerning man would have found irony in the thought that a painted old trollop like Long Tooth Emma should finally have brought Kurt face to face with himself and a solid realization that crime did not pay. The finer nuances of the scene he had just been through were lost on Kurt; he was occupied solely with the most obvious aspect of what he had heard—that the wolf-fanged old slut of a parlor house madam should imagine he was importing high-priced hookers because a looker who had asked for him happened to be acquainted with a lunger whose living came from pounding out tunes on a flophouse piano!

It was enough to make a guy heave up his breakfast. But the part that got Kurt was them *knowing* each other! And her from St. Louis!

With an oath, he plunged into the loamy blackness that concealed the racks and hitched horses. He knew pretty well where he had left the dun, but it was so goddam black you couldn't hardly see your own hand before your face.

Then he remembered he'd trained Snuffy to come at his whistle. He gave him a call and the dun stallion nickered. Further over to the left and back a little.

Kurt moved toward the sound, thinking what a hell of a trap this would make if some fellow who had it in for him happened to know about him leaving old Snuffy out here. Be a natural for him. When Kurt opened his mouth to call out to the horse, all the guy would have to do would be to haul out his gun and start triggering.

A sweat came out round Kurt's collar, and he

stopped and stood listening. He couldn't hear anything but the restless stomp of some hitched pony's hoofs, but something told him not to whistle again.

He was in a fever of impatience to be out of this town, to begin that respectable Christian life he envisioned for himself so soon as he could separate from past activities and present personnel. As is generally the way with reforming characters, old associations were become abhorrent to him; he was in a lather to remove himself from all corroding influences.

But he was not in such a sweat he meant to risk being tagged by any powder-sped blue whistler. There were times when speed was best made slowly when the better part of valor had nothing to do with poking your chin out.

He moved with extreme caution, eyes raking the shadows, feet testing out the ground before he put his weight on them. This was plain horse sense, a part of the pattern by which his kind were enabled to continue a precarious existence. The graveyards were filled with damn fools who'd got careless, and he was more than half convinced that, somewhere in this devil's brew of blackness, some belly-crawling sidewinder was waiting to pot him.

He spent a long ten minutes scouting out the dun's position, afterwards swearing in a relieved kind of anger when it became at last apparent, he had the place to himself.

He tightened the cinch and stepped into the saddle.

By God, it would be *good* to get out of this business. Another couple days and he'd be shooting at his shadow!

He let out a tired breath and kneed Snuffy toward the street.

It was just as he reached it, where the light fell full on him, that a figure stepped out of the harness shop doorway.

"I'd like a little talk with you."

THIRTEEN
"DO YOU RECOGNIZE THIS PICTURE?"

CARDIGAN STOPPED, turned completely still.

Cold sweat came out on the backs of his hands and a risen wind, clouting in off the desert, lifted a spiral of dust from the street and sent it spinning off into the darkness.

A flat moment of silence followed. Then Esparza's voice said: "Do much ridin' at night?"

A look of smoldering violence brightened Cardigan's stare, but he fought down the urge of his roaring blood. "You stop me to find that out?"

"Just wondered. Been out to your place at night twice kinda recent. Seemed funny not findin' nobody home. You been losin' any horses?"

Cardigan considered. "Not that I know of. Hard t' tell without checkin'."

"Thought mebbe your boys was out watchin' for horse thieves."

Cardigan looked at him then, quick, and quiet, thin of lip. "If you come out to buy horses why'd you come at night?"

"Came the first time one mornin'. No one home but your cook."

A kind of stillness settled.

"Well?" said Kurt sharply.

Esparza shrugged. He lifted his pipe stem and rubbed at his chin with it. "Lot of ranchers been losin' horses round here. Too many. They don't like it. As a breeder yourself you can understand their feelin's."

Cardigan nodded. "Stealin' horses," he said, "is a bad fine of work for a man to be in."

"Yes," Esparza said, "a very chancy business. When a horse thief's caught, more often than not he's found with his neck stretched, danglin' from a tree limb. You ever think about that?"

Cardigan sat very still in the saddle, with his head slightly tipped, looking down at the man. He searched the marshal's face with a hard, steady probing.

But there was nothing to be read from Esparza's wrinkled features. Neither friendliness nor hostility. The pale surface of his eyes looked back at Cardigan unwinking.

The big rancher's control was beginning to wear thin. Bright flecks, like wildness, danced through his stare and the refracted light from the yonder saloons showed a glistening of sweat along the curves of his cheeks. But in the end, some tag-end of caution made him softly say: "Why should I?"

Esparza made a gesture with his pipe stem. "Want to tell you a story, Cardigan. Chances are it won't much interest you, but I'd like you to hear it anyway. It concerns a young feller of about your age who come into this country several years ago. We didn't have much law around here at that time but there was plenty of room an' plenty opportunities for a man that didn't mind takin' a little chance."

Esparza tapped the dottle from his pipe, rummaged round in his pockets, and brought up fresh tobacco. "This feller could of made him a stake at most anythin' he felt like turnin' his hand to; he was smart an' likable, had some wheels in his think-box. He took a whack at minin',' tried some freightin',' a little ranchin'. Could of done all right at any of 'em, but the work was hard an' the money come a little too slow for his likin'.'"

He looked up and studied Cardigan a moment. He finished packing his pipe and put the tobacco away. "This feller had a broad streak of recklessness in him. Patience wasn't one of his virtues. He looked around, sized up the layout, saw what other men were doin'. Some of those gents were skatin' on the thin edge of turnin' into what Judge Honnifer describes as 'undesirable citizens.'"

Cardigan's shape did not relax in the saddle. His lips made a solid, bitter roll across his face and his eyes were bleakly expressionless, watchful.

Esparza said, "Our friend was no crook. He didn't aim to become one, but that reckless streak in him was beginnin' to turn yeasty. Men were maverickin' cattle an' gettin big at it; gamblers were livin' off the fat of the land. Our friend saw no reason why he shouldn't take a little fling at quicker profits himself.

"Up north in Colorado, in Wyomin' an' Montana where the grass was good and the ranches far apart, there was a lot of good horseflesh driftin' round without brands. Yearlin's an' two-year-olds—some aged stuff, too. Horses was cheap in that country but down here they would fetch a good price. If you had them.

"Originally, he prob'ly figured on payin' for 'em, but there was this brash streak in him. All he really needed was an organization an' there was plenty of young sports, brash as himself, that would jump at the chance once they knew what the plan was."

Esparza dug out a match and looked up at Kurt slanchways. "This stuff borin' you?"

"Go on," breathed Cardigan.

"Well, this guy started to work an' made a pretty good thing of it. Got his horses up there an' sold 'em down here. Prob'ly had a few hideouts along the way, relay stations with other gents workin' 'em. Lot of ranchers'll rest horses if you can show 'em a profit in it. This feller was smart. Worked the business two years without crowdin' his luck. Built up quite a spread in this country, an a name for horses of the very top quality—stock with run in it an' plenty of bottom.

"Then the picture changed. Those fellers up north got hep to themselves. Small colt crops an' too much shrinkage in their usin' stock made them start to look around. They put some men on the job an' caught an' swung a few fellers but our friend slipped through them; he was still in the clear, tracks covered. He'd enough stock on hand that he could be what people thought him an' become an honest breeder."

Cardigan sat there, neither speaking nor moving while fiddle scrape and the clink of glasses mixed with drunken shouts and laughter became loud sounds in the increasing quiet that stretched between himself and Esparza.

Time stood still.

Impatience lifted Cardigan's shoulders.

The marshal sighed and scratched his match. Smoke came out of his mouth round the pipe stem.

"Here was a feller growin' up with the country, gettin' his start like too many others; still, I'm bound to admit, no worse than buildin' up a spread with one cow an' a runnin' iron. He wasn't takin' no bread from the widders an' orphans. When them northern boys clamped down on his game it left him two choices—he could quit an' go straight or he could shift his operations to some other locality.

"I'd like to tell you he quit, an' he may have done so. He commenced sellin' mounts to the cavalry an' nobody kicked there was anything wrong with it. But a man don't readily pass up an easy profit—or shake loose of a bunch he has et, stole an' slept with. It was hard to believe his whole crowd had gone straight or that he'd got rid of them an' had a new honest crew. Once a man goes in for that kind of thing it's a pretty tough business tryin' to feel content with the smaller profits an' hateful routine of square livin'.

"Times had changed. Law of a sort had come into this country. Its enforcement was bound to change things still more, cramping down a man's freedom, puttin' a fence around initiative. It was not a harsh law or an avengeful one; but it was there all the same. Although plainly inclined to let sleep-in' dogs lay, this law—with its rigid set of rules an' forbiddin's—must have represented to a man grown used to doin' as he pleased an intolerable restraint, a constant challenge and irritation.

"Do you follow me?"

The glitter of sweat was on Cardigan's forehead. "You talk," he said, "like that Camp Pickett preacher."

"A sharp man," the marshal nodded. "I wish our friend might have known him better. Might of been the means of improvin' his outlook. Of mebbe keepin' his feet on the straight and narrer."

He sucked at his pipe in a thoughtful silence. "I want you to see the Law's position. If this feller had quit, he was entitled to a break. We had no proof he hadn't quit. But about three months ago, more or less, a bunch of ranchers usin' land in the north end of this Territory started howlin' they was losin' horses—not culls or colts but top usin' horses, the cream of their remudas.

"They carried their complaints to the Governor. All sheriffs an' marshals was warned, descriptions of some of the horses sent out—cattlemen's associations alerted. Maybe our friend wasn't aware of this; he got to doin' a lot of night ridin', keep-in' out of sight in the daytime. The word got around. Nothin' definite, of course, just loose straws in the wind, little draw-in's apart, a look in folks' eyes when his name was mentioned."

The silence closed in and got deeper and deeper till it shut out completely all sound from up yonder. The run of Cardigan's breathing became audible.

"You—you think this guy was doin' it?"

Esparza shrugged. "Somebody was—and still is. Forty head of horses was lifted two weeks ago from the neighborhood of Chandler. Bunch of mares an' colts were run off a couple nights later from a ranch in Oak Creek Canyon; then this bunch hit Amado, then Cortaro, then Florence."

A wildness lay in Cardigan's eyes.

"This same bunch?"

Esparza said: "There's a pattern to these things that

a man can't escape. A thief starts small, but the habit grows on him. Violence breeds violence. The man who'll snatch a purse today will be in the mood to rob a bank tomorrow. Do you recognize the picture?"

FOURTEEN
THE TASTE OF DEATH

CARDIGAN'S LAUGH was short and ugly. "I don't think your man will rob any banks."

Esparza considered him and then looked at his horse. He had his own private thoughts but no reflection of these was permitted to alter the planes of his face. Yet his glance, when he finally lifted it, held the look of a man who has lived too long on the edge of violence, who has gone too long with the run of the pattern.

"I do not think your opinion or mine will much help him. He, or the men he thinks for, have turned their backs on caution. The bank at Douglas was gutted two nights ago. A stage south of Tombstone was stuck up yesterday morning. In broad daylight, yesterday evening the same pack of wolves robbed the Copper State Bank at Bisbee."

"If you're suggestin'—"

The marshal held up his hand. "You can be hung just as high for a sheep as a goat and humans, generally speaking, like horses, are mostly judged on past performance." He regarded Cardigan quietly. "If you should happen to bump into him, tell this man he's through. There is just one thing that might possibly straighten him out—complete restitution and the prompt apprehension of every man connected with what happened at Bisbee yesterday."

* * *

DOCIE BALINETT, seated on the leather covered springs of the buggy seat alongside the consumptive Britisher, thought she had never seen anything quite like this country in all her twenty-two years. The vastness of it was immeasurable and the effect both majestic and terrifying. Rugged mountains, great upthrust slabs of barren rock by their look, hemmed it in with barbaric shades of blue and purple, a burning waste of sand, silence, and desolation.

"But what do people find to do out here?"

Top Hat Charlie's rheumy eyes showed a twinkle. "Ranching, mining, and hell raising, mostly. I say, it's not really bad once you're used to it. Some fine chaps out here—quite heroic, really. Take this fellow, Cardigan."

"Yes?" Docie prompted.

Charlie looked at the back of the horse a few moments. They had already covered the past pretty thoroughly, the people they'd known, the places they'd been—Abilene, Dodge City, Cheyenne, Deadwood, Virginia City, Brady, San Saba, Coffeeville and a hundred other places a shade less hectic in between. Neither had dwelt at much length on current affairs. "I make out to keep on eating," the Britisher offered with a little smile. And Docie explained, "I haven't met this man Cardigan—yet."

Charlie's look, when she'd mentioned that, had seemed a little queer; and it was queer again now, Docie thought, regarding his profile. Not a look you could take apart and label. More a kind of withdrawing; a tightening of the mouth, a general air of reticence—as though his eyes were windows, she thought, and someone had drawn the blinds.

She said, "Heroic? I thought he was a rancher."

"I guess he is, after a fashion. Has a place just south of Oracle—sells horses to the cavalry. Don't know much about him, really. Keeps himself to himself if you know what I mean. We don't see him much down around Tucson."

"But why call him 'heroic'?"

Charlie studied the horse's tail. "Perhaps," he said, "'remarkable' would be a more apt description," and lapsed off into silence.

For a time, as the buggy creaked and groaned toward the hills, Docie gave her attention to the country about her, to considering the thorny bushes and different kinds of cactus. Charlie clucked to the horse and made occasional small talk, commenting on flora and fauna, the condition of the range, weather prospects, and mineral deposits.

But at last, Docie seemed to have had enough of it. She said: "Charlie, I want to know more about Cardigan."

He nicked a fly off the horse's flank with a shake of the lines. "What do you want to know about him?"

"I want to know why you looked funny when I mentioned him."

"Did I?"

"And why you called him remarkable."

Charlie said, reflectively: "Wouldn't you call a man remarkable who showed up in a place about three years ago with nothing but a horse and the clothes on his back and is now generally regarded as the greatest horse breeder in that section of country?"

"Well...yes," she nodded, "I guess perhaps I should. But that doesn't account for the way you looked, does it?"

He didn't immediately answer. Instead, his eyes came around and considered her. There was speculation in his look, a little embarrassment also. "Must we talk about him?"

"I'd rather." She said soberly, "You've either said too much or not enough, Charlie."

He studied the lines in his hands for a moment. Then he lifted his eyes and looked straight ahead. "It's absolutely none of my business, Docie, but I can't help wondering what interest you'd be having in common with Cardigan. He's— Well, to put the thing politely, he's a pretty tough character."

"Don't be stuffy. Say what you mean."

"You can't pin the man down that way. I could tell you he's a ruffian but that wouldn't give you the picture. Half the people in this country would fit that description."

"In what way is he different from the rest of the ruffians?"

"Well, he's no bully. He don't go around picking fights, yet he's not the kind of a man you'd want to cross."

"Why not?"

"I can't tell you that. I am not at all certain I know the answer myself. He's a hard man to know."

"You mean deep?"

His hand described an irritable gesture. "I don't know what I mean. The man's an enigma—you could question a dozen people and get as many different answers. He looks like a brush popper and talks like one. Most of the time he acts like one, too, but he's a long way from being just another dumb bruiser. When Cardigan speaks men listen."

"Quite a character," Docie smiled.

"He's more than a 'character,'" Top Hat Charlie said darkly. "He's a very dangerous man, my girl, and I'd advise you to keep away from him."

Docie's hazel eyes twinkled. "Have you not ever noticed what a compelling attraction a dangerous man has for a woman?"

He met her smile with a strange severity.

He drew a troubled breath, and his glance searched her features with a sustained and dark conviction. "You're a mighty beautiful woman, Docie, but you're not the girl I knew in San Saba."

Docie lowered her eyes. Color passed through her cheeks. "You're bound to leave a few things behind when you set your foot on the rung of a ladder."

"You were very determined," he remembered. "You were going to be someone—"

"Yes," she said quickly, "but values change. As a person climbs, he finds the view widening. I have discovered that a fence creates an optical illusion; it does not change the quality of the grass on either side."

He shook his head. He said regretfully, "I am afraid Abilene and Dodge City were not good for you."

She patted his knee. "Let's put that song away, Charlie. I've found it doesn't pay to look back. We all strike our bargains sooner or later; I've struck mine and I'm going through with it. Now tell me about yourself."

Charlie shrugged that away. "What are you doing in Tucson?"

"I came out here to marry a man," Docie said. "I came out here to marry Kurt Cardigan."

Charlie almost stopped the buggy in his shock. He looked at her with an expression of incredulity. "Are you crazy?"

Her eyes met his straightly. "What's so crazy about marrying a rancher?"

"But... Cardigan!"

He was plainly disturbed. It was in the quick lift of his chin, in what she saw staring at her out of his eyes.

She said, "Have you never been disgusted with the life you are living—with everything it stands for and all its surroundings? Two months ago, in St. Louis, I made up my mind that I had all I could take of it. A fresh start was what I wanted; a man to take care of me, a feeling of security. I put an ad in a paper offering to marry a rancher and Cardigan answered."

"You can't do it." His voice said bitterly: "I won't let you."

"It's not your concern."

"We'll see about that! Half this country thinks the man's a damn horse thief—do you think I will let you get mixed up with that?"

"I have made my bargain," Docie said, "and I will keep it"

* * *

CARDIGAN WAS two hours out of Tucson before he could do any coherent thinking and he was almost to Rickven's cabin before the marshal's words began to make any sense and uncover the picture in its proper perspective.

Anger ran through him like the feel of hot iron. Someone in his outfit had turned wolf and double crossed him. But the damage was done now, and he was caught in the toils of it, caught like an ant in flypaper.

He had reached this point in his thinking when the nester's shack loomed up before him, a deeper black against the low-riding stars.

A cold wind flapped and fluttered in the trees, damp with the smell of the yonder pool. He had no illusions about Espar-za's reasons in tipping his hand, about the marshal's purpose in showing a horse thief just where he stood.

Frank Esparza was smart, a great deal smarter than Cardigan had figured him. He knew his own limitations. He knew how far he would get fetching a badge-packing posse onto Cardigan's land. He knew he'd either find nothing and give the show clear away or he'd catch them with the goods and get a lot of men killed.

He never had much cottoned to gunplay and killing; it was one of the things folks liked him for. He never dragged a gun if he could manage to get around it. Handing Cardigan that line had got him round it very neatly. He'd shown Cardigan where he stood without presenting any occasion for gunplay. By the terms of his strategy if powder was burned it would be burned in the hills among a pack of wrangling chaparral wolves.

He'd put the whole business right square up to Cardigan. He hadn't mentioned Cardigan's name at all, but anyone would know he had been talking about Cardigan. Of course, he'd made it appear like he didn't suppose Cardigan connected with this recent stuff, but he'd made it clear enough whose men he figured was doing it—and it was Cardigan he proposed to make responsible for their actions. Which was all fair enough if those banks and that stage had been stuck up by the KC crew.

But what if they hadn't?

Supposing Esparza was just guessing—was just presuming, because he'd pegged the KC crowd for a bunch of crooks, that it was Cardigan's men that had pulled those raids at Chandler, Amado, Cortaro, and Florence?

He scrubbed a damp hand across bristly jowls. If the KC crew *had* pulled those raids it was quite in the cards, they'd robbed the banks and stage also; but if the marshal had proof, would he have wrapped the deal up in this kind of a package? Wouldn't it have been a heap more natural for him to have put Kurt Cardigan under arrest?

There was the crux of all Cardigan's thinking. Did the marshal have proof or didn't he? He could maybe have got on to what had happened up north but if he had any proof to what had happened around here—any proof he could give to a jury—why in hell would he be asking someone else to rake the chestnuts?

That wasn't the way a marshal worked in Cardigan's experience.

The smell of this night was strong in Kurt's nostrils as he sat idle in the leather trying to think his way through this. One thing was clear and one only. Regard-less of how much or how little Esparza knew or suspected, the play left Cardigan right out in the open. He either played the cards Frank Esparza had dealt him or he became in full fact an out-and-out outlaw. No other interpretation could be put on the marshal's words.

He got out the makings and twisted up a smoke. Still absorbed in his thinking he was about to scratch a match when a voice said:

"Cardigan?"

Cardigan stiffened.

The voice said hurriedly: "It's me—Rickven. Over here by the door."

Cardigan said, half angry, "You pick a damn funny time to call out to a man."

"I'm not myself, I'm that worried. It's Lula—if you kin spare a couple minutes I sure wisht you would look at her."

"What's the matter with her?"

"She keeps moanin' an' groanin'—"

"I don't hear no moanin'," Cardigan said, but he got out of the saddle and followed the nester into his shack.

Rickven lighted a lamp. He was an ineffectual man, hollow chested and meaching, with a ten days' growth of whiskers on his face. "I tried t' hail thet other feller down, but..."

Cardigan brushed past him, his eyes going at once to the red headed girl he had seen by the waterfall. He was shocked by the change in her appearance.

She was on a bunk in the corner with a shift twisted round her. Her red hair didn't look as though it had seen a comb in weeks and the lovely face he'd remembered was twisted and drawn, unnaturally flushed as with fever. The staring eyes didn't know him.

"Hell's fire!" he said, turning. "You can see what's ailin' her! What the hell you been thinkin' of? This ain't no place for a woman in her condition!"

Rickven's hangdog look slid away and came back again, sly, and emboldened. "Who got her this way?"

Cardigan caught him by the shirtfront in a twisting grip. "You don't need t' look at me—an' you can wipe that damn smug look off your face! You know the kinda guys I got on my payroll—why the hell didn't you keep your eye on her?"

He flung him back against the wall. Going over to the bed he stood there scowling down at Lula.

"You're a hell of a father," he said, coming back. "Her time's about here. Ain't there some woman you could get t'—"

"What woman?" Rickven whined. "What woman would come up here, an' what would I be payin' her with if she did come?"

Cardigan pulled a roll of bills from his pocket and tossed them on the table. He saw the gleam that came into the nester's eyes, and said sharply: "That's for her—understand? It ain't t' buy you no whiskey with. You get a pill-roller out here an' do whatever he tells you t' do."

He started to go out and then paused with his hand on the door, looking back again, looking at Rickven carefully.

He said, "If you was a sheriff an' had got the deadwood on a bunch of damn rustlers, what would you do?"

A kind of sweat came out on the nester's cheeks.

"Say you caught the big dog right in town, had the

drop on him. Would you spin him a story an' tip your hand or would you throw 'im in the jug?"

"I... I'd throw him in the jug."

Cardigan nodded. He didn't seem to notice the man had licked his lips twice before any words came. Or that his cheeks had gone a dirty gray as Cardigan had spoken.

He went out and climbed into the saddle and turned Snuffy's nose in the direction of the ranch.

* * *

THE MOON WAS UP NOW, a silver disc above the blue-black slopes of the mountain. Its argent light spilled across the range in a flood of ghostly radiance, lending commonplace things a majesty they seldom attained in daylight.

But Cardigan's mind was not concerned with beauty. He was listening again to the nester's words and nodding his head to the wisdom of them. It is easy to believe where one's own convictions are handed back in another man's voice.

Esparza had no proof. He'd been pulling a bluff in the hope Kurt Cardigan would do his work for him. A pretty sharp biscuit—and he'd come mighty near putting it over. Not that Kurt would have turned his own crew over to the law, but...Even now Kurt grimaced when he thought how near he'd come to playing the fool. He must be losing his grip or going soft in the head. The KC crew must be sharing that thought to go out on their own and be sticking up banks and stagecoaches! By God. He tipped his shape in the saddle to fling a quick look at the black piled-up

shadows of that brush on his left and was like that, turning, when something like a gigantic sledge smashed him
out of the saddle and dropped him, breathless, in the
shale of the trail.

The flat, dry crack of the shot split into fragments of
sound that rolled through him and over him and off
through the hills like stampeded cattle; and saddle
leather creaked, and a horse broke out of the brush and
ran south.

FIFTEEN
OVERTURE TO VIOLENCE

THE STAGE from Pearce was forty minutes late when it came rolling into Tucson at twenty after twelve that night and drew up with a flourish before the Cosmopolitan Hotel.

Two elegantly dressed girls, very obviously not ladies, were assisted to the ground with great ceremony and a considerable babble of eighty-five cent words by a couple of inebriated knights of the saddle.

The last person to leave the coach before it rattled down Pennington in the direction of Pearl was a man in a derby. He'd been riding the box with the driver and had a fat cigar jutting out of his mouth which he rolled across sun-chapped lips as he ogled the girls and their tipsy companions.

After a moment, his green glance went beyond them, quickly scanning the front of the white-plastered one-story hostelry. Apparently satisfied, he turned and moved leisurely off toward Main with his hands in coat pockets and the smoke floating back from his fat cigar.

One of the drunken punchers stared after him. "Y' know, I sheen that dude b'fo' someplaish..."

The taller girl tugged at his arm. "It's the bed you was lookin' for, dearie—remember?" And the other puncher said: "Hell with 'im. Whatsa use a lookin' at a goddam dude when you gotta sweet armful like—"

"Gawd," the other girl said, "but I'm hungry! Can you get a T-bone steak in this joint?"

"Honey," Ed assured her, "you kin git ever' damn thing yore little heart desires." And they all moved off.

* * *

WHEN FRANK ESPARZA stepped into his office at a quarter to one, he paused with the door still open and, with shoulders hunched, stood quietly, unbreathing, with his glance grimly raking the black room before him.

"Never mind the drawn shade," said a voice from the blackness. "Come in and shut the door. An' put the lamp on, damn it. I ain't fixing to bite you."

Esparza scratched a match, found the lamp and lit it, and took a long look at the man in the corner. He looked him over from yellow shoes to brown derby. Then he nodded.

"You're the dude that left town in a hell of a hurry. The coffee drummer that got the bad news and had to light out for El Paso. Did you get there?"

The man's sunburned features broke apart in a grin. "Nope. Didn't seem so necessary after I lost Cardigan. Quite a character. He been around here long?"

The marshal grunted. "Long enough to know

better." He said, after a moment, "You have trouble with Cardigan?"

"I'll take care of that. I guess you'll be Frank Esparza. My name's Sollantsy—call me Sam for short." He took out his wallet, flipped it open so the marshal could see his credentials. "I'm reppin' for the Tri-State Cattlemen's Association, work-in' out of Billings."

Esparza went over and sat down at his desk and hoisted his booted feet onto a drawer. "Go ahead," he said. "What's your problem?"

"Horses. Lot of our members been losin' 'em, we—had a regular epidemic of horse stealin' up in our neck of the woods two-three years ago. Must've lost right around about seven hundred head."

"So, your members took their troubles to the Tri-State?"

"You said it," Sollantsy grinned. "They knew we'd give 'em some action. We caught a few guys and the law strung 'em up. Some of our members weren't quite satisfied though. Old R. C. Hale—he's the Tri-State's president—had been hit pretty hard. He'd been breeding some mighty top cowponies. Mostly ropers an' cutters when you got 'em finished out. He went in strong for duns an' these horse-thievin' sons seemed to take a real shine to 'em. They got twenty-five or thirty of the best, includin' Hale's top studhorse, Jubal Jo.

"We put a few men out and turned up some horses —around forty or fifty head, I reckon. Most of this stuff had been bought up by small ranchers, one or two to the spread. Took a lot of time and a lot work to find 'em, but gradually a picture began to build up. We began to catch onto how these crooks had been operatin'.'"

Sollantsy got a cigar from his vest and bit the end

off. He went over to the lamp and puffed it into life. "The ones we had caught had mostly been locals. We had worked on a few but we didn't find out much. Most of the stuff we picked up we got in Colorado an' Utah. That showed the stuff was goin' south.

"Then one day we hit the jackpot, following a lead, we jumped a two-by-four rancher on the Colorado line. He had a place tucked away in the mountains about a hundred miles north of Estes Park. What he really had was a relay station. Stuff comin' out of our country would be driven to his place an' left to rest up. Same way with stuff bein' pushed north. He had a right sweet setup and didn't much cotton to being put out of business. He had three fellers with him. an' we caught 'em flat-footed but they went for their irons an' we had to rub 'em out. We didn't get a nickel's worth of information out of 'em."

Sollantsy rolled the cigar across his mouth disgustedly. "You know how it goes. Just when you figure to bust a case wide open, along comes a shoot-out an' all you got is corpses. Stopped the stealin' though—our members ain't lost a damn horse since."

Esparza said, "Maybe that was their headquarters—"

"Not a chance," Sollantsy said. "Feller that run that place didn't have enough sense to pound sand down a rat-hole. He knew his job an' that was all. The guy that's roddin' this gang is big caliber. We don't figure the ones we've got was even members of the gang. The way we've got it doped out there probably ain't more than five or six men in the gang. All these others is extras — probably workin' for wages. They do the spottin', furnish the tips and maybe hide out the horses while they're bein' rested up. Way we've got it doped out the guys on the outside edge of this deal are mostly just scouts. All they do is get a line on good stock—where it's at, how much an' Ivhen's the best time to grab it. They pass this dope along to one of the boys in the pay of someone that's got him a relay station, and this guy passes it on to one of the gang."

"Sounds pretty complicated," Esparza commented.

"It's pretty cagey," Sollantsy nodded. "But that's one thing about Tri-State—when they fasten onto a thing, they stay with it to the finish."

He puffed his cigar as though he really enjoyed it, savoring the smoke as it came out through his nostrils. "I never seen a job yet the Tri-State couldn't crack."

"Then you think they'll lick this one?"

Sollantsy grinned. "That's what I'm here for. We got it ready to scratch off the books right now."

Esparza looked at him thoughtfully. "Are you trying to tell me this gang holes up around here?"

"Within twenty miles of where we're sittin' right now."

"You've got proof of that, I reckon—"

"We got enough to turn the trick. You know how Tri-State works; We round up the evidence. We go where it takes us. When we get what we figure is enough to do the job we send in a report and contact local authorities."

Esparza nodded. "You'll be seeing the sheriff—"

"I've seen the sheriff. You got a damn big county here. Sheriff tells me he's up to his ears in work now and that you're the man to handle this end of it."

Sollantsy grinned. "He says these people around here elected you to keep down the rustling as much as anything, and that you're a bonafide deputy sheriff with full powers to go out into the county—"

"All right," Esparza said. "I can see you've got in touch with him. Who do you want me to arrest?"

"Kurt Cardigan, for a starter."

"Cardigan's a rancher, a big man around here—"

"I've looked him up. I know how big he is, an' how standoffish. And I know what his neighbors think when they hear that tough crew he's got go by in the dark."

"That's not proof," the marshal said.

"I've got proof enough to flush him out into the open!"

"Legal murder is what you're proposing. We don't do things that way around here."

"You mean you'd coddle a horse thief—"

"Wait," Esparza said. "You don't understand the background or the issues involved—"

"I understand the law—"

"The letter of the law, perhaps. The law as it's administered in more thickly settled country. Out here it's a little different. We try to temper justice with a little bit of mercy. Laws are conceived and passed to hold down crime and—"

"I know all that!"

Esparza smiled patiently. "I want you to get the picture in its proper proportions. If Cardigan's a horse thief I'm not condoning his actions or proposing to ignore them. I've heard the same rumors you have and I've gone to a lot of work trying to dig out the truth. Though I've found no proof I could take to a jury, I'm pretty well convinced in my own mind he was stealing horses up north and selling them later as stock of his own raising—"

"Then what the hell you waitin' on?"

"Proof," the marshal said stubbornly.

Sollantsy took the cigar from his mouth and said harshly: "I've got all the proof we need! That guy run me out of this town at gun point. He was so hellbent to get rid of me he bought me a horse at Reagan's livery, a dun filly with a white mane and tail that I happen to know was raised by Bob Hale at Big Timber, Montana —one of the horses he lost to this bunch of damn horse thieves! An' that ain't all by a long shot! That stallion Cardigan rides around is Jubal Jo, Hale's top studhorse!"

He got his cigar going again and said grimly, "I've been out to Camp Grant lookin' over some of that stuff he pushed off on the cavalry. I didn't turn up a thing I could put the finger on but there's a lot of their horses I didn't get to see. If you want to force my hand I'll go back there, but why fiddle around? You handle this right an' we'll get all the proof anybody will ask for."

"Sure," Esparza nodded. "Bullet proof."

"What's the matter with that?" Sollantsy bristled.

"It's not the way we do business—"

"It's results that count, not the way you get 'em. When you're dealin' with a horse thief—"

"You figure when Cardigan's bunch sees a posse comin' they'll either break and run or start throwing lead. Either way, they're guilty accordin' to your book. They're guilty before you ever start after them. You're not stopping to count the cost in misery and dead men or the chance that Cardigan might happen to be innocent—"

Sollantsy snorted. "If that guy's innocent I'm a sidewinder's uncle!"

"Not innocent perhaps of stealing Jubal Jo, but he could very well be innocent of the things that have been going on around here since then."

Sollantsy stared. "So now you're splittin' hairs! What kind of a setup have I walked into? How much of a graft are you gettin' from this guy?"

Esparza said quietly, "You have to realize the powerful influence of this country. This isn't Texas or Kansas or even Montana; the laws of those sections do not fit into our problems. They do not fit our conditions or these peculiar times. We're in transition, Sollantsy. This country puts its mark on every man who tries to live here—it actually does this, bringing out in him swiftly—even oftentimes magnifying—whatever tendencies he has toward either good or evil.

"It is a big, tough country and it's always attracted a pretty rough kind of man. Weakness is not always just a matter of muscle; there can be weakness of character, too, Sollantsy, and many weak characters have come into this country, and the effect of this country on them has generally been unfortunate. Such men, if they survive, very frequently become outlaws—"

"Hell!" Sollantsy sneered, "I didn't come to your office to listen to no sermon—"

"I'm trying to show you why your suggested method of handling Cardigan is wrong," Esparza said. "Let us admit for the record that Cardigan has deliberately acquired brand-less horses that did not belong to him—let us even go so far as to admit that this is stealing. At the time in question—the time you fellers up north were losing horses—a great many men were doing the same thing in cattle and were considered none the worse for it. Some of these mavericks became cattle barons—"

"We've passed laws against it—"

"We didn't pass them here until just a couple of months ago. Since that time, you have no proof whatever that Cardigan hasn't been completely on the square."

"You sure do love that guy, don't you?"

"He could be a very useful citizen and I think he's trying to reform," Esparza said.

"He should've, done his reformin' before he run off with them horses." The Tri-States man knocked the ashes off his smoke. "If you think Bob Hale is gonna forget Tubal Jo—"

"I think I can handle that part of it. I believe Cardigan will pay a good price for that horse, and for everything else that came out of your country—"

"Well, buddy, I'm glad to meet up with you," Sollantsy said, with his hard bright eyes going over Esparza carefully. "I thought your kind had all died in the Crusades."

"Don't you believe in giving a man a break?"

"Not no goddam horse thief! All I've got for his kind of skunk is a rope thrown over a juniper branch."

Esparza said quietly, "We'll have none of that here."

"Are you tellin' me you refuse to take action? If you think Tri-States—"

"I'm not thinking about Tri-States at all. I'm thinking of a man who may be trying to go straight, and of the probable results to this country if such a man happened to be pushed the wrong way."

He took his feet off the desk and picked up his hat. "An ounce of prevention can be worth a pound of cure. We've had a bad outbreak of violence in this Territory during the last couple of weeks," he told Sollantsy softly. "I don't think Cardigan's mixed up in it, but I *do* think he may help to put a stop to it and perhaps recover some of the money that's been stolen—if he's given half a chance."

He considered the other man steadily. "I may be setting a thief to catch a thief, but in my book it's a form of prevention and I intend to stay with it until I see what it can do."

The bright green stare of the Tri-States man showed a plain and bitter outrage. "Then you aim to keep settin' right here on your fanny—that's what you're tryin' to tell me, ain't it?"

"I intend, first of all, to try and get back the loot that was taken from the Copper State Bank and the bank at Douglas," Frank Esparza said mildly. "I've sent a deputy clown there to look things over and I shall wait for his report. If that report should show definite evidence against Cardigan or if, in the meantime, Cardigan appears to have ignored the warning I gave him, I shall then be ready to consider other measures."

* * *

CARDIGAN STAYED where he was in the shale of the trail until the last flogging hoofbeat of that horse had faded out. He felt, during those moments, no pain at all; he felt only the shock and a strange frightening numbness that seemed to encompass the whole left side of his chest.

He knew his chances of getting up were a lot better now than they would be later after the numbness wore off. He twisted over on his side and drew one leg up. It astonished him to find that it could take him so long.

Getting shot this way was no one's fault but his own. A man who had tampered with the law as long as he had should have known a heap better than to ride through moonlight on a giveaway horse. Hadn't he given the crew hell for stealing Snuffy in the first place? And hadn't Lahr told him the horse would get him killed?

He got a knee under him and gathered his strength. What was it Rickven had said about someone before him? Someone going too fast for him to hail the man down. A pity, by God, he hadn't thought of this sooner. Or at least kept his eyes peeled. He was in a hell of a shape now to do what had to be done.

He staggered up with a groan and almost fell down again. He stood there, dizzy, and giddy for several moments, feeling exhausted beyond the strength it took to move—but that was crazy. He had to move. He *had* to. He had to get to the ranch, though he couldn't remember why.

He tried to whistle for Snuffy, but his whistler wouldn't work. His mind wasn't working too damned good, either. What he needed was some action, something to get him woke up. He said: "I got to get out of here."

He tried to whistle again but finally gave it up. He tried to think where he was, looking wearily about him, but he couldn't seem to get up much enthusiasm for it. Thing to do was start walking. He started.

It gave him a weird kind of funny sensation like he didn't have any connection with the ground—like he was a bird or a balloon or something. His feet didn't seem to have any weight, or the ground beneath him to have any substance. Sometimes he didn't hardly know whether he had his feet hoisted up or down, but after a while, it seemed they must have turned to lead, and it was all he could do to even drag them along after him.

But he knew where he was now, five miles beyond Rickven's in the Bent Creek bottoms. Less than a mile to the house. He wondered if he'd make it.

And then feeling came back and pain stabbed through him like a saw-edged sword. It came in waves that left him shaking but he kept on going. Sometimes he cursed the bushwhacker who had tried to dry-gulch him, but more often he cursed himself that he should have been so damn careless. If he'd had enough sense to drive nails in a snow bank, he might have guessed someone would try this. It was the obvious thing to look for if the crew had double crossed him and stuck up those two banks.

One of them, of course, might have been in town tonight and seen him chinning with the marshal. But if the crew had robbed those banks—which was what Esparza had hinted—it was fifty-seven to one that Shiloh Frayne or Curly Lahr had got fed up with two-bit stakes and decided to take the lid off. And if this was how the thing had gone, the next step, of necessity, was to rid the gang of Kurt.

He remembered then that the horse had gone south, had gone crashing off in the direction of town; and he shook his head and gave it up. If someone in town had got an urge to waylay him there were a hundred places handier than this. No feller from town would have come way out here in the middle of the night. It was one of the crew, that was all there was to it; and when he got home and saw the horses he'd know.

He concentrated on getting there.

But he couldn't keep from thinking.

His gun was still wedged in the waistband of his trousers, and he was damn glad it was because there wasn't much doubt, he'd need it.

He wished the hell his mind would take a rest, but it kept going round like a wound-up clock, like the whirlpool down in the Broken Bit narrows, always churning up things that he'd just as like stayed buried. Like his childhood on the south Texas ranch, an endless miserable stretch of back-breaking labor because his old man had been too tight to hire the help the outfit needed. When most kids his age had been going to school, he'd had to ride fence, break broncs and tail bogged steers up. A hell of a happy time he'd had; and the two years they'd made his old man send him hadn't been much better. The kids had laughed their heads off to see a guy so big so goddam dumb.

He'd run away finally, thinking to improve his lot, but all he'd found was work and more of it, and trouble, of course— he'd always found trouble. He remembered the cook on the XIT, the wagon boss on the Diamond A, the strayman at the Gourd and Vine. Then he'd tried his hand at freighting and a rival line had wrecked half his wagons and he'd beat the boss up and had to quit the country.

He recalled his first gun fight, one of the few chunks of trouble he hadn't brought on himself; and a girl he had known in Corpus Christi, and that fetched his mind back to Docie. Docie Balinett who was waiting for him now; and suddenly he felt he couldn't take another step.

But he did. He scowled into the silver-dappled shadows and kept on tramping with the stubborn tenacity that was the most enduring thing he'd ever got from the Cardigans; and the ranch lights threw their yellow beacons through the interlacing branches of the cottonwoods and catclaw.

He did not find it queer that any lights would still be showing. He was remembering all at once the look on Rickven's hangdog features when he'd asked him what a sheriff would do if he had the real dirt on a rustler. There'd been something almost furtive, almost frightened in that look. There'd been sweat on Rickven's cheekbones and something in his voice that, now he thought it over, bordered mighty close on panic.

And then he remembered Esparza, and it came to Kurt like a bolt from the blue what had put that look on the nester's face. It was Rickven, that Kurt had let squat on his land, who had tipped Frank Esparza off!

The knowledge stopped Cardigan dead in his tracks. He forgot where he was, forgot all the pain in his sudden black fury; and he was that way, half turned and half minded to go back, when a girl's frantic cry swung his face toward the house.

SIXTEEN
A VERY POTENT QUESTION

WHEN TOP HAT CHARLIE drove the hired rig into the yard at Cardigan's KC ranch headquarters, the girl who shared its seat was not feigning astonishment when she said, looking about her with an intake of breath, "Are you sure this is the place?"

"Quite." The Englishman's nod held only a studied civility.

"But, Charlie, it's *big!*" Docie cried, with her gray-green glance wholly approving the arrangement of the sturdy log buildings scattered among the trees. "I'd no idea he had a place like this."

"A matter of some three hundred thousand acres, I believe. Not patented, of course—just held..." He seemed about to say more but let it go with a shrug. "Yes, it's big," he said cryptically—" "big as Cardigan himself, and just about as vulnerable, given the right set of circumstances."

Docie turned her head to regard him. "You think Cardigan's vulnerable?"

"Like glass."

"I'm not sure I understand."

"You will if you stay around here." He leaned toward her impulsively. "I'm concerned for you, Docie. Chuck this, won't you? Let me take you back to town—"

"It's too late for that, Charlie."

"It's not too late yet. Look. There's nobody here—"

"They're probably in the house."

"Look at the corrals. No horses in them. Let me—"

"You *are* sweet, Charlie. Perhaps you're right in not liking Cardigan, but it just wouldn't work. This isn't a thing I've gone into rashly."

"I'm afraid it is," he answered quietly. "It's something you're doing on the rebound, Docie. You can't run away from things. Believe me. You can run to the very ends of the earth but the thing you would escape remains as near you as your shadow."

"But I'm not running, Charlie. There's nothing in my past that I'm ashamed of. Regret—being sorry for a thing isn't necessarily shame. I have made my mistakes but I'm not running from them. I want a different kind of life."

"Did you find the old so bad?"

"I want trust and security. I want a set of values I can depend on. When I see a thing that's white, I want it always to remain that way. I am tired of sham and shifting shadows. I want to feel that I matter—I want security, Charlie."

"Nevertheless, you will not find it. You will never find it here. You don't know the man you are trying to do business with."

Docie said, breathing deep: "I would rather belong to one honest rustler—"

"It isn't that."

"What is it then?"

Charlie spread his hands in a gambler's gesture. "The man has built a house of cards. A strong wind is gathering. When this house falls down, I would not like to see you pinned underneath it. Believe me, Docie, there's no future in Cardigan."

She looked a long moment at his handsome face, seeing how the evening breeze ruffled the silvering hair at his temples, noticing now how gray he had become in the years since those carefree days at San Saba. But she had put the past behind her, and she meant to keep it there.

He said: "I think—" and paused to look at her sharply; and he shook his head and let the rest go and put his thin lips together, locking his thoughts away behind the impassive look he customarily wore while taking his turn at the Gold Plate Saloon.

"We all have our own lives to live," Docie said. "A woman takes the best she can get—"

"All right," he said. "At least you can wait for Cardigan in town. Get a room at the Cosmopolitan or Palace."

Something in her eyes silently thanked him, but she said, "I will wait for him here," and he helped her down in the hard bright sunlight and fetched her bag from under the seat.

She knew suddenly, watching him, that here was a lonely man; and then he turned his head and caught the reflection of that thought on her face.

"Good luck." He smiled and lifted his head and climbed into the buggy and drove away.

They had been like two ships that, going in opposite directions, meet and pass in the ocean. Like the ships, so alone against the vast panorama of sky and water, they had a certain routine and their aloneness in common; nothing more. She halfway wished, for Charlie's sake, they might have found their destiny beneath the same star, for she was a full-bodied woman, rich in all those things for which a man eternally searches; and there was much in the Englishman that she could admire.

A sadness touched her lips and she sighed. A person never should look back.

She picked up the bag and started for the house, a substantial looking place with curtains at the windows; but partway across the yard she stopped, struck by the incongruity of a feminine touch peeping out of a structure that looked more like a fortress than it did a stockman's ranch house.

Curtains at the windows.

It didn't fit anything she'd heard about Cardigan.

"Hello," she called. "Hello! Hello!" came the echo.

With a shrug, she went on. The massive door stood open, and she paused beside it, listening; and it seemed to listen with her.

She smiled at that and, setting down her bag, went in.

Notwithstanding the curtained windows, the place looked masculine enough in all conscience. This was the living room apparently, an immense and lofty barn of a place with an enormous fireplace at the far end. The walls were unfinished pine sheeting. Dark furniture was set about the walls and a massive table made a dark and uncompromising island in the center of the room. Indian rugs were scattered splashes of color against the yellow boards of the floor. There was a lamp with a round glass shade on the table and a handful of brass-jacketed cartridges that flung back the blaze of the lowering sun. Chairs that were barrel-shaped lattices of parti-colored slats with hide stretched over their upper framework were set about at regular intervals; there was a saddle in one, a pair of saddlebags in another, and the rest were draped with discarded sweat-stained clothing. And a buff-colored dust powdered everything.

Docie shook her head. It was time Kurt Cardigan got himself a woman if this was a sample of the rest of the house.

And it was. The kitchen was cluttered with dirty dishes. There was a bed in one room with no bedclothes on it, a cracked pitcher, and basin. A chest of drawers had another room all to itself. There was nothing soft in the entire place but the curtains.

With spirits somewhat dampened Docie returned to the living room and was trying to make up her mind if she should pitch in and clean it when the sound of approaching hoof beats drew her glance to the door.

A rider came into her line of vision, a hard-faced fellow in the garb of a cowboy. She watched him ride into the corral and dismount with an irritable mumble that had the sound of profanity. She noticed that he limped as he set about unsaddling. She watched him turn the horse loose and hang his saddle on a pole, afterwards leaving the pen and coming toward the house, still muttering.

She wondered if this were Cardigan and went reluctantly outside to meet him.

He seemed too busy with his thoughts to notice her. He was a gangling, loose-shackled specimen who looked seven shades rougher than hell itself. Midway of the yard he swung left toward a long narrow building that had a bench outside it on which reposed one bent pail and a rusty basin.

He must have felt her looking at him for he spun round of a sudden with his hand flashing hipward. He had his gun clear of leather before he got a good look at her. You could see realization hit him in the way his jaw sagged and the way he went rigid.

Docie said: "Is Mr. Cardigan here?"

"Who the hell are you?"

"My name is Balinett. I'm looking for Kurt Cardigan. I—he's expecting me."

"First I heard of it. First I heard of you, either," he said, putting his gun up, but with his face still hostile. His eyes kept boring into her. "You musta got off on the wrong foot or somethin'—he don't want no women around this place. Them's his orders. No women. You better pick up that bag an' head back where you come from."

Docie looked at him coolly. "I believe I'll just wait."

"Wrong guess," he said. "Get that bag an' get outa here."

She shook her head, meeting his look with that direct way she had while their wills clashed and locked, and a dark surge of color crept above his open collar.

He said, loud and angry: "Do you know what kind of a place this is?"

"It's a horse ranch, isn't it?"

"You didn't come out here to buy no horse."

"No." She smiled a little then. "I came out here because Mr. Cardigan sent for me."

She could see him turning it over, could see he didn't believe her. She said, "He sent me the money to come here."

He didn't believe that at all and didn't like it. He closed his jaws so tight it brought a scar out lividly the length of his chin. The black look of his eyes became more unreasoning, and a kind of violence beat through him, making her draw back a little.

He said, "You're wastin' your time."

Docie's cheeks showed a touch of color. "After all," she said, "I'm the best judge of that—"

"You fool," he cried bitterly. "The man's gone, pulled his freight! He don't live here anymore!"

"Nevertheless, I shall wait," Docie told him and ignoring the outraged look of him, turned and went back into the house.

* * *

THREE-QUARTERS OF AN HOUR later she had the living room looking as though people lived there. All the dust was swept out and all the clothes and gear picked up and put into the room with the chest of drawers. In the drawers, she had found a couple of clean blankets which she put on the bed. Then she fetched in her bag and started in on the kitchen.

By the time she had it looking as a kitchen ought to look, she was ravenously hungry. The feeling was probably accentuated by the tantalizing odors of a cooking meal that were emanating now from the long skinny building into which her surly interrogator had gone. He was probably the cook, which was one blessing anyway. At least she wouldn't have to cook her own supper.

While she was waiting for him to call her, she decided to clean up. What with trail grime and house grime she felt dirty all over.

She went into the other room and got clean underthings and a fresh dress from her bag and brought them back into the kitchen, laying them on one of the recently scrubbed chairs. She put another chair under the knob of the door. She really needed some hot water, but she didn't feel like bothering to build a fire to get some. Cold water from the well would have to do, she reckoned and proceeded to pump the sink full. At least there was plenty of soap, great brown blocks of it stacked on a shelf.

She looked around at the windows, of which there were two; one above the sink and a bigger one back of the stove. The one above the sink faced the yard. The other one was in the back wall of the room and gave out on a wide sweep of grass covered hills that were yellow from long drought. There were no shades at either window and no curtains. There were solid slabs of board that could be closed across the windows, but she didn't feel like going to all the bother of that. The cook was getting supper and had made it very plain he wasn't interested in women.

She pulled off her dress and got out of her crumpled underthings. Sometimes, she thought irrelevantly, it must be nice to be an Indian. She got a washcloth from her bag and a big soft fuzzy towel. She laid the towel on the drain-board and put the washcloth in the water. It was then that she remembered she didn't have anything to stand in.

Should she get the cracked pitcher and basin from the bedroom? She looked out into the yard which, as before, was hotly empty. She could hear the cook banging around in his shanty. She really wanted that basin. It would only take a moment. With a shrug, she decided to risk it and pulled the chair from beneath the knob.

She crossed the long living room, the yellow boards of the floor feeling warm beneath her feet. Moving into the bedroom she lifted the heavy pitcher and got the basin out from under. Turning then, she caught the reflection of her sunlit shape in the window and paused a moment, not entirely satisfied.

It was nothing to be ashamed of. A little slim, perhaps, but adequately rounded in the most appropriate places. It had never been her fortune though she knew it could have been.

She was halfway across the living room when the sound of men's voices startled her. She flew into the kitchen most becomingly flushed, whipped the towel around her, and got the spare chair beneath the doorknob again. Then she took a deep breath and cautiously peeked out the window that was over the sink.

There was another horse in the yard. Still saddled, it stood on dangling reins before the cabin where the man who didn't like women was rattling pots and pans. By the mutter of voices both men were in there, but their talk was more unintelligible here than it had been in the other room.

Leaning forward, Docie raised the window a little. She still couldn't hear what the two men were saying.

Fearing any moment, they might call her to supper or, worse, that one of them might come to fetch her personally, she hurried through her bath and got into her clothes. A girl liked to spend a little time with her bath—it was bad enough having to take it standing in a basin—but she couldn't afford much dawdling with a couple of unattached males on the premises.

Hastily combing out her hair, she put it up without brushing and supposed she looked a sight but there was nothing she could do about it. Cardigan, apparently, had never found the need of investing in a mirror.

She looked out the back window. The sun was dropping behind the hills and, already, the shadows were turning purple black. She wished that cook would shake it up a little. She could have cooked supper twice in this length of time.

She picked up her discarded clothes and carried them into the room where she'd put all the stuff, she'd picked up in the living room. Then she went back and tidied the kitchen and took the basin back into the bedroom. She couldn't see her reflection in the window now...

After a while she went back in the living room and sat down in one of the hide-bottomed chairs; the dry leather creaked abysmally but she found it surprisingly comfortable. The vast silence of this country seemed to reach all through the house. A pleasant lassitude stole over her, a peace she hadn't known in months.

It was dark when she realized the cook wasn't going to call her. Really dark. She could see the winking gleam of stars through the lesser black of the open door. She had no idea how long she'd been dozing; it must have been a good while.

She got up and went to the door and stood a moment looking out. The whole yard was dark, and the foliaged branches of the trees made great patches of blackness against the deep blue of the star-girded night. The men were sitting on the bench before the cook-shack. She could hear their occasional movements and, now and again, the desultory murmur of their voices; she could see the fitful glow of one man's cigarette.

So, they had eaten their supper and now were smoking, taking their ease, and neither of them had bothered to give her a call. Surely horse thief hospitality had little to recommend it.

She wondered what time it was getting to be, and abruptly realized she hadn't seen a clock since she'd come into this house. No clock and no mirror. Cardigan certainly needed some lessons in housekeeping.

Groping her way to the kitchen she got a match from the box hanging back of the stove. She stood a while then, carefully thinking things over; but finally, with a shrug, she scratched her match and lit the bracket lamp appended to the kitchen's back wall. Then she got another match and went back and fit the lamp on the living room table.

The voices of the two men were louder now; lifted in some kind of altercation. But she paid them no attention. What she wanted now was to get some food inside her. She hated like sin having to fix her own supper, but she hated even worse the thought of going to bed hungry.

She was glad she had put on this gingham dress; it was cooler than the taffeta and a lot more comfortable. She was not a bit sorry she'd done her cleaning in the other. Taffeta, someway, seemed out of place around here.

She looked out the door. A silver moon was coming up. The men seemed to be having some kind of an argument. She heard the cook say plainly: "You kin be a goddam fool if you want to, but I don't want no part of it!" And she went back to the kitchen to see what a search of the curtained shelves would turn up.

It didn't turn up much in the way of food. A couple of boxes of biscuits the rats had been into, three still-unopened cans of sardines, three Bermuda onions, a sack of dried beans, a ten-pound bag of salt, and a scant half sack of weevilly flour.

Docie turned away with a grimace.

She'd rather go to bed hungry than to ask a man like that cook for anything. Nor did she very much relish the thought of going to bed. It wasn't that she was afraid exactly, but...

Supposing the cook had told the truth about Cardigan? If Charlie's gambling house rumors had been based on anything stronger than jaw-wagging... She recalled then what the cook had said first and felt better. *He don't want no women around here. Them's his orders—no women.* He'd not have opened up that way if Cardigan had gone.

But why would Cardigan have given such an order?

Hoof sound turned her face toward the window and a kind of excitement brightened her cheeks. She would soon have all her doubts set at rest; surely this was Cardigan coming now. What would he be like? And what would he think of her? Would she suit him—would she be the kind of woman he was hoping and expecting?

Well, why not? Not an inconsiderable number of the men she had known, including Top Hat Charlie, would have felt themselves fortunate to get a woman like her. She didn't guess Kurt Cardigan would be much different from the rest; at least, so far as what he wanted was concerned.

She tried to see out the window but the light in the room threw back too many reflections. She heard a jingle of spur chains and went hurrying into the living room to pull up with an unaccustomed fluster when she saw the man in the open door. It hadn't occurred to her before that she might not like Cardigan.

He stood in scuffed boots with big-roweled spurs and his long legs were covered with brush-clawed chaps. There was a glisten of sweat on his hard burnt face and his thumbs were hooked in a heavy black belt that gleamed with cartridges and held a bone handled gun in a tied-down holster. His chin-strapped hat was broad-brimmed and low of crown and a grin pulled thick lips from his tobacco-stained teeth.

"Hello there, honey. Reckon it's been pretty lonesome fer you hangin' around here."

"I finally got here."

"Yeah. Sure, sure, you did." He came into the room, and she felt frozen in her tracks. "Sure, you did." He grinned, and stood there, looking at her.

He had yellow, lashless eyes that were unwinking as a snake's.

She felt she had to say something. "What—what took you so long?"

"That goddam cook. I had t' git rid of him. Didn't even know you was here till we got all done with eatin'—sometimes I don't think that guy's got 'em all."

He grinned at her again. "I bet you're hungrier'n a bear."

It was this consideration, this reminder of her hunger, that threw her off guard. He got his arms around her before she knew what was happening. He covered her mouth with his. With a furious effort, she wrenched herself free and stood back from him, panting.

There was surprise on his face. "Gosh, honey," he said, with contrition, "I didn't reckon t' scare you—Christ, I wouldn't scare you fer anythin'! Guess I never expected you would be so danged beautiful... I—I guess I jest sorta broke plumb away from myself." His voice came down a notch. "I—I'm sure sorry if I was rough."

Docie felt for a chair and dropped into it suddenly, feeling weak as a kitten.

She didn't know what to do, or what to say, or what to think. He *did* look sorry. She guessed she was acting like a fool, but she hadn't been prepared for anything like this. Mostly these cowboys were shy, timid fellows when they got around a woman. She had forgotten how wild they could sometimes be.

She just stared at him, wondering. She felt all tangled up inside. She didn't know whether she wanted to laugh or to cry. After all, she'd come out here of her own free will to marry him. If he had been a little precipitate, wasn't it probably no more than natural when you considered the kind of life he led, the lonesomeness of it, the hard work and danger?

She lifted a hand and pushed back her hair. She took a deep breath and tried to smile at him. "I—I'll be all right in a minute." Sure.

She put out her hand so that he could help her up.

"Sure, you will." He grinned and came over and took it.

She knew, too late, she'd made another mistake. His hand closed around hers like a bear trap. As it pulled her onto her feet his other hand came forward and tore the front of her dress loose. Then he had her in his arms again and was bending her backward with his mouth crushed tight on hers. She tried to get his gun, but he slapped her hand away, and she could feel him laughing deep down in his throat as he caught her overbalanced weight against his thigh.

She twisted her head and got her mouth free and screamed.

He laughed openly now, exultantly.

"Go ahead—yell. The cooks rode off. Who the hell you think'll hear you?"

She could feel the hot breath of him against her cheek. She tried again to break loose, and he bent an arm behind her, twisting till she quit. There was a roaring in her ears, a sound of running feet. The hot, gloating, bright yellow eyes were gone off focus. She was like a swimmer going under for the third and final time when she heard a man's voice quietly say:

"Don't you reckon you've gone about far enough, Frayne?"

SEVENTEEN
DANGEROUS BUSINESS

SHE HAD no trouble getting clear of him now. His shape was still as though turned to stone and all the steel was gone out of his fingers. They still gripped her arms but there was no strength in them, and she tore herself from them, staggering back against the support of the table.

Only then did she see the other man, the one whose voice had set her free. He was by the open outside door, a yellow-haired man in trail-grimed garb with a spatter of dust streaked across granite features. There was blood on his shirt and his cheeks looked ghastly, but a hard smile twisted his saturnine lips.

"Turn around, you cheap tinhorn, and let's have a look at a skunk on two legs."

All the flush of hot blood had fallen out of Frayne's face. And all the boldness. There was not much difference between his tawny eyes now and the painted glass buttons tied into the head of the elk above the mantel.

"Turn around," the man said, and Frayne did so, stiffly.

He tried to shake himself together. He licked parched lips and life crept cautiously into his eyes and sent ragged glances this way and that like the eyes of a weasel backed into a corner. It wasn't a pretty thing to see.

But the man in the doorway wasn't pretty either with that blood all over the front of his shirt, with his cheeks so gray and glance so bitter. He was like a man skewered above the fires of hell. It was his calm, she thought, that made him seem so alarming. Whatever it was, you could not fail to be conscious of this man's deadly power. It was an aura about him, a suggestion of violence held in leash by a hair.

"What do you reckon will be the end of you, Frayne?"

Frayne flushed and scowled. He appeared to have gotten back some of his assurance and there was, just back of those yellow eyes, intermingled with the fright, an arousing anger compounded of thwarted passion and injured pride. You could see it gnawing him, burning like acid across all those barriers of care and caution flung about him by the look of this other man's eyes. You could see it battling with the fright that was in him: but the fright was strongest, and it shaped his answer.

"Hell! I thought you an' me was friends, Kurt."

Kurt! Docie stiffened. So, *this* was Cardigan, this yellow-haired man! A deep breath lifted the swell of her breasts and she looked at him carefully.

He was a solid shape with the look of hard living ground into his features. The scars of his trade had left their marks on him in the high voltage look of his saturnine eyes, in the lines around his mouth, in the whole appearance of him. Here was no man to be dismissed with a tag. A tremendous energy was in this man, a dynamic something that colored his every look and gesture; a quietness that bordered on insolence.

"Friends, eh? Was you thinkin' of that when you was maulin' this woman?"

"Hell's fire! I wa'n't maulin' her—"

"What was you doin'?"

Frayne threw out his hands. "I was jest sorta honey-fussin' round with her a little—"

"Do you always tear their dresses when you're honey-fussin' round?"

Cardigan's words flung a bright color into Frayne's face. Stung pride and resentment worked their yeasty way through him and he blew out a gust of breath and cried wildly: "You got no call to be ridin' herd on me! I knew this skirt when she was up at Dodge City—"

"She ain't up at Dodge City now," Cardigan said. And his eyes grew darker as he stared at the man. "You know my rules about women. Get on your horse and ride out of here. An' don't bother to fetch yourself back."

Frayne stood perfectly still. Then he shook his shoulders together and the resentful, corrosive rage that was in him burned through to his cheeks and he yelled in a high half-strangled voice, "You can't kick me off like a empty boot! By God, I got some rights around here!"

A cold grin tugged the set of Cardigan's lips. "Sure you have. You got a gun in your belt. If you want to fight for 'em, use it."

Frayne's eyes came wide open.

He went back half a step, and then he went back another. All the anger fell out of his face and left it ashen.

"You want your rights." Cardigan sneered. "Go on an' pull it."

Sweat made a shine along the side of Frayne's cheeks. A moment ago, he'd been a bundle of fury. Rage and resentment had obscured his judgment, blinding him to where his wild words might take him. Now he found himself shaking.

He could no more have lifted that gun off his hip than he could have scratched his right ear with his own left elbow.

"Just a four-flusher, eh?" Cardigan taunted. "I reckoned all the yeller wasn't used up in your eyes. Toss your gun on the table—an' if you wanta die quick hit the lamp an' I'll oblige you."

With a ludicrous care, Frayne did as commanded.

Cardigan shook his head, dissatisfied. "By Gawd, but you're a beauty. Plumb cultus!" He sneered.

Frayne said nothing at all. He closed his heavy jaws and kept his thoughts to himself.

Cardigan said: "Pick up your gun."

"What's that for?" Frayne said, making no move to go near it.

"I like you better with a gun in your fist. You don't look so much like a rabbit."

"I'll get by."

"Pick it up!" Cardigan said.

Frayne's malign stare licked at Cardigan darkly. He never lifted a finger, never moved from his tracks.

"What's the matter? You froze there?"

"Do I look crazy?" Frayne sneered.

"You look like a woman-baitin', white-livered sneak that ain't got enough guts to take a slap at a sand flea. I reckon I could take a batch of corn shucks an' lightnin' bugs an' make you run till your tongue flopped out like a calf rope. You musta lost all your sand tryin' t' best my woman—Christ!" Cardigan snarled, "ain't there nothin' I kin say that'll put a spark to your powder?"

Frayne's cheeks were the color of butcher paper but he kept his hands stiffly held in plain view. It was no great feat to guess what line his thoughts were taking. There was not much fear in his tawny eyes now; they were baleful and hating and scheming out a course that he might take some other day.

It was plain enough to Docie. Frayne had shed his fright with that gun; he was gambling that Cardigan would not shoot an unarmed man.

She amended that conclusion after considering him a moment. Shiloh Frayne wasn't gambling; he was confident Kurt wouldn't shoot him and, considering his former agitation, he could only have one basis for such confidence—the fact that his gun was in plain sight on yonder table.

But, if Cardigan had ever entertained the thought of killing him, why had he disarmed Shiloh Frayne in the first place? He hadn't disarmed Frayne actually; he had told Frayne to toss his gun on the table. A mistake?

Looking at Cardigan Docie didn't think so. She thought it much more likely he had wanted Frayne to draw; that Cardigan's deliberate intention had been to put a gun in Frayne's hand in the hope Frayne would try to use it.

But Frayne had been too frightened. He had not risen to Cardigan's bait. And now he saw Cardigan's purpose and would not go anywhere near the gun.

Even Cardigan seemed to know the chance was lost. He looked at Frayne with a biting contempt. "Get up on your hind feet, skunk, an' git outa here. I'm goin' to have my woman blow out the lamp an' fetch me that rifle over there on them elk horns. If you know when you're lucky you won't be doin' no stoppin' till you've got yourself clean on outa the country. Go on now —git!"

EIGHTEEN
INTERRUPTED JOURNEY

IN THE DARKNESS of the room after the lamp in the kitchen also had been snuffed and she had fetched Kurt Cardigan the rifle off the elk horns, Docie did what she could to repair the bodice of her dress. But her fingers seemed all thumbs and she kept remembering the grip of Shiloh Frayne's hands. She had never felt so terribly alone and defenseless.

She looked to where Cardigan stood in the doorway, a solid black shape with a rifle, watching Frayne's progress across the bright yard. This was the man she had come here to marry, the man with whom she had hoped to find security; but the sight of him standing there failed to reassure her, and she shivered again, thinking into the future.

After all, what did she know of him?

Even remembrance of his forbearance in the matter of Shiloh Frayne did not greatly brighten her outlook; she had a disquieting conviction there'd been something about that business which she had not fully grasped.

What kind of man was he underneath that grim exterior?

She thought now that perhaps she had been a little hasty in turning down Charlie's suggestion that she go back and do her waiting for Cardigan in town. Supposing he were to treat her as Frayne had? She'd come here of her own accord. He was a bigger man than Shiloh Frayne and a rougher one by the look of him. Suppose he didn't care to wait for any marriage lines? He had told her very bluntly that what he wanted was a woman.

And there was Frayne. Who could say what any man might do after coming on her and Frayne the way he had?

She remembered the icy blaze of his eyes.

St. Louis, of a sudden, seemed a very desirable place.

She felt an uprush of panic, an almost overpowering urge to run away and lose herself in the yellow grass of the windswept hills. She had to bite her lower lip to keep it from trembling.

She was moving with stealthy care in the direction of the kitchen when the sound of Frayne's departing horse brought her to her senses. She must quit this foolish nonsense. She'd come out here to marry Kurt Cardigan; she mustn't let the thought of Frayne unsettle her in this fashion. All he'd actually done had been to steal a couple of kisses; his ultimate intentions had nothing to do with reality. Because Frayne had been a beast was no good reason for thinking Cardigan one. The only thing she knew of Kurt was definitely in his favor. Though under great provocation and with ample opportunity he hadn't been able to bring himself to shoot an unarmed man.

She turned her head for another look at him, and caught her breath sharply as she found herself staring at an unbroken rectangle of moonlit yard. The black shape of Cardigan was no longer in the door.

She fought down a wild impulse to scream. There must be some explanation, some perfectly natural reason...

She went hurrying forward, almost plunging head-long when her foot rammed into something soft and yielding. Even before she heard his groan she knew, with a sudden sick remembrance of that blood on his shirt, that this was Cardigan.

She found the sulphur matches and got the living room lamp lit. She wouldn't let herself think as she brought the lamp over and put it down beside Cardigan. She was afraid now— really afraid with a cold and sinking feeling that was creeping all through her. She knew she mustn't give way to it. His life—perhaps her own, might well depend on what she did now.

She had had some experience with wounds; her father had been a doctor, though much too frank for the good of his family.

Cardigan lay sprawled just inside the open door; he seemed more to have slid down the wall than to have fallen. She dropped to her knees beside him, steeling herself against the sight of his wound. Very carefully she opened and folded back the grimy shirt.

The lonesome sounds of the night drifted in; she heard the distant rush of the wind. *Keep cool,* she told herself. *You've got to keep cool.*

But when she looked at his chest the breath caught

in her throat. She must have hot water. She remembered the salt on the curtained shelf and hurried to build up a fire in the stove. She put on a big pot of water.

While she was waiting for it to boil, she went back and again looked at Cardigan, worriedly. She ought to get him on a bed; she felt distrustful of her ability. She was a long way from puny, even when judged by current standards which seemed inclined to weigh a woman after the manner of a heifer, but she doubted that her strength would prove sufficient to lift Cardigan. He was a pile of man any way you looked at him.

And it sure wouldn't do to go dragging him around. By the looks of that wound, he was due for a fever.

He was probably better off left right there on the floor.

She fetched a clean petticoat from her bag and tore it into strips for bandaging. The pot of water on the stove was beginning to boil and she stirred in some salt from the bag on the shelf. When she judged it had boiled a sufficient length of time, she lifted it off and took it into the living room. Cardigan was groaning but was still unconscious.

She went back and washed her hands and returned with the spoon she had used to stir the salt. Dropping two of her cloths in the steaming mixture she twirled them around till she felt sure they were disinfected and then fished one out and held it on the spoon until the steam went out of it.

Carefully then, she washed the clotted blood away from the ugly hole. She got him on his side and pulled the shirt up over his back. She washed more blood off there. One thing she had to be thankful for, the bullet had gone straight through. It could have been a lot worse. Passing straight through his chest it had left a comparatively clean hole separating his ribs and grazing the sack of his left lung as near as she could judge. He was probably in great pain and would continue to be.

She fished the second cloth out of the steaming pot and when it had sufficiently cooled, bathed the wound as well as she could. With the rest of the dry strips, she bandaged it, rolling him from side to side as she worked. He did a lot of groaning and it hurt her to hear him, but she knew it had to be done if she would keep down infection; and there was no guarantee that she could, even so. He had ought to be in bed.

She carried the water back out to the kitchen and poured it down the drain. Then she filled the pot with fresh water, poured in a little salt, and put it back on the stove where she would have it handy.

She washed her hands again and went back and slumped down in a chair by the door. All the time she had worked with Cardigan she'd kept listening for the sound of approaching riders, and she was listening now.

After a while, she got up and took off her dress in the bedroom, and mended it. She put another dress on, a gay yellow-and-white print, in the hope it might serve to kind of buck up her spirits. Taking the rifle with her she went over to the cook shack and ate some cold beans which she found on the back of the gone-out stove. Then she went back to Cardigan.

He was moaning again but his eyes were open.

They considered each other for a bit without speaking. There was a kind of grudging admiration at the back of his eyes, but he didn't put any of it into his words. "In that letter, you wrote you didn't mention

Dodge City." The way he said it sounded like he was accusing her of something.

She said: "I don't recall that you mentioned being a horse thief, either."

"What's my politics got t' do with it? You claimed you was wantin' to tie up with a rancher—that you wanted some feller livin' west of the Pecos. That's me on both counts."

She let that go. "Can you get up if I help you?"

"I'll git up when I'm ready an' I don't need no help."

She lifted her chin and looked him straight in the eye. "You better get up now then. You ought to be in a bed."

She could see the bright anger boil into his stare. She had a temper herself and she put the whole business right square on the line. "I'm not one of your punchers. If we go on with this thing, I'll expect to be treated as a wife and a partner. If I don't measure up to what you were looking for you can say so right now, and I'll go on back to town."

The look of his eyes was like the smash of a hammer. "Back to that pianner-thumpin' tinhorn, I reckon!"

He climbed onto his feet then and stood towering over her with all the wild fury of a goaded bull. "If you're stay-in' round here there's somethin' you better git straight right now. I don't want no pardner an' I ain't about t' hev one! Bein' a woman's your job an' what goes on outside of these rooms don't concern you. I told you straight out when I sent you that money—"

"I know what you told me. *'I ain't aimin to buy no*

pig in a poke. I ain't reckonin to be under no obligation till—"

"Correct," Cardigan scowled.

"All right. I'm here. You've looked me over. Now get into that bed before you're down with a—"

"Hold your lip," he glared, "till I git done with my talkin'. You'll git plain grub here an' plain talk an' no fripperies. I'll put food in your belly an' clothes on your back, but I'll run this spread any damn way I feel like an' I don't want no jawin' outa you about it, neither."

"Are you through?"

"No, I'm not through!" He seemed angered to hear his own voice going up while she stood there so cool, giving him back look for look. "You better know what you're gittin' into. I don't trim my lampwick fer no one. There's tough sleddin' ahead an' come I find that it's needful you'll do a man's work same as everyone else. I ain't runnin' no rest home—"

"I didn't ask for any rest home."

"You ain't gettin' one, neither! This ain't no country fer weaklin's. You'll tend to the fire wood an' cook fer the outfit such times as they're here, an' such times as they ain't you'll take care of all stock that's bein' kept round the yard. You'll turn your hand to whatever needs doin' an' you'll pleasure my bed whenever it suits me."

She said with plain scorn: "What you want is a squaw."

The words didn't shame him, didn't bother him at all. She was not quite certain of the way he looked at her; he appeared to be watching her. Almost, he appeared to be waiting. It came over her suddenly what he had in his mind, and she laughed to herself to see the way his face changed when she said, quiet and scornful, "Though I suppose I could learn to be one if had to."

The chagrin that darkened his eyes proved her right. His talk had been designed to scare her off, to get rid of her; to turn her away from here without delay.

She did not seek just then to uncover his reason; she was much too engrossed with the discovery she had made—that there was a lot more to Cardigan than showed on the surface. Oh, he was dangerous, all right, a rough man and a tough one, but not nearly so tough as he would have people think. He could have told her straight out that he had had a change of heart; instead, he had resorted to subterfuge, had tried to paint so dismal a picture that she would withdraw from their arrangement of her own accord.

So, there was softness in him, white mixed with the black. Good hidden back of that hard blasphemous bluster. A kind of modern Robin Hood with a code that would not let him shoot an unarmed man.

She felt considerably better about her prospects for the future.

She found he was still looking at her, obviously disgruntled. "You mean you're figurin' t' stay here?"

"And where else would I go?"

There was no doubt but that he found her decision disturbing. Plainly he had counted on her going back to town. He seemed to want to speak out, to reveal some further disadvantage; and a perverse humor suddenly prompted her to say:

"You wanted a woman, so you sent me the price of my transportation. You weren't expecting too much for you didn't even bother to ask me for a picture. You couldn't believe your luck; the moment you laid eyes on me you made up your mind there was something rotten somewhere. You couldn't forget you'd found me being pawed by Frayne; your suspicions were confirmed when he told you he had known me in Dodge City."

Some memory darkened the look of her eyes. "Does every woman in Dodge City have to be a harlot? You don't even ask me *if* I were there, or what brought me there, or what I was doing! You've heard I came out here with Top Hat Charlie and so because he deals faro at the Gold Plate Saloon, you—"

"What *were* you doin' there?" Cardigan growled.

"I was with a variety show from St. Louis. I don't say Frayne didn't see me there—a lot of people saw me that I wouldn't know from Adam. But he had no right to say that he had 'known' me. No man can say that."

There was color in her cheeks when she finished, but it was the color of embarrassment and not of shame.

It would have been nice in him to have said he believed her, but he didn't say anything. Nor did he appear much impressed.

He unbuckled his cartridge belt and dropped it over the back of a chair. He shoved the door shut and dropped the bar into place.

"A hoofer, eh?"

Docie bridled. "If you think—"

"My head ain't workin' too good right now. I'm goin' t' catch a few winks," he said wearily and grimaced. He licked at his lips, and she suddenly realized how haggard his face looked. He took a long breath and let it slide out of him. "When the crew comes in wake me up," he grunted.

Then he paused and looked back at her. "You were right about one thing." A twisted grin lit up his tough face briefly. "You're a choicer piece of baggage than I'd any right t' look for."

* * *

WHEN HENNESSY, Cardigan's cook, quit the ranch he had his meagre belongings stuffed into the bedroll lashed back of his cantle and no least intention of ever coming back. Enough was enough and if on top of everything else, Shiloh Frayne had no better sense than to start horsing round with that black-haired filly, it was time for a smart gent to roll his cotton.

He'd about made up his mind to do it anyway. Things was moving a sight too fast for any stove-up man who craved to keep on living. It was one thing to rustle maverick horses up north and something else again to start stealing from your neighbors. He'd seen some of those horses from Amado and Florence and the worked-over brands wasn't even healed yet! Lahr had claimed this new stealing was by Kurt's orders, and maybe it was, but that didn't take the damnfool craziness out of it.

Nor out of setting in a deal where the deck was being stacked by any jasper like Lahr. You might's well ask for a rope and be done with it. People was getting fed up with this night riding and blood would be spilled in mighty grim earnest if it ever leaked out the KC was mixed up in it—they was plenty suspicious of the outfit already.

He'd been a fool ever to listen to Lahr in the first place. If Lahr would double cross Cardigan he would double cross anyone—Hennessy included.

With cold sweat on his neck, he lifted his horse into

a lope. He drew the carbine from its scabbard and rode with it cradled across the pommel of his saddle with his eyes jabbing this way and that through the shadows. He should have shaken the dust of this country right after Lahr put the deal up to him.

It had looked pretty slick the way Lahr had first told it.

A cinch, Lahr had said. Just as easy as knocking off skunks with a club.

There'd be just him and Hennessy; with the ranch for a stake and whatever they grabbed from the bank jobs. Not a chance for a slip-up—he'd got it all figured out. Alibis and everything. There was an old hat of Cardigan's hanging in the cook shack, and that's what they'd use to pin the whole thing on Kurt. They might look a little simple being tied in with a bunch of damn outlaws like that, and some folks might even make a few ugly cracks, but they could never prove anything. Not the way Lahr would play it.

He had it all fixed up. Stapleton, that owned the Gold Plate Saloon in Tucson, had been mixed up in some crooked deal Lahr had found out about, and that was the wedge he aimed to use for their alibi. Him and Hennessy only. Just the two of them. Clean as a fresh diaper.

Lahr would fix it for the bunch to rendezvous down at Frenchy's, a hole-up they knew about just east of Naco. It would take them a while to drift down there. Each man to ride separate so as not to attract any suspicious attention. Meantime Lahr, with Hennessy, and unbeknownst to the others, would ride into Tucson and make themselves conspicuous in the Gold Plate Saloon where they'd proceed to tank up and, presumably, get plastered. Stapleton, ostensibly to forestall trouble, would publicly have words with them and apparently, persuade them to take their arguments and their liquor into the privacy of the Gold Plate's back room. Where they would proceed to go on a three-day bender—according to Stapleton.

There were no windows opening off that back room and the only door was the one they'd go in by. Once they had shut it and locked it, however Stapleton—in the room above it—would lift an already-loosened plank from the wooden ceiling, let down a rope and haul them up. After which, from this upstairs room's window, with the same rope he'd let them down into the alley. And he'd take care of the appearances after they'd gone.

Rejoining the others at Frenchy's by a relay of horses they would crack the Douglas bank the following night. Lahr would be wearing Kurt's old hat and would manage to lose it during the Copper State holdup at Bisbee. This, once the hat was traced back to its owner, would pin the whole thing right on Cardigan. Of course, Jupe Krailor and Frayne would be in for it, too, but with their Gold Plate alibi, Hennessy and Lahr would be strictly in the clear. And Lahr already had a bill of sale with Cardigan's signature faked slick as anything.

This was the way Lahr had put it up to him that hot afternoon while he'd been peeling potatoes; and the deal, so far, had gone just like clockwork. The Douglas bank was just like gutting a slut and that stage they'd stuck up hadn't fanched them none, either. It was the butchery at Bisbee that had upset the applecart and first shown Hennessy what kind of a bastard he had gone and tied up with. There had been no need of Lahr killing that star-packer. It still sent cold chills all through Hennessy's marrow to remember Lahr pumping slugs into the lawman.

"Hell, I had t' make sure they'd get to work on that hat," Lahr said callously. "We can't grab the ranch until we git rid of Cardigan."

Hennessy groaned as he flogged through the shadow-dappled moonlight night. He'd been a fool to get mixed up in this thing. Any guy as slick as Lahr was at fixing things up wouldn't find no trouble getting rid of a partner.

The best thing now, Hennessy told himself, was to head straight south and get on over into Mexico. And he was there in his thinking, bemoaning the follies of a misspent life when something jerked tight about his arms and chest and dragged him headlong from the saddle.

Roped!

The truth raced like fire across the havoc of his thoughts. And then the whole world exploded in a million glittering lights.

The next thing he knew a rough hand had hold of him and he felt himself being hauled to his feet. Then his head cleared a little and he mighty near fainted when he found himself peering into the face of Curly Lahr.

Lahr's expression was not pleasant.

Hennessy swallowed twice and shuddered.

Jupe Krailor held the end of the rope with his weight on his boot heels thirty feet away.

Hennessy gagged and Lahr said thinly: "Where the hell did you figure to be goin' in such a lather?"

There it was. Right there was the crux of this whole situation.

Terror broke Hennessy's brain from its paralysis. His thoughts flew round like a fly in a bottle, but his tongue couldn't seem to get hold of any words.

"Well?" Lahr said, his tone sharp and vicious.

"I...uh...wasn't goin' anyplace, partic'lar."

Hennessy sweated.

"You always go no place in such a hell-tearin' hurry?"

"I was lookin' for you. There's a woman at the ranch; right young an' damn good lookin'. Says she's waitin' fer Cardigan."

"What kind of a yarn are you tryin' to patch up?"

"By Gawd, it's the truth! Someone fetched her out from town. She was there when I rode in—had her bag right on the doorstep. Wanted to know where Kurt was an' when I tells her he's pulled out she wasn't bothered even a little bit. Jest give me a grin. 'He's expecting me,' she says, an' takes her bag on into the house.

"Then Frayne comes ridin' in. I kept my mouth shut till we was plumb through eatin'. Then she put on a light an' of course I had t' tell him. He was hog-wild to go over. I done what I could an' when I seen he was goin' over anyway I piled into a saddle an' come huntin' you—an' I kin prove it. You kin see her for yourself jest as quick as we git back!"

Lahr eyed him for several moments, never saying a word. Then he signed Jupe Krailor to ease up on the rope and, when Jupe did, he loosened the loop and let Hennessy get out of it.

Hennessy plainly had the fidgets. "You're goin' back there, ain'tcha?"

Lahr tossed the loop to Krailor and grinned and shook his head.

"But— You know what Frayne'll do!"

"I ain't Frayne's keeper."

"But-"

"There's times I find it pretty good business to let nature take its course," Lahr said. "You can take the hulls off these nags, Jupe. We're goin' to stick right here a spell an' give Frayne's talent a chance to exercise."

Krailor guffawed. Hennessy looked worried. "What if—"

Lahr said, "That's why we're waitin'. Kurt'll be back if he told that filly t' meet him there. If he walks in on Frayne it's. goin' to be too bad for someone. There's a fair-sized possibility it might be too bad for Kurt."

NINETEEN
COMMON GROUND

SAM SOLLANTSY FOLDED up the week-old copy of the Tombstone *Epitaph* and, with a snort of disgust, chucked it over with the others on the marshal's desk. He had been through them all and was no nearer solving the Douglas and Bisbee bank robberies than he'd been last night when Esparza had refused to go after Kurt Cardigan. The brief accounts in the *Star* and the rambling through colorful diatribes taking up half the pages of the Brewery Gulch *Gazette* only gave additional fuel to his contempt of local law.

"It's plain as the nose on your face," he said bitterly. "A kid in three-cornered pants could see the same damn bunch is pullin' all this stuff. Settin' on your tail ain't going to slice no pickles! Four men stick up the Tombstone stage; four men go larrupin' hell-for-leather out of Douglas right after the safe at the bank was blown; three men stick up the Copper State at Bisbee while a fourth waits outside with the horses. God a'mighty, what more do you want?"

"Proof of their identity," Esparza said quietly. "We

have nothing but conjecture to connect the same four men with all three jobs and nothing but suspicion to hook them up with Cardigan. I want facts, not surmise and suspicion. Show me one fact that ties Cardigan into this and I'll—"

"I've shown you three facts an' you won't act on any of them."

"You've said the yellow stud Cardigan rides is the Hale stallion, Jubal Jo, from Big Timber. You've said the buttermilk filly Cardigan bought for you at the livery is another Hale horse, and you've said Cardigan forced you out of town at gun point. But the livery keeper, Reagan, says he didn't buy the filly from Cardigan; he says he didn't see Cardigan throw a gun on you. And *I* didn't see him throw a gun on you and, for all you know, Kurt may have bought this Jubal Jo from somebody else. —"

"Then why not go out there an' ask him? Make him produce a bill of sale. Make him round up the stock he's got out there an' let us look it over." The Tri-States man said bitterly: "You know damn well in your own mind that crowd's guilty!"

The marshal shook his head. "I think the KC crew may be implicated in some of this violence that's been going on, but thoughts are not proof. And we've nothing at all to connect them with those bank jobs. As a matter of record, and according to Stapleton and several others, at the time those banks were being robbed the KC cook and the KC range boss were having themselves a bender right here in town in the Gold Plate Saloon."

"Just because those two didn't happen to be in on it doesn't alibi the whole outfit, does it?" Sollantsy snorted. "The bulk of his gang may not work on the ranch, may not have no connection with the KC at all. If he's got any cogs in his noggin he'd have his bunch scattered out, one guy workin' here, another one there."

Esparza said, "There's no point goin' all over it again. You may be absolutely right in callin' Cardigan responsible for the stealin' in your country and the Tri-States crowd may have enough to convict him, but until it's put before me, I'll consider this end first. I'm a lot more concerned with getting back that bank loot, and the men responsible for those killings at Bisbee, than I am with somethin' that happened somewhere else. And, since the fellow you're after happens to be the very man I'm dependin' on to help me get back the money that was stolen in those—"

"But it's the same goddam man!" Sollantsy shouted. "An I'll be campin' right here until I take the bastard back with me!"

"That's your—" Esparza quit talking as a man in dusty range garb stepped through the door. He looked at the man carefully. "Glad you're back, Hankins. What'd you find out?"

The deputy tossed a hat to Esparza. It was old and sun-faded and grimed about the band with an ingrained coating of dust and sweat. "This hat was dropped by the leader of that bunch when they went poundin' away from the Copper State —the guy that cut down the Bisbee marshal. If you don't recognize it," Hankins said, "turn it over an' hev a look at the sweatband. Notice them initials? I just been talkin' to Kransfeldter down at the Mercantile. He stamped them initials in that hat for Kurt Cardigan."

* * *

CARDIGAN DIDN'T SLEEP WELL. The pain in his chest was like a white-hot iron and its heat spread all through him. Awake he could fight back the pain, could clamp his jaws shut and ignore it, but in sleep it kept him twisting and groaning. Sometimes he was a luckless prospector caught by the Apaches and staked out on an ant hill; at other times he was afoot in the burning glare of the desert, trying to track down his burros with an empty canteen. But always, when the dreams or the pain finally woke him, the black-haired girl was either close by or bending over him, wiping his face, or putting cold rags against the heat in his forehead.

God, but he was hot!

The funny part of it was he didn't seem to get delirious. He always knew who she was and what she was doing there. Each time he woke up her face would bring it all back. He'd had a damn close call and he knew it. An inch either way and you could have what was left of him.

Sometimes he was awake when he'd make out like he was sleeping—playing possum, kind of, just to see what she'd be up to, or to have himself a look when she bent over to put the clothes on. She was a damn good-looking baggage—best he'd ever laid his eyes on; a cool hand, too, and gritty, he thought, recalling the way she had fought against Frayne and the way she'd faced up to him afterwards. Too bad this deal had got so loused up. Mebbe, if things had been different...

He said one time: "You better git some sleep," but every time he come to himself, there she was, still with him. Still wringing out cloths or putting their dampness against his hot face. She had the lamp turned way down and the shutters barred over the window and his rifle propped ready not two foot from her hand.

Practical. By God, you had to give her that much. Practical and pretty as a basket of chips.

He said, "Why don't you go an' git yourself some rest?"

"I'm doing all right. Besides, it's almost daylight. Do you want me to fix you something to eat?"

"I don't seem t' feel like eatin'."

"I'll get you a drink," she said; and he heard her working the skreaky pump in the kitchen. And then she was back with a dipperful, holding his head up, and its smooth, soothing freshness was cooling to his throat.

"Bleedin' stopped?" he asked as he sank back again.

She gave him a nod. "You don't get much with that kind of wound; it had stopped when you got here." She took another rag from the pan she had handy. "How'd you happen to get it?"

"Carelessness. Some guy took a shot at me out in the brush."

Pain laid hold of him and tightened the line of his jaw for a moment. She leaned impulsively forward. "I know it's bad, Kurt. I wish I might bear some part of it for you. If you can think of anything I *could* do..."

He shook his head and grimaced. And afterwards, he looked at her with a long, searching stare. There was a depth to this girl, a steadiness and fortitude he had not previously noticed. Looking at her this way made a man feel—But there was no good in building pictures. Perhaps, if he had managed to come across her sooner—

He said abruptly: "You'll find my horse around here someplace. Big yellow stallion with a red mane an' tail— name's Snuffy. Wisht you'd take an' pull the gear off him an' put him in the corral so's he'll have a chance t' roll. You might throw him an armful of hay while you're at it, an' get him a can of oats from the bin in the barn. Uh..." He said, carefully picking his words, "You might do a sight better t' git on him an' get outa here. There's more to this thing than you know about an' it ain't goin' t' git no better."

The shadows of the room etched and clarified her features, and her eyes explored his face with a quiet yet quick attention. She laid another cool rag against his forehead and sat back again, gently shaking her head. "I'll stick to my part of the bargain, Kurt—"

"I made no bargain!" he reminded her sharply.

"I know." Her eyes looked black in this light. He had not noticed before how they slanted at the corners or how her lips revealed each shift of her thoughts. He watched them now, how they parted and met again, full and red against the ivory smoothness of her face. And he saw the black shine of her hair while she held herself still, almost as though she were inviting this inspection.

And something robust and intense and unsettling ran between them; and he looked at her with a sultry thoroughness, seeing how completely she was the end of every trail.

He swung his feet to the edge of the bed and sat up, still eyeing her, as unconscious of pain as he was of the damp cloth sliding off his forehead. He seemed completely engrossed and they came to their feet as of one accord. Color showed and fell out of her cheeks and her arms came up and crossed her breasts; and then she let her hands fall to her sides and he pulled her against him roughly and kissed her.

They came apart breathless and trembling and she

watched him with eyes that were wide and searching. She looked queer standing there like that and just staring. He felt queer himself; nothing like such a feeling had ever got into him.

He reached for her again, but she stepped back away from him.

"No, Kurt... not yet." There was something high and proud and shining in her eyes; and he said, "Docie!" and started toward her again.

But she cried: "Wait—" and stopped, as though she would offer some further explanation. He saw it fade out of her and saw the quick rise and fall of her breathing and was profoundly disturbed.

He took a deep breath; and she said, "After we're married—"

His harsh laugh stopped her. "What give you that idea?"

"But you said..."

"I said what you could expect if you stayed here—I didn't say nothin' about gettin' hitched up. A variety show hoofer ain't my idea of wife material."

TWENTY

"AND TAKE THAT CARRION WITH YOU!"

HE DREAMED he was lost in the desert. That he'd been wandering for hours in that trackless waste trying to reach a shimmering lake of water; but every time he got to where he thought the lake was, there was no water there, just the blistering sands. Again and again, he clawed to his feet and went staggering on; and always, ahead of him like a will-o'-the-wisp, was the beckoning gleam of that tranquil lake with the white gulls wheeling and flashing above it. So real it looked—so cool and blue! And then he saw the tall shape of a comely woman. Young and handsome, she was and coming toward him with the black hair flying round her face like a veil. And then her red lips parted, and he recognized Docie. "Come," she said, "and I will show you the way." And then someone was shaking him violently, and he came out of the dream with a cold sweat on him to find Docie bending over him.

"There are riders coming into the yard," she said quickly, and he was awake on the instant.

He saw the sun's yellow pattern of brightness on the

floor and knew he had slept a lot longer than he'd aimed to. He swung his feet off the bed, and she handed him the dipper. He threw her a slantways look as he emptied it.

There was no sign of tears, and she met his glance coolly.

He set the dipper on the bed. "Get me a shirt—in that chest over there. I don't want them bastards t' know I been wounded."

From the drawers, she said, "There's nothing here but this pink thing—"

"What's the matter with that?" He growled: "Fetch it here."

She handed it to him and then brought his gun belt and watched while he strapped it about his lean hips; watched him dig out his pistol from under the pillow. "You ought to stay in that bed."

He flipped open the cylinder, making sure it was loaded, and swapped one cartridge for another from his belt. Then he tucked in his shirt and slipped the gun's barrel between the shirt and his pants; it was only then that she noticed his belt had no holster.

He tossed her another of those close, searching glances. "So, you made up your mind to be the dog at my table."

She bit her lip, but she was not the kind to cry or dodge round a thing. She met his eyes straightly. Flat and level, she said: "I haven't decided what I will do." Her voice faded down to a throaty whisper. "I hadn't expected to fall in love..."

He looked at her sharply and stopped in his tracks. For the space of three heartbeats, he stood entirely still, considering her with his completest attention.

The sound of talk drifted in from the yard; horse sound, too, and the tiny melody of a tinkling spur chain; but Cardigan's eyes never left the girl's face.

There was incredulity in the way he regarded her, and outrage, despair, and, beyond these things, a startled and brightening gleam of real pleasure which he could not quite hide.

He reached out and took hold of her shoulders, and the hope was still there and the doubt and uncertainty. "You mean...with *me?*"

She said with her lips pulled back from her teeth: "Do you imagine yourself the only man in this country?"

One moment longer he stared at her, then he clamped his jaws shut and wheeled out of the room.

* * *

JUPE KRAILOR WAS STRIPPING the gear from the horses when Cardigan opened the door and stepped out. Hennessy's look was plainly uneasy, but a wry grin twisted Lahr's florid face and he put up a hand and said, "Glad you're back."

"Didn't you reckon I'd be?"

Lahr ignored the black truculence in Cardigan's voice and said, "Sure—but ten days is ten days an' we was beginnin' t' git worried. Thought mebbe you'd run into trouble or some-thin'-"

"Wouldn't of figured you had much time to be worried with all of the runnin' around you been doin'. What have you done with that stock you been grabbin'?"

Lahr's green eyes shifted warily. "What stock is that?"

"All them horses you run off from Chandler, Amado, Cor-taro an' Florence."

"Why," said Lahr easily, "we've scattered 'em round the place like we always do—"

"Who you been workin' for, yourself or Esparza?"

Lahr must have felt the startled looks of the other two for he stood with a visible strain on his features. Then he laughed, over loud, and said, "Hell, fer a minute I thought you was serious.

"You thought right," Cardigan said: "an' you ain't answered the question."

"What the hell you gettin' at? All we been doin' is follerin' your orders—"

"That's a goddam lie an' you know it!"

Lahr's green eyes narrowed "Be a little careful with that kinda talk. Them's fightin' words—"

"I'll repeat 'em if you want. I've never run off a branded horse in my life, or ordered one run off, or stole off my neighbors—an' you damn well know it."

Lahr's brick-red skin was tight as a drumhead across the jut of his cheekbones. He said to the others with a lean, hateful smile, "You see how it is? He's got a woman here now an' he wants t' git shut of us. Any excuse'll do when a man gits a hankerin'—"

"You doublecrossin' dog!"

Lahr put on the look of a martyr. "So, I'm a double-crosser now. You lay out the orders an' I shove 'em through, an' then you get a woman an' a new set of notions an' that makes me a doublecrossin' dog. I guess you'll try t' say next you never even told me to stick up them banks—"

"I'll tell you somethin' right now!" Cardigan snarled, striding toward him. "Gather up your stole horses an' git offa this ranch—the whole pack an' passel of you!"

But Lahr stood his ground. Malevolence flashed in the look he gave Kurt. "You heard the boss, boys. He don't need us no more so he's throwin' us out. Us that's built up this place for him, livin' in the leather for weeks at a time, takin' his orders an' riskin' our necks like a bunch of pelados so he can play the fine gentleman an' be known all over as the biggest horse breeder in five hundred miles. Don't stand there like fools—take off your hats to him! Ain't he known all up an' down the Spanish Trail for the quality of the stock we've run his brand on?

"We better pack up our duds an' git goin', I reckon, 'fore he gets around t' siccin' that marshal on us. We ain't good enough for him now he's turnin' respectable on the money you an' me put into his pockets."

Lame Hennessy scowled. Krailor licked at his lips and dropped a hand toward his belt gun.

Cardigan never took his eyes off Lahr. His face was black as the wrath of God. And each grim stride fetched him nearer the range boss.

A slow wind lifted the flaps of Lahr's vest. Some dark remembrance thinned his lips, and his upper body tipped a little forward, settling his weight on the balls of his feet. But the look of his eyes did not back up that pose and Hennessy stepped back away from him quickly; and Lahr cried out: "Stop right there—stop it, Kurt!"

But Cardigan kept coming, slow stride by stride,

inexorably nearer, the steady crunch of his boots the only sound in that stillness.

Lahr's eyes sprang wide and grew bright with panic. He went back half a step, but it wasn't far enough. He threw up both arms, but they weren't enough, either. Cardigan's rock-hard right ripped through that defense and smashed him full in the mouth.

Lahr's head rocked back. His eyes rolled wildly. He bared his teeth and spat out two broken ones and Cardigan's left fist flattened his nose.

The range boss loosed a great yell and, beyond thinking now, made a frantic and desperate grab for his gun.

Like a pile-driver, Cardigan's right struck Lahr's belly.

At that time, exactly, Docie came to the door. She heard the agonized outrush of Lahr's expelled breath, saw him fold and go crazy-like round in a circle with his chin on his knees and an animal whimper dribbling out of his throat. Then his knees let go and he pitched face down in the hoof-tracked dust and lay there writhing like a snake with its back broke.

She heard Cardigan then, the wheezy rasp of his breathing, and caught the white look of his twisted cheeks. He stood wholly alone out there in the open with his big hands still fisted and the look of his eyes holding Krailor and the cook grayly frozen in their tracks. She was reminded of a huge and battered grizzly at bay; there was no give-up in him, no consciousness of odds.

She found it hard to untangle the effect it had on her, seeing him standing out there like that. The pain of his wound must be setting him crazy; yet nothing but a dark and blazing fury looked out of him as he stood there waiting for whatever the others would do.

Both men were watching him closely and both kept their hands well away from their pistols. There was a strange, puzzled look in Jupe Krailor's stare as though he could not believe what he had just seen happen. Hennessy's look was an expression of pure fright.

Cardigan's lips flattened out and thinly showed the white of his teeth, and the wind that ran whispering through the overhead branches ruffled the yellow hair at his temples and molded the sleeves against the muscles of his arms.

Hennessy's cheeks had turned gray as wood ash and, under that prolonged scrutiny, even Jupe Krailor began to show his disquiet.

Lahr groaned and stirred. With both hands in the dust he came onto a knee. He groaned again and looked stupidly around him. And then he got to his feet and his eyes found Cardigan and turned brightly wicked.

"Got enough?" Cardigan said.

The range boss weaved away a few steps and drew a hand across his mouth and wiped the hand on his trousers.

"Get his horse for him, Krailor."

Lahr looked up with a scowl. "You're feelin' mighty proud, but don't overdo it."

Cardigan said to Krailor: "Put the saddles on all three of them"; and Hennessy took the first full breath since he had come here.

Behind the blood and dust ground into them, Lahr's roan cheeks turned suddenly bitter. "What about that money we banked with you—the money for that stuff we got up north?"

"It's goin' back to the men who lost those horses."

"Do you think I'll let you get away with that?"

Cardigan's mouth showed a meager smile; it was all the answer he bothered to give and there was no smile in his eyes at all. Krailor came up with their mounts and Lahr reached for his reins in a shaking fury.

"You ain't done with this—"

"Go on—go on," Cardigan said. "Get out of here."

It was then, while Kurt had his back to her, watching them, that Docie heard the rasp of some sound and stared, cold with horror, as Shiloh Frayne came around the corner of the house behind Cardigan, immediately throwing the rifle to his shoulder.

But the sound of that movement, or the bright wink of metal, warned Cardigan. He dropped flat and whirled as the crash of Frayne's shot clouted the fronts of the buildings. He rose up on one knee and flame licked from his pistol. The rifle fell out of Frayne's loosening grasp and he spun half around and collapsed, choking, sideways.

Lahr snatched a dropped hand clear away from his gun butt and threw both hands high over his head as Cardigan's glance swept around with his pistol. And then Kurt got up.

"Now get out," he said bitterly, "and take that carrion with you!"

TWENTY-ONE
THE FINGER WRITES

THERE IS ALWAYS a certain excitement attendant to any kind of chase or hunt. When the hunt happens to have a man as the recipient of its interest the concomitant furor customarily mounts in direct proportion to that man's importance, position, or the number of dollars which have been offered for his capture. When Sam Sollantsy let it be known that Frank Esparza was gathering a posse to go after Kurt Cardigan the excitement became terrific.

The news spread like wildfire. All over town men suspended their regular employment to speak of it; the cobbler quit his last to run out into the street, knife in hand, and shout the tidings to the Mexican barber; the barber left a customer half shaved and dashed off with his razor to impart the news to the Italian butcher; the butcher dropped his cleaver, wiped his hands on his apron and went to the nearest saloon with the tale; half the men at the bar rushed off with the story and one of them took it to Big Tooth Emma who told her girls who told their customers who promptly purveyed it all over town. And, after the manner of stories, the news lost little through these many retellings.

Inside a half hour, there were half a hundred versions being circulated with gusto. Cardigan was exposed as the chief of the horse-stealing gang which had been harrying ranchers all over the Southwest. He was king of the gang which had been robbing the stages. He had 'blown' the Douglas Bank several nights ago and, with ten masked Yaquis from below the border, had stuck up the Copper State in broad daylight, killing the Bisbee marshal and the agent at Butterfield's Bisbee station. He had raped a nester girl north of town. With a gang of forty tough night-riding rustlers, he was trying to take over the entire Territory and turn it into an outlaw's paradise with himself as overlord...

Whatever you wanted to hear, you could hear it. He was an escaped lifer from Yuma. He was Curly Bill. He was one of the James boys. He was one of the gang who'd been riding with Bonney who was being driven out of New Mexico and aimed to set up headquarters at Tucson. He was the right-hand man of Billy the Kid. He was a cousin of Chisum, the cattle king...

Everyone was going to join the posse. Everyone wanted a crack at this killer who was turning the Territory into a shambles. Killed four men at Amado—a dozen more around Florence. He had sixteen notches on his gun right now and swore he wouldn't quit till he had a round two dozen...

Talk was cheap and as usual, noisy; but it took a bit of intestinal fortitude or a good private reason to have your name bruited round as being connected with a posse sworn to bring in a man as expert with a gun as Kurt Cardigan. Hard as Sollantsy worked—and he was indefatigable—it was nightfall before Esparza's posse was ready to take to the field.

It numbered nine men, including Esparza and Sollantsy, when it left the marshal's office at 9:00 p.m. Sollantsy had rounded up about as many more, but Esparza had refused to swear them in on the contention that justice would be poorly served by men of debatable character. The rejects were drifters and barroom bums. Sollantsy was not too disgruntled; be bad spent the intervening time since his arrival in pinning down an abundance of local gossip and felt reasonably confident that most of the men sworn in would do their best to fix Cardigan's clock.

There was himself and Esparza. There was the Flowerpot owner and his foreman, Zeke Smith, who had no more reason to be tender about Cardigan than had Joe Nettleton of the Straddle-Bug, an outfit which had also lost heavily to horse thieves. There was Esparza's deputy, Hankins, who had fetched Cardigan's hat back from Bisbee. There was Ed Reagan, the livery stable proprietor, who may or may not have purchased stolen stock from Cardigan. There was Tom Steins, the local gunsmith, and finally, loudly sponsored by Sollantsy, there was the piano-playing gambler, Top Hat Charlie.

Five miles out of town these watchdogs of the law were joined by the nester, Rickven, who vociferously held Kurt Cardigan responsible for the present unwonted condition of his daughter and who declared, with some justice, that no one in the posse knew Cardigan's layout and the adjacent country as thoroughly as he did. After considerable argument, Sollantsy prevailed upon Esparza to include him.

Before they'd left town Esparza had routed out two other men for posse work, a man named Hazelton and Farquas Torney. Hazelton was an up-country rancher for whom Kurt had worked when he'd first come into the country. Torney was a blacksmith from up around Oracle whose young son Cardigan once had rescued from a runaway horse. Both were favorably disposed toward Cardigan and Sollantsy had howled about "prejudice" until Esparza had crossed them off the list. The way the deal stacked up now, the Tri-States man felt pretty well convinced that justice would be done without a lot of red tape.

* * *

AFTER THE DEPARTING KC crew had reached a point some half mile or so from Cardigan's headquarters, Lahr flung a hand up and called for a halt. "Go up ahead a piece, Jupe," he told Krailor, "an keep your eyes peeled while Hennessy an' me git rid of Frayne's body."

When Krailor was out of earshot, Hennessy said, "What's—"

But Lahr cut him off. "This'll work out better than the way we had it figured. That bastard dealt us the ace of spades when he put that slug through Frayne an' made us pack ol' Shiloh out of there. I been doin' a little thinkin' an' we really got him now."

There was a smug satisfaction about his look as he hooked a knee round the horn of his saddle and, digging out the makings, started rolling up a smoke. "Here's the way it stacks up. Two months ago, Kurt sold me the place, but there was a clause in the deal that I wasn't to get possession till he'd got all his stock moved off the KC range. In the meantime, you come to me with a hint that you figured Kurt was crooked—that you'd noticed a couple horses with some damn peculiar brands. You got that?"

Hennessy nodded.

"All right, then. We decided to look around an' see what Cardigan was up to. He had always seemed like a pretty good guy an' had always seemed to be squarely on the level; but them two horses had got us t' thinkin'. We begun to watch Cardigan; we found he was doin' a heap of night ridin'. Every few nights he'd slip off from the ranch; sometimes we'd find out in time t' take after him but, until last night, he'd always give us the slip. Last night we was ready for him. We had let Frayne in on it an' he was with us. We trailed Kurt up t' that draw near Black Mountain. There was a shack up there an' a bunch of horses tied round to the back. We left ours in the brush an' injuned up there an' me—I got a look in at the winder. There was Cardigan an' three-four other guys splittin' up the cash from them bank jobs.

"You come up then an' had a look, too. You heard Cardigan say t' some beetle-browed gent with chin whiskers that the game around here was about played out an' that it might be smart to clear out of these parts. The beetle-browed guy says it would of been all right if Cardigan hadn't gunned the Bis-bee marshal. Then a consumptive-lookin' jasper with a limp wants t' know what they're figurin' t' do about the horses, an' Cardigan says they can be sold just as good over around Ajo an' that might be a pretty good place t' work out of. Beetle-brow wants t' know when Kurt figures t' leave here, an' Kurt says they'll pull out the day after t'morrow.

"We don't wait for no more but light a shuck out of

there. We spend the rest of the night ridin' the KC range an' what we find is a bunch of stock wearin' fresh-altered brands in a little hole up near the Ironwood Seep. Looks to us like this is some of that stuff that was run off from Florence an' Amado.

"We're struck pretty hard, findin' out what a skunk Kurt has turned out t' be. We'd always figured he was straight— never had no cause t' think otherwise; an' prob'ly, if you hadn't spotted them two horses the other day, he'd of got clean away with it an' skipped the country. But now we understand a whole pile of queer things which we hadn't never give much thought to before—like Kurt bein' off on so many trips an' all, which we'd figured he was just off buyin' an' sellin' horses."

Hennessy said: "What about the girl?"

Lahr scowled a moment, then he shook his head. "She don't make no difference. It was close to eleven when Cardigan got home—she can't prove where he was before he got here."

"She kin prove where Frayne was."

"All right. We leave Frayne out of it. You an' me follered Cardigan. You an' me rode the range an' found the stole horses. This mornin' we told Frayne. This afternoon the three of us rode in an' Frayne pops it at him. Frayne says: 'What do you know about that bunch of stole horses we found—' That's as far as he gits when Kurt grabs his gun an' goes t' smokin'. We was still on our horses. Frayne manages t' stick in his saddle till we git outa range. Meantime his horse goes lame. We turn the horse loose, knowin' we got t' git Frayne to town quick or he'll cash in. I take him up on my horse, but he passes out anyway before we can get there—an' here, by

Gawd, is his body t' prove it!" Lahr grinned at the cook. "An' what's wrong with that?"

"Esparza will wanta know where you got the money t' buy Cardigan's ranch—"

"Hell, my uncle in Kokomo left it to me in his will."

"Well, but..." Hennessy hesitated. "What about the girl?"

"It's just her word ag'in ours. They got nothin' against us. We got a cast iron alibi for the time of them bank robbin's." Hennessy ran nervous fingers around the inside of his collar. "I got a feelin'—"

"Hell, you always got a feelin'." Lahr pitched his smoke away and shoved his boot back into the stirrup. "Look, there ain't no sense us leavin' empty-handed. Once we've told Frank Esparza our story, he will surer'n hell bring a posse out here an' they'll clean this range of everything we got on it. We might's well gather up a little of the cream—wouldn't take us more'n a little while t' shove twenty or thirty head of the best down into them river bottoms south of the mission. Frayne'll keep limber f'r another five-six hours. We could leave 'im right here an'—"

"What about Jupe? Where you fittin' him in?"

"Yeah," Lahr said, "Jupe Krailor. That's right. He ain't the kind a man could put much trust in. Kinda weak in the head. No tellin' what he'd do—liable t' open his mouth an' put his foot right in it... I guess," he said at last, "we better salt Jupe down. We'll let him help us with them horses..."

* * *

NIGHT HAD long since rolled the range up in its blanket. Docie, after the departure of the sacked KC crew, had seen Kurt back into bed, had caught a few hours' sleep, and then had got up and fixed herself a little supper from the ample supplies she had found in the cook shack. She had changed her dress.

She had looked in on Kurt and given him some more water. She didn't know when he'd last eaten but she didn't dare give him any solids with that fever. His bout with Curly Lahr had fetched it way up again and she could hear him in there now, twisting and groaning in his sleep; but there was nothing she could do for him she hadn't already done. There was no good fooling with that hole in his chest. It was up to God what happened to him now.

He was tough as an ox. She had never seen a man with as much vitality. Yet if that wound became infected...

She pulled her thoughts away from that.

She tried to consider what she herself had ought to do, but she gave that up, too. Somehow it didn't seem to matter. In the vast reach of this country, this monstrous hush and desolation, the acts of any one man or woman appeared trivial and commonplace, almost without significance. She was astonished she could think of herself in that fashion.

She watched the moon come up, round and red, behind the rugged outline of blue-black mountains and felt the welcome coolness of a breeze rising off the desert. She couldn't see it but knew it was down there below her, mile on tawny mile of it, brooding, waiting, patient as the eternal slopes that ringed it.

She had no conception of passing time. Of what

account was time in a land so vast? The mystic radiance of the risen moon was now all about her, silvering the yonder ridgetops and spreading before her incredulous gaze a whole new world of ethereal beauty. A great peace stole over her, and she listened to the run of the wind in the branch tops. She let the rifle rest in her lap and settled back comfortably against the doorframe. The last thing she heard was the stomp of a hoof in Snuffy's corral.

She must have slept.

The next thing she knew she was sitting bolt upright, the rifle clutched in her hands, listening into the wind-driven night. She could not guess what had wakened her. The yard was filled with the movement of shadows, and she heard the wind tearing through the cottonwoods; and fear pressed cold fingers against her heart.

She got up thinking Kurt, while she slept, might have called her. Her frightened glance raced round the yard. Nothing moved there. The shapes were just shadows. Faintly, far off, through the rush of the wind, she could hear the ululating cry of a coyote, and then a spatter of sounds that might have been shots—that *were* shots; suddenly she knew it.

In the corral, Snuffy nickered and flung up his head.

There was a rumble of hoofs in the teeth of the wind, now loud, now soft, but at each loudening nearer. The wind flapped her skirt and fear closed round her heart with the stark omniscient grip of foreboding. She whirled and ran through the house to rouse Kurt.

But he was already up and pulling on his spurred

boots. He stamped his heels into them and reached for his gun.

"What is it?" she cried.

He shook his head grimly. "You should of gone while you could—you're trapped into this now." He scowled as he buckled his shell belt around him. He sloshed on his hat and caught up the rifle. "Git into a pair of my pants an' come into the yard just as quick as you're ready."

He swung on his heel and went hurrying doorward.

She had boots in her bag; they'd been a part of her act-boots and a hat and a red bandanna. While she kicked off her pumps and got into the boots, wind fetched her the pound of those oncoming ponies and she ran to the door, stood there breathless and staring.

Cloud half covered the face of the moon. In the corral, Snuffy blew out a gusty breath and his shrill, whistling challenge rang over the yard.

Out yonder was tumult, a gray blur of movement. Horses tore through the brush by the gate and came thundering past with dilated nostrils, and a second wave of shapes knifed through the dark trees, and the clatter of slithering hoofs was all around her.

Three hatted heads showed against the white clouds and the moon came out and she saw these men's faces—the faces of the crew Kurt Cardigan had fired!

TWENTY-TWO
A NIGHT IN THE HILLS

CURLY LAHR STOPPED his horse within ten feet of her, a high black shape against the sky, as Cardigan came up with the yellow stud.

"Didn't I tell you, Lahr, to git off this ranch?"

"Well, Jesis Christ, we been *tryin'* t' git off it! We started roundin' up them horses like you told us t' do—had 'em all bunched an' strung out for the border. Comin' onto the Tanque Verde flats we run smack into a goddam posse an' that loco fool, Krailor, opened up with a rifle! Knocked Zeke Smith off his horse first crack—"

"What'd you *want* me t' do—git hung fer a hoss thief?"

"This ain't no time fer jawin'," Hennessy growled. "That bunch'll be onto us if we don't git outa here."

"How many was they?"

"Hell's fire," Krailor snarled, "must be fifteen-twenty of 'em. They was spread all over the goddam flats."

Cardigan said: "We'll head for Mammoth. They

can't track us in the dark an'—" He swung a look toward the house and saw Docie. "What the hell are you waitin' for? Thought I told you-"

Docie's chin came up. "I'm not one of your dogs."

Even in the moonlight, he could see her eyes flash, could catch the hostile tone of her. Then contempt edged her voice and something else came into it. "You're a fool if you go with them. You fired these men and their troubles with the law are no concern of yours."

Lahr laughed harshly.

Docie kept her eyes on Cardigan, "Listen to me, Kurt. Don't throw your life away. I heard you fire these men this afternoon for stealing horses. "I'll tell the sheriff—"

"You wouldn't get the chance," Kurt said. "Any talkin' they do'll be done with rifles. Some them moguls round Tucson have been layin' for me. I'd be shot dead-er'n hell 'fore you could open your mouth. Now get into them pants."

Docie stood her ground. "If you go with these men, you can't ever come back here; when you run from the law you have to keep on running—"

"For Chri'sake," Hennessy snarled. "How long you goin' t' jaw with that woman?"

And Krailor said: "Listen!"

Down the wind came the thunder of hard-running horses, still faint and far, but getting louder every moment.

"Get into them pants!" Cardigan told her.

"I'll go with you on just one condition—"

"You'll go with me an' like it, just the way you are.

You had your chance t' pull outa this—a sight better chance'n I ever had."

Hennessy cursed. "You goin't' gab all night?"

The sound of the posse was drawn immeasurably nearer. Even Krailor showed tension in the spasmodic way he kept roweling his pony.

"Jupe," Cardigan growled, "find Miz Balinett a horse."

"I won't go," Docie said; but Cardigan was onto her before she could slam the door. She struck at him with her fists, and he slapped her across the face with an oath. He caught her behind the knees with one arm and scooped her, kicking, up onto his shoulder.

"You can take Jupe up behind you," he told Hennessy, and dumped her, still kicking, into Krailor's saddle. In the moonlight, her pantalets looked like white trousers and he grinned at her futile attempts to hold her dress down. "I told you t' wear pants."

Krailor came up. "I can't find her no—Hell's bells! She can't hev *my* hoss!"

"Climb up behind Hennessy," Kurt said unfeelingly, and to Docie: "You gonna behave or do I got t' tie you on there?"

He didn't wait for an answer. He took Krailor's rifle; shoved it into the man's hands. "Git up behind Hennessy." He took Doeie's reins and strode over to the dun and swung into the saddle.

Sound of the posse's oncoming horses seemed ominously close but if Cardigan noticed it seemed not to bother him. "Swing left of the house an' go through the back pasture. House'll keep 'em from seein' us till we've got out of rifle range. They'll waste a little time tryin' to pick up our trail-Here," he said abruptly, tossing Lahr Doeie's reins. "You fellers go ahead—"

"Where the hell d'you think *you're* goin?" Lahr demanded.

"Go on," Cardigan said, "I'll catch up with you." Swinging down off his horse, he ran into the house.

Lahr swore, glaring after him, but kicked his horse into motion. The KC crew passed out of the yard.

* * *

THEY PULLED up in a grove of scrub oak just beyond the north pasture and waited. Hennessy was all for pushing on, but Lahr said: "We'll wait. If that bastard's fixin't' sell us out, we better know it now."

Doeie's look held contempt. "If he'd wanted to do that—"

"I don't want no lip outa *you!*" Lahr snarled; and Krailor said, "More likely he went back t' dig up that cash he done us out of."

Lahr sat silent, plainly turning it over. Then he shook his head. "Good part of it's in silver; he'd need a couple extra broncs if he was figurin' t' fetch that with him."

"Here he comes," Hennessy growled. And, when Kurt came up, "How come we don't hear them horses no more?"

"I put a lamp in the window," Kurt said with a grin. "It'll give us another mile's start, anyway, while that bunch is injunin' up on the place. They can't be sure you boys stopped an' they won't want t' miss me."

They rode steadily for a quarter of an hour, holding their horses to a ground-eating walk. The way angled upward in easy stages and Krailor laughed when they heard shots behind them. Grass carpeted these slopes and some of the earlier roughness fell out of the wind.

The country grew wilder, the upgrades steeper and the grass petered out and left shale underfoot. The horses' hoofs slithered and clacked in it and Docie had to lean forward to stay in her saddle.

There was a ridge shoving up in front of them, a bare expanse of rock-studded slope which the moon made almost as bright as clay. Lahr swung his horse toward it. Now and then from the sides of her eyes, Docie had quick glimpses of trails running crosswise, and of great boulders which had fallen from the mountains, and which now strewed the slopes like miniature houses.

It was a desolate region they were into now where nothing but cacti and rock abounded, some of the cactus towering forty feet high. They crossed the ridge and found another and higher one bulking before them with a thicket of squatting cedar at its base.

Cardigan's voice came up to her. "You smell anythin', Lahr?"

Lahr sniffed and looked back and shook his head.

"Well, keep your eyes skinned," Kurt said grimly. "The Phoenix road crosses this trail just beyond that next ridge."

They went on again, slowly, Lahr picking his way with more and more care. It was colder up here with a kind of dry stillness that made every sound seem uncommonly sharp.

Branches slapped at her face as they passed through the cedars, and then they were quartering up the steep slope, the horses slipping and sliding through the clattering talus. They struck the rim and climbed over and saw a whole world of timbered uplands before them, the black shapes of the nearest trees but a scant quarter mile ahead.

Cardigan passed her, spurring up beside Lahr, and they went on that way for a hundred yards and came out on a wagon-tracked road and stopped.

Cardigan held up a hand for silence. To their right the road, climbing up from Tucson, came out on the ridge in a tangle of juniper. To the left, it followed the line of timber and was lost in the moonlit distance.

Twisting in the saddle, Cardigan sent a long look toward the right. Though she herself heard and saw nothing, it was plain to Docie that Kurt was disturbed. She saw him jerk a look at Lahr and saw Lahr's head dip. "Dust," Lahr murmured, and then she smelled it herself. It was very faint.

Cardigan threw another look at that tangle of juniper, then his glance went slowly over the road and picked at the black stand of trees beyond it. "More than one," he said softly. "Been through here in the last five minutes and, since they didn't use the road, they must have cut through the timber."

He said more and more thoughtfully, "If they're headin' the other way, they came from town an' may be huntin' us. What's your idea, Curly? You reckon Frank's split up his posse figurin' we might do just what we have done?"

Hennessy said in a lather of impatience: "Fiddlin' round here ain't goin' t' solve nothin'. While we're settin' here jawin' them fellers at the ranch will be on their way up here—"

"So, they'll be on their way up here," Cardigan said,

"an' if this other bunch is part of 'em and we're trapped in between 'em it ain't goin' to be any picnic."

Lahr said, "I'm for turnin' left an' takin' the Phoenix road fer a spell. We'll make better time—"

"An' we'll be easier seen," Cardigan pointed out. "Besides, if it's part of Frank's posse, they'll expect us to do that. I got a hunch we better—"

He went suddenly still. Below them, in a south southeasterly direction, there came the sharp flat crack of a rifle.

Cardigan and Lahr exchanged glances. Before either man could speak there came a long high yell from above and to the left of them, and at once the night was filled with the crash of breaking brush as hard-ridden horses came plunging toward them through the timber.

"They've cut us off," Cardigan said. He grabbed Docie's reins and thrust them into her hands, and immediately swung the dun stallion, sending him into the road toward town and lifting him into a headlong gallop.

Flame in two places knifed out of the junipers and Lahr swept the thicket with a blast from his rifle; and then they were past, tearing down the white road. But, almost at once, Cardigan left it again, driving the big dun into the timber and up a narrow lane through the trees. Then he held up his hand and they stopped, grimly waiting, and saw two horsemen rush past on the road.

Hennessy started to lift up his reins, but Cardigan reached out and stopped him. "Wait." They heard the men then who had been in the junipers; they were angling uphill through the trees, coming toward them; and then the sounds stopped, and a six-shooter spoke three times very rapidly. Down on the road, another gun answered, and not fifty yards from Cardigan's crew Reagan's voice shouted: "They're up here someplace—in the timber!"

Lahr cursed under his breath and, from the road, the voice of Esparza's deputy, Hankins, sent a clear *"How you know?"* from the entrance to the lane.

"We heard 'em," the liveryman answered. "We've got them horse-stealin' bastards now. Spread out down there an' work this way."

Cardigan said in the quietest of voices: "Four men, or could be five. Two in the timber, mebbe three on the road. What's it look like to you, Lahr?"

"Duck soup." Lahr grinned. "All we got t' do is foller those orders; them birds in the timber won't know us from their own crowd. We drift up t' them two an' shut their mouths. When them fellers from the road shove up, we drop 'em. Slick, quick an' easy."

Docie shuddered. She didn't see how Kurt could work with such a man, or how Lahr would much want to work with Kurt either after the trouble they'd had at the ranch this afternoon. Kurt was a fool to throw in with them again...

Toward the road, but much nearer, she heard the hoofs of a horse crush fallen limbs, and she saw the dark blob of Kurt's head abruptly nod. "All right," he said quietly. "You take the far right of the line, Lahr. Hennessy an' Krailor will advance in the center an' me an' the girl will come up on the west—"

"Just a minute," Lahr growled, swinging round in the saddle. "You wouldn't be fixin' t' run out on us, would you?"

"How far do you think I would get runnin' out?"

"Not very damn far!"

"Let's go," Cardigan murmured, and swung off to the left, Docie following. She heard the others drift off and then their more cautious sounds were lost in the noise of the men from the road.

She kept watching for Cardigan to turn the dun's head up into the timber toward Reagan's position, but he kept heading west, and then she saw the moonlit road through the trees and knew that Lahr's suspicion had been right. Kurt had had no intention of joining in that slaughter, and suddenly she felt better than she had in a long while.

Cardigan stopped the dun just short of the road and waited for her to come up with him. She put a hand on his arm. "Thank you, Kurt."

He looked at her a moment. Snuffy let out a sigh and watched the road with his ears cocked. She couldn't make out Kurt's expression with his head turned that way, but she squeezed his arm.

He said, "We ought to—"

The crack of a rifle sheared off his words. It came from the direction of Reagan's position, and three further shots laid their explosions through the timber. One high, wild cry went into the night; and then a tremendous racket of gunfire broke loose, and Docie heard the crash of running horses up there. Someone yelled, "Cardigan! Cardigan!" and Lahr's voice slammed through the uproar with a wilder and wilder fury.

"Come on!" Cardigan said, and spurred his dun stallion into the road, turning him up the road toward Phoenix, but soon letting him drop into a walk on the grade. They passed the juniper tangle and were cresting the rise when Cardigan reached out and grabbed her bay's bridle, pulling both horses up sharply. "Listen!"

But there was no need to listen. They could both hear it plainly, even above the fight in the timber. There was a pounding rush of hoofs on that road; like a roar of surf, that sound ran toward them.

"Quick!" Cardigan cried, and swung the yellow horse crossways of the road, pulling her bay around with it. "We'll have to drop back down." He put his quirt in her hands. "Lay it on!" he said, and then they were pelting across the bare ridgetop, pushing their horses to the limit to get below the rim before those others should catch sight of them. But they were seen anyway. Docie heard three guns cry out in unison, one of those bullets whistling past her cheek.

They were below the rim then, their horses slipping and sliding dangerously as they went plunging down the rocky face of the slope. She could hear shod hoofs pound the hard ground above them and then they were plunging through the dark line of cedars, crashing through the low brush, and racing across another bare ridge.

"Swing left!" Cardigan yelled, and she swung with him into a narrow defile which the trees had concealed until this moment. The floor of this gulch was littered with rock and pitched steeply downward in an easterly direction between tree-masked walls. After five hundred feet it bent south again and then once again east and came out in a tiny deep-grassed basin about a thousand yards across.

Cardigan stopped and she pulled up beside him, hearing the pursuit roar across the bare ridge and dive into the cedar brakes, the sound of its progress afterward dying to a distance-dimmed rumor. She saw where the moon hung low in the south, seeing how the grayness of the eastern sky was commencing to show the ragged tops of mountains. It would soon be dawn, she thought with astonishment.

She looked at Cardigan, wishing it were lighter so she could make out the expression on his beard-stubbled cheeks. He must be terribly weary. She knew his wound must be giving him a lot of pain, too; and she marveled anew at his capacity for punishment.

She said, "That man, Krailor—he was with those men who robbed the Bisbee bank. He took care of their horses. He was the one who shot the man in the stage office."

Cardigan said, "I oughta be kicked, draggin' you into this thing," and sat a while, silent, staring into the south. "Funny," he said, "the way things..." and let the rest go.

He got out of his saddle and loosened the cinches; came around, helped her down, and then loosened hers. "I reckoned on gettin' through, but it looks like now that was damn foolish figun'n.' Like about all the rest of the things I've done." "You mean... like sending for me?" He stood a while thinking or perhaps, just watching her. When he finally spoke, it was to counter with a question. "Would you still of bought that ticket, knowin' what you know now?"

"I don't know," she said honestly. "Probably not." He said, "I remember the first time I saw you. You were right when you told me I couldn't believe my luck." She saw the brief glint of his teeth, then he said: "Time t' go," and went over and retightened his cinches, then came back and retightened hers.

He gave her a hand to the saddle and his hand, going back, brushed across her bare knee. It brought his glance down at once and he stood absolutely still. She guessed he hadn't noticed before what the brush had done to her clothes. His head tipped up and she knew his eyes were searching her face. A kind of sigh welled out of him. He said: "I want you t' know I'm goddam sorry about everythin'."

He stood looking at her a moment longer and then went over to his horse and got into the saddle.

They crossed the basin at a steady walk and Docie was shocked to see how much nearer the day had come. Above the eastern mountains, the sky was brightening rapidly. In almost no time at all the sun would be up, throwing its revealing light over all. She had a strong and unwelcome conviction Esparza's posse would not look such fools once the confusion of darkness had left the land.

Even as the thought took shape in her mind a sound of rifle fire threw up its clatter again from some place far below and a bit to the left of them; and Docie stopped with her eyes flown to Cardigan, hearing the echoes of this madness roll and break and fade through the hills.

Cardigan sat with his shoulders bowed, listening; and she tried to put herself in his place, but she could only think how it would be with her if she found herself being chased by a posse. Of course, she *was* being chased, but it was Kurt they Were after.

"Lahr," he said, and put his horse on the trail again.

"What are you going to do?"

"Keep runnin', I reckon."

"Wouldn't you have a better chance if I ... if I weren't with you?"

"Probably," he said, without looking around.

"At least you don't have to be so blunt about it."

He looked around then and she could see his eyes. They were not the eyes she had remembered. "I don't have much talent for your kind of talk. You asked me a question. I answered it."

"Where are you going?" she asked, after a moment.

"I'm takin' you back to the ranch."

"But...but isn't that dangerous—for you, I mean?"

"Sure." A twisted grin streaked across his cheeks. "I want t' be a martyr an' fix things up so you can go back where you come from an' get this hand dealt over."

He spat at a pine and drew the rifle from its boot and gave her a look that was anything but flattering. "Now suppose you give your jaw a rest an' let me get in a little figurin'."

Trees were all about them and he rode with his eyes raking each patch of shadow. She could see the sun now where it touched the high crags and gilded the ramparts of the black eastern mountains. And, abruptly, he lifted a hand for quiet

The report of fast traveling swelled out of the east to a sustained and rapid onrush of sound, passing loudly across some nearby corridor with a lifted voice saying sharply, "Try that left fork!" and the shod hoofs dropping at once to a whisper as though the mouth of some gulch had gobbled them.

"Esparza," Cardigan said, and leaned forward as though he might see beneath the down-drooping branches. Then he moved the dun on, and she fell in behind again.

Almost immediately they were out of this wood and staring down the length of a shallow ravine that was half blocked with windfalls. Presently Cardigan stopped and sat eyeing the ground, and when she came up, he pointed out the deep tracks. "Four of 'em. Here's where they crossed. Game's tightening up."

These hours in the saddle had left their mark on him. He looked older and leaner, much less sure of himself, and two days' growth of bristle blurred the line of his jaw.

She bit her lip and looked away and then looked back at him again. And color ran through her cheeks, and she said, very low: "You don't have to take me back."

He didn't look round. He stared a while longer at the brush up ahead and then, as though satisfied, turned the dun into the trail out of which that fragment of the posse had just come. A rifle cracked once far above and to the left of them, that sound followed by a distant hallooing. Kurt said, "I'm goin' back anyway."

"But that's crazy!"

"I do a lot of crazy things."

"But *why*? What is there in it for you? I tried to get you to stay there in the first place and you wouldn't. You said—"

"I know what I said. You wanted me to stay there and face that posse an' I told you there was people that would ask nothin' better than for me to be caught with a bunch of cheap crooks."

"But I told you I'd tell—"

"An' I told you that posse would do its talkin' with rifles. You been hearin' 'em, ain't you? I don't know what fellers are with that bunch but there's bound to be some Lahr has turned against me that would like nothin' better than a chance t' cut me down."

"Then why go back now?"

Cardigan grinned without mirth. "A little matter of business. Lahr ain't the only one around can set traps. That slick son will be back an' when he comes I wanta be there."

"I guess I'm not very bright."

"You ain't no dumber than I was. Took me quite a spell to understand that feller. Not sure I do yet, but I *will*. Ha tied up with my bunch about a year ago. We'd been roundin' up unbranded horses up north, fetchin' 'em down here an' sellin' them for good money. You'd be plumb right t' call it crooked, though there wasn't no law against it then. It was just a plain case of take your own chances. If you got by with it, fine. If you, didn't you got handed your comeuppance muy pronto."

The trail crossed a dry wash and came into a region of rocks and scrub oak. Cardigan seemed more to be putting his own mind in order than doing this talking for Docie's benefit.

"Lahr was right slick. I guess right from the first he knew what he wanted. There was a girl there in town had her cap set for him; I never give it much thought, but it all adds up. He was after my spread, which is the biggest one round here in point of importance, rep an' stock quality. He must of seen from the start where his big risk was me; he had to figure some way to get me took care of if he ever was goin' t' git his hooks in KC. He had t' get rid of me—an' he sure done his best to.

"I can call t' mind now a whole passel of things I couldn't quite savvy when they was bein' dealt out t' me — that marshal, fer instance, an' this give-away horse. But I was playin' in luck an' not even the lyin' rumors he spread was enough in themselves t' pull me down.

So, he began buildin' up for a powder smoke show-down: his lies might still help, an' the horse an' the marshal; but to make sure a posse would ride an' do the job for him he needed spilled blood an' a gutted safe.

"Soon's, I took off huntin' you he turned wolf. He robbed two banks an' a stage carryin' money, killin' two guys an' the Bisbee marshal. He raided Amado an' drove stock out of my neighbors' back yards, worked over the brands, and left the stuff runnin' around loose on my range. I don't know how he figured t' get loose when the crash come, but it's a cinch he had some sly way figured. An' he can still get away with the whole stinkin' business if I don't git back there t' stop him."

Docie rode a little way without speaking. Then she said, "But won't the posse...won't Esparza suspect—"

"He prob'ly will. But Frank's a square-shooter; he can't act without proof. An' he won't have no proof Lahr was anyplace round this business tonight. All Lahr needs is an alibi, an' a guy slick as him'll have five or six handy."

"Is that why you're so sure he'll come back to the ranch?"

"No. By my figurin' he would come back anyway. The money—cash an' currency—we took in from that stock we stole up north is still there in the house, an' he'd come back after that if for no other reason. Twenty thousan' dollars would take him quite a long ways."

TWENTY-THREE
LAST ACT

IT WAS a strange world of stone they were riding through now. Great blocks of rock, broken loose from the mountain flanks, lay all about them in weird assortment, the trail tortuously curving between and around them. The shod hoofs of their horses rang unconscionably loud though Kurt if he noticed, seemed to give no mind to it. She guessed the pain of his wound might be at him again, or perhaps it was fatigue that pulled his broad shoulders down, or the both of them together. He had the rifle across his saddle again, but he didn't seem to be doing much looking around.

She was bone weary herself and would be glad to be done with this endless riding. She hadn't been on a horse in five or six months, and she dreaded to think how she would feel tomorrow; but mostly, she just thought of Kurt and his problems and, very briefly, of her own. Her own after all, compared to his, were pretty simple. She could stay on in Tucson or go back to St. Louis.

But where could Kurt go? He didn't even seem to

give a thought to that himself. All of Kurt's thoughts seemed to begin and end with Lahr; about half the time, she guessed, he even forgot that she was with him. And yet ... that time that he had kissed her...

The crash of a rifle brought the chin off her chest. She saw Kurt sway wildly and go out of the saddle. Saw the roll of his body and the dust beat up round it, and the flame going out of his extended right hand. And then a scream, high and frightened, tore through all of that racket and she saw Kurt, up on his feet again, go zigzagging into those rocks on the right; heard his gun bang again and then his voice calling out to her.

She kneed her horse off the trail and in between two great rock slabs, hearing Snuffy, who had stopped, cautiously coming along behind her. Over against a bright patch of sunlight, she saw Kurt bending over something that was hidden from her behind a three-foot rounded boulder. And, coming nearer, she saw the man.

He was propped with his back up against the rock. He had a derby on his head above a scared white face. The left leg of his rumpled store-bought trousers was pulled above the knee; there was a tourniquet about it and Kurt was bending over him doing something with a knife. Then she saw the dead snake, a big diamondback rattler with his head blown half off.

The man's eyes had a crazy half-glazed expression and great beads of sweat stood out on his face. He looked like some kind of traveling salesman, and then she saw with alarm the widening stain on Kurt's shirt.

"Take this gun," Kurt said, passing her a short-barreled pistol, "an' keep your eye on this guy while I try t' suck out that poison."

"But Kurt!" she cried, beside herself, "don't you hear—"

"Yeah, I hear 'em. Some of this feller's playmates comin' down from above, I reckon. Heard the shots," he said, with a twisted grin. "But they wouldn't get here in time t' help him."

Bending down, he went to work on the leg. And, when he had finished and spat out the last trace of rattlesnake venom, the noise of the oncoming posse was a racketing noise of all too near sound.

"Get into your saddle, Docie," Kurt said; and, to the man: "What you done with your horse?"

"Shot down in a brush with some of your gang."

"Here? When?"

"None of your goddam business."

Kurt looked at him. "Well, thanks," he said, and swung into the saddle. "If you don't want t' spend the rest of your life here you better get out an' flag them boys down."

* * *

IT SEEMED to Docie the posse might be right on their heels; but Kurt said no, it was the rocks made it sound that way. "We oughta make the ranch three-four minutes ahead of 'em—barrin' accidents."

They rode for ten minutes and came out of the rocks on a dry drab carpet of drought-stricken grass. Far off to the south, she saw the trees and log buildings of Cardigan's ranch.

"You ought to let me take care of that—"

"Later," Kurt said. "Hell—don't worry about me."

She looked back after a while, but the posse still

hadn't come into sight. She told Kurt. He nodded. "We been savin' our horses a lot more than they have. But Frank Esparza's no fool. They'll be along in time t'—"

"They're comin' now!"

Cardigan looked back over his shoulder. "Yeah. That's Frank, all right. Looks like the Flowerpot boss an' Joe Nettleton with him. We got three-quarters of a mile on 'em an' double that t' go. We'll make it.—"

"But you can't stop now, or they'll catch you!"

"I'll be stoppin'."

She looked at him worriedly. "But—"

"Some things means more to me than gittin' away, I reckon."

He let the big dun out another half notch and Docie gave up trying to talk to him. The wind plucked the words straight out of her mouth like chaff from a threshing. Her bay horse was game, but he was tiring fast; he lacked considerable of being the horse Kurt was riding.

She looked back again and saw they were gaining. The men with Esparza were flogging their horses at every jump but the gap kept widening. She felt a little encouraged. Perhaps after all Cardigan ripped out a curse.

She saw him staring toward the ranch. And then she saw what had caught his attention, and her own eyes widened with a dawning horror. About three hundred yards this side of the buildings a man on horseback was dragging a burning something across the range at a headlong gallop, and in a great arc behind him, the dry prairie grass was leaping into flame.

The sharp glitter of anger was in Cardigan's eyes, of an anger more terrible than any she had seen, and all the bones of his face stood out; she knew then he would kill Curly Lahr if he could. It was a wildness in him, the yeastiness of an affronted pride. He had enjoyed a certain prestige in this country, a reputation for toughness and shrewdness; he'd been Lord of the Hills—a bad man with a gun. And Lahr, by his acts, had torn this to shreds.

These things she read in Cardigan's look. And then he was gone in a swirl of dust, seeming to forget what horse was under him. Consumed by his hate, by his need for revenge, he was spurring the big dun without mercy, driving him straight at that brightening blaze.

She called on the wearying bay for more speed, wondering if the whole range were threatened; wondering, too, why Lahr had set this fire which must surely wipe out everything he had schemed for. If he'd planned, as Kurt thought, on bluffing this through, what had ever possessed him—

And then, of her knowledge, the answer came to her. Lahr had naturally thought to be rid of Kurt as a culmination to Esparza's visit. It must have come as a terrible shock to the man to have looked up and seen Kurt Cardigan coming across these flats with the posse behind him.

That was it—Lahr had panicked. Had been filled with a sudden overpowering fright on beholding Cardigan riding toward him. She had seen Kurt put that fear into men; into Lahr himself and into Shiloh Frayne. Curly Lahr cared for life even more than he cared for the fruits of his treachery and, abandoning all, he had set this fire in the desperate hope that it might cut Kurt off, might hold him back until Lahr could hide his trail and get out of the country.

She beat her heels against the bay's heaving sides,

sending him tearing after Kurt's stallion, her dilated eyes glued to Cardigan's shape. Smoke was commencing to roll up now as the burning grass sucked wind like a draft. Fifty yards from the yellow-red glow she could hear the rising roar of the flames, and her heart almost stopped when she saw Jubal Jo rearing up before them. But Kurt fought him down with an iron hand and they whirled to the left, plunging recklessly on, trying to find some way past that wall of flame.

Docie turned the bay and gained thirty yards, felt him lift to the call of the singing quirt. But he was failing fast. She could feel the great muscles quivering under her, could see the slow fall of that gallant head; only his fighting heart kept them going. But she dared not stop here—to stop here was death; they must get beyond reach of these ravening flames.

Her smarting eyes were filled with tears from the smoke and sometimes now she couldn't see Kurt at all. But always she could hear the yellow stallion's hoofs, even through the roar of the flames she could hear them —even above the groaning breath of the bay.

She felt the bay falter, felt the changing rhythm of his pace—felt him stumble. She stood in the stirrups, held him up with main strength; heard him cough. The smoke in great billowing gusts was all about them, recurringly pierced by the brief orange tridents of crackling flame that winked and danced and fluttered. And again, the bay faltered; and she knew, this time, by his staggering strides that the end was at hand. And then—

Oh, blessed relief! Amazing, incredulous—they were out of the smoke and beyond the fire's reach in a splendid great open of hoof-tracked dust where nothing at all grew to give the fire purchase. Twenty yards the bay ran and then he started to fold. She kicked free of the stirrups and struck heavily, rolling.

But the deep dust cushioned her fall and she got unsteadily onto her feet and, because some way it seemed the thing to do, began slapping the burned spots out of her dress. When she was satisfied there were no live sparks on her, she looked toward where she judged the ranch to be, but a burned-over hogback cut off her view. She heard no horses, no blast of gunfire. She guessed Kurt was trying to track down Curly Lahr.

She saw now that she was in a kind of depression that looked to have been made by the hoofs of penned stock. Climbing to higher ground she found her view increased considerably, though she still couldn't see whether or not the ranch were burning—the buildings, that is. Out on the flats of the north pasture, great clouds of dark smoke showed the fire was still marching inexorably toward the foothills and she guessed it would not stop before it reached that boulder basin.

Turning around she saw that in the opposite direction, which was dead against the wind, the fire had burned freakishly, skirting the shallow ravine over there, yet leaping a creek to go tearing across a stretch of high ground and then, balked by a forty-foot ledge of buff sandstone, dipping east through a thicket of chaparral. That arm of the fire was now creeping toward a flimsy shed and pine board shanty some thousand yards to the south of her.

And then she saw Cardigan.

* * *

HE WAS on his yellow horse, sitting straight legged in the saddle and moving at a snail's pace across the smoking high ground south of the ravine and west of the creek beyond it. He had his rifle across the pommel so, presumably, he had not yet found the man he was hunting.

If he thought to find Lahr in this neighborhood— and it was obvious to her that he was working back this way—he must already have looked to the south and west, the most natural directions for Lahr to have run. This meant Kurt had someway cut the man off and prevented the getaway Lahr's panic had prompted. Therefore, Lahr must have taken to cover.

She felt suddenly afraid for Kurt on that ridgetop. He seemed very tall limned that way against the sky and the stringers of smoke curling up from burned timber. He had his hat shoved back and, on that yellow horse, the sun turned the edges of his hair a bright gold.

So alone he looked—was it pride that made him expose himself so? Did he think it the quickest means to his purpose? She wanted to cry out *Get off that ridge!* but she dared make no sound or move which might even for an instant divert his attention.

She tried to think where Lahr might hide if he were round here, and her glance sped at once to the shed and board shanty. They were down in that hollow to the east of the creek, and the fire working down that side of the creek was less than a hundred yards from them now. If the man were there, he'd have to pick up soon. Perhaps that place was out of range for a rifle or, if someway Kurt had cut him off from his horse, perhaps he had no rifle but only a belt gun.

And then she saw why it was Kurt didn't look

toward that place. He was working the west side of the ridge just above the ravine; the shed and the shanty would not be in his vision until he rounded the rock strewn base of the slope.

And then she saw Lahr.

He was in the ravine, fifty feet below Kurt, well concealed among the vine-covered branches of a windfall. But now the sound of the dun stallion's nearness had drawn his lank shape very carefully erect; and he was crouched, bending forward, with his outstretched arm along the gray barked trunk. It was the sunlight glinting off the barrel of his pistol which had shown her where he was.

Even as she spied him a snake's head of flame winked wickedly upward from the snout of that pistol. She saw Cardigan flinch. She saw the shine of his teeth as he lifted the rifle and coolly fitted the butt to his shoulder. Snuffy stood like a rock. She saw Cardigan's lips move but all she could hear was the trip-hammer pounding of Lahr's flaming pistol. But the man's nerves were ragged, he was in a panic of haste, firing wildly and furiously as fast as he could trigger.

The flat crack of Kurt's rifle came through that sound cleanly.

Lahr's head tipped back and, with his mouth stretched wide, his arm slipped slowly off the bole's gray bark. Docie didn't see him fall. Some compulsion stronger than anything in her had turned her startled eyes toward the pine board shack.

The breath caught in her throat. The fire had reached its east corner, but it wasn't that inferno of flame that blanched her cheeks. Aghast she was staring at the white-gowned figure that on hands and knees was crawling from the now open door.

Docie screamed and pointed.

Cardigan, across the ravine, took one look. He lifted the big dun on hind legs and whirled him, sent him recklessly plunging across the shale littered slope. Down the creek side, he flashed at a hard pounding run. She saw Cardigan lift him and put him across it—saw the stallion dive, squealing, between blazing trees and slide into the dooryard on locked, sliding heels.

Before he stopped Kurt was out of the saddle, tearing the rolled slicker away from his cantle. Docie saw him run forward, slicker over his shoulders, to where the girl lay in a crumpled white heap not ten feet from the flames. Fire enveloped the shanty; in a gust of bright sparks flame swirled from the doorway and curled over Kurt as he stooped, gently rolling the unconscious girl in his slicker.

She saw the girl's red hair flying loose and wild as he gathered her up in his arms and straightened; saw him bend again—holding the girl with one arm and a knee—and scoop the hair into his hat, putting it on her. Then he turned, still bent, using his body to shield her, and carefully moved toward his horse.

Docie couldn't help it. She screamed again when she saw the blazing tree fall square across Kurt's path. A volcano of sparks and flaming branches obscured him; then she saw him again, still holding the girl, trapped away from his horse by the tree's blazing length.

Her heart almost failed when she saw Snuffy bolt.

She heard Cardigan whistle; heard him whistle again and saw the big dun stop and look back uncertainly; heard him whinny and snort. Saw him shake himself violently. Even from here, she could see his shape tremble, could see the wild roll of his terrified eyes.

Kurt whistled again and Snuffy pawed at the ground. He took a few nervous steps and stopped, shaking all over. She could see how he watched Kurt, though; and then, with head held so as to keep up the reins, he went reluctantly toward him, whinnying softly. Step by step he moved nearer, terribly frightened and nervous but with his trust in Kurt bringing him always in closer until he stood just across the burning tree from his master. Kurt fought his way across it with the unconscious girl held aloft in his arms and, with clothes still smoking, got into the saddle.

* * *

THEY WERE WAITING for him when he came out of the flames.

"Some hoss," Collquist said—he was the owner of Flowerpot. And Rickven, with tears streaming down his stubbled cheeks, took the girl from his arms. Top Hat Charlie nodded.

"Well," Cardigan said, looking down at Esparza, "let's get it over with."

"No hurry," Frank said. "She bad hurt?"

"I think she'll make it, all right. If there's anythin' left of my place!—"

"Main house an' cook shack."

"Better take her up there then. My woman'll help."

Esparza looked briefly at Docie and nodded. "I got your note—the one you left on the table."

Cardigan scrubbed a hand across his chin, leaving

another streak of soot in its wake and smearing one that was already there. He let out a sigh. "You'll find the cash on a coupla pack horses I tied out in the brush about a mile south of here." He licked his cracked lips and said: "All of it."

"So, he was all set to run, eh?"

Cardigan shrugged.

Docie touched Frank Esparza on the arm and said shyly, "I'd like to say a few words if you'll let me. I know Kurt's too proud to speak up for himself—he thinks a man ought to stand or fall by his actions; but it seems to me a man's actions could be misunderstood—he misunderstood Lahr till it just about ruined him. I want you to know that man Lahr was a scoundrel!"

"I've suspected as much," Esparza told her gravely.

"I can prove it, too," Docie said emphatically. "I was at the stage station when the Bisbee bank was robbed, and Lahr was the leader—I saw him shoot that marshal, and our crew was in it with him. Jupe Krailor didn't even have a mask on, and I know Lahr was the leader because his hat came off when they were making their getaway and I saw his green eyes and red hair! I think he was the leader of those night-riders too; we've got misbranded horses all over our range."

No one stared any harder than Kurt, for all he was so weary he wasn't catching half of it.

"Kurt and me," Docie said, "were going to round them."

"We'll take care of that, ma'am—"

"Well, that will surely be a help, short-handed like we are. Kurt fired the whole crew, but they came through here last night with a big bunch of horses—"

"Yeah. We know about that."

"Did you know Kurt and me were trying to track them down?"

"We kind of suspected as much," Espraza nodded. "That Lahr was a pretty bad actor. Did you know he wrote Sollantsy here—Sollantsy's a rep for the Tri-States cattle crowd-that your husband was riding a dun called Jubal Jo that was stolen from a rancher at Big Timber, Montana?"

Here it comes, Kurt thought; and was too pooped to give a damn, though it had kind of halfway made him mad to hear Docie putting her oar in that way—who the hell did she think she was kidding! And that puking dude—imagine that guy being a Tri-States range dick!

Docie said, "I'm not a bit surprised. You should have heard some of the lies he told my husband."

The marshal nodded. "Just for the sake of the record though, Sam, do you reckon this could be the horse Lahr was jawin' about?"

Cardigan saw the dude stepping forward. He had a hard time bringing the guy's face into focus. To hell with him, he thought, and wished to Christ they would hurry and get it over.

"You mean this nag?" the dude said with a sneer. "Jubal Jo was a *horse*—not a goddam pony!"

You could have knocked Cardigan's eyes off his cheeks with a stick. It was the damnedest thing he had ever heard tell of; yet there the guy was, tramping off with Joe Nettleton, Hankins, and some other birds, heading for their saddles. Hell, it must be Docie, he thought, plumb astounded. She seemed to have pulled the wool over everyone!

"Guess we better be shovin' along," Frank was saying; and the next thing he knew there he was alone with Docie. She looked kind of scared, and well she had a right to be. "I never could stand a lyin' woman," he told her, "But if you figure you could reform, I reckon we better git hitched up." A grin cut across his tough face, changing it. "I sure wouldn't want Frank thinkin' he'd been deceived!"

GUNFIGHT AT THE O.K. CORRAL

PART ONE

FORT GRIFFIN

ONE

THIS WAS BUFFALO COUNTRY. All that vast stretch of uncharted prairie west of the river was stomping ground for uncounted thousands of the shaggy-shouldered animals, worth from four to five dollars a hide in the aggregate, and the hunters and their crews were coming in from all over. In the town, Conrad's store was taking in $4,000 a day, this was in the time when a dollar was a dollar, and the bulk of this trade was done on guns, lead, and powder. Hides were piled everywhere, bloody feasts for the flies. It took a strong stomach to live with that smell.

Fort Griffin on the Clear Fork of the Brazos was booming. "The Flat" itself, as the town was called, had three inexhaustible sources of revenue: the hide men, the troopers, and the free-spending drovers who rode in from the trail herds to "see the elephant jump to the moon." Treeing the town, this sport was called later. The merchants hadn't yet become fed up with it. Gamblers waxed fat, and the liquor peddlers likewise. Pimps and their whores were thicker than fleas, and fourteen establishments catered to thirsts. Many of these employed "girls" in addition to derringer-packing tinhorns to help separate the fools from their money.

The post, established in 1867 by Lieutenant Colonel S.D. Sturgis topped a mild rise known as "Government Hill," with the houses of ranchmen and other settlers strung about it like a brood of chickens. Nearby was a village of friendly Tonkawa Indians, many of whom acted as guides and scouts for the constant comings and goings of the military. Some of the Tonks' Women also found employment in the post and the wild town as well. Bugle calls regulated the round of activities: reveille at daybreak, stables shortly after, sick call at 6:45, breakfast 7:00, drill 7:30, recall 8:30, guard mount 9:30, water call 11:15, orderlies 11:45, recall from fatigue at 12:00 sharp, and so on, these calls permeating and having a considerable influence upon all life within hearing.

It was just after orderly call, with the brassy notes still quivering in the glittering sun-flushed air, when three horsebackers clothed in the garb of range hands came in sight of the town on a bluff across the river and hauled up against the haze-cushioned blue like a circling of vultures to give the place a sharp-eyed scanning.

This was Ed Bailey with his right and left bower, Alby, and Rick, three of a kind, dark against the sweeping lift of the sky, not yet identifiable above the sun-yellowed grass, but in some singular fashion synonymous with trouble. It was a feeling oozing out of the way they sat their saddles, dark faces scrunched and unblinking, no loose talk or laughter.

Having had his look, Bailey lifted the reins and

heeled his bronc into a surly canter. The three passed the cemetery, turned into the fetlock-deep dust of the road, and came jogging on, eyes narrowed beneath the cuffed brims of their hats.

It wasn't much of a town, even for the frontier, being more a helter-skelter conglomeration of jerrybuilt shacks whipped out of green lumber which had never known paint and was already warped and grotesquely twisted at every joint and hit-or-miss angle. Bailey eyed the freight office, his glance passing over a mired-down wagon that had been there for three weeks and never dug out through the mud which had trapped it was now stiff as baked bricks. He saw the three wagons crammed high with stinking hides creaking in from the west, and the government supply train, crawling specks in the distance. His angry glance picked up the cavalry detail, with its two Tonk scouts, jogging in from the north. No trilling bit of activity on that street escaped his notice. He showed a hard and sullen face darkly burned by the sun and heavily stubbled. Two big pistols in tied-down holsters joggled at his hips, and the stock of a Spencer rifle stuck out of the scabbard under his left leg. Here was no kind of man to slap your hip and yell boo at. Danger was reflected in every crease and dust-grimed wrinkle.

They turned into the street, Bailey slightly in front, Alby, and Rick with their horses' noses just back of his saddle skirts, one at either side. These two looked what they were, just a pair of tough hands, paid gunslingers, and none too happy to be where they were.

Several lounging men on the roundabout porches silently eyed them as the trio rode past the Astor Hotel. Bailey twisted his head and gave the place a hot stare.

Two loafers playing checkers on its verandah stopped their game to scan the riders with knowing looks, and a buxom woman with a prominent nose came into the open doorway to glare and turn quickly back into the lobby.

The three riders, reining up across from the hotel, stepped out of their saddles in front of John Shanssey's Saloon & Gambling Hall. Four men, coming out, stopped cold to regard them with shocked and clearly watchful eyes. A man with a deputy's star on his vest, coming out of an alley, very nearly ran into them, then pulled back for a cold prickling instant of silence. Bailey snorted and pushed through the batwings, his two dogs at his heels. The deputy, Wayne, tramped hurriedly off down the street, dust spurting up in little bursts behind his boots.

The inside of Shanssey's place resembled most others of its kind. Lighted with hanging Rochester lamps whose wicks were only snuffed for refueling, it was perhaps a little more ornate than its competitors and had the added distinction of offering more floor-space and, it was said, a greater variety of feminine "pulchritude:" There were not many customers on hand when Bailey came in with his gunhands, but these were quick to note the look on his face and step back to leave ample room at the bar.

The sleeve-gartered, bald-headed barkeep made haste to move up.

"Whiskey," Bailey said. "An' leave the bottle."

John Shanssey, every inch a dandy in frock coat and flowered waistcoat, his stomach crossed with a cable of gold watch chain, was ensconced in a rear booth feeding his face. He got up, spotting Bailey. He put a cigar in his mouth, flicked a match into flame, sent out a few puffs of smoke that ballooned ceilingward like signals, and came down the mahogany. "You back again, Ed?"

Bailey said, "Where's Holliday?"

"Expect he's probably over to the hotel. He laid a bet you'd show. You better think this over, Ed."

"Get him word I'm waitin' for him."

Shanssey looked at him coldly. "All you'll do with a play like that is get yourself planted. You better just stick with your watered-down rotgut and leave shootin' business to them as understands it."

"No sonofabitch is goin' to cut down my brother an' get away with it."

"Your brother came in here stinking drunk. He was spoiling for a fight, Ed. He made a passel of talk not many gents would take. Doc let it roll off'n him. Then your brother went for his gun."

"You keep out of this, Shanssey. I know what I'm doin.'"

"Well," Shanssey said, "it's your hide, Ed. If you're bound for a burying I guess he'll oblige you."

Bailey, snatching the bottle from the bar, shoved past. Shanssey said over his shoulder, "Leave your guns with the barkeep if you aim to drink here."

Bailey wheeled around as though he'd been hit by a wasp. His men swapped glances. Bailey finally nodded.

"Okay." All three laid their unbuckled belts on the bar. They went back to a table near the rear and sat down where they could watch the batwings.

* * *

UPSTAIRS IN THE HOTEL, in a shade-drawn shadowed room, a knife blade flashed and thunked point-first into a wall. Across a rumpled bed a gangling, pasty-faced, wire-thin man slaunched in a hard-bottomed chair, rocking it forward and back on its spindling hind legs. On a stand beside him stood a half-filled bottle of whiskey, an empty tumbler, and a dozen throwing knives, their sharp blades glinting in the uncertain light. The large-breasted woman with the prominent nose, the one who had watched Bailey & Company ride past the hotel, had her face to the curtain edge, angrily watching the street. She said, "You haven't got a chance if you step out on that street, Doc. He brought a pair of hardcases in with him, Alby, and some other whey-faced rat."

The consumptive dentist who called himself Holliday chunked another knife beside the first one in the wall. He poured the tumbler half full of whiskey, tossed back his head, and downed the whole drink in one gulp.

"Jesus, honey," Big Nose Kate said, "let's quit this town while we've still got the chance. This whole goddam place, includin' that cold-footed marshal is layin' for you!"

Doc, ignoring her, bedded another blade.

"Right or wrong, your neck's due for stretchin' if you kill another man. Don't you understand?" she cried, desperate. "Goddam it, you ain't even listenin'!"

"Now, Kate," Doc said, "Mr. Bailey's come all the way from Fort Worth for this business. Wouldn't be polite for me to light a shuck now. You wouldn't want me to disappoint him now, would you?"

"Spare me that stinkin' Southern gentleman routine. I'm thinkin' about your neck, not your face."

Holliday grinned. "Purely a case of ethics, my dear. Of course, I know you don't know much about ethics."

"You always got to treat me like I'm dirt under your feet"

"Well," Doc said and heaved another knife. "Ain't you?"

"Sometimes, by God," Kate said, looking plumb driven, "I think I ort to poison you! Lemme tell you somethin,' Doc. Them fancy duds and that smart talk don't make you out no gentleman to me. I know what's underneath them things an' don't you never ferget it! Maybe I'm dirt, but there's good women, too, girls you ain't fit to be around even."

Doc yawned. "That's debatable." But he was irritated, too. He snapped another blade into the wall with a force that buried almost half its length.

Kate's lips twisted scornfully. "Ain't this about the stage where you tell me about your family's aristocratic Georgia plantation and all your fine proud friends an' the wenches."

"One of these days I'm like to strangle you, Kate." He grinned beneath his debonair mustache but there was nothing pleasant about it. He looked deadly as a rattler, tail up and warnings posted. After a moment he turned away from her and slammed another blade into the wall. He was touchy about his family.

But Kate couldn't let it alone. "Your folks must've scraped the barrel after the war to put you through that tooth-yanker's school. You're a real credit to 'em. They'd be sure enough proud too."

A knife quit Doc's hand and drove into the boards about an inch from Kate's head. She blinked and winced, stunned. Yanking the steel from the wall she rushed wildly at him, furiously lunging, mad enough to disembowel him.

Doc quit the chair in one bound and grabbed her. She was a chunky, husky woman who knew every trick of barroom brawling, but she was no match for Doc. He twisted her knife hand behind her, shoved it up her back, not giving a damn whether he broke it or not. With his free hand twisted into her high-piled hair, he forced her head back, his eyes as hard as stones.

"You're hurtin' me!" Kate gasped.

"Let go of that knife."

She tried to struggle, to jerk loose of him. Doc put on more pressure, bringing her almost to her knees. The knife got away from her. She slumped panting against him. "Ah, lover," she moaned, "let's don't fight."

Doc, stepping back, said colder than frogs' legs, "Don't ever mention my family again."

He straightened his string tie and the hang of his coat, wiping his hands irascibly on the skirts of it. Kate, nervously eyeing him, said, "God, you sure are jumpy today, honey. Look, why don't you forget this guy, Bailey? Let's you an' me go off someplace and have a little fun. Maybe we can do something about that cough... Sounds to me like it's gettin' worse."

"Your concern for my health deeply touches me," Holliday said with his lip twisting down in a sneer.

She flung her arms about his neck. "You know how I feel about you." She shoved the fullness of her breasts against him, grinding her hips, but the man wasn't interested. "I know," he said nastily, "exactly how you feel."

Kate looked at him, big-eyed, a little breathless. "I don't know what I'd do if anything was to happen to you."

The natty killer pulled her arms from around his neck, threw her off, and stepped distastefully back. "Worrying about your meal ticket, are you?"

Kate's chin came up, and there was plenty of it. "That's a hell of a thing to say to me. I've been good to you, Doc. It's about time you thought a little bit about me."

He looked at her slanchways and grinned thinly. "Well, I suppose the *girls* would be happy to regain a charter member."

Kate slapped his face, her own turning ugly with the fury surging through her. Heaping insult on injury that nasty smirk appeared again around Holliday's mouth and in the cut of his stare. His hand half raised as though to return the blow, but she did not cringe, and he finally dropped it. Then he reached out, patting her rouged cheek, and smiling. "Get over to Shanssey's. Tell him I'll be around later, soon's I work some of the kinks out of my system."

"Please don't go there!"

"Do what I tell you." Holliday scowled and Kate, defeated, said bitterly, "I've got to have some money."

Doc dug a bill from his wallet and held it out without comment. Kate took it, tucked it into the crevice between billowy breasts, and stomped from the room like a wet-footed cat. Doc, laughing, poured himself another generous slug and walked over to the mirror, patting down his hair. He was a handsome man by any standard, handsome despite his almost constant dissipation and the ravages of tuberculosis. He took no care at all of himself, aside from his personal appearance, about which he was inordinately vain and upon which he focused a most fastidious attention. He was invariably groomed to the nines. He stood for a few moments poking at his mustache. Then he opened a watch which he took from the lower right hand pocket of his magnificent vest.

He stood lost in thought, staring at a picture that was just inside the cover. This showed an attractive woman and a man in a Confederate uniform. Snapping the cover closed he stared a further moment at an engraved inscription which read: *To our Beloved Son, Doctor John Holliday.*

Doc took another frowning look into the mirror past the whiskey glass, a cartridge belt, and holstered pistol, and the hilts of the knives he'd driven into the wall. He could not seem to stand the sight of the dough-colored face reflected back at him. A violent seizure of coughing came over him.

When this was finally quelled, he scrubbed the blood from his lips and looked again at the face, flushed now, mouth twitching.

Doctor John Holliday.

"You sonofabitch!" he shouted and sent the watch crashing into the mirror. The flash of gold bounded back from the broken shards of glass, fell to the boards of the floor, and rolled. Doc, kneeling contritely, picked the watch up, gently cradling it in shaking fingers. His eyes were watery, his white teeth clenched...

TWO

IN A LAND WHERE THE LAWS, and the order these were fondly propounded to establish, were most frequently the subject of inordinate belly laughs ox caustic comment, one man at least was rumored to take them with deadly seriousness and was, in consequence, pretty thoroughly disliked by the element which provided most of the noise in that locality. This man, six feet tall and weighing a hundred and fifty without his boots and shell belt, was a blue-eyed blond. The whip of the wind and the blaze of the sun had baked many lines in his face, particularly about the eyes, and the cold-jawed mouth almost hidden behind the luxuriant bristles of an elegant jowls-sweeping handlebar mustache.

The name of this fellow was Wyatt Earp.

In the dust and bright glare of that windy afternoon when the trail of Dave Rudabaugh fetched Wyatt into Fort Griffin, he was twenty-nine years old, veteran of many things and places. He'd known Kansas and Nebraska when Omaha and K.C. were hell tearing border towns. As a freighter, he'd driven bull teams on the Overland and Santa Fe trails. He'd hunted buffalo and Injuns and been a professional gambler. He'd policed Wichita when that place was considered one of the wildest towns on the "Circuit" and knew most of the rougher toughs of the time through firsthand or, at least, a sort of nodding acquaintance. Some of them he knew more thoroughly than their mothers, for he had heard the owl hoot and the owl had heard him. Currently employed by the Atchison, Topeka, and the Santa Fe, he was, in the freewheeling parlance of the day, a railroad dick.

Life on the Flat hardly got under way, generally speaking, before the middle of any evening. Only a few Yankee shopkeepers hunting transient customers were earlier astir; the Big Guns seldom strolled into view before the fashionable hour of chimney smoke and supper preparations. It was scarcely three o'clock now. Wyatt had dawdled deliberately these last few miles, aiming to reach Griffin in time for a look around before his man should hear any whisper of his advent.

Turning his mount with one toe toward a hitching rail he called to the hostler at the stable across the street: "Hey!"

The old man limped over, scrubbing at his neck with a grimy once-red bandanna. Wyatt, stepping stiffly out of the saddle, said, "See that this horse gets bedded down, then fetch my saddlebags over to the hotel."

The man commenced to bristle; then, taking a more careful note of this stranger's hard stare, he mumbled, "Yessir."

Inside the Marshal's Office, into which Earp tramped with the heaviness of a man who'd been long off the ground, Cotton Wilson, the incumbent star packer, and a reluctant acquaintance of Wyatt's from away back, looked up with a grunt from his rifle cleaning and scowled. He'd about as soon have tangled with the Old Itch himself as to see Wyatt Earp stepping into his bailiwick. There'd been a time when Cotton Wilson was a hard man with a pistol, but this was far in the past, on the very fringe of memory. He had a good thing here and wasn't minded to turn loose of it.

"Howdy, Wyatt," he finally growled.

"Hello yourself. Been a long time, Cotton."

Cotton reluctantly put out a hand, involuntarily wincing as Earp vigorously shook it. Getting up, the marshal replaced his rifle in the gunrack, turning back with a wary slanchways stare. Wyatt, yawning and stretching, wearily plopped down into a chair. "By God, I'm plain wore out. Hope you've scraped up some good news for me... Got my message, didn't you?"

Wilson, nervous, reluctantly nodded. He studied his gnarled old hands, wheezing and glowering.

"Well? Speak out. Didn't he show?"

"You're talkin' about Ike Clanton, I reckon." When Wyatt just stared, Wilson said, desperate, "He come through here three days ago, headin' east. Ringo was with him."

"Headin' east? Rode through. Didn't you get my wire?"

"'Course I got it. Don't lookit me like that. Jesus Christ, I'm only one man!"

Still, Wyatt stared. The marshal squirmed. Wyatt, getting up, said, "Why didn't you hold him?"

"I got no quarrel with Ike," Wilson flared. "Ain't nothin' round here I could hold him *for!*

"What do you call 'nothing'? There's twenty charges hangin' over that ruffian!" The Santa Fe's man looked both disgusted and outraged. "Rudabaugh's trail was already cooled off when they put me on it, but I cut Ike's tracks when the grass hadn't hardly sprung back from his passin.' He was headed this way, that's why I sent you that wire."

He looked like for two cents he would work Wilson over. "I played this whole deal so's he'd be forced into Griffin. Seemed like if there was one star in Texas I could depend on to stop him, you'd be the man."

"Now don't go rilin' yourself into no lather," Wilson said, raising his voice some. "I got to walk a pretty tight line in this place. Clanton had friends here."

"I never heard tell of you duckin' a fight before."

"I...well...we just got a different way of runnin' things now. Politics is gettin' so's a man can't hardly spit, half the time, without finding himself backed into some corner. Goddam it," Wilson said, warming up to this subject, but the Santa Fe's man waved his bluster away.

"This is Wyatt Earp you're a-talking to, Cotton. Ten years ago, I watched you walk singlehanded into that saloon back in Oklahoma City and drop three of the fastest pistoleers that ever whacked leather. What's the matter with you, man?"

Wilson stepped around his desk and slumped into the chair like a sack of burst oats. "I know it, but that was ten years ago. I'm gettin' old, Wyatt."

"Is that what you call it?" Earp shook his head. "If any man would of told me Cotton Wilson was going to turn yaller I'd have called him a dadburned hypothecatin' liar."

He went over and settled a hip on the corner of Wilson's desk.

The red-faced marshal said, "You've got no call to make a crack like that. You don't know what I'm up against. You don't know the misery I got in my back, boy. There's times I ain't got no hand for it at all. Things ain't like they used t' be. Marshalin' ain't the same no more, it's all politickin' now. It's who you know an' how you set with 'em. I've bucked some of the toughest gangs in the West."

"Then whyn't you stop Ike Clanton an' Ringo? If you can't handle fellers like them anymore whyn't you peel off that tin?"

"Goddam it," Wilson snarled, "I told you! My hands is tied. I can't cross up them boys. I got too many irons in the fire, too." He chopped the rest off, badly shaken, watching Wyatt like a mouse would a cat with his eyes rolled up until only the whites showed between his scrunched lids.

He blew out an exasperated breath through the yellowed stumps of tobacco-stained teeth. "I been a lawman now for better'n twenty-five years. What else could I do? I've worked more hellholes than you'll ever see! An' what have I got to show for it? A twelve-dollar-a-month room in the ass-end of a cruddy boardin' house, an' this goddam star!" He said with a squeal of indignation, "You think I *like* endin' up in a place like, this? I've reached the end of the line, same as you're goin' to someday. I'm gettin' mine now anyway that I can!" Wyatt shut his mouth on the things that were struggling inside of him for utterance. He walked out of the place without again looking at the congested face of a man he had once admired and called friend.

* * *

THE AIR inside of Shanssey's saloon was tight and piled deep with the threat of an explosion. Every eye in the place was fixed either openly or guardedly on the glowering Bailey and his two tough hands. Ed Bailey, flushed and sweating, bolstered his nerve with another stiff slug from the bottle, but his shaking hand spilled half of it on his chin. He could feel the eyes, and the contempt, skepticism, and speculation back of them. It rasped against him like a clawing of nettles. Damn the whole stinking push! His eyes flared back at them, red-rimmed from his riding and the whiskey inside him. Everywhere he looked the frozen faces gazed back at him, troopers and bar girls, hunters, gamblers, macs, and aproned bartenders, all of them watching in avid expectation. The bottle was nearly empty; he found it hard to focus his attention, but he wasn't forgetting what he'd come here for.

"Where is that yellow-livered skunk?" he snarled.

Rick, his left bower, said, muttering it, "Take it easy, Ed. This whole crowd's in it with him. They're settin' it up to git you riled." And Bailey's other hand said, "You better lay off that bottle, boss."

Down the bar about twenty steps Shanssey had his head tipped, talking into the ear of the head barkeep. Now the apron nodded. He said back of his hand, "What's keepin' Doc anyway?"

Shanssey grinned. "Doc's figuring to let him dangle a while."

Cotton Williams came in with his chief deputy, Wayne, and two others armed with shotguns. These last two posted themselves beside the green-painted batwings, hats low over eyes that were narrowly alert for the first sign of trouble.

At his table, Bailey slung the empty bottle into a corner, not much caring if he hit anyone or not. "Let's hev some decent whiskey here!"

In the archway over by the grab-and-stomp part of Shanssey's establishment just beyond the free lunch, a bevy of girls in rather scanty attire made bright splotches of color as they stood in a huddle, peering into the saloon. Beyond them, under the balcony overhang, Kate of the prominent nose sat as though she was held by fiddle strings at a glass-ringed table in the silent company of another soiled dove. Kate's white-knuckled, garishly be-ringed, and over plump fingers nervously twisted a handkerchief that looked damp with handling, but no damper than her cheeks behind the rouge and rice powder. She wasn't a bad-looking dame if you didn't mind that nose or her too-ready willingness to meet ardent males somewhat more than halfway.

Rumors concerning her were rife in the town. It was said she was a girl Doc had married and discarded after snatching her out of a St. Louis finishing school. She habitually packed a gun and could use it. She did not wear it in sight, but it was always about her somewhere whenever she had occasion to resort to it. Some of the more malicious-minded claimed she was a whore by preference, ready to peel off her clothes at the lift of an eyebrow, but she lived where she pleased and paid tribute to no one. She was equally at home on the plains or in town; she was as self-sufficient and as fearless, as fiery-tempered as Doc.

She'd been hanging around Shanssey's place for several months. Doc had been dealing cards there.

They saw quite a bit of each other although it was a generally accepted fact that Shanssey herself was paying most of her bills. Doc had been here two months and gave every evidence of regarding himself as a more or less permanent part of the menage. He had no regard for the law whatever and Wilson left him strictly alone.

Kate lifted her half-filled glass and abruptly drained it.

The batwings flapped back, and Wyatt Earp stepped into the barroom. A kind of visible relief ran over the place, some of those nearer faces relaxing visibly as, clean-shaven below his yellow sweeping mustache and wearing fresh linen underneath his black vest, he went past Cotton Wilson as though the marshal wasn't there. The whole feel of the place turned easier as a number of the men and even a couple of the unattached girls gathered about him as he stepped up to the bar.

The girl beside Kate got out of her chair and started uncertainly across the dance floor. Kate grabbed her wrist.

"Who's that they're making all that fuss about?"

"Wyatt Earp."

"You mean the railroad dick? Is that who he is? What's he doing here?"

The girl twisted loose. She went into the saloon, pushed into those around Earp. "Hi, Wyatt. Bet you don't remember me."

"Wichita," Earp said with a grin. "Sadie's dance-hall. How could I forget?"

"See you later?"

"I'll probably be around," the detective said, eyes twinkling.

He winked at the girl as several others pushed up to him. John Shanssey elbowed into the circle, grabbed Wyatt's arm, and drawing him away from his admirers, led him into a semi-separated booth at the rear of the room.

Pumping Wyatt's fist, he said, "You old son of a gun! Whyn't you let us know you was figurin' to ride in?"

"Good to see you, John. Matter of fact, I came here on business."

Some of the bunch the saloonkeeper had dragged Wyatt away from had followed them all the way back to the booth. As Earp doubled into a seat at the table Shanssey threw out his hands as though to push them away. "Look, boys, give us a break." He partially hid his annoyance behind a quick smile. "I'll turn the famous man over to you later." He said to Wyatt, "You eaten yet?"

"No." The detective watched the others drift reluctantly away. "Seems like I'm gettin' to be a marked man."

"Price of fame," Shanssey chuckled. He caught the glance of a passing waiter. "You've sure as hell come quite a piece since Cheyenne. Everybody, I guess, has heard of you now. Ellsworth, Wichita, Dodge." He shook his head. "Never had you pegged for a lawman, Wyatt. Seemed to me you was always pretty reckless and wild."

"Still am, some would tell you. In those days," Wyatt said, referring to the crossing of their trails in '67, "I figured the world was my oyster. Not so sure of it now." He put his elbows on the table, thinking back to Cheyenne of ten years ago. Shanssey, a pugilist then, had fancied himself ready to take on Mike Donovan, the Champ. Wyatt had refereed the fight. Shanssey had been so thoroughly drubbed he had never gone into a ring again.

"Guess I never really figured myself for a lawman," Earp said. "I just sort of drifted into it. I was standin' in a real bind one day when somebody handed me a star and six-shooter. I haven't been able to get rid of either one."

The waiter came up. "Fix a prime steak up for Mr. Earp," Shanssey said, "and fetch a bottle of the best from my personal stock."

"Coffee'll do," Wyatt said as the man departed.

"You gone temperance?"

"Not really." Wyatt frowned. "I've just found that drinkin' and packing a gun don't go so well together. Never seen a drunk yet that could hit the side of a barn."

Shanssey regarded him thoughtfully. "You take that badge pretty serious, don't you?"

"I've got to," Wyatt nodded. "My life depends on it."

"How's your brothers?"

"They're gettin' along. Scattered all over the country. Virgil and Morgan are married, you know, though I must say none of us appear to have settled down too well. Guess the Earp's ain't the kind to put down many roots." His eyes focused keenly on Shanssey's face. "John, I ain't much of a hand for sayin' so, but I could use a little help."

Shanssey fired up a stogie. "Anything I can do."

"Ike Clanton an' Ringo rode through here three days ago. I went to some trouble to make sure they would, and wired Cotton Wilson to hold them. What's the matter with that feller?"

"He's not the same man we used to know. You see that bar?"

Wyatt's glance drifted bar ward. He nodded.

"Every one of those boys behind the mahogany is gunfighters. Only way I can keep order. I hate to say it, but I can't help you. I don't know a thing about, say, wait. Let me think." He snapped his fingers. "Doc Holliday set into a game with that pair. He might have heard something."

Over at Ed Bailey's table, a clatter went up. The man's mean eyes flicked about him impatiently. "If that two-by-four bastard," he said loudly, "ain't here in twenty minutes I'm goin' after him!"

"That Ed Bailey?" Wyatt asked.

Shanssey nodded. "Poor damn fool's just askin' to get planted. Doc killed his brother, but there again the guy was begging for it. Mean drunk he was. Cheated at cards, tried to put it on Doc an' yanked his smoke pole." Shanssey rolled the Long Nine across his teeth. "You ever met Holliday?"

"Briefly. Once. He was tooth pullin' then. Wonder what turned him into a gunslinger?"

"Never heard. He ain't one to talk about his past. I've yet to see him pick a fight. Far as that goes he don't seem to have to; trouble just naturally gravitates toward him. Bailey's the third man he's killed in the Flat. Gotten so every would be pistol pusher in the Territory seems to want the name of havin' put him under. You know how it is when a man gets a rep."

Wyatt nodded soberly. "I certainly do."

Shanssey said, "I've got Doc figured for a mighty

short life. Never seen a place so against a man as this one is. Even if Doc fixes this one's clock, mean even if he come out of the smoke, the crowd'll lynch him this time sure. He ain't got a real friend in this camp."

Wyatt said, "Where can I find him? If you think there's a chance he might have heard something."

"He's got a room at the hotel."

Wyatt got up. "Keep the steak warm."

Shanssey smiled. "You wouldn't be missing too much. It's plain Texas longhorn."

Wyatt moved past Bailey's table. The man was opening a fresh bottle.

* * *

IN THE HOTEL Astor dining room Doc, at dinner, was just setting down a glass. As usual, the gambling dentist was immaculately clad. The big room was about deserted. His dinner finished, Doc pushed back the grease-smeared dishes and began to lay out a hand of solitaire. He moved a few cards, sat a while in concentration. Moving the jack of spades off a turned-down stack, he looked up to see Earp standing over the table.

"Mr. Holliday, I believe," Wyatt said.

Doc said nothing, just kept moving the cards. Pulling out a chair Wyatt sat down across from him. Doc, without raising his head, said sarcastically, "Make yourself right at home."

Wyatt, ignoring his tone, leaned forward. "Don't know if you remember me."

"Wyatt Earp," Doc said. "I pulled one of your bicuspids ten years ago. If I'd known when I had you in that chair"

"Understand you've taken up a new occupation. You were a pretty fair dentist."

"Patients couldn't stand my coughing in their faces."

He kept on moving the cards. Wyatt reached over to shift a queen for him. Doc grabbed his wrist. "The name of this game is solitaire, mister."

Wyatt settled back, grinning patiently.

"Mr. Earp, I'm busy."

"I'm huntin' information."

"Hunt somewhere else."

Wyatt said expansively, "Let's say I'm in a position to do a little horse trading."

"Not interested in horses."

"I think you'll be interested in what I've got to tell you."

"You couldn't know a thing it would be worth my while to listen to."

"Don't bet too heavy on it." Wyatt said, smiling, "What would you say if I was to tell you Ed Bailey's got a lady's gun hidden in his bootleg?"

"Left or right?"

"Left."

"I'd say that was good information. Happens Bailey's left-handed."

Once again Wyatt leaned forward. "Ike Clanton an' Ringo rode through here three days ago. You know which way they were heading?"

"Beats me," Doc said.

"Thought we were tradin' information?"

"I didn't make any deals."

"You probably know where they went, or where they were figurin' to go."

"You're playing hell with my game."

Wyatt, glaring at Doc, got stiffly out of his chair. "You've got no use for the law at all, eh?"

"I'm not hugging and kissing it. Last year, in case you don't know, your fine brother Morgan ran me out of Deadwood. Impounded ten thousand dollars of my money. I should like that?"

"I should be blamed for it?"

"You got brothers wearing tin all over the goddam country."

"Perhaps I'll run into you again," Wyatt remarked thoughtfully.

Doc, unperturbed, went on shifting his cards.

THREE

WYATT, coming back into the saloon, was met by Shanssey. One glance at Wyatt's face seemed to give him the whole story. "Wasn't talking, eh?"

"Hell with it. I'm headin' back to Dodge City."

"Too bad," Shanssey said. What he said then was just like putting the old X straight down on Doc's character.

He said, "You know, he's in my debt for a few things. I believe he'd help you out if I was to ask him."

Wyatt shrugged it away. "Ringo and Clanton are probably headed for Tombstone. Ike's old man has a big spread there."

"Isn't your brother Virgil the marshal at Tombstone?"

"Last I heard, he was. I'm gettin' off a wire to him to keep his eyes skinned for them."

"Doc say when he's coming over here?"

"What he said you could put in your eye and never feel it."

Shanssey sighed. "I sure wish this night was done with."

* * *

DOC, over at the Astor after Wyatt had left, played another couple of cards, and tossed in the deck. He poured himself a stiff drink and downed it, wiped his mouth, and got out of the chair. Heading for the lobby he put on his hat and stopped by a mirror to adjust his string tie and straighten his coat.

There was no one in the lobby except the bored clerk.

"Oh, Mr. Holliday," the man said. "Would you care to settle up your bill? What I mean is...ah...we didn't know whether you'd be checking out or not."

Doc gave him a hard stare. "If I do you'll be the first to hear about it. I'm not in the habit of running out on my debts."

He stepped out on the porch, stood there a few moments gazing across the road at Shanssey's. Perhaps he was thinking about Earp, a little jealous of the man's high standing in the country. Whatever his reflections were they obviously gave him no pleasure, but he did not miss seeing the pair of shapes that came out of the Cottonwood's shadows to dart with some furtiveness into the saloon. A smirk tugged at Doc's lips. Whistling softly he moved down onto the walk and, finally, striking off through the dust, he crossed over. While he was still some steps away from the batwings, Shanssey came out and intercepted him.

Shanssey wasted no words. "You're walking straight into trouble if you go into my place. If Bailey don't get you Cotton Wilson will. You'd be smart to pull your freight while..."

Doc, brushing past him, headed for the doors.

Shanssey said disgustedly, "You tired of livin,' Doc?"

Doc paid him no attention at all. He pushed through the half-leafs and heard the place go still as the news of his presence ran like a wind through the chip clatter and gab. A lane, like magic, opened up between Holliday and Bailey's table. Wyatt, standing a few feet from Cotton Wilson, marveled at the stillness that was, in its way, a kind of tribute to Doc's prowess as a corpse maker. Shanssey trailed the gambler in. Not once, so far, had the consumptive dentist looked at the man who had come here to bury him.

Cotton Wilson said, "Wait a minute, Doc. Check in that gun. We don't want no trouble in here."

Doc, considering the marshal, appraising his determination, finally walked over to him, unbuttoning his coat. Smiling thinly, he pulled it open. There was no gun belt and no gun. He gave Wilson a sour grin and, whistling through his teeth, stepped nonchalantly up to the bar, halting about a yard from Bailey's table. People standing around there scattered. Not by even a lift of the eyebrows did Holliday acknowledge Bailey's presence. Turning his back on the man, he propped a foot on the rail and held up two fingers. The nearest apron set a bottle in motion.

Wyatt shook his head. "He's got guts, all right." Shanssey, somewhat tight about the mouth, nodded silently. Cotton Wilson continued to watch Doc edgily, a half-opened hand beside his gun butt. Kate stepped out of the archway, coming a few steps into the room.

Ed Bailey's hands nervously drummed the tabletop. Sweat put a greasy shine along his jowls.

Doc held up three fingers and the barkeep poured. He must have been as tightly wound as Bailey, but he put every drop of the drink inside the glass. Doc was watching Bailey in the back bar mirror.

Now he said to the barkeep in a voice that carried plainly to the ends of the room, "I understand there's a gentleman here from Ft. Worth, but I don't observe any gentleman, aside from myself." He tried the whiskey for flavor, even passed the glass back and forth beneath his nose. "This fellow should have taught his brother the difference, between Hoyle and a deck of marked cards." While the people standing about visibly held their collective breaths, Doc said to the barkeep in the way of one sport confiding in another, "If anyone should happen to lay eyes on this ranny, kindly pass the word along I'll be waiting at Boot Hill. I'm referring to this son of a yellow-bellied sow."

Bailey staggered to his feet, upending the table. Doc could see every move the fellow made in the mirror. As Bailey bent grotesquely to jerk the pistol from his boot leg Doc dexterously produced a knife from somewhere adjacent to his collar and, abruptly spinning about, caught Bailey in the act of leveling his six-shooter. There was a glint of streaking steel. The gun drove a slug through the tin of the ceiling and Bailey, staggering back, collapsed, and doubled over the reddening hilt of the bedded blade.

Alby and Rick, Bailey's hired toughs, started for Doc and were stopped in their tracks by the rock-steady focus of two pistols in the hands of the barkeeps.

Unruffled, Doc tossed off his drink, put the glass on

the bar and, colder than hell on the stoker's day off, stepped through the stunned crowd, plainly aiming for the batwings.

Wilson's deputies closed in on him. "No funny business, Doc."

"What's the charge?"

"We'll think of something," Cotton Wilson said nastily.

After the batwings had flapped behind Doc and his coterie of badges the saloon seemed to pick up a new lease on life. A crowd gathered wordlessly about Bailey's body.

Shanssey came into it with uncaring elbows. "All right. Break it up." He beckoned over a couple of his girls. "Get a sheet or one of them table covers; a thing like that can put a cramp in business. You," he growled, putting the finger on another frail, "tell them fiddlers to hit up a hornpipe." He took stock of the crowd that was beginning to pinch off in knots with their heads together. "Step up to the bar, folks! Drinks on the house!"

While Shanssey was still trying to get his customers back to normal Wyatt drifted into his orbit and carried him down to the far end of the bar. "It's always a mess after something like that," the ex-pugilist growled.

"There's one thing you got to say for Doc," Wyatt said. "He was plumb at the front when they was passin' out guts."

"Shanssey! Mr. Earp!" Kate cried, hurrying toward them. "They hadn't no business taking Doc up for that. You saw what happened! What else could he have done? It was him or Bailey."

"Now, now," Shanssey said, harried eyes flicking about, "Cotton knows."

Wyatt's hand fell on his arm. "Who's this?"

"Huh? Oh, Kate Fisher. Friend of Doc's. Kate, meet Wyatt Earp."

"They're going to frame him!" Kate cut in. There was fright in her eyes, in the jump of her voice. She was twisting her chubby jeweled hands together. Her face looked blotchy in the lamp's yellow gleam. "Do something, can't you? Don't just stand there! This whole pack saw Bailey pull that gun on him."

"Why don't you just relax," Wyatt said. "The law will take care of everything."

Kate was not to be put off or consoled. She whirled on the detective furiously. "You fool! There ain't no law on the Flat!"

"Well, it's no business of mine," Wyatt said, shaking free of her. "But I'll say this, lady: I never saw a man more determined to get chopped down. And I'll tell you this! I don't like Holliday. I don't want any part of him."

Kate peered at Wyatt more intently. "Please, Mr. Earp."

"Sorry," Earp said gruffly. "Good night."

He turned with a stiff-necked bow and went out.

Kate turned desperately to Shanssey. The saloon-keeper tiredly shook his head. "I can see that a pair of fast horses are put around at the back of the hotel, that's about as far as I'll be able to go. I wouldn't stay in business ten minutes if it was ever to get out I helped him. A man's got to look at the facts of this matter."

"Then he's finished," Kate said, looking stonily at him. "He hasn't another friend in this town."

Shanssey's glance drifted over the grumbling crowd.

He saw anger there, and a bleaker note was creeping up through the talk. Kate's knuckles shone white. There was a look on her face he wasn't able to meet.

* * *

IN THE LOBBY of the Hotel Astor, Earp stood against the counter talking to the desk clerk.

"Be sure you get this telegram off first thing in the morning."

The clerk nodded as Wyatt signed his name and pushed the pad of yellow paper toward his hand. Cotton Wilson, just then coming down the stairs, spotted Wyatt and froze. But only for a moment. Anger tightened his cheeks and a wave of color crawled up his neck as, with a glance averted, he came off the stairs and, stomping across the lobby, went out.

"What's he doing here?' Wyatt said.

"They're holding Holliday upstairs in his room."

"In his room?" Wyatt's focus widened. Looking puzzled he rasped a hand across his jaw. Twisting around he stared at the street into which the marshal had stepped. Then, chousing his glance toward the stairs, grunting unintelligibly, he started up them.

As he came onto the second landing, he saw the deputy Wayne with his shoulders settled against a closed door. Wyatt went on to his own door, shoved it open with his hand near his pistol, and when nothing untoward happened, went in, and cuffed it shut. He stood there beside the bed, grimly thinking. The whole business *did* have a kind of smell.

He finally shrugged and sat down and pulled off his boots. Going over to the dresser he turned down the gas lamp and presently pulled off his shield-fronted shirt. He was hunched there staring at the things in his head when a quick knock rattled the door. Kate Fisher, not waiting for his permission, came in, shutting the door behind her.

She was panting a little from the climb, the agitation of her more obvious charms a bit overpowering seen thus at close quarters stacked against the closed door. She gave him a tight and practiced smile and, when he didn't respond, she caused her bosom to heave agitatedly. Her low-cut gown only emphasized the flesh pushed deliberately by her corsets against the confining cloth. She seemed about to burst from the dress, but Wyatt stayed where he was through the gamut of her swift-changing tactics. Now, face twisted, the panic showing, she rushed to the window, ran up the blind, and stared into the night-shrouded street below.

"Look," Wyatt said. "Like I told you, Miss Fisher, this is none of my business."

"Think what you will, but that's a lynch mob out there. You've got to do something! Wilson won't lift a finger and they're—listen to them! You hear that?" She was almost beside herself, shaking all over, her eyes like great coals in the pallor of her cheeks. "They're goin' to hang him, mister! The rights of it don't matter; he's a human bein' ain't he? You goin' to sit there and let them take him out an' string him up?"

Wyatt pulled on his shirt, and got up, and shoved the tails in. He went over to the window. He could hear them all right. They were heading for the jail. Kate snarled, "A pack of goddamn animals!"

He met the full force of her desperation. "No

matter what he done he don't deserve that," she said hoarsely, grabbing hold of his arm like a bear trap.

Her scent swirled around him in a musky fog. He extricated himself and stepped back. "I'll do anything," Kate said. "Anything you say."

"Not necessary, ma'am." Wyatt sat down and pulled his boots on. "First place, Doc ain't over in that jail, he's right here under this roof."

He studied her a moment. "Get down to the end of the street there someplace and watch this window. When I wave a lamp set fire to whatever comes handiest." Getting a bandanna out of his pocket he tied it over his nose and mouth, jammed on his hat, and lifted the gun from his holster. Suddenly she came hard against him with the staves of her corsets, the bulge of her breasts. "Bless you!" she cried above the noises from the street.

Wyatt pulled open the door. He moved down the hall with a cat-quick stealth, stopping a moment where it turned, his mouth squeezed tight. If this thing backfired there'd be hell to pay. When Earp rounded the corner the big deputy, Wayne, was still lounging against Doc's door. Pistol leveled; Wyatt leaped.

The man, caught cold, stood gaping, frozen. His eyes bulged as though he couldn't believe what they told him. Too late he grabbed left-handed for the doorknob, his right streaking hip ward. The barrel of Wyatt's up swinging pistol took him sharply under the jaw. The man went limp and slid down the jamb like a busted sack. Wyatt kicked the door open.

Doc, in a chair by the window, was moodily eyeing the activity below. A startled deputy on the bed blinked incredulously into Wyatt's gun snout. "Git your paws up!" Wyatt growled.

The deputy let go of his shotgun. Wyatt, stepping in, rapped the pistol against his head. The man folded. Doc's watching face displayed hardly any interest. Smiling thinly he said, "Guess you're what might face-tiously be called an 'advance scout' for the necktie."

"Choke off the blat," Wyatt said, "and get out of here!"

"You don't really think I'd be fool enough, do you? Hells fire! The minute I got off this chair you'd turn that gun on me and claim I tried to duck out on you."

"We got no time to play games. Get movin'!" Wyatt snapped.

He had dragged Wayne into the room and was binding and gagging the pair methodically. He picked up one of Wayne's pistols and flipped it to Doc, at the same time divesting his face of its mask.

The gambler, now staring, looked genuinely surprised. "A little out of your line, ain't it, busting loose prisoners?"

"Nothing personal about this," Wyatt said impa-tiently. "I just don't hold with lynchings." He lifted the lamp from the dresser, went over to the window, and waggled it back and forth.

* * *

AT THE FAR end of Main Street, there was an abandoned barn that had once been part of a horse change station. Kate, dressed like a man, saw the flare of light in the hotel window. She took a lighted kerosene lamp off a manger and pitched it into a great pile of musty hay. Flames shot up. She watched them spread, then ducked out the side door.

Back in Doc's room, both men stood calmly. Out in the street, a loud voice yelled, "Are you with me?"

A chorus of angry growls rose in answer.

"Somebody git a rope!"

Doc grinned at Earp. "I'd say that right here and now would be a pretty good time to get out of here if this deal's really on the level."

"We'll wait a bit."

"It's your show." Doc shrugged.

Wyatt, pointing through the window, brought Doc's head around. He saw the leap of red-flecked flames and softly whistled. "Mighty handy bonfire."

"Go down the back way." A discovery shout went up from the street. "They've seen the fire. Wouldn't lean too hard on my luck if I was you."

"I'm obliged to you, Tin badge." The gambler lifted a hand. "Look me up some time in Dodge City and I'll try to render a more proper thanks."

"You can thank me properly by staying out of Dodge."

Doc, chuckling, stepped into the hall and disappeared. Wyatt took another thoughtful look from the window. The ruse was pulling the mob down the street. Men with buckets were hustling to join them.

Down behind the hotel, Doc found Kate with two saddled horses waiting. On the front porch of his establishment, John Shanssey smiled and puffed on his cigar as towering flames lit up the back of town.

PART TWO

DODGE CITY

FOUR

A RATTLING coach behind six horses beat up the dust of the pot-holed road, flinging it over the borders of rabbit brush and thousands of thirsty wild sunflowers. Dead ahead loomed a hill thatched in a haphazard fashion with slabs of weathered wood and a scattering of drunken crosses. A sign, bullet-riddled, read:

BOOT HILL CEMETERY, DODGE CITY.

Some distance along the far side of this hill, not in sight at the moment to driver or passengers, was a yellow-painted depot and the sidings of a railroad. A man with a sweeping well-cared-for mustache stepped out of the depot carrying a packet of letters. For perhaps forty feet he strode along beside the tracks; then, shaking loose of his obvious preoccupation, he crossed the rails and bent his lengthening stride toward the main part of town. He passed a sign, hesitated, turned, and stared back at it. He considered it perhaps a bit longer than necessary. There was nothing subtle or elusive about the proclamation. It said bluntly:

DEADLINE, CHECK ALL FIREARMS AT MARSHAL'S
OFFICE, BY ORDER OF DODGE CITY COUNCIL.

He moved on into the traffic, a tall man with springy stride yet with the saddle bound carriage of a man more at home on the back of a horse. His eyes were sharp and cold as he scanned passing faces. A number of people spoke to him. He touched his hat to the women and managed a nod for the men, but he did not pause or become engaged in conversation. Straight ahead of him now was the Long Branch Saloon. Across the road from the Marshal's Office was the Dodge House, a smart looking and eminently presentable hotel.

The man paused to stare a moment in the direction of the saloon, then shook off the thought and cut toward the Marshal's Office and the barred windows of the jail. As he came up to the door, Charlie Bassett stepped out.

"By grab, I'm glad to see you, Wyatt!" Bassett was Earp's chief deputy and a very well-known marshal in his own right. He said, "Bat Masterson's in there waitin' to see you."

Wyatt nodded, got his watch out, and checked it. "Stage is due. Take a squint at the passengers."

Bassett took off across the street, as Wyatt moved into the office.

He found Masterson sitting behind the desk with his boots propped on it and a stump of cigar sticking out of his mouth. Wyatt slapped Bat's feet off the desk, shoved the chair away. Putting one hip on the desk, he placed the letters beside him and opened the top one. The stagecoach pulled up in front of the Dodge House and commenced unloading, as could plainly be seen through the plate glass of the window.

Masterson lit the ragged end of his cigar and puffed in silence. Wyatt, busily reading, said, "Letter from Virgil."

"Understand things are really humming in Tombstone what with that silver strike and the bunch any boom will always draw in its wake. How's Virg doing?"

"Hey!" Wyatt exclaimed. "He's bought himself a house! Makes the first of us Earp's to really put down roots. He says Betty is expectin' again this summer."

Dropping the top page, Wyatt's face as he continued reading, began to take on the granite set of annoyance. "Thought so!"

"Bad news?"

Finishing the letter Wyatt tossed it on the desk. "I was right about those two. Virg tells me Ike Clanton and Ringo rode in a couple weeks ago. Virgil arrested them, but you know how that goes. Ike's old man owns that county. The judge, who's square in the old bastard's pocket, turned 'em both loose. Freed 'em of all charges. Damn! Those lousy killers, turned them scot stinkin' free!"

Tipping back his derby, Masterson rubbed some of the sweat off his forehead. "Guess I'll never get used to risking my neck pullin' in these hardcases an' watching some tinhorn judge set 'em free."

"He says Ringo's headin' back up this way."

"So? What about Ike? He's the one I'd like to get *my* hands on."

"Virg says Old Man Clanton got killed in an

ambush. Ike's staying on to take over the ranch." Wyatt slammed a fist on the desk. "I tell you, Bat, I just don't understand it."

"No thanks in this business, you ought to know that."

Wyatt shook his head. "You know, I'm just the town marshal here. But some of the things I've seen and had to put up with." "You're the sheriff, Bat, so you see more even than I do. How many of these peckernecks have tried to make you a deal?"

"Oh," Masterson said with a chubby grin, "I get propositions worth about a thousand bucks a month."

"Doesn't it bother you?"

The county sheriff shrugged.

"I sometimes wonder," Wyatt said with a scowl, "if we wouldn't be exhibiting considerable more sense to take them."

"Now you know mighty well you couldn't do that."

"I've sure been givin' it some thought," Wyatt growled. "We ain't getting no younger. Be kind of nice to have a stake tucked away."

The pair of them simultaneously came to their feet and were drawn to the plate glass to stare across the street. A "classy number," as Bat himself put it, had just gotten off the stage and now was standing beside it, graceful as a willow, pointing out her luggage to an attentive half dozen of the town's derby-hatted sports.

Wyatt exclaimed in a gusty breath, "Talk about your children in the fiery furnace! God above, Bat, who's that?"

"Looks to me like Delilah," Masterson said, fingering his tie. He ran a considering hand across his cheeks, unconsciously smirking. "Or Salome, wasn't she the dame that asked for that preacher's head on a platter?" He continued to watch the newcomer admiringly as, trailed by her escort of smitten swains, she moved into the shade of the coach's lean shadow, exchanging a few words with the driver before striking out with her retinue of baggage carriers straight up the street in the direction of Miss Deed's boarding house. "What do you suppose she's doing in a place like Dodge?"

He got no change out of Wyatt. The Dodge City marshal was staring after her raptly. Bat said, "Watch out for the flies. You got your hatch dropped open like a hungry bird's."

Wyatt, flushing, pulled up his jaw.

"That's strictly big city fluff," Sheriff Masterson said.

"School teacher?" Wyatt guessed.

"Too fancy a getup."

"Lady rancher, maybe?"

"Too soft, too frilly." Bat shook his head as the young woman moved out of their sight leaving a myriad of turned heads peering after her. Some cowhand whistled. Several laughing loafers dug each other with their elbows. All up and down the street were visible unmistakable signs of male reaction. Wyatt said reflectively, "Must be fixin' to stay a while. Two trunks would hold more than an overnight change."

"Yeah," Bat said scowling. "And I've got to take out a posse, fact is, that's what I come to see you about. That daddratted Injun's on the warpath again."

"Dull Knife?"

Masterson nodded. "I'm going to have to borry your deputies, chum."

"Damned if you ain't always shortest of men at the most inopportune times," Wyatt growled.

Charlie Bassett came in.

"Who's the frail?" Wyatt and Bat popped the question almost in the same breath.

"What frail?" Bassett said, and both the other men groaned.

"Hell, I been too busy to be lookin' out fer wimmen," Wyatt's chief deputy grumbled, "Hold your drawers now, I got some real news. Doctor an' Mrs. John Holliday just checked in an' have put up at the Dodge House!"

Both officers blinked. Wyatt said, "*Mrs.* John Holliday, I didn't know he was married!" And in the next breath, he growled, "I told that damn fool to stay out of Dodge!"

Masterson caught Bassett's arm. "Lottie Deno? A redhead?"

"Big Nose Kate," Bassett said, enjoying their concerned surprise.

Wyatt scowled. "I better get over there before he unpacks."

"Wait a minute," Bat grumbled. "You going to loan me your deputies?"

"All right, all right," Wyatt gave in, plainly distracted. "I'll have to keep Charlie, though; he's needed right here. You can have the rest, but you better be back before those trail herds pull in. You know what it's like when those cowhands hit town."

Wyatt paused at the door as though of two minds about something. Coming back he pulled his shell belt from a peg and strapped it about his lean-hipped middle.

He found the consumptive dentist-turned-gambler in the barber shop with his feet up and the towel and apron covered the rest of him stretched out flat in the chair. The barber removed the steaming towel from Holliday's face and painted it with a froth of lather. The gambler spotted Wyatt at once but made out not to notice him. The famous boots were unpolished, the thinning soles were about to show holes, and both heels were run over. For a celebrity, Wyatt thought, Doc looked downright seedy.

"Mario," Wyatt said, "go out and get some fresh air."

"Si, signor." The barber hurriedly vanished. Wyatt locked the door. Doc, pumping the chair, raised himself to a sitting position and with the apron smeared some of the lather off. "Ah," he said caustically, "I see the mayor hasn't forgotten me."

"I thought I told you to stay out of Dodge City." Wyatt wasn't one to beat around any bushes.

Doc, climbing out of the chair, picked up Mario's razor. He ran it back and forth a few times over the strop and tested its edge with the ball of his thumb. "I like a sharp razor. You come in for a shave?"

"No, thanks," Wyatt said. "And this ain't no time for jokes."

Brushing fresh lather onto his face Doc stepped over to the mirror and started shaving himself.

"A stage," Wyatt said, "leaves for Abilene in the morning. You be on it."

"Can't. Marshal of Abilene sent me here. Matter of fact, I wish some enterprising chap would draft a new speech for tin badges. In the last five burgs, there hasn't hardly been a changed word even."

"Then you'll hole up in your room until day after tomorrow. I will personally escort you to the westbound train."

"It seems we are faced with a hard fact, Wyatt. You find me in a state of complete financial collapse. I don't even have the price of a ticket."

"There's still Kate's jewelry. You can fall back!"

"Alas," Doc said, "those rocks are but a fond memory. I've had a terrible streak of luck."

"You had a roll in Fort Griffin thick enough to choke a cow."

"As you may recall," Doc smiled, "I shook the dust of that town in something of a hurry. I went off and left twenty thousand in your friend Shanssey's safe."

Twisting his head, he regarded the marshal sadly.

Wyatt, hunkered now on the arm of the mechanical chair with his gun hand propped upon the grip of his pistol, returned the stare without noticeable feeling.

"And do you know," Doc sighed, "what that sonofabitch did? Those two broncs he staked out in back of the hotel cost me exactly ten thousand simoleons apiece! Fancy!" With a philosophical shrug, he went back to his shaving. "Everyone," he said presently, "seems to put a most outlandish value on my life."

Done with his shaving he stepped over to the water bowl and dipped his face into his hands. Groping blindly, he gasped, "Don't just sit there like a fly in molasses. Pass me that towel before I run into something."

"You're going to run into something if you don't haul your freight out of here." Wyatt flipped him the towel, watched the man wipe his face off. Now Doc stepped along the shelf, inspecting the labels of the displayed stock of bottles, sniffing with a variety of facial contortions. He uncapped a lavender bottle and helped himself to a swig. "Not bad," he said, smacking his lips, and put some on his hair.

"Wyatt," he said finally, wheeling around to face him squarely, "how much do you make in a year handling trouble? About a hundred a month and two bucks an arrest? If you were the sort to stash some by on the side you could make quite a bundle. I don't suppose you are, so I'd imagine most of the time the cupboard goes bare."

"Come to the point if you've got one." '

"I feel compelled," Doc said delicately, "to offer you a proposition. How much money can you lay hands on?"

Wyatt considered him, cold faced, in silence.

Doc was not moved to blush. "Not much, I gather. A few hundreds you've been saving for a ranch or country store? Look," he said, getting down to bedrock, "I can make it easy for you to own a *big* spread. I mean something in the neighborhood of a couple thousand head. Stake me for a start and I'll split my winnings with you. When the trail drives hit this burg there'll be real money for a man with his eyes open."

"Of all the trashy gall!"

"Tish tash," Doc grinned. "Don't be so goddam holy! Any number of gents would be delighted to back me for even as little as five percent. You consider yourself better than the mayor of this town? Damn it, I like you, feller. I like your cut."

"You're a generous bastard," Wyatt said, getting up.

Doc picked up the folded razor, tossing it up from one hand to the other. "Look at it this way: What would a barber be without his razor? A boat without a rudder? A church without a steeple? You're a peace officer; how far would you get without a gun? About as far as a carpenter without saw or hammer. My tool is money, coin of the realm." He considered Wyatt whimsically. "Don't be a goddam piker. Put up your widow's mite. It'll be in good hands, believe me."

"You guaranteein' not to lose?"

It was hard to tell if Wyatt were stringing him along or actually thinking of taking Doc up on it.

"You got a good poker face," Doc sighed. Suddenly he twisted over, taking time out to cough. When the paroxysm passed he wiped his mouth with a white square of linen, studying it a moment before he put it away. "I never lose when the moon is right. Poker is the game of desperate fools lured on by hope and the need of hard cash. The man who has nothing to lose rakes the pots in. And that's the way I go into a game. It's the game."

"It's a cinch," Wyatt scowled, "you don't care about your hide."

"With this cough?" Doc laughed bitterly. "I certainly don't intend to wind up in white sheets! Come on, what are you scared of?"

They stared at each other like a couple of strange dogs.

Doc said with a snort, "Well, it figures. Dig into that hoard, you damn Simon Legree. If you want me out of here you'll have to pay the train fare." He said with a contemptuous slanch of the eyes, "Maybe your precious City Council can be talked into making it up to you!"

Wyatt laughed. "I've done some pretty stupid

things. I think I'm about to do another one and let you stick around."

Doc cried, "My God! Such generosity!"

"Guess it's a kind of damn fool admiration for a sport who don't know when to yell calf rope. You can stay," he said sobering, "and you can play on one condition. No knives. No guns. No killin's."

Doc bowed formally. "You have my word, as a gentleman."

"One thing more," Wyatt said. "You ought to treat that woman decent or leave her."

"You mean Kate? She's a cross, no getting around it. Stands for every last thing I hate in myself. I don't know..." He sighed. "I'll try, Wyatt. Leave me two bits for the face-scraper, will you?"

* * *

IN HIS OFFICE, Wyatt tipped back in his chair, was filing down the firing pin of his new Buntline Special, a pair of which had been presented to him by the author of that horrendous thriller *Buffalo Bill: King of the Border Men* which, in the marshal's candid opinion, was a heap of sure enough garbage. But the gun, as he twirled it and sat clicking the trigger, he admired pretty highly.

"Hey," Bassett said, stepping in off the street, "where'd you get the new pistol? By the way," he went on, without waiting for an answer (which is the way with a lot of folks even now), "I found out all about your elegant obsession."

"My what?" Earp said, peering around the barrel.

"That dame that got off the stage a while ago. Some gun!"

"That's the one that feller Buntline had made up for me special. What about her?"

"Sure beautiful," Bassett grinned. "But ain't that barrel too long?"

"You talkin' about this gun or the girl?"

"Hand-tooled, too," Basset said, sounding envious. "Some cannon."

"What'd you find out?" Wyatt laid the gun on his desk.

"Why, she's stayin' over there at Miz Deed's place. Along with them drummers. Some of the' most elegant foofaraw you ever seen come outa them trunks, they tell me. Some of them things come clean from Paris, that's in France, by godfries! Five-foot-four, weighs a hundred an' twenty pounds."

"What's her line?"

"Gambler."

"Very funny, Charlie."

"Well, I thought so muself, but it's the Gawd's own truth. Hell don't take my word for it. Take a hike down to the Long Branch an' see fer yourself."

Wyatt jumped up and stomped out, Basset trailing him.

* * *

A PLUSH JOINT, the Long Branch, whole notches above the average of its kind. And there, sure enough, sat the girl at the faro bank, bucking the house man, Cockeyed Frank Loving, who was nobody's fool even though he did favor ladies' garters for keeping his sleeves from dropping down over his fingers. A cowhand, half plastered, was also in the play and very evidently endeavoring to impress the girl with his manly charm. At least a dozen men were gathered about the table, including Mayor Kelly, the owner of record. His triple chins were dripping sweat like a Kansas City hydrant. Wyatt, still trailed by Charlie Bassett, came up and stopped behind the outsize pants Kelly had to buy to cover his bottom. Neither Wyatt nor his deputy was armed.

Kelly looked around. "What's the trouble, Marshal?" Wyatt, indicating the girl, said, "I'm going to bust up the game."

"Now, wait a minute," Kelly said, plainly riled. "You can't come in here and stop my game just because a woman's got her money on the table."

"Every time we get a woman in a place like this there's a fight. My job's to keep the peace. Close her out."

When the fat mayor made no move to comply, Earp stepped forward, grabbed the girl's cards, and flung them over his shoulder. "Game's closed."

The cowhand got to his feet. It appeared to be considerable of an effort, but there was no mistaking the jut of his jaw. "That's no way to do to a lady!"

"You shut your mouth an' stay out of this, feller."

The young lady smiled. "It appears the marshal is laboring under the mistaken idea that he's not dealing with a lady."

"No *lady* plays cards in a gents' saloon. Not in my book, anyway," Wyatt said.

"No *gent*," the cowboy growled, "would talk like that to a lady."

The marshal's hard stare made the fellow back up a step. Turning to Kelly, Wyatt said, "If you'll think back, Mr. Mayor, you'll recollect we both agreed there'd be no women gamblers on the north side of the street."

"But, Wyatt," Kelly cried, "this here is Laura Denbow. Miss Denbow's marker is good for ten grand anyplace in the West. She's considered an exception."

"Not in Dodge City, she ain't."

"Come, man, be reasonable!"

"So you're the famous Wyatt Earp," Laura said. With a flash of dark eyes, she added, "Lawman, judge, and jury."

"That's right," Wyatt grinned. "Start with you an' we'll have every tramp on the south side over here."

"Who's a tramp?" the cowhand bristled.

"Keep out of this, buster."

Laura stood up and Wyatt nodded toward the door. "On your way."

"Is this an arrest?"

"If you mean are you going to jail, the answer's yes."

Her chin came up. "On what charge?"

"Expect I'll likely think up a better one. In case I don't, we'll book you for disturbing the public peace."

She smiled at him, angered. "Don't you think you'd better wait for a few of your deputy marshals?"

"I think I can manage," Wyatt said, taking her arm.

The cowboy shoved forward. "Git your paw offa her!"

He yanked open his jacket, palming a concealed pistol. The crowd backed off with an audible gasp, leaving a good fifteen feet of silence open all around them. Wyatt eyed the man carefully.

The fellow was enjoying the sensation he was creating. He fell into a crouch. "Go for your gun!"

"Happens I'm not heeled."

The fellow stared stupidly as the marshal, outwardly cool as the proverbial well chain, moved a couple of steps nearer. The drunk flung up his pistol. "Stand where you are!" It seemed as though he would surely fire if the badge packer wiggled so much as a finger.

The marshal was used to handling drunks. "I can see you don't know what you're doing, feller. Better give me that pistol before it gets you into real trouble."

Bleary-eyed, weaving around on his feet like a rudderless ship in the grip of a tempest, the big slob eared back the hammer of his gun.

Wyatt said with a sneer, "You haven't got the nerve to pull that trigger." The cowboy commenced again to back away. "Stand still!" Wyatt said. "I'm goin' to take that peashooter away from you."

Every face around them reflected the tension of not knowing what that damned fool would do. The girl had a hand tight against her lips. The mayor's eyes looked bigger than slop buckets. Sweat beaded the house man's upper lip and Bassett's face was rock stiff with repression as he stood locked in his tracks.

Wyatt bored in, holding the man with his bitter stare. The fellow couldn't back away any farther, the blades of his shoulders were hard against the wall. Sweat ran off his chin, the pistol waggled in his fist, the roll of his eyes showed fright and fury and then, in desperation, he fired into the floor at Wyatt's feet. Wyatt came steadily on until the brims of their hats weren't a foot apart. The fellow, snarling, rammed his gun into Wyatt's belly. Wyatt's hand came up and took the pistol away from him. The man's drunken curse cut the quiet like a sob. Everybody started to talk at once.

The cowboy's voice, crammed with earnestness, whined, "I didn't aim fer to shoot you, mister. It was jest..."

"Sure, feller. I understand. You just wanted to impress the little lady."

The whole place, it seemed, heaved a sigh of relief. Bassett stepped up. Laura said to Kelly, "*He's* a showoff, too."

The fat mayor shook his head, mopping his face. "Not him!" he exclaimed. "I've seen him do that too many times. He can read a man's mind like he owned him."

"Charlie," Wyatt said, "take him in the back room and sober him up. Then get him out of town." Wheeling, taking hold of Laura's arm, he started her toward the door. Kelly, intercepting him, said, "You're not really serious about this, are you? About arresting Miss Denbow?"

"Out of the way, Kelly. I've had enough for one evenin.'"

"That's all right, Mr. Kelly," the girl smiled. It took some of the strain out of her cheeks, but her tone made it plain she considered the marshal two shades lower than the belly of a snake. "I intend to know every cranny of this town, and I might just as well start in with the dungeons."

She pulled her arm away, brushed his touch from her sleeve, and walked, head erect, ahead of him to the louvered doors. There she stopped and stepped aside.

Wyatt looked at her, puzzled.

"Aren't you going to open them for me?"

Wyatt's cheeks turned red; his eyes flashed with annoyance. Then he shoved the doors open and followed her out, leaving Kelly and the others staring after them open-mouthed.

FIVE

THE GIRL GOT under Wyatt's skin as no other woman had been able to do. She was different, a type he had never before come up against though he'd met many kinds. Her cool, aloof self-sufficiency rubbed sparks from his temper, and the more he tried to figure her out the greater was his hotly baffled confusion. She was a beauty, he gave her that, and she had courage, but it was a kind of courage bluntly bordering on boldness he couldn't understand. If she *was* a lady, and she sure as hell looked it, why was she determined to spend her time in saloons?

The jail back of his office held a long line of cells, and he steered her to one near the farther end. Directly across from the one he had in mind was the nauseating sight of a beat-up and passed-out drunk loudly snoring. Laura, taking in these unpleasant surroundings, visibly stiffened, and faced him indignantly. "Do you have to put me here?"

"You could get ten days for this, and ought to. I treat everyone' alike. No preferential treatment regardless of sex," Wyatt said, remembering the opinion of him she had so freely expressed to the mayor.

"But all I've done..."

"You can tell it to the judge."

"Are you always so obnoxious?"

"Don't push me, ma'am. I can git a lot more so."

She was riled, all right. Her chin came up. She looked about as put out as he felt. "Very well. Do your damndest."

Wyatt grinned. "You can leave right now if you want to give me your promise to do all your gambling south of the line."

She had herself in hand now. She said, smiling sweetly, "I wouldn't want you to break any rules for my benefit." She stepped into the cell, nostrils quivering daintily. "Go ahead, lock me in. We can't have you being remiss in your duty."

Wyatt glared. Seething, wild with frustration, he grabbed the grille and slammed it shut.

"My, what a temper! Well, perhaps the judge, at least, if he isn't more impartial may not be so sternly righteous. Hell hath no fury like a righteous man." She was laughing at him openly, enjoying his indignant confusion. "Here," she said, reaching through the bars to push into his hands a number of Long Branch chips she'd come off with. "I won't need these here. Go out and buy yourself a new halo."

Wyatt gnashed his teeth, wishing he had a dog to kick. Then, reluctantly, a sort of parched grin cracked his lips as he studied the straight slim line of her back. He was a man who could not pass up a challenge, and the sparks this girl had so easily struck from him stung like nettles in his mind, stirring unaccustomed thoughts and sleeping desires he had figured to be done with.

* * *

NIGHT AGAIN SHOOK out its sable blanket and the lights of Dodge gleamed over the prairie like a swirl of thrown brilliants. Doc, lugging a bottle, came into the Marshal's Office, steadily enough but in an aura of fumes that threatened to lift the paint right off the walls.

Charlie Basset, elbow-deep in paperwork, threw down his chewed pencil and pushed back with a groan. "Man, this twelve on twelve off is playin' hell with my home life."

These goddam papers would rub the ass off an elephant. What's stickin' you?"

Doc, hauling up a chair, brushed the papers aside and set down his bottle and an unopened deck of cards. "Have a nip?"

"I wouldn't mind, by Gawd," Bassett said, "but I reckon not. Wyatt won't stand for drinkin' on duty. What's the occasion?"

Doc poured a slug down his throat and corked the bottle. He broke open the cards and laid out a deal of blackjack. "Well," he said, examining his hand, "I'd like to bail out that woman."

"Denbow?"

"That her name? Never seen a piece that looked any better put together."

Bassett squinted at his cards. "Hit me, damn it. I've got nineteen."

"Twenty," Doc said and dealt again. "How about it?"

"She's got to appear in court tomorrer. No bail's been set. I'll stand on these."

Doc hit himself three times hand-running. "Twenty-one. I'll wait for Wyatt."

Bassett vigorously scratched his head. He watched Doc toss around the pasteboards. "I sure hope Masterson gits back with our deppities before them goddam cowboys hit town. Blackjack!"

"I've got one, too."

"You musta fell in the manure pile." Bassett glared. "Nothin' personal, Doc, but you know, if we was playin' fer real, I'd be compelled, by Gawd, to hev a look at that deck."

"An' I'd be forced was that the case, to see you try and get it," Doc confided imperturbably.

Charlie Bassett made a playful pass at his pistol. Doc's lightning reflexes took hold at once. Before Bassett's gun was half out of its holster, Doc's pistol was looking him square in the face. Bassett gaped and Doc grinned. "You could get yourself killed trying that sometime."

"Hell, you didn't think I was sure enough tryin,' didja?" He peered at Doc slanchways. "It's almighty lucky Wyatt don't let us go around draggin' our irons or this goddam place would be depopolated!" He scowled around at the clock. He got to his feet. "Time to check the pris'ners an' lookit the horses. Watch the office, Doc, will yuh?"

"Sure thing, Charlie."

Bassett tramped through the door to the jail.

Doc sauntered over to the gunrack and lifted down

a rifle. He sat down at Wyatt's desk with it cradled on his knees. Presently, still sitting there, he cocked his head to one side and slipped a finger through the trigger guard. A man never knew in a place like Dodge if the sound of a boot heralded friend or foe and the chances, to Doc's practical mind, looked overwhelmingly in favor of it being the latter. He thought it better to be ready and worked the bolt of the weapon. Propping both elbows in the desk top he took dead aim at the door.

Wyatt stepped in.

Doc pulled the trigger.

The unloaded rifle clicked.

"You know," Doc said, "I never could get the hang of these things."

"Move," Wyatt growled. "Where's Charlie?"

Doc got up and replaced the rifle. Wyatt, taking Doc's seat, began to leaf through the batch of papers the deputy had been working at.

"He just stepped out for a minute," Doc said. "Wyatt, I'd like to bail out Miss Denbow."

Earp glanced up. "This personal or otherwise?"

"Otherwise, naturally. Anyone with half an eye could tell she's a sure-quill lady."

"No favors," Wyatt said, scowling.

"How about releasing her in exchange for some information?"

"I can't think what you might know that could be of any use to me."

Doc said, smiling, "How well do you know Shanghai Pierce?"

"Well enough to stay away from him. Owns about a third of Texas. Used to drive his cattle up the Chisholm to Wichita when I was marshal there a few years back."

"Expect you've likely had a few run-ins with him?"

"Know of anyone who hasn't? Had to bat him over the Cabeza one time when he got tanked up on tarantula juice and tried to shoot up the town. He ain't no creepin' terror, just another damn fool that forgot to grow up."

"They tell me he's got a real sharp memory."

"I hurt his pride probably a heap worse'n I did his mule-stubborn head."

"Well, mister, he's fetching a herd to Dodge City. On his way right now, coming over the Western Trail to save money. I understand when he heard you were packing tin here he vowed to bust this town wide open. Hear he's hired Ringo to make mighty sure you don't spoil his fun. In addition to that, the story is he's put a thousand dollars on your scalp if it's lifted."

Wyatt grinned. "What else is new?"

"That ought to be new enough for most anyone. I find it pretty amusing, putting a price on a lawman's head."

Wyatt said patiently, "You know what's the matter with that bunch of wild Indians?"

"I'm always interested in the other man's theory."

"They're lonely men. That's what's back of all these benders they go on. Those yahoos hit civilization about once a year and by that time they've worked up so damn much steam they've got to do something scandalous or bust their britches. They're just little boys, really, screamin' for attention."

"They generally get it," Doc said dryly.

Wyatt nodded. "We give 'em whiskey and women and action at the tables, so long as they keep to the south side of the street. But as long as I'm the law around here not one of that bunch crosses the deadline with a gun. Not if it's Shanghai Pierce or Jefferson Davis."

"Spoke like a gent," Doc nodded, grinning. "I'll make sure those words are repeated at your funeral. Now how about turning the little lady loose?"

"She's in good hands right where she is."

"But, damn it, man, we made a deal!"

"You made the deal. I don't remember agreeing to anything."

Charlie Bassett came in. "Charlie," Doc said, "you're working for a crook."

"Go on home and turn in," Wyatt told him. "I'll finish up these blasted reports."

Bassett, stretching, said, "Obliged. The town's quiet. Night, gents." Almost through the door, he turned back. "You really ought to turn that girl loose, boss. She's got no business cooped up behind bars."

"That's just the way I want it," Wyatt scowled. "No business for her means no broken heads."

Bassett, shrugging, went out.

"I think Charlie's right," Doc put in.

Wyatt, grinning sourly, flipped a set of keys across the desk. "I guess I'm gettin' old. Go ahead and let her out."

"It's your conscience, Earp."

Wyatt sighed. "I don't know what it is. Soft spot in my head, I guess likely. That girl's got something."

"Wouldn't have guessed you'd taken the trouble to notice."

"I noticed, all right. Tell Kelly she's got to play in the side room. I won't have her gamblin' on the main floor. I mean that. Now clear out of here before I change my mind."

Doc set off for the cells. Wyatt, taking a deep breath, scowled morosely at the mess of unfinished papers before him. He could hear the mumble of Doc's voice back in the corridor, the tap of high heels, and the tramp of Doc's boots that, once again, shone like bottle glass.

The pair came in. Doc tossed the keys on the desk.

Wyatt, frowning formidably, made out to be powerfully busy but he heard Laura come up behind him, stand waiting. Grinning in spite of himself he got out of his chair and held open the door for her.

"Thank you, Mr. Earp."

"You're entirely welcome, Miss Denbow."

She went out, followed by Doc, who threw an amused glance back across his shoulder at the marshal.

For a while Wyatt just sat there, peering out across the street in the direction in which she had vanished.

SIX

IT WAS EARLY in the morning, almost time for the sun to get up. The interior of the Long Branch, practically deserted, presented a pretty dreary picture and one that stank to high heaven of dead cigars, spilled beer, human sweat, and other noxious odors too numerous and well mixed at this hour to be accurately cataloged even by a connoisseur, of which several haggard-looking specimens were still wandering, ghoul-like, about among the wreckage.

Behind the bar, the town's fat mayor and one of the house men, natty dough-faced, quick-fingered Luke Short, were counting up the cash. The main floor with only a couple of lamps still burning looked a rather unpalatable cross between an abandoned parlor house and a mortician's workshop after the corpses have been scrubbed and planted. Only Kate was still standing there pouring it into her.

For the past forty minutes, she had been dividing her flushed and venomous attention between the oily roil of what she was drinking and the split curtains off yonder beyond which a poker game was still in grim progress. Killing the bottle she dropped it thumping on the floor and with a do-or-die expression moved belligerently to the curtains which she flung somewhat viciously apart to disclose the heads bent over the table.

First to come under her bitter scrutiny was Doc in his shirtsleeves and black silk tie. There were four other players, including Cockeyed Frank Loving, but Kate's glare lingered longest and most uncharitably on Laura.

Laura said, "Calling my raise, Doc?"

"Nope, you can have it." He tossed his hand in.

Laura, grinning, raked in the checks (they were seldom called "chips" in those days) and teasingly turned over her hand to reveal nothing more ominous than a pair of lone deuces. Doc laughed, gulped some whiskey, and broke into a cough.

While the cards were going their rounds again, Kate, coming forward, stopped behind Doc's chair. "Don't you fools know it's damn near morning?"

"Eh?" Loving said.

Doc ignored her, concentrating on his hand.

Kate, cheeks darkening, put a hand on his shoulder. "For Christ's sake, Doc! You going to sit here all day?"

Doc, shoving a stack of checks into the middle, said, "I'll open for a hundred." Reaching into a pocket then he pulled out a bill which he passed over his shoulder without ever lifting his glance from the cards. "Here, go buy yourself a drink."

Kate grabbed the banknote and stormed back out to the bar.

The deal went around three or four times more. "I guess I'll call it a night," Laura said. "Frank, cash me in." She did look tired, for a fact.

All the men stood up as she got out of her chair. Doc put the wrap from the chairback over her shoulders. Wanly smiling her thanks she stowed her winnings in her purse. "Gentlemen, good night."

Doc bowed over her hand, quite the gallant.

Laura pushed through the curtains and came up to the bar where she stopped beside Kate.

"Good night," Laura said softly.

Kate turned her back and, snatching up her glass, drained it.

Laura, turning away, went over and touched up her hair at a mirror and headed for the batwings.

Kelly, peering across Short's shoulder, said, "Good night, Miss Denbow."

"Good night, Kelly."

Wyatt was leaning against a porch post as Laura came out. "Ah, Miss Denbow!"

She attempted to brush past him, but he moved into her path.

"It's late," she said, "and I'm pretty well beat, Marshal."

"Figured to walk you home."

"I can find the way, thanks."

Stepping around him, she set off down the echoing scarred planks of the walk. But Wyatt, coming up behind her, caught hold of her shoulders and compelled her to face him.

"Now, look here," he said gruffly, "we'd better have an understanding."

"About what? I've already sampled the hospitality of your jail."

She had, Wyatt thought, an exceptionally nice voice. It could do things to him, even cool as it was now.

"Well," he said, trying to make out her face in this rather poor light, "I think you're onto the fact by now my main obligation around here's to keep the peace. This afternoon, for instance, there could easily have been a killing. I believe I'm entitled to your' full cooperation. Going along with this assumption, I'm afraid I've got to insist you keep off the streets at this time of night without you're suitably escorted."

"I think I've discovered the drift of that thought. You, being so devout, righteous, and dedicated, no doubt feel there is no one so eminently suitable to accompany me as yourself. I find this extremely flattering but I prefer to enjoy this fresh air by myself."

"Look!" Wyatt pleaded, coming as near an apology as he could manage to bring himself. "I had to do what I did. I'm sorry if you were humiliated. The safety of this whole town was involved. Can't you see that?"

She considered him intently, finally shook her head. "I'm afraid not. Now, if you will please let me go."

"Not," Wyatt said, "till we call off this war."

She took a step. She took another, then turned slowly.

"You're truly sorry?"

"Indescribably."

"Well, I do admire a man who can be big enough to admit he may have been mistaken." He thought her eyes looked brighter, gayer. "Do you go that far?"

"I think I could go a heap farther with you."

"That was nice."

He offered his arm. "May I see you home?"

She hesitated so long he thought she was going to refuse. Then she nodded, smiling, and took hold of his arm. "I suppose you always get your way?"

"I was never in my life so scared I wasn't going to."

They both laughed at that and moved off down the walk.

Presently, arriving at an intersection, they paused to consider a dark row of frame houses set behind white picket fences. "Nice here now," Laura said. "It seems so peaceful."

"It can get pretty rough when the cattle drives hit town."

"Aren't you ever afraid? You live so dangerous a life."

"I've been afraid plenty. It's something a man never really gets used to." They moved on, walking more slowly. "Laura, I sure ain't hankering to run any chances of damaging this new friendship, but there's something I'm kind of curious about."

"Nothing ventured, nothing gained."

"I guess I'm just old-fashioned about women. Call it what you will, but, dang it, you just don't belong in a gambling hall."

She was silent so long he was certain he had offended her perhaps irretrievably. In a low voice, she said, "Where do I belong?" Then she said, her tone more brittle, "With the girls south of the line?"

"You know I didn't mean anything like that."

"I don't suppose you did. I expect you would like to see me behind a desk teaching school, or running a dry goods store, or perhaps as the wife of some broad-backed horny-handed farmer. Look, Wyatt: If you prefer to go through life as a human target, grant me at least the right to live mine. I don't question your business. Why should you question what I do?"

"Because you're a *woman*," Wyatt growled.

"And it's a man's world, isn't it? Men have all the fun. Women are expected to stay home and have babies. Women have got to be above reproach, it's all so ridiculous. Why should you think women are greatly different from men? They're not, believe me. They have desires and needs and areas of fulfillment, very often the same dreams and motivations which actuate men. Try to understand that women are human, too. We have our weaknesses, and not always the ones most attributed to us."

"But can't you see that people will talk?"

"That's one thing you can't stop, marshal or no. Talk is a universal failing, what is it the Scriptures say? Out of the mouth?" She looked at him steadily. "Really, Wyatt, you can't change human nature. You just have to live with it like anyone else."

Wyatt said stubbornly, "Where are you going? Where have you been?"

"Where I've been is my business; it concerns no one else. As for where I am going, who knows? Who really cares? How many people you know have any real convictions of what they want out of life? Do you understand what *you* want? Perhaps I'll have a house in Frisco someday, a white house with green shutters on top of Nob Hill."

"We all get what we set our sights on."

"You don't really believe that, do you? Do you honestly imagine the poor enjoy their poverty? Or that the bad enjoy retribution? There are compulsions in people, deep dark places filled with all manner of."

"Laura," Wyatt said impatiently, "what do you want?"

"I want a little time in the sun, my share of fun,

adventure, excitement. Do you find that so strange? I can tell you very quickly what I *don't* want. I don't want what my mother and sister had. You'd call it 'home-steading.' I call it legalized slavery."

"You could marry some big cattle raiser."

"Why should I? I'm not interested in cattle. It's people that intrigue me."

"You'll meet some pretty poor types in a gambling hall."

"Anyone will gamble, given the price and opportunity. Don't be so stuffy. The reason what I'm doing gets under your skin is that I simply refuse to play by the rules a bunch of men have set up to govern a woman's conduct. If you were a woman would you be satisfied with the crumbs?"

"We're not talkin' about me."

"How like a man," Laura said, turning her back on him.

"Why try so hard not to be a woman?"

She came around with a soft little laugh. "Oh, Wyatt," she exclaimed, "sometimes you're so veritably a man I could scream. I've seen most of what the West has to offer, from brawls and gunfights to marauding redskins. I don't care what you say about me, or what you think. No man alive is ever going to make me pull a plow for him."

"That pretty face of yours is sure deceivin.' You've got a heart that's nothing but solid rock."

"Let's just say," Laura smiled, "I don't intend to be bound by old-fashioned ideas about womanhood. Women ought to have the same rights as men. What's sauce for the gander is cream for the goose."

"At least you play your cards in good style."

"Why not? I like to gamble. It's my trade. I expect we had better say good night here."

"Do we have to? I mean, right now?"

"Tomorrow's another day in my business. Good night, Marshal."

Wyatt stood there, silent, watching the swish of her skirt disappear in the shadows of the lilacs about the porch to Mrs. Deed's boarding house. Even after he heard the soft close of the door he continued to stand there, lost in his thoughts.

* * *

THE NEXT DAY in the office, seated back of his desk, Wyatt, his hands smeared and oily, was cleaning a gun when Charlie Bassett came in and tossed a telegram before him.

Unfolding the message Wyatt scanned the lines, frowning. "From the Attorney General. More trouble, goddam it. Here, see what you make of it." Wyatt went back to his gun.

Bassett, reading, said, "Old Ritchie Bell, eh? So him and a couple more halfwits cleaned out a bank at Salina yesterday. Nipped off with some government dough and left a dead teller. Took off down the River trail."

"An' would I go out and intercept them please!" Wyatt snorted and then sagged back with a sigh. "Left Salina yesterday. Ought to be somewhere around here tonight, or tomorrow mornin' early. That Bell's a mean actor. I better find someone to go with me. Charlie, you're going to have to hold down the town yourself."

Wyatt stood up and clapped on his hat.

Bassett grinned. "Oh, and Jud says he can wangle

you an appointment as U.S. Marshal any time you want it."

"United States Marshal. Yeah, that's all I need." Wyatt took down a rifle from the rack and went out the door stuffing cartridges in his pockets.

* * *

DOC, over at the Long Branch, was whiling away his spare time at the bar, appearing extremely debonair in his usual brushed and black immaculate coat and trousers, ruffled white shirt, and black string tie. No one else appeared to be about except Kelly, who in galluses and shirtsleeves, sat at a nearby table looking over his inventory sheets. Wyatt, coming in, stopped by the mayor. "I got to borrow Luke Short. Ritchie Bell pulled a job in Salina. I just got a wire the bastard's headed this way."

Kelly shook his head, peering up at Wyatt as though it bothered him real bad to have to be so disappointing. "Damn, I sent Luke over to Abilene." He clucked his tongue three or four times against the clack of his dentures. "How soon you have to pull out?"

"Right away," Wyatt scowled, "if I'm going to do any good. Of all the lousy...With all my boys bein' away, Luke was the likeliest man still around. It's got to be somebody who can handle a gun. Wire says there's three of them..."

"What about Charlie Bassett?"

"Somebody's got to keep an eye on this town."

Doc, coming down off his stool, caught hold of the marshal's shoulder as Wyatt was about to step into the street. "I can handle a gun. I'm not busy."

"You?" Wyatt grunted. "No, thanks. Some other time maybe."

"I know which end the smoke comes out of. Of course, if you're looking for testimonials....Those best able to give me the nod are regrettably not available."

Wyatt, not warming to his grin, said, "I'll handle it."

Doc, shrugging, turned away. "Makes me no difference. Go on out and get killed if you want to. I don't guess anyone's going to cry in their beer."

Wyatt pulled up. He *could* use Doc. To think, with Wyatt, was pretty generally to act. "It ain't like to do those duds any good, but if you can stand it I can. Raise your right hand. You solemnly swear to uphold the laws... Oh, for Pete's sake! This is ridiculous! Consider yourself deputized. Hustle over to my office and get yourself a rifle. I'll go pick up the horses."

"Hell, don't I get to wear a tin star?" Wyatt measured him sardonically and laughed. "Not on your life!"

* * *

ONCE THEY GOT onto the road and away from town Wyatt and his unaccustomed deputy put their horses into a lope, regularly alternating between that gate and a walk, making good time, pausing occasionally to let the horses blow. This was rolling country, a lot of it brush-covered, ideal for an ambush. "That Bell," Doc said, "is a pretty sorry specimen, tricky as a part-time whore."

"Man gets all kinds in this business," Wyatt said. "Sometimes I wonder why the hell I stay with it."

They talked in a desultory fashion during the times

when they were letting the horses catch up with their wind, but it was mostly small talk, nothing of any importance. Doc was in a philosophical mood; a good many of his remarks were strictly over Wyatt's head and sounded pretty loco. After some while, climbing a long hill, Holliday said, "Don't you reckon it's about time we were getting off this road?"

"We'll have a look from the top, there. Be getting dark before long."

"You think they're going to stay with the road?"

"Right around here they haven't got much choice. Broken land over to the left there, pretty stony off to the right. Ritchie'll probably be trying to make time, riding with one eye peeled on their back trail. After killing that teller he won't be hunting no posies."

They, by this time, had gotten pretty well up to the crest. Wyatt put out his hand and got down, Doc somewhat stiffly following suit. "We'll sneak us a bit of a look," Wyatt said. "Main thing is, don't stand out where you can be spotted. Take off that hat. Get a handful of brush you can hold in front of you. We'll have to get down and belly up on it."

"I'll leave that to you," Doc said. "I'll just stand here. This rig set me back too much to screen gravel with."

Wyatt injuned up to the high ground. The sky was ablaze with the sun's dying plunge, all streaky with cobalt and copper. Below him now was a considerable view, fairly level open country. He beckoned Holliday up with the horses.

"You think they've got across those flats already?"

Wyatt shook his head. "They won't come that way.

Probably swung east at the river fork. It's my guess those polecats are heading for Newton."

"Maybe we'd better get whacking." Doc, taking another look at the country, pointed, and said, "Why wouldn't they come that way?"

"Too apt to be crawling with Indians. I think we'll camp right here for the night. In the morning."

"You mean we've got to sleep on the *ground!*"

"Hell, that ground ain't so bad. You'll be asleep before you know it."

"Yeah? And who do you thinks going to watch out for my hair?"

Wyatt laughed and commenced unsaddling the ponies.

Their camp was a little below the rim and on the Dodge City side in the lee of some house-sized boulders. Doc, hunkered as near the tiny fire as he could get, was feeding himself beans with a spoon from a tin plate on his knees. Their only other nourishment was coffee; Doc had forgot to bring along a bottle and was feeling its absence keenly. Wyatt got up and cleaned his plate out with sand. It was full dark now and off to the west somewhere a coyote was yapping like a roomful of women. Saddles and bedrolls were spread close by. After Doc got through with his plate he had a sharp coughing spell that left him gasping. "Must be this goddam altitude," he wheezed. "Sure you didn't fetch along a little nip?"

"Never use it."

"Sometimes I find it hard to think of you as human."

Wyatt grinned. "You'd be better off yourself if."

"Don't tell me how to run my life."

"For a smart gambler, you sure play sucker odds

with that whiskey. Keep on and you'll be dead inside a year."

Doc snorted. "This kind of a cough doesn't go away."

"Get out of those stinking saloons and find out. Go live in the mountains. Keep regular hours, get plenty of sleep. You might even live to a ripe old age."

"Not me. I've seen too many of 'em dodderin' around. When my time comes I figure to go quick. No dragging it out in a bed for me!" He contemplated Wyatt darkly. "The only thing I'm rightly scared of is dying, by God, in a lousy bed. Never could stand pain. Fair gives me the willies even to think of going little by little like the drip of a faucet. I'm waiting for some sonofabitch to out shoot me so don't bother preaching me sermons."

"That why you come along? To get shot?"

"I've been sticking around Dodge hoping to even the account, to find you in some kind of jackpot where the quickness of an eye, a finger on the trigger, could make the difference. I'm giving you the God's unvarnished truth. I've got just one debt in the whole stinking world, and I don't like owing it to you."

Wyatt wasn't sure whether he could believe that or not, but he said in a tone that sounded equally belligerent, "You don't owe me a thing. I been shiftin' for myself ever since I could button my pants. I never leaned on anyone yet and I don't; by God, figure to lean on you!"

He got up and prepared to turn in, still scowling. From his own pad over in the rocks, Doc said, "I sure would like to depend on that."

"Far as I'm concerned you can get on that horse an' take off right now."

Doc grinned nastily. "I'll stick around a spell. You might crack up yet."

"Don't hold your breath for it."

"Well, Doc croaked, "I give in that you may fool me, but the odds are eighty to one that you don't. Tougher they come the harder they fall. A man can only live so long under pressure; something's got to give and when it does you've seen the end of him. Show me a tin badge, I'll show you."

"You won't show me nothing!"

Doc, crawling into his blankets, laughed. "How many lawmen do you know that's old as Wilson? You want to wind up like him? Licking the boots of a bunch of cheap grifters! Never was a star packer didn't have an Achilles' heel. You ever hear the story of Achilles, Wyatt?"

Wyatt's face in the dim curl of firelight looked taut. His eyes winnowed down; his lips writhed but only a splutter of snarl came forth.

"What's the matter, Preacher?" Doc said with sly malice. "Aren't you enjoying the sermon? If the boot don't fit kick it off; a man don't have to drink just because somebody shoves a glass at him. You know, honestly now, you and I have got a lot of things in common. We're actually pretty much alike if you want to scratch under the external."

"Oh, for Christ's sake," Wyatt cried, "shut up an' go to sleep."

* * *

HE DIDN'T KNOW how long he'd been lying there, blanket up to his chin, staring skyward, trying to count stars, and not having too much luck with it. Doc's gurgling snores had choked off in a fit of coughing. The marshal, getting up on an elbow, tried to make out the gambler beyond the fire's feeble shine. The coughing continued. Wyatt, getting out of his blankets, gathered them up and, stepping over the fire, put them down across Doc and went back to his saddle and hunkered there beside a rock, staring drearily into the flaking coals. Though he hated to admit it, Doc's words had stuck with him. What if the sonofabitch was right?

Wyatt shivered in spite of himself. Didn't make no difference how much iron a man had in his nerve he was bound to have some off moments. You only had two eyes and with the deck rigged against you the chances of survival in a place like Dodge...

The fire, the next time Wyatt jerked his head up to check on it, only showed a few cat-eye embers dully gleaming through the smudge of its ash. Evidently, a considerable time had elapsed. Doc lay flat on his back, hat over his face, sounding by God just like old Petey's saw mill that time it had been getting ready to break completely down.

There wasn't any moon. He couldn't make Doc out none too plain, what with all the shadows; he couldn't even manage to doze off again, either. Some sixth sense, call it a hunch if you want to, had set off some kind of alarm in Wyatt's head, and the longer he possumed there furtively and, yes by God! *Spookily* flirting his eyes around, the stronger this conviction of peril became.

He was too old in the ways of violence to tip his

hand by any quick movement or an attempt to alert his companion.

The feeling got ranker, became an alien presence, split up, and gradually materialized as three deeper darknesses, creeping nearer, growing plainer, abruptly reared up into the shapes of men with guns drawn.

An arm lifted and pointed out Wyatt's rifle, too far from Wyatt's reach to break any bones in this bastardly bind. While its discoverer bent down to remove it from temptation, the other pair turned their attention on Wyatt.

These were lifting their pistols when out of the blanket-shrouded mound of Doc's raucous snorts and sundry gurgles came three hammering reports and lances of orange flame. At almost this very instant Wyatt's own pistol blasted the night. Three caught cold shapes toppled grotesquely in their tracks as the marshal sprang up with lifted Colt to make sure certain.

"I thought," Doc said querulously, "you were asleep."

"No," Wyatt said. "Not quite asleep."

"Well, it's done now. Let's head in. I've had enough of communing with nature. Take me a week to get these cricks ironed out of me."

"What's your hurry? Settle back. They're not goin' anyplace. I've got me some sleep to catch up on."

Doc peered at him, disgusted. But, finally twisting the riddled blankets around him after carefully making sure he'd whacked out all the sparks, he lay back in smoldering silence.

SEVEN

THE FOLLOWING sun-blasted hours looked well into the shank of another hot evening when Wyatt and his consumptive deputy, jogging tired horses down Front Street, pulled up and dismounted in front of Wyatt's office. Charlie Bassett stepped out with a grin. "Welcome home." Doc looked just about fit for the scrap heap.

"Guess I'd better fix up the coroner's reports." Wyatt cuffed the dust from his clothes. "You're relieved of your obligation, Doc."

"Not, by God, until the debt's paid in full!"

"It's paid as far as I'm concerned."

After the marshal went into his office Bassett said, cocking an eyebrow curiously at Doc, "Get all three of them, did you?"

"I never done so much digging before in my life."

"Must have been some fancy shooting."

"Look," the gambler said irascibly, "I don't want to hear no more about it." He surveyed his ruined finery with a scowl. "You want to do me a favor, go find Kate and tell her to get up to the hotel straightaway. By God, I never felt so tired. Just tell her to get over there, will you?"

"Matter of fact," Bassett said, "Kate hasn't been around today."

Doc blinked at him stupidly. "Hasn't been around?"

"Nobody's seen her on this side since you rode out."

Doc broke into another coughing spell. He really looked bad, Bassett thought and moved forward. But Doc brushed him away. "Send a sawbones up." He turned and staggered away.

Inside his room, some couple of hours later, Doc sat sprawled rather woozily in an overstuffed chair with the usual bottle and glass propped beside him, a book in one hand, a pink-smeared handkerchief in the other. He was coughing again as Kate, without knocking, pushed open the door and stepped inside.

Gravel-voiced, Doc said, "Where the hell have you been?'

"Out."

"Where!"

"For a walk."

"A two-day walk?"

"Well, you've been away, ain't you? Gallivantin' all over with high and mighty Mr. Virtue."

"I was sick last night. Sick when I came in today. I should think since I'm paying the bills, you would."

"Why don't you put a rope around my neck an' jerk on it when you want me?"

Doc rockily picked himself out of the chair. "You were across that goddamn line, that's where you were!"

"What if I was!"

"Don't get flip with me, you whore! You can't stay

away from them, can you? Always got to be gettin' back into your gutter."

"Way you treat me that's where I belong! What the hell do you care?"

"Who was it this time?"

"Why don't you leave me the hell alone!"

"I think I will," Doc told her grimly. "I've had about enough of your whims an' tantrums. You're getting out of here for good. Go on, you slut, go on over there and wallow with the rest of the Good Time Gerties."

"You ain't ditchin' me," Kate snarled. "Not after all I've put up with!"

Doc staggered wobbly-legged over the carpet and reeled through the door that let into Kate's room. He stumbled over to the closet and started throwing out her dresses.

"That damned Wyatt Earp!" Kate screeched. "He's the one that's turned you against me!"

"You're loco. He's got nothing to do with you. I owe him a debt of honor and I'll pay it, by God, if it kills me!"

"You still playin' the Georgia gentleman? What the hell do you know about honor! You an' your hoity-toity."

Doc, with a snarl, shoved her sprawling onto the bed. He went back to the closet and yanked down more dresses, whirling to pitch them out into the room.

"Mr. Virtue! Mr. Virtue! Mr. Virtue!" shrieked Kate.

Doc kicked the dresses across the floor to the window, jerked up the sash, and pitched the whole tangled mass of them down into the street. He hauled her trunk through the doorway and out onto the stairs.

With an angry shove of his brush-scarred boot, he sent it crashing below. Then he whirled, grabbed Kate, and, dragging her swearing and scratching across the floor, shoved her after it and slammed the door. The balustrade saved her. She came back to stand pounding and screeching like a fishwife.

"Let me in! Let me in!"

Doc, slumped exhausted against the locked door, was doubled over, gasping, face congested...

* * *

WYATT, several days later, riding along at a canter over the roll of yellow prairie, turned abruptly off the road and at a walk reined his horse up the rise of a boulder-strewn ridge. Reaching the top, hardly daring to hope, he stood up in his stirrups and peered under the shade of his hand toward a distant arroyo, a shallow gulch off to the left that greenly flanked a dry wash.

She was there. His heart leaped when he saw her standing beside her calico horse beneath the over-hanging branches of a huge cottonwood. Not the lady gambler he knew in town but a different Laura, less austere, more piquantly feminine in boots, split suede skirt and an open-necked blouse of pale blue silk, and with her corn-colored hair braided in pigtails. To Wyatt, she looked wholesome and fresh as he sent his horse cantering down the decline.

"Morning, Laura."

"I never thought I'd be so glad to see you," she said.

"Something wrong?"

She grinned. "Nothing personal. My horse pulled up lame."

Wyatt swung down. "Let's have a look at him."

He stepped up to the horse, talking to it softly, bent and lifted the leg, carefully examining the hoof. He put it down, patting the animal. "Split," he said. "He'll be all right but I'm afraid you'd better not ride him in."

She considered him dubiously, pulled a lip between white teeth. "It's a lucky thing you happened along."

"Well," Wyatt said, rasping his jaw, "I didn't exactly happen along. I know you've been riding out here pretty often of a mornin.' Here, give me your hand; my pony can handle both of us. Be a pleasure to give you a lift back to town."

She continued to study him, not moving, not saying anything either.

"Six miles," he urged, "is a right brisk walk in the heat of the day." Then he grinned. "I won't bite you."

Her lips twisted faintly but her eyes were not altogether free of misgiving. Wyatt, tying the reins of her mount to his horn, swung up and reached down for her. She still did not appear entirely satisfied but six miles on shanks' mare was no salubrious prospect. She finally put out her hand and permitted Wyatt to swing her up behind him.

He didn't make the suggestion, but in this position she found herself compelled to put her arms about his chest. Or risk bouncing off. She naturally had no desire for a spill.

Wyatt grinned behind his mustache and put the horse up the ridge.

She clamped hold of him more tightly, blushing, furiously aware of and considerably affected by the close proximity of their physical contact. "Better keep a firm hold." Wyatt's words floated back to her. "This ground here's pretty rough." Laura stretched her arms a little farther around him. "Tighter," Wyatt called and put the big roan into a canter.

She suspected he was grinning. She grinned reluctantly herself.

* * *

CHARLEY BASSETT, foot on the fence, peered into the stockyards cattle pens. His reins-trailing horse stood hipshot beside him, desultorily flicking his ears at the flies. There was a mort of dust. Cowboys were hazing the stock into pens, tally men were counting, one of them tying knots in a rope, the other man setting little marks in a book. Several railroad men were looking on and cracking jokes. Doc Holliday appeared, coming up behind Wyatt's chief deputy. Charlie, sensing another presence, glanced over his shoulder, goggling as if he couldn't believe it. "Heavens to Betsy! What's got you up at this time o' day? Why it ain't hardly three o'clock yet!"

"All right, all right. Matter of fact, I'm on a health bender. Up before noon and take a twenty-yard cruise, regular as clockwork. This is the first day." He glanced about, covering his nose with a handkerchief. "Terrible lot of beef coming in. What'll they ever do with it all?"

"I guess someone'll eat it. This is just the beginning. You ain't seen nothin.' The really big herds'll be rollin' up soon."

Doc took up a position alongside Charlie, both of them staring into the pens. Doc couldn't see enough of Charlie's face to gauge his expression. "Where's Kate?"

He practically had to shout to make himself heard above the cowboy yells and bawling steers.

Charlie Bassett scrunched a quick peek out of the corners of his eyes. Doc was still peering through the dust and bars trying to discover what was happening to all those horn-clacking cattle. While Bassett was fumbling around for words, not wanting to break it to Doc in a way that might turn the gambler's wrath upon him, Doc, twisting round, snarled, "Where is she, man? Can't you understand plain English?"

"It's, well, it's kind of a touchy subjeck. I..." Bassett's lips fluttered like those of a female about to bury her head in an apron. He saw Doc sway toward him. He wanted to run. Doc's eyes laid hold of him like strangling fingers and twisted him around. He could feel his knees half push out from under him. Doc hawked loudly and spat. The bastard might as well have fired his pistol. Charlie choked back a sob. He began to sag.

Doc's eyes looked like fish scales. Old Charlie damn near fell down, he was that scared.

"Where is she?"

By God, he *had* drawn a gun! The snout of it was boring straight through Charlie's middle.

Bassett's arms flopped. His knees turned to rubber. "Wiley's Hotel." He couldn't seem to get it out quick enough now. "Ringo's there. Kate's taken up with him."

Doc turned slowly. He got his foot back up there onto the rail and kind of hunched over, staring into the pens again. After perhaps thirty seconds he said, "What's the action here?"

Charlie, puzzled, tried to scrape himself together. "We been collectin' their hardware fast as they hit town. Leastways we sure as hell been tryin.' Don't look like Bat's goin' to git back with our deppities. Doc, you just can't do it. A gunfight right now would bring old Wyatt a heap o' misery. Goddam it, it might even git him kilt! Can't you..."

"Sure is a lot of cattle," Doc said. "A mighty lot of cattle."

* * *

BUT BACK IN his room some ten minutes later the torment in Doc could no longer be hidden. Back and forth he paced like a cooped up cougar. He whirled over to the dresser, stood for moments with fingers drumming against its dusty top. Impatient, he yanked open a drawer, got his shell belt off. Rolled about the holstered pistol he dropped it into the drawer, grimaced, and shut it.

About to turn he swung back. One hand went out and fastened itself to the haft of a knife. He stood there, face working; flung the blade viciously into the wall. He was in a hell of a temper as he walked across the room and yanked the knife free.

* * *

IT WAS night again and full dark now with Front Street stippled in light and shadow. There was plenty of business and noise and whooping as the crew from the herd, hard cash in their pockets, set out to catch up on things too long denied them. Doc looked neither to right nor left. Like the tracks he rolled down the middle of the street in his black frock coat and gambler's string tie until he came to the DEADLINE sign and crossed over, deliberately moving onto the south walk.

He pulled in his stride to move slower now, peering into the shabby, cheap rundown dens of vice and iniquity, out of many of which issued roars of laughter, drunken talk, maudlin songs, fiddles' screech, the tinpanny clang of out-of-tune pianos. From some, nickelodians ground out their tunes, from others came wrangling, shouts, and curses. Their lights flicked across him, briefly illumining that cold, and set face. At one point a drunk came reeling out onto the walk. At another, the gambler stepped over a prostrate body. A girl swept up to him, mouthing endearments, caught a gleam in his eyes, and backed away. Now and again someone, recognizing him, stopped dead in' his tracks.

Doc went on like the march of doom.

Like the wrath of God, he passed Wiley's Hang tree Gambling Hall, boots banging out a hollow thunder from the planks that rattled and sometimes gave with his step. Now he stood stopped before Wiley's Hotel. There was not so much noise here and very little light.

He stepped into a lobby that was cavernous with shadows. A solitary lamp, its wick turned low, burned untended on a counter beside an open book.

Doc entered a hallway where the distant sound of a ragtime piano grew as faint in the gloom as the frightened beat of a moth's fluttering wings. There was no light here but that seeping out from behind closed doors. Doc studied the doors, moving cat footed now. He found one that he appeared to favor and paused a long moment to crouch there eyeing it. The sound of feet came up behind him. A dancehall girl with a laughing cowhand turned into a room just across the way.

Doc, finally stirring, moved up to the door he'd been so steadily watching. He put out a hand as though to knock, decided against it, and twisted the knob. The door swung back, and Doc was into the room...

A lamp showed Kate on a couch, drink in hand. Between couch and door was a grimy table with a dozen bottles on it.

"What are you doing in this dump?" Doc growled.

"Well, well!" Kate laughed. "If it isn't the little deputy,"

"I certainly called the turn on you. A goddam whore, bed an' all! You're every last thing I named you, taking up with a crazy gunman like Ringo. Or maybe," Doc said, "you've got something in mind, something having to do with Wyatt."

"What the hell difference does it make to you where I go or who I take up with?" Her red lips writhed into a belligerent sneer. "Maybe I do have something in mind."

Doc's contemptuous stare let go of her and moved to Ringo standing with gun half-drawn in another door...

"If you're fixing to use that hog leg," Doc said, "use it."

Ringo snarled. "You got no right to come bustin' in here."

"I do what I please, whenever I please, where I please."

"You'd look good with your neck folded over a crate top, with your shiny boots flopped from its bottom. Now get the hell out."

"I came to see Kate. We've got some talking to do."

"Anything you got to say," Kate sneered, "you can say in front of him."

Doc's burning eyes whipped back to her. "I guess I've said it all. You slut."

He turned to go.

"Just a minute," Ringo growled, coming forward. "You don't talk to my woman like that."

"Save your blather. You can have your cheap whore."

"By God, I'm goin' to blast you apart!"

"I don't have a gun."

"Ain't you the brave one!" Ringo holstered the gun that was in his hand and, catching hold of its mate, lifted it out of his belt and slid it over the table where it stopped on the edge, scant inches from Doc's hand.

"You got one now," Ringo said.

Doc smiled coldly. Ignoring the pistol he reached up to rub at his neck. "I'm not fighting."

Ringo laughed, eyes jeering. Doc reddened. Doc's fingers squirmed.

"Go on," Ringo said. "Grab it."

When Doc just stood there the gunfighter guffawed. "The terrible Doc Holliday!" He laughed uproariously.

Kate said, "He won't fight. He promised Wyatt Earp to be a sweet little boy."

"I always figured," Ringo said, "you made that rep putting away a bunch of drunks." His lips curled back. "You're a yellow skunk."

Doc's hand inched toward the back of his collar.

"Watch him!" Kate screamed.

Ringo backed away a couple steps. Then he snorted.

"No more harm in him than a chambermaid. An old maid could chase him with a bundle of shucks. Have a drink, Holliday. Mebbe it'll put some backbone into you."

Picking up a glass half-filled with whiskey he dashed the contents into Doc's face.

Though he went stiff as a ramrod and white as chalk, Doc made no move. He gave Kate a long look, then turned and walked out. Ringo gaped, then doubled over with laughter. Kate ran to the door and fell against it, sobbing.

"Oh, Doc... Doc..." she cried in a whisper. She spun about. "Shut up, you ape!"

Doc stood trembling with rage in the hall. Through the door, he could hear the continued guffaws of Ringo. He shook as with an ague. Seething, face contorted, he stomped into the lobby and out onto the street.

EIGHT

THIS WAS a gala night at the Dodge House. A banner stretched over the side door read: DANCE AND CHURCH BAZAAR. Gay strains of music floated over the environs. There were a lot of folks catching their breath on the verandah, the ladies waggling their fans, the gents attempting with fingers to stretch too-tight collars, as Mayor Kelly and Laura stepped out for a moment.

At the nearby intersection, a shay was pulled up in the gloom of box elders, Wyatt impatiently fiddling with the reins. He'd been watching the exits for almost a half-hour. On seeing Laura he hauled in the weight, picked up the whip, and got ready to move. But Laura hadn't yet departed from Kelly. "It's a lovely dance; I'm truly sorry to have to be running off so soon."

"The floor," Kelly said, on an outgoing breath, "will be covered with busted hearts."

Laura laughed. "Good night, Mayor."

She came over the street and stepped up on the walk. She seemed to move slowly passing Wyatt's office, at least till she discovered the head-tipped shape with his boots on the desk could not possibly be the marshal. Just as she reached the intersection. Wyatt's shay drove up beside her. The marshal jumped out.

"Evenin,' Laura: Can I give you a lift?"

"What, again? I guess not." She smiled. "For such a short way I believe the walk will do me good. I seem to be inclined to eat more than I can afford."

She started to turn away, but Wyatt wouldn't leave it there. "It's early," he urged. "I've got to ride out to the bluffs. Thought you might care to keep me company."

"Thanks, but I have to get home."

"You're an expert on percentages. Let's analyze the situation."

"What situation?"

"The lady gambler who has convinced the town she's completely untouchable and the poor but honest marshal who's convinced despite all evidence that under her grand manners is a heart that beats in a real she-male woman."

"Wyatt, I'm *not* about to ride out of town with you."

"Why not? You're a gambler. You know all the odds. It isn't as though you had anything to fear. Everyone will tell you I'm devout, righteous, and completely dedicated to my work. In fact, I believe you said as much yourself. Now, who in the world could you be safer with?"

She was plainly intrigued, but oddly nervous, too. After studying him a moment she said, "I suppose the bluffs at night *are* rather splendid if there were light enough out there to see anything."

"Oh, there is," he assured her. "We might even hear a coyote howl."

"If you're sure there aren't any wolves around?" She reached out her hand.

Wyatt lost no time helping her into the vehicle. He hadn't really expected so much luck. He climbed in after her and got the horse moving.

The bluffs were only a few miles out of Dodge and in the daytime presented a rather exciting view of the town and the rolling country that lay roundabout it. There wasn't any moon but driving along the bluffs on the old dirt road one did catch a pretty stimulating view, what with all the lights of the town spread out like a glimmer of jewels against black velvet.

"It's beautiful," Laura said. "I'm glad you persuaded me to come. I hadn't realized Dodge had grown so much these last weeks."

Wyatt stopped the rig, wrapped the reins about the whipstock. "Want to step down and walk a bit?"

"Well, just a little," she said dubiously.

He lifted her down.

"You're very strong, Marshal."

"You don't need to look so scared," he said.

"I'm not scared. Not really."

"All right," he said. "Now tell me why you came."

She tipped her head, watching him. "I've been wondering what makes a man like you tick. I've been wondering about you ever since that evening you arrested me in Dodge, watching you drive yourself and the men around you, walking into terrible danger every moment you're on duty. I've wondered if what everyone says is really true."

"What do they say?"

"They say you're not a man but a machine, a 'killing' machine. I don't very often let myself get curious about people, but I have to admit to being curious about you. Are you human, Mr. Earp? Or are you just a trigger finger?"

He caught her to him and kissed her fiercely. At first, she struggled to break the embrace, then relaxed against him, eyes big as teacups. When he turned her loose, she drew back, puzzled and half frightened.

"Doesn't that answer your question?"

"Oh, Wyatt...Wyatt...."

He brought her into his arms again, her own coming up to close about his neck. His lips closed on hers and she came fully against him. How long this went on neither one of them knew but suddenly, gasping, she broke away. She moved blindly off a few steps, panting. He came up behind her. She said, "We'd better stop this."

He grasped her shoulders, forcing her to face him. "No, Wyatt, no!"

"Who's the one that's not human? Stop making yourself unreachable. You've got a heart. Why not listen to it?"

"There's nothing in this for me," she said. "You're a legalized gunslinger. I'm not going to end up like Kate Fisher."

"Laura. Good Lord, I want to marry you!"

"I can't understand that. You hardly know me."

"But well enough to know I love you."

She slipped out of his hands. "It wouldn't work, Wyatt. I'm not falling in love with any badge toter."

"But I wouldn't be a badge toter all my life. We could start a ranch."

"You haven't a life to share. Your life belongs to the law. I've seen too many marshals' wives dry up and wither away before their time. You're Wyatt Earp, the Iron Marshal. You'll never be anything else, I wouldn't want you to."

"I could be anything you wanted me to be," Wyatt said earnestly. "We'll buy some cows."

"No," Laura said with considerable emphasis. "My mother had cows and so did my sister. I told you about them."

"But if we want each other, Lord, there's plenty of other work I could take up."

"Is there? No, Wyatt." She shook her head. "You'll never get away from your reputation. Wherever you go there'll be a badge and a gun."

He dropped his arms. "I expect you're not much of a gambler, after all." He pulled himself together. "Let's get on back to town."

* * *

FRONT STREET APPEARED DESERTED. In front of the Marshal's Office Charlie Bassett lounged with his shoulders braced against a post, humming somewhat off-key a dancehall tune called the Cuckoo Song in time with the music coming out of the Dodge House. Charlie tapped one foot and then tapped the other.

There was nothing rowdy about the Dodge House. Everything there moved with utmost decorum as befitted a church sociable. Take that table with the punch bowl-real punch, no spikes. The platform was provided with a fiddle, a banjo, and a piano, and three sweating men who were top hands at making them talk. All about the sides of the room little knots of people were engaged with their various conversations and, out on the floor in embraces of varying closeness, about twelve couples were doing the Little Foot. A group of the town's leading citizens, mostly merchants, were gathered off to one side about the corpulent shape of the Dodge City mayor. Right in the midst of the most earnest part of whatever it was that Kelly had on his mind a racket of gunfire shook the room's windows. A gabble of yells burst out of the street and chin music, band music, and everything else including the mayor came to a stop in a kind of stunned silence.

Charlie Bassett flew jangling into the room. "It's that long-legged, fat-assed sonofabitch, Pierce! His crew has treed Front Street. No one's to step outside of this room. I mean that!" He caught Kelly's eye and the mayor waddled over. Bassett said, "Climb out a back window an' try to find Earp. Go on, get a wiggle on! I'll do what I can to keep them in hand."

Outside it was pretty bad, sure enough. Through the wind and dust and the Rebel yells twenty-five big-hatted horsebackers flourishing pistols were filling the street with a bedlam of shouting, riding their horses up and down the walks and some of them even into places of business, shooting out windows, roping stovepipes, and going skallyhooting off with them, and otherwise acting like a bunch of wild Indians, while a trio of others, non-participants, lounged in their saddles enjoying this frivolity. One of these was Johnny Ringo, mean, vindictive, and full of rotgut. The larger of the other pair who were taking this in with a vast satisfaction was Pierce himself, old Abel Head Pierce, better known as "Shanghai," the Rhode Island-born son of a blacksmith who had come into Texas at the age of nine-teen and got into the cattle business through the back door by building a fence. He was an extremely loud talker and frequently given to exaggeration. He was also tight-fisted and seldom forgot an injury and at this particular tier of his life, he was at the height of his arrogance as a Texas cattle king, wealthy, powerful, and bossing a tough crew. He had a foot-long cigar poled through his fat lips and both his saddle and gear blazed with silver.

"Lively bunch, eh, Ringo?" he said, and back-handed the gunfighter unexpectedly in the belly, laughing uproariously at the man's pained expression.

"Yeah," Ringo managed to grunt somewhat feebly.

"Can't you show a little enthusiasm?" Shanghai demanded, vigorously puffing his cigar. "This here oughta learn them once an' fer all who owns the cow towns, don't you reckon?"

Ringo spat and said "Yeah," and looked like for two cents he'd blow the big auger plumb loose of his saddle.

Amid the dust and the confusion of all that yelling and horsing around, Shanghai's foreman, the other gent sitting there, spied Bassett approaching from out of an alley, He didn't know who this was but had caught the glint of the badge on his vest and, lifting out his six-shooter, laid the long-barreled weapon ready for service across the knobs of his drawn-up knees.

Bassett, stomping out of the dust, yelled. "Call them fools off before somebody gits hurt!"

"Who the hell are you?" Shanghai roared.

"I'm the deppity marshal."

"You go tell your boss I'm not about to settle fer anythin' less'n his personal attention."

"By Gawd, I'm puttin' you under arrest, Pierce!"

Shanghai laughed. "You hear that, Ringo? I'm under arrest."

"Yeah," Ringo said, and put a gob of tobacco juice within an inch of Bassett's boot.

The deputy marshal caught hold of Shanghai's coat. Ringo's hands dropped over his gun butts. There was a noticeable tightening of the supercharged air; then Basset swearing, went for his gun. Two reports cracked out before Bassett cleared leather. Charlie staggered, arms flopping, backed a few hurried steps, and went down like a log.

* * *

IN THE BACK room at the Long Branch, Cockeyed Frank Loving, dealing faro, put his head to one side in an attitude of listening.

Doc, looking up, rubbed the back of his neck. "Reminds me of hell emigrating on cartwheels."

"What say we quit? I'd like to get out there."

"Frank, my boy, just keep passing those pasteboards. I'm not breaking this run."

Half a dozen slugs crashed into the room. Great shards fell out of the room's single window and a nude lady in a frame resting against the far wall suddenly became endowed with a second belly button that went all the way through her like the tunnel of a mine. A bottle shattered on a table by Doc's left elbow. Loving's face turned livid. Doc, never turning a hair, eyed his cards.

"For Chrissake, Doc!"

"Deal."

Back at the church sociable in the ballroom of the

Dodge House, everyone but the piano thumper was huddled in a corner with the shaking women. A great and pervading quiet appeared to be spreading over the street outside. Some of Pierce's crew came stumbling through the doors, wild-eyed and powdered with trail dust. Shanghai tramped in with Ringo and his cold-jawed foreman.

"Well," Pierce said, "What've we got here? Look back there, Johnnie. I'd say some of them jaspers has been havin' a hoedown. You wanta dance with them hoors, boys?"

Shocked gasps flew up from the outraged gathering. Pierce put on a scowl. His foreman said, "This ain't a very hospitable outfit. Mebbe we ought to learn them some manners."

A merchant said from a group at one side, "Better get those bums of yours south of the deadline."

Shanghai roared, "You hear that, boys? These here bluenoses don't appreciate friendliness. We ain't good enough for 'em! They like our money but don't figure we're fit to take hold of their women."

Several of his whiskered trail hands grinned. One fellow yanked out a six-shooter and brought down a lamp in a cascade of oil and shattered glass. The rest of them whooped like a bunch of Comanches.

Shanghai dug out his own cannon then. He put a couple of slugs above the piano man's fingers. "Strike up a tune!"

With the command, Pierce's crew bolted for the heifers. Several of the crowd made an effort to interfere and were promptly knocked sprawling. Ringo and Pierce's foreman covered the crowd with their pistols while his crew seized the women and, dragging them out into the cleared center of the hall, began to wrestle them about more as though they were steers than anything human. The man at the piano pounded out the Sailor's Hornpipe. Two of the trail hands, dancing in rapt togetherness, burst suddenly apart and started pummeling each other.

The fight swiftly spread, sweeping over the bandstand as the pair's compadres joined the melee with an assortment of whoops and swear words. The banjo picker and the violinist leaped incontinently from the platform, abandoning their instruments, digging for the tules. In less time than it takes to relate, the banjo became a short-lived club and some unfortunate shopkeeper with blood and deep scratches on the sides of his face went howling from the shambles in a froth of splinters and fiddle strings.

One trail hand got knocked into the punch bowl and sat there grinning from ear to ear. A horse charged snorting and squealing through the carnage, the cowboy astride him catapulting from his back in a flying leap for the chandelier which came down like the walls of Jericho. All this while the pale piano pounder's nicotine-stained fingers had been flying over the keys like a bat out of Carlsbad. But now, in the very midst of *Miss Mulligan's Piano-Fortay*, the ivories went astonishingly still with the effect of a Fall River factory shutting down. All over the room, there was a hiatus in the racket as men and even the ladies, what was left of them, paused to catch second wind and exchange bewildered looks with those nearest.

As ripples spread out across rocked waters the vortex of the hush appeared to be thickest about the main entrance and the reason for this was pretty soon apparent as increasing numbers of those present discovered Marshal Wyatt Earp standing there with a rifle.

The fool in the punch bowl clambered out and stood shamefacedly dripping while the rest of his outfit, cautiously shifting, took up a stand behind Shanghai and Ringo as the women took refuge in the arms of their men. Neither moving nor speaking, Wyatt stood like something hacked out of stone, the hot glare of his eyes ominously fastened on Pierce. Shanghai himself looked like some lout of a kid caught with both paws in the cash box. His long neck turned red, and he swelled up like a carbuncle. "I thought this would pull you out of your hide hole! Now, you goddam gun-whackin' sonofabitch, you're goin' to pay up with interest fer this scar you give me in Wichita!"

Wyatt said, whisper-soft, "If you varmints are itchin' for a real jamboree I may only get two or three of you, but the first one down is going to be Pierce. Get out of those shell belts an' belly up to the wall. Anybody I see with a gun in his fist will sure as hell get it broken. Start peelin.'"

"You better start prayin'," Shanghai blustered. "You've pulled your last bluff!" And Ringo chipped in, "He sure has, Boss. Let's work him over."

But it was all too apparent that none of the rest of them thought Earp was bluffing. Belts and pistols were dropping all over like a flight of tired geese coming down for water. Then, just when it looked as though the frolic was over, Pierce's foreman palmed up his cutter and started blowing out the lamps. "Take him, boys!" Pierce yelled, and the whole crew surged forward with a howl, grabbing up their weapons.

But the avalanche stopped as if it had hit a stone

wall when dapper Doc Holliday with a gun in each fist stepped through the side door. He didn't have to say a word. One look at the killer blaze of his stare was enough to take the starch from pretty near anything. Doc grinned like a wolf and the guns dropped out of their fists in a hurry.

But not all of them. Pierce still had his and, with his eyes shuttling back and forth between Earp and Holliday, he looked like a man who was plumb hankering to use it. Ringo, still armed, growled, "Call the play, Shanghai," and Pierce's cold-jawed foreman said, "We kin take them buggers!"

"But you'll get it first, Shanghai," Wyatt said stonily. "They will be scrapin' up your pieces all over Ford County."

Doc bored in on the flank. Those nearest fell back before his advance. You could smell the death on him, you could see it in his face. He stopped about ten yards away from Wyatt.

Pierce didn't know what to do. He'd been waiting a long while for a chance to cut Wyatt down, but he sure wasn't craving to die in the process. The muzzle of Wyatt's rifle was leveled straight at his brisket.

"You may get me," Wyatt said quietly, "but if you don't unbuckle inside of five seconds there's goin' to be a double funeral, and I'm starting the count now. One... two... three..."

Sweat popped out all over Pierce's face. That goddam Earp would just as lief do it. He said like he was talking through a mouthful of worms, "You heard him, boys. Throw down your irons."

Doc laughed nastily. "First sensible thing you ever said."

There was a halfhearted grumble of protest from those of the crew who were not directly in the immediate line of fire. Wyatt paid no attention to this face-saving gesture. He stepped forward, the snout of his gun barrel not ten inches from Shanghai's paunch.

More guns dropped. But Ringo, thinking he saw a chance, tipped his up. A blast from Doc tore the weapon from his fingers and he spun onto his knees clutching a shattered arm.

"Anybody else feel lucky?" Doc asked.

"Scrape him up," Wyatt said, "an' let's move."

Shanghai and his foreman pulled Ringo onto his feet. The gunfighter snarled, "You. ain't heard the last of this, Holliday!"

"That's because I'm in a charitable mood."

Pierce and his gangling foreman, half supporting the cursing Ringo between them, led the way to the street, the sullen crew straggling after them under the guns of Doc and Earp. At the door, Wyatt turned, "Anybody hurt here?"

Several of the least cowed townsmen shook their heads. "We're all right," one of the merchants said.

"Somebody get a doctor for Charlie Bassett. A couple of you boys pick up that hardware and bring it over to the jail. The rest had better go home. We'll hold court on this business first thing tomorrow morning. I want all of you there."

As Wyatt came into the street it appeared that Doc had things well under control. No one was giving him any trouble. "I guess," Wyatt said, "you don't want my thanks."

"Can I put thanks in my pocket? Will it get me back

that good run of luck? Let's just say the account is paid in full."

Wyatt said, "That suits me fine." He looked at Pierce's outfit. "All right, get going. You'll find the jail straight ahead."

* * *

SOMETIME LATER, with all the drovers locked up, Wyatt, at an open shed stable behind the Dodge House, went through the business of bedding down his horse. Just as he started away from the place Laura's voice came worriedly out of the shadows.

"Wyatt?"

"I'm all right," Wyatt said.

She came against him. "Oh, Wyatt!"

"What are you shaking for? Good lord, girl!"

"I was so frightened. I've never been so scared in my life. What if you'd been killed?"

"Would you have cared?"

Her arms tightened. "Everything's changed. All my values have gone topsy turvy. I don't seem even to know my own mind anymore. I don't know what's wrong or what's right, and I don't care."

NINE

THE NEXT DAY when Wyatt stepped into the Long Branch Saloon on his rounds he found Doc alone at a table, hardly yet well started on his afternoon whiskey. Wyatt said, "How's tricks, Doc?"

"Pretty tricky." Doc scowled.

Wyatt dropped into a chair. "Just thought you might like to know," he said smiling, "there's about to be one less star packer around here."

"Charlie worse?" Doc asked, looking up.

"Charlie's all right."

Doc peered at him quizzically. "So you're turnin' in the tin."

"Heading for Californy," Wyatt said. "Going to try ranching. I've decided to take that good advice you were passing out a while back and get out of this business before I turn into another Cotton Wilson."

"Smart man."

"Laura's coming with me. We're going to travel in double harness. Would you like to congratulate the prospective groom?"

"She's a lady," Doc said. This, coming from him, was quite a testimonial.

"We'd take it kindly if you could see fit to come to the wedding. That is, if it won't take you away too long from your poker game."

Doc delicately hoisted his whiskey, grunted unintelligibly, and tossed down the slug. "Deal me out," he said, putting the glass down. My forte is funerals. I'd be no good to you there."

Wyatt stood up. "Well," Doc sighed, "good luck to both of you. You're smart to be getting out of this country."

"Why don't you try your luck down the road?" Doc shook his head. He poured himself another whiskey.

* * *

LATER, up in his room at the Dodge House, Doc wearily sat down and stretched out on his bed. Kate came in without knocking and put her back to the window. Her face showed lines of dissipation and weariness went deep into her. Doc didn't even bother to get up.

Lips trembling, she said hardly louder than a kind of forlorn whisper, "Doc, for God's sake, take me back!"

"No."

"Please. I'll do anything, anything you say. I don't care how you treat me."

Doc, getting up, went over to the dresser, leaning on it, head hung over like a beat-out horse, with his back about all Kate could get a good look at.

"Give me another chance," she pleaded, only one blink away from tears.

Doc swung around and faced her. "I never gave you much of a chance. But I'm not blaming you, either, not for anything, Kate. Maybe, maybe it could have been different if I'd been right for you in the first place. But we can't turn back the clock."

"It ain't too late. I'll be good to you, Doc, I swear it!"

She rushed over, intending to fling her arms around him, but he pushed her away. "It's too late for the both of us. Do something better for yourself while you can."

Kate, openly begging, said, "Doc... Doc, don't let me go back there."

Holliday turned away as though exhausted. "Go," he sighed. "Just leave me alone."

Color sprang into Kate's face. Her eyes flashed. "I'll see you dead!" And she went storming out, the door slamming behind her.

Doc reeled over to the bed and fell onto it.

* * *

AT THE MARSHAL'S Office Wyatt, cleaning out his desk was throwing things into the trash can, practically everything he figured to have no further use for. A clean sweep, he told himself, nodding and whistling.

Charlie Bassett came in with his arm in a sling. Wyatt eyed him and grunted but, not seeing the telegram Charlie was carrying, paid him no particular attention. Chances are, in his present frame of mind, all perked up with the thoughts of the future he envisioned with Laura, he would not even have noticed had Charlie stuck a gun in his face. He went blithely on, throwing away old dodgers and whatnot.

Dumping a pile of records, he said, "These are all dead ducks, Charlie; no use clutterin' the place up with 'em. But these," he grinned, tossing a handful of expense vouchers across to the deputy, "I guess you'll be finding a use for. Every time you step out to the backhouse the Council will expect to get one of these from you."

He sent his marshal's badge spinning across the desk. "That's yours, too. Keep a good shine on it. Well," he grinned, slamming shut the empty drawers, "I guess that winds me up as a lawman. For good, I hope."

Bassett's continued silence appeared abruptly to register with Wyatt. His head came up, wheeled around. He stared for a long still moment at the disturbed expression on Charlie's face. Then he saw the telegram and stretched out his hand. Bassett pushed it across the desk.

He tore open the envelope, peered at Charlie again, and dropped his glance to the lines of type. His jaw turned grim as the message got home to him.

Out on the bluffs Laura said, sometime later, "I should have known you couldn't quit. Something like this was bound to happen."

They were standing under the big tree near *the* wash, their horses behind them on dragging reins munching at whatever grass they could find.

"Laura, please. After all, Virgil's my brother. He's in trouble. He needs me. Is that too much to understand?"

"I understand I've been rather foolish to have imagined you could ever love anyone. Go if you must. I won't stand in your way. But we're not going to start anything at all as long as you've got a gun in your hand."

"But, honey?"

"What makes you feel he needs you more than I do?" Her lips firmed; her chin came up. It's your choice, Wyatt. Either you cut clean away from guns."

"Or what?" he said, frowning.

"I've given up my way of life for you. I told you when we first met, right here on this very spot, I wouldn't follow you from town to town, sitting in the dark, expecting every moment someone to come riding out with news that you've been killed. I won't do it, Wyatt. If your love isn't strong enough."

"I'll swear I'll never touch a gun again after Tombstone."

"You'll never be through with it. Your reputation will find you wherever we are."

"But Laura, this is my brother!"

"And I'm the girl you were going to marry. If your brother means more to you than a wife."

"That's not fair!"

"It's as fair as what you're proposing to do."

"Don't ask me to let Virg down."

"But it's all right to let *me* down. Is that it?" she said sharply. "I told you once no man would ever get me to pullma plow. Those were pretty empty words, I guess. I'd give up anything, go anyplace for you. I'll face anything with you, except a gun. You've got to meet me halfway, Wyatt."

He said, barely breathing, "I've got to go to Virg."

"Then go!" she cried. "Clean up Tombstone! There's a hundred tough towns on the frontier practically begging for the great Wyatt Earp. Go ahead, clean them all up."

She turned her back on him, stood there shaking. Coming up behind her he softly kissed her neck, but she stood there stiffly, completely withdrawn from him.

"I love you," he said, and let his hands drop tiredly. He looked at her a moment and, sighing, went over and caught up the reins of his horse, pulled himself into the saddle, and rode off up the road in the direction of town.

There was anguish in Laura's face as she stared after him. She half lifted a hand but, even with the tears, her chin stayed up. She would not let herself call him back.

ON THE ROAD from Dodge City that same afternoon, in the dust and glare and rattle of wheels, an Army caisson slowly crept through the heat.

Wyatt, a weary and saddened man lost in bleak thoughts, was hunched over the driver's seat listlessly holding the reins in gloved hands.

Behind him, a horseman was hurrying to catch up. Not until he'd yelled half a dozen times did Wyatt come out of his brooding and pull up. He must have recognized Doc, but his expression held no particular interest and, certainly, no curiosity.

"Afternoon, Marshal," the gambler grinned, reining in. "You just out for the ride?"

"About seven hundred miles' worth."

"Tombstone, eh? A remarkable coincidence," Doc said dryly, lighting up one of the crooked stogies he favored. "I was heading that way myself. Thought the climate down there might be better for my cough."

"At least you won't have so far to go when you leave."

Never knew you to be interested in your health. What is this, something recent?"

"Well," Doc said, rasping a hand along his jaw, "to tell you the truth, it's a matter of finances mostly. Nobody will give me any play around Dodge; I haven't any choice in the matter. It's move or starve. I don't suppose, even if I still had those nags, I could sell them back to Shanssey for anything like what he charged me for them. Took my whole roll," he said with a parched grin. "Twenty grand. Still, he wasn't a bad coot. Mind if I ride along?"

"It's a free range, they tell me." Wyatt sighed. "Where's your gear?"

Doc, taking a deck of cards from his pocket, held them up. Then he got off his horse, twisted the reins about the horn, headed him for town, and slapped him on the rump. He climbed into the empty half of Wyatt's seat. Wyatt joggled the lines and the wagon moved on.

"Be a dry ride," he said presently.

Doc had taken off his coat. He reached back now and got a bottle from the pocket. He exchanged a look with Wyatt. Both men grinned.

The days slipped past.

About the middle of an unusually warm afternoon as they were traveling through a region of gray shale ridges, deep cut banks, and stony outcrops festooned with wolf's candle and Spanish dagger, Wyatt staring off across that gray haze of baked rock, remarked, "Another town up ahead."

Doc scrunched his eyes against the glare. "I don't see it," he said irritably.

"Over there," Wyatt grunted. "On top of that mesa. Don't you see those mine hoists?"

"I'll take your word for it."

"Where there's mines," Earp said, "there ought to be money. And where there's money there'll be people."

"Never knew it to fail." Doc waved a hand. "There's a hell's smear of cartridge cases strewed along the sides of this road."

"There's a rusted six-shooter," Wyatt said, pointing.

"And a rifle without any stock," Doc added. "You reckon this is the place?"

"Looks enough like it from what Virg said."

"Well, we'll know when we get there."

Wyatt pulled up after a bit and sat stiffly listening. "Sounded like shots."

Doc said irascibly, "Them cartridge cases don't just grow there."

They went on, steadily climbing, gusts of wind whipped up out of the gullies blowing hotter and rougher through the gray immensity of baked desolation. Doc growled presently, "You ever see the beat of this? Must be the back door to hell. Even the goddam creosote bushes ain't hardly bigger than burro weeds. If this is Tombstone she's rightly named."

They came out of their climb on the brow of a hill that was studded with headboards and whitewashed wooden crosses, both of them bearded and grimy and haggard. Doc, peering around, had a bad coughing spell. "Boot Hill," he croaked when he got back his breath. "We've come seven hundred miles to reach a land of gray rock and corpses!"

They saw the town spread out ahead of them. "Must be three thousand people still unplanted around these diggings," Wyatt said.

"Well, there's still a mite of room on that hill," Doc said dryly.

Wyatt drove on. Doc said suddenly, "You know, by God, I feel cooler. Breathe better, too. How high do you reckon we are?"

"About as near to heaven as we're likely to get." Wyatt pointed out a sign that read O.K. CORRAL. "Want to pull up there?"

"Let's drive on a ways."

Wyatt pointed down a side street. "There's the Wells-Fargo office."

"I'll try the tables first."

Wyatt's mouth tightened somewhat but he kept his thoughts to himself. He pulled over to the side, pulled around in a wide circle, and stopped the wagon in front of an old man lounging against the fence. He looked like a stable hand and talked as if he had stock in the local Chamber.

"Welcome to Tombstone, gents," he hailed, straightening up. "You're a-standin' right now on the very spot where Curly Bill downed Marshal Fred White. Yes, sir, biggest town in the entire Southwest. Bar none. You figger to be here long?"

"We'll be around for a spell," Wyatt said, getting down with a noticeable stiffness. "Put these horses and wagon up for sale. We want a fair price."

Doc, peering around, said, "Where's a decent hotel?"

"Next street down." The ancient waved. "Cosmopolitan, absolutely first class. None finer. I'll fetch a buckboard an' take your gear over."

"Where at," Wyatt said, "does Virgil Earp live?"

"The marshal? Straight down Fremont Street.

That's this 'un, right back the way you come. Can't miss it. On the corner of First, only house there." He peered at them curiously. "Don't believe I caught your name."

"Didn't throw it." Wyatt gave Doc a wave of the hand. "Be seeing you around," he said, and tramped stiff-legged off, following the toothless gabber's directions.

PART THREE

TOMBSTONE

TEN

IN THE VIRGIL EARP KITCHEN, Wyatt sat at the table with his assembled brothers, Morgan, Virgil, and James, swallowing the last few mouthfuls of a bang-up dinner. It was full dark out now. In the light of the coal-oil lamps Betty (Virgil's wife), cleaning off the plates, looked about eight months gone with child. Tommy Earp, age four, was ensconced on Wyatt's knee.

"Lordy," Wyatt exclaimed, passing a hand across the tightness of his belt. "That was the best assortment of groceries my stomach's got hold of in more time than I care to think back on. I'd just about forgot a home-cooked meal could be that good."

He slipped an affectionate hand about Betty's waist. "I think I'll have to steal you from Virg."

"By golly, Wyatt," Morgan said after the laugh, "you're goin' to be the only bachelor Earp left in the tribe. I got a family goin' in Deadwood an' even little Jimmy here is tyin' the knot quick's he can git back to Californy."

James Earp said indignantly, "What do you mean, 'little' Jimmy? I'll be nineteen next month."

Betty, rumpling his hair, said, "You'd better be having a man-to-man talk with your brothers."

James blushed. "I know a heap more'n you figger I do."

They all laughed again.

Morgan said, "When are you fixin' to get hitched, Wyatt?"

Wyatt, frowning, shook his head. "I don't know," he sighed on an outgoing breath. The silence got a little uncomfortable. Betty lugged off an armload of dishes to the sink. Virgil drummed his fingers on the table.

Betty, looking back, said, "I guess it's time for the women and kids to run out and play. Come along, Tommy. As a matter of fact, it's high time you were in bed."

"Aw, Mom. Do I got to?"

"Come along. Your uncles will all be here tomorrow."

"Good night, Uncle Wyatt."

"Good night, Deputy."

Tommy said good night to the others and his father kissed him. Reluctantly the lad took hold of his mother's hand. As they were going through the door, Betty said over her shoulder, "It was mighty nice of you to come. I... I only wish it were under pleasanter circumstances."

"Seems pretty upset," Morgan said when she was gone.

"It's the pregnancy." Virgil frowned. "She's all the time after me to give up the badge. Hell, you know how women are. Any of you boys want cigars?"

They all lighted up, the older three watching with

some amusement as James, the youngest, got his going and vigorously puffed on it. But soon, he surreptitiously set it aside. "Think I'll go out and take a look at the horses," he said.

Virgil said, "Morg an' Jim know the setup here. The whole trouble's them Clanton's," he told Wyatt. "You know, Ike has a ranch outside the city limits. Got the toughest bunch of gunslingers for a crew you ever laid eyes on. Been rustling Mexican cattle, an' he owns the county sheriff."

"Who's that?" said Wyatt.

"Old friend of yours, Cotton Wilson."

"He's here?"

"Yep, an' sittin' pretty as a hawg on ice."

"I tell you," Virgil growled, "we was sure enough sick when we found Ike owned him, lock, stock an' barrel. Boils down to this: Clanton's runnin' wild in the county and Cotton is protectin' him. He's got a ranch full of Mex'kin cattle and he's sure as hell got to move 'em. Handiest place he can ship from is Tombstone. You see where that leaves us? He can't realize a nickel so long as we control the town."

"That's about the size of it," Morgan agreed. "The bastard's organized, and he's mean. We can't keep him out of this town forever, not without we get help. That's why we sent for you."

Wyatt said, "What about these people around here? They stand back of you?"

"John Clum will, anyway. He was Apache Agent here. Now he edits and publishes *The Epitaph*, Tombstone's paper. Some of the other city fathers will probably swing in line once they know you're callin' the shots."

"We've all agreed," Jimmy said, rejoining them still somewhat green about the gills, "you're to ramrod this go around."

"One thing," Morgan said, "that bothers me, and I'll get it off my chest right now. That's this: there'll be a mort of gabble about you ridin' with Doc Holliday."

Wyatt stiffened and set his jaw, but Morgan went on doggedly. "He's about the worst damn killer on the whole frontier. I had to run him out of Deadwood account of him borin' a couple of prominent citizens. It don't look good, him comin' here with you."

"The straight of it is Doc saved my bacon in Dodge, and more than once. I can't go back on that. Also, in spite of his faults, he's a man of his word. He's got a place here, boys, so long as he deals straight and keeps his gun out of trouble."

"I didn't know you were huggin' an' kissin.'"

"We're not. But Doc's showed me he deserves a square deal. If I stay, he stays."

"Well, hell," Morgan gruffed, "if you say so, that settles it."

Wyatt said, "Let's get down to cases. First thing, as I see it, we've got to let the Clanton's know this town is closed to them, and we've got to keep it that way. Then we've got to get the run of the county." He regarded them thoughtfully. "I'll get a letter off to a feller that can mebbe iron that out for us. Now let's have a look at that map."

Virgil spread out a map on the table and they all got up to peer over his shoulder.

* * *

THE NEXT MORNING, Wyatt stepping into the *Epitaph* office, found J.P. Clum, owner, and publisher, back of his desk thumbing through a stack of freshly printed quarter cards.

"Mornin'," Wyatt said, and introduced himself. "I'm here," he added, "to see what we can do about this matter of Ike Clanton."

Clum scrutinized him sharply. Presently he nodded and handed Wyatt one of the cards. "That ink's a little wet, but I would think this might bring him right out into the open."

Wyatt read it and grunted. "It ought to make him squirm."

"Mr. Earp," Clum said, "I'd like you to know how glad this town is we've got a man of your caliber interested in our problems. You may count on the full support of my paper. I know twenty men you can make special deputies. I can get fifty more if it turns out you need them."

"That's a nice thing to know. I certainly couldn't do much without some public support."

"We're with you. We're right behind you. If you believe we need vigilantes."

"I'd like to do this legally." Pointing to the cards, he said, "Like this."

* * *

COTTON WILSON WAS REARED back in a chair trying to stir up a breeze with his hat when Wyatt stepped into the Sheriff's Office. He had a stack of

Clum's cards tucked under his arm. Nodding at Cotton he placed these face down on the desk.

"I've been rather expecting you to drop in, Cotton. You're looking fine, real prosperous. Understand you've done a first-rate job looking after the interests of the outlaws hereabouts."

Cotton grinned somewhat edgily. "I ain't complainin' none. This here's the best-payin' job I ever latched onto."

"I can well believe that." Wyatt was hard put to treat the man with even a show of courtesy. "I don't suppose," he said, "you dropped by to shoot the breeze. Now that you've laid down your character, Cotton, maybe you'd like to turn your cards up and say straight out what errand you're on."

Wilson said unabashedly, "Ike wants to make you a deal."

"What kind of deal?"

"Well, he's got all these cattle pilin' upon him. If you'll give him the nod so's he can ship out of Tombstone, you an' him' U git along powerful easy." He grinned at Wyatt boldly. "There might even be a few bucks in it fer you."

"That's very generous of Ike."

"We think so. Then I kin tell him it's a deal?"

"I didn't say that."

The sheriff, frowning, eyed him more carefully. "Don't be a goddam fool all your life! Lemme draw you a picture. Someday, mebbe, when you're so stove up you can't hardly put one foot ahead of the other, they'll stake you out on a pension of prob'ly twenty stinkin' dollars a month, an' I'm talkin' about if you live that long. Say what you want, Ike's a good guy to work for.

I've got me a ranch now an' twenty-five thousand tucked away in the bank. It don't bother my sleep a particle."

Wyatt said coldly, "It might bother mine, though."

"Seems about time you got offa that pulpit, Ellsworth, Wichita, Dodge, Jesus Christ! What's it got you but a assload of misery? A woman who..."

"I think you better get out of here, Cotton."

"Be smart for once in your life. Clanton's big. Too big fer you to monkey with. He's got friends, even a Congressman. Owns two judges an' every piss-ant lawman in three counties except you Earp's. He's got a million dollars' worth of steers on his place an' he's sure as hell goin' to move 'em."

Leaning close, with his breath closing round Wyatt like a fog, he growled, "Your cut adds up to fifty thousand cash."

"Golly. Hard to believe I could be worth so much."

"You ain't. Like I said, Ike's a good man to tie to."

"So's the devil, if you don't mind getting singed in the process."

"Ha-ha!" Wilson laughed, and then his eyes winnowed down. "Fifty thousand's a heap better than a hole in the ground. You think about that."

"Tell me," Wyatt said. "How would you feel about me running for county sheriff?"

Wilson's lips skinned back. "That ain't scarin' me."

"I guess everybody sees things different." Wyatt picked up one of the cards from the face-down stack and pushed it over to the sheriff. "Here's a little souvenir you can tote back to your boss."

Wilson turned it over, FIREARMS FORBIDDEN IN THE CITY LIMITS OF TOMBSTONE.

The skin of Wilson's cheeks pulled tight. He said on an outrush of anger, "Think you can make that stick?"

"I guess we'll pretty soon find out."

* * *

WILSON LOST no time getting out to the Clanton ranch. He found Ike Clanton tipped back in a chair against the front of the house catching himself a little shuteye in the shade of a pulled-down hat. He pushed the felt off his face when he heard the approaching horse. Wilson swung down without opening his mouth, walked up to Ike, and dropped the card in his lap. Ike read it casually, tore it up, and got out of his chair. "That his answer?"

"He figures to pull the town from under you, Ike."

The sheriff followed Clanton into the house. Finn and Billy Clanton, Ike's brothers, were at the kitchen table, eating. Their mother, tired and worn and half sick from work, was scrubbing out a blackened skillet over a tub of greasy water. "Earp's barrin' guns in Tombstone," Ike said.

Finn looked up, scowling. Considerable older and meaner than Billy, he shoved back from the table, wickedly cursing.

"Ain't but one thing to do, Finn," Ike told them. Round up Wes Fuller, Ringo, Claiborne an' the McLowry brothers. Tell them I want 'em heeled to the teeth. Tonight we'll ride in an' put this business to the test."

"Hey, Ike!" young Billy cried. "How about me?"

"If you're growed enough, you're old enough. Come along if you want."

Mrs. Clanton stepped away from the tub. "You can go and get Finn and yourself shot to dollrags, but you leave Billy out of this! He's only a boy."

"He looks big enough to me. You had tried workin' my tail off when I was his age."

"You ain't gettin' that boy killed."

"Don't worry about me, Maw. I kin outshoot them Earp's left-handed."

"Get aboard your horse an' get whackin,' Finn," Ike Clanton said, looking hard at the old woman. "If the kid wants to come along with us you're not stoppin' him."

* * *

A PLACARD on the Fremont Street front of Scheiffelin's Hall announced:

EDDIE FOY & COMPANY—IN PERSON
—TONIGHT.

Wyatt, near the entrance, stood unarmed in front of this poster checking over the miners and other patrons standing in line as they filed past. There was a deal of racket coming out of the place. A roar of applause shook the windows and the voice of Eddie himself, as the din somewhat abated, could be heard greeting the vociferous crowd. Wyatt, turning out of the line one fellow wearing a pistol, said, "Sorry, pardner. You'll have to take that gun to the Marshal's Office."

"Since when?"

"Since right now. There's placards all over. New city ruling."

"I don't go no place without my gun."

"You better take it right out of town then."

"You Wyatt Earp?"

"That's right."

"Well, hell. If I got to, I got to."

Farther down the street, behind the picket fence fronting the O. K. Corral, Ike, Finn and Billy Clanton, Wes Fuller, Billy Claibourne, and Tom and Frank McLowry were getting off their horses with a clinking of spur chains. John Ringo, coming out of the shadows, walked up to them. "He's at Scheiffelin Hall, no gun."

Ike grinned. "Let's go."

* * *

WYATT'S back looked broad against the light as he stood in the doorway peering into the semi-darkened hall, listening to the singing.

"Earp!" a voice said sharply.

Wyatt casually turned, holding his hands well out from his body to signify his peaceful intentions. His glance took in the shapes of eight waiting men. Eddie Foy sang on, but around Wyatt now was a creeping stillness. It was plain by their faces they were here for a purpose which had nothing to do with the performance going on inside.

"Been a long time, Ike," Wyatt said, smiling easily. "Hello, Ringo. Still renting your gun to the highest bidder?"

Ike started for the doorway. Wyatt stepped into his path. They stood face to face, Clanton burly and scowling, Wyatt coldly watchful. "Where do you figure you're going?" he asked.

"We come to take in the show. You got any objections?"

"Not if you figure to check those pistols."

"What *is* this!" Ike Clanton's powerful shoulders tipped forward as he bent at the knees to drive a hand belt ward. Before his spread fingers got hold of the weapon, Wyatt's right fist crashed into the big rancher's jaw. In the same split second, his left snatched the pistol from Clanton's holster. Ike staggered back, cursing. His friends were about to make a play for their own guns when Virgil Earp said back of them:

"Hold it!"

Ike, twisting a look blackly over his shoulder, saw Virgil, Morgan, young Jimmy, Clum, and Doc Holliday in the middle of the street with leveled shotguns.

"I guess you know most of my brothers," Wyatt said. "That jasper in the middle is Doc Holliday, and the gent on his right is Mr. J. P. Clum, esteemed editor of the local paper and presently head of the Tombstone Citizens' Committee."

Ike made a loud noise. "That bunch of old grannies are a laugh. If you're smart, you'll haul freight. You're a marked man, mister."

"You're the one who's marked, Ike. You'd better put on some specs and take a good look at yourself before they start shoveling dirt in on you. This town is fed up with you and that bunch of plug-uglies you run with. There's a new deal in Tombstone. The next time you ride in leave your guns at home, or you'll go out feet first."

He gave Clum the nod, and the group around the

publisher closed in on the Clanton hardcases and started moving them off toward the edge of town. Wyatt stood fast, and as they tramped sullenly past, he reached out, catching young Billy Clanton by the arm.

"Just a minute," he said, pulling the boy off to one side. "Aren't you a little bit young to be packing a six-shooter?"

"You wanta try me?"

"I would like to prevent you from getting yourself killed. I think you're the one who likes to fancy himself another Billy the Kid, isn't that right? Well, let me tell you something, son. The real Kid's dead, and that's where you'll be if you don't snap out of the way you're heading. How old are you, sixteen?"

"I kin take care of myself," Billy scowled.

"You'll never make seventeen hanging onto that attitude. You go on home and think it over."

Billy, starting to turn, went for his pistol. Wyatt kicked it out of his hand. "Your brothers teach you to draw on an unarmed man?"

Billy, bunching his fists, wading in, started swinging. Wyatt spun him around, roughly shoved him away. Then, picking up the pistol, he tossed it to the boy. "You don't have to prove anything to me," he said gruffly. "Go on home before you get into trouble."

Startled, bewildered, in a maze of indecision, young Clanton turned and went scuffling off.

* * *

NEXT DAY, Wyatt tilted back in a chair on the porch of the Marshal's Office, watched the stage pull in with his brothers, Morgan, and Virgil. They watched John

Ringo weave up to the coach, pull open a door and haul a laughing Kate Fisher out into his arms, kissing her loudly, then spinning her around to slap a hand against her bustle-covered bottom.

"And there comes trouble," Wyatt said, softly swearing.

Morgan peered at the woman. "Who is she?"

"Kate Fisher. Doc's bed partner in Dodge. Damn her mixed-up soul, she just couldn't stay away."

Virgil said, *"The* Kate Fisher?"

"I said so, didn't I?" Wyatt watched her and the gunfighter cross the street arm in arm. "Virg, find out where she's stayin.' I better get hold of Doc."

* * *

IN THE ALHAMBRA SALOON, Doc and five others were engaged in draw poker, Doc being currently elbow-deep in chips.

One of his companions said, "Two pair. Aces over."

"Three small deuces." Doc grinned and raked in the pot.

As it happened, he looked up just as Kate and Ringo came into the place, still loudly talking. Ringo steered them, without noticing Doc, over to a table right next to him. Apparently, Kate had not discovered Doc either.

Doc, though endeavoring to ignore them, was plainly uncomfortable.

Ringo yelled, "Hey, waiter! Whiskey down here, an' leave the bottle."

"Wake up Doc, your deal."

Doc flipped in his ante, dexterously shuffled and offered the cut. "Three-card draw, jacks or better."

"Nice town, huh, Kate?" Ringo said loudly.

Kate, more guardedly, "You're going to take care of what I wrote you about?"

Ringo laughed. "Didn't I say so?"

The muscles stood out in Doc's cheeks like white worms. The player across from him said, "Beats me." The one on his left said, "I'll open."

At the table back of Doc a bottle thumped against wood. The eyes in Kate's twisting head incredibly widened. She came around in her chair, shaken but glaring. "Well, well," she said hoarsely, "if it ain't the little deputy!"

"I pass," Doc said and put down his cards. He sat there, waxen, his knuckles white against the table.

Kate leaned over him. "Can't you say hello to a flame that's fallen into sparks among the ashes?"

"Cards?" Doc said.

The man next on his left said, "Three," and dropped his discard.

The fellow next around, face twitching with fright, desperately managed to whisper: "One."

"Say, deputy!" Kate's voice carried over the room. "Mr. Virtue still keeping you under his wing?"

The whole saloon sat frozen. Doc put down the deck, the sound of it loud as a face being slapped in that brittle quiet. He stood up without haste and got into his coat.

Kate cried shrilly, "Not leavin' are you, deputy?"

"Sure he's leavin'," Ringo sneered. "He's fixin' to run over and get his pal."

"You're drunk," Doc sighed, looking full at him then.

"Ain't that the way you made your rep, shootin' down drunks?"

"I'm warning you," Doc said thickly.

"Hear that, folks? Killer Holliday is warnin' me! What am I supposed to do now, drop dead?"

Doc said harshly, "You're a fool for letting her get you steamed up."

"An' I say you're yeller!"

"Good night, Ringo." Doc picked up his hat.

"Oh, no you don't. You ain't skinnin' out till I git done talkin.' I got somethin' to settle with you from Dodge City. I'm goin' over to the hotel and get my persuader." Ringo stepped up to him, sneering, and tapped his chest. "I'll be standin' outside, waitin' for you, in about two minutes. You hear? Two minutes!"

Ringo walked around him and pushed through the doors.

The room was a sea of white faces, but none so livid as the face of Doc Holliday, so humiliated and furious it looked as though he would strangle.

"I said I'd see you dead," Kate whispered.

Wheeling, brushing past the spectacular bosom which seemed in imminent prospect of bursting in all its surging magnificence from the downy nest Kate's skill had fashioned, the consumptive dandy, shrugging out of his coat, walked the length of the bar and went still-faced around it to reappear in the harness of fastened straps that held a shoulder gun in place. A lane opened up before the push of that stare down which Doc, traveling as though to a gallows, slowly made his trek to the doors:

When he appeared on the planks, weirdly illumined in the wavering leap of the orange flares, Ringo, coming off the steps of the Dodge House verandah, moved inexorably into the forty feet of open road which was all that lay between them now.

Ringo's whisker-stubbled lips were pulled apart in a snarl. Doc looked colder than the proverbial well chain. The two shapes paced into point blank range and were that way, crouching when a gun blast ripped the groan of silence and scared the quivering bejazus out of half the avid watchers. Both men whipped about as though jerked by a single string.

Ringo's wide-sprung eyes looked frantic. Doc's gray stare was hotly furious.

Virgil Earp, cutting out of the streetside shadows with a shotgun gripped in his white-knuckled fists, called: "Go for your guns and I'll cut you in half!"

Ringo, reckless with the whiskey inside him, tipped back his head in a derisive guffaw. "Sure... sure," he chortled, flapping his arms. "I wouldn't hurt that little bastard fer nothin.'" Doubled up with his guffaws he staggered around in a circle holding onto his sides.

Doc, bitter as gall, stalked off down the street with a towering indignation in the direction of the Cosmopolitan. Virgil, pounding up behind him, got hold of an arm and swung him about just as he reached the hotel door. He was white with an outrage that matched Doc's own.

"What kind of a sucker play was that! That would have been all the excuse Ike Clanton's hunting to start a goddam war around here!"

"What the hell do you think I'm made of?"

"We'll bust those owl hooting sons of bitches," Virg said, "but we'll by God do it *our* way!"

"You keep on playing pattycake they'll cut you to pieces!"

Virgil began shaking Doc in a temper. "You stay out of this!"

"Get your hands off me!"

Virgil slammed him against the door. Doc's pistol jumped into his hand quick as the flick of a lizard's tongue. Shaking with rage, he snarled into Virg's face, "You better thank God, you're Wyatt Earp's brother." Knocking the marshal's hand away, he spun on his heel and jerked open the door.

"Wait a minute!"

Doc went still in his tracks, but he didn't turn. Virgil said back of him, "If you care anything about Wyatt you'll get out of this town. Having a killer like you on our backs is makin' this job about three times as tough."

ELEVEN

WYATT FOUND Doc sitting in his room with a bottle. Doc looked ugly as a teased snake. Wyatt sat down on the bed with a sigh. "Doc, I understand you're about to pull out of here."

"You bet your goddam boots I am! I'm taking the stage out of here in the morning!"

"Kind of figured this climate agreed with you. Didn't you tell me you thought it would be good for that cough?"

"I'll tell you something, I've taken enough!" He got onto his feet and stomped round the room. "Being here is causing me one hell of a pile of embarrassment. Why some of these halfwits even think I'm a lawman!"

"Well," Wyatt said thoughtfully, "I can't really blame you for cuttin' your string. If things had been different, but this isn't your fight."

"It sure as hell isn't!" Doc glowered at him, pacing, chewed his lip, and came back. He said, more reasonably, "I could get along in this town if... Well, there's no use pushing it at somebody else. What's done is done and no one but a fool would waste time looking back." He said, watching Wyatt's face, "I *would* kind of like to square with Ringo though. That sonofabitch really gets in my hair."

"Don't worry about him. He'll be taken care of along with the Clanton's." Wyatt stood up. "One thing: I don't want you shovin' out on my account."

"*Your* account! Are you loco? You got nothing to do with my leaving."

They looked at each other through several moments of silence. Wyatt said abruptly, "Well, take care of yourself," and reached for the door.

"Too bad," Doc said, "we can't be in at the finish together. I feel like I'm leaving the best part of me here." His eyes tightened up; he cleared his throat noisily.

"It's just not in the cards," Wyatt said. He paused as though he might say something more, maybe making it some harder for Doc to haul his freight. But, shutting his mouth, he turned and went out.

Doc stood there, listening to him go down the stairs. Then, gritting his teeth, he smashed the fist of one hand angrily into the other.

* * *

VIRGIL, the next morning, was in the office reading a batch of mail he had just fetched back from the postal premises when Wyatt with Clum stepped in off the porch. Virg tossed a folded paper at Clum. "Here's the answer to that letter Wyatt wrote."

Wyatt, reading over Clum's shoulder, said, "That's it! You'll get all the action you're wanting now. How long will it take to round up those fifty deputies you promised?"

"Not long," the newspaperman said grimly. "I can probably produce them inside of three days."

"All right, get busy. And try to keep this as quiet as you can."

"Right!" Clum said and, squaring his shoulders, departed like a sergeant who'd been stepped up two full grades.

Several minutes later Morgan and James came in packing a passed-out Billy Clanton between them. Virgil, frowning, said, "Where'd you pick up that?"

"Alhambra," Jimmy grinned. "He was stretched out in the sawdust taking up room for three at the bar."

"He's got a snootful," Morg said contemptuously.

"Expect we'd better throw him in and let him sleep it off?'

"Hold on," Wyatt said. "Let me think about this." He tapped the letter they'd discussed with Clum. "Let me have him."

Stooping, he flipped young Billy over his shoulder like a sack of oats. "Think I'll take a little ride out toward Charleston."

"You droppin' in on the Clanton's?" Virgil asked sharply.

"Just a neighborly visit."

"You crazy?" Morgan growled.

Wyatt carried Billy through the door. On the porch steps, he smiled. "I don't think so."

"You better take your gun," Virgil grumbled.

They had fetched Billy's horse. Wyatt untied it and his own from the rail and, laying Billy over the saddle, he took the reins of the Clanton horse, climbed aboard his own, and said, "Pass him up to me." He waved the letter at them. "This is all the ammunition I'll need." He gathered up the reins of both mounts. "If I'm not back in a couple or three hours you can have John Clum and his Citizens' Committee come drag me out of there," he said with a laugh.

* * *

WYATT, still riding the cruppers behind his saddle and with the prostrate Billy draped unconsciously across it, jogged along through the bright slant of morning sunlight as apparently unconcerned as though this were something he did every day of the week. The whole country figured the Clanton tribe to be rougher than cobs and Wyatt reckoned they probably were, but when he came up with a hunch to do a certain thing he pretty generally did it, come hell or high water. There was some good in this kid if a man had the patience to dig it out. He kept his eyes skinned, not being minded to ride into an ambush, but about all he saw on the ride out was cattle. There seemed, giving credence to the stories he'd heard, to be thousands of head tramping over this range, a whole heap too many for the grass that was on it. Ike could mighty soon be in a bind unless he moved them, and there was another angle that would be gnawing at Ike. The most of these critters were almost certainly stolen stock, though a man might find proving this difficult. These were longhorns, wild but good rustlers. Trouble was, there wasn't much left on this range, including cactus.

After a time, Wyatt picked out the buildings of the Clanton headquarters. These were sun-warped and paint less, appearing sadly neglected. Most of the windows were shutterless; several of them did not even have any glass. A board above the twelve-foot top of the horse gate bore a single word: CLANTON. Below, attached to the two center rails with baling wire was another reading bluntly: TRESPASSERS WILL BE SHOT ON SIGHT.

Wyatt put his horse through the gate, hauled Billy's horse after him, and pushed the rickety affair shut, dropping a wire loop over the end pole. He rode on toward the house. There were a few parched geraniums in a circle of stones a few feet from the pump.

Wyatt, getting down, hauled Billy off and vigorously shook him. He looked about as sick as the geraniums, but he was conscious. Wyatt shook him again, finally slapped his face when the lad showed signs of buckling at the knees. "Stand on your feet, boy."

Billy shook his head and peered around like a halfwit. Mrs. Clanton came out, gnarled hands half hidden in a twist of her skirt.

"Afternoon, ma'am." Wyatt touched his hat. "Sorry to be the bearer of unpleasant news, but Billy here got himself liquored up."

"I don't know what in the world's to become of that boy. I can't think what I'm goin' to do with him."

"I'll get him sobered up."

The old lady, distraught and obviously in a flutter, led the way into the house which, though scrupulously clean, was frowsy as to furnishings. Wyatt propelled Billy by the scruff of the neck. Turned loose, Billy slumped into a chair he pulled out from the table, sheepishly avoiding his mother's eye. She fetched them both steaming mugs of coffee. "The way he's goin',"

Mrs. Clanton said, "he'll end up like his father, shot down stealing cattle. Ike and Finn are well along the road."

She scooted a worried glance at the marshal. "I can't stop them. I've preached till I'm hoarse. It's too late for them but why in the name of God."

Wyatt nodded. "Think you're pretty touch, son? I've never seen a gunslinger yet that lived to celebrate his thirty-fifth birthday."

He stood up. "I thank you for the coffee, ma'am."

"Mr. Earp," Billy stammered, "I... nothin,' nothin,' never mind."

"Think I don't know what's inside of you? I had two older brothers. They fought in the war. I was too young. But, by gollies, I sure done my best to live up to them, just the same as you're tryin' to live up to Ike an' Finn."

"You, you really know about that, huh?"

"It's a natural thing. But I've learned one thing about gunfighters. No matter how good you are there's generally somebody just a shade faster, and the more you work with a gun the quicker you're goin' to meet that man."

It was plain enough that Wyatt was reaching the boy. Billy was turning over Wyatt's words, frowning, wary but confused, not knowing what to think. Wyatt sat down again, close to the boy, waving Mrs. Clanton back.

"It ain't," Billy said, "that I want to be a gunfighter. It's... it's, just that sometimes I... I get so goddam lonesome."

"Gunfighting, boy, is a pretty lonesome trade. Matter of fact, I get lonely myself."

"You? Aw, you mean that?" The marshal's words appeared to have a considerable impact on the boy.

"Gunfighters are the loneliest men on the face of God's earth, Billy. They live in fear, generally die without a dime, or a woman. Without even a friend."

"I... I never thought about it that way. I always figured, gosh! You ain't pullin' my leg are you, Mr. Earp?"

"I surely ain't, Mr. Clanton." Wyatt chuckled. "My friends all call me, Wyatt, Billy."

Billy's eyes were round, but something was troubling him. He said in a voice that was wistful, uncertain, "I always kind of had a cravin' to be."

"To be what, Billy?"

"You ain't goin' to laugh, are you?"

"I won't laugh."

"Well, I'd sure would like to be a vetinery. You know, one of them docs that takes care of animals. I like to be around dogs an' horses. Seems like I got away with them, only, only Ike an' Finn, they claim that's sissy stuff. Is it?"

"I don't think so. Wanting to be a vet is a right fine thing. Seems to me like it is." He got up again. Billy grabbed at his sleeve...

"Could I come talk to you sometime about it? I mean."

"Come anytime, son. Maybe we can work it so's you can go to one of them veterinarian schools."

Mrs. Clanton came forward. "You listen to the marshal. Never mind what your brothers say, you listern to the marshal. He's a man whose word don't need no bond. When he says a thing's so, it's so forever."

The boy put his arms around his mother, hiding his

face behind her head. "I won't do it no more, Maw. I swear I won't. I'll die in bed like you wanted Paw to, with my boots off."

"Oh, son!" she cried. "Son...."

Wyatt walked softly out of the house.

He was about to mount up when the sound of hoofs coming fast pulled him round. Ike and Cotton Wilson in a fog of dust came tearing down the lane from the gate. Ike Clanton came off his horse in one jump. His face was wild. "What you doin' here?"

"I brought your kid brother home, drunk." Wyatt tried to step past Ike to get on his horse, but Clanton grabbed his arm. Wyatt yanked the arm free. Ike's other fist slid down to his gun.

"You're leavin' all right, but not on no horse. Start hikin'."

"That would be a mistake that might get you killed. Some of my friends in Tombstone are apt to get the wind up if I'm not back soon."

"That don't cut no ice with me! You're outa your bailiwick."

"You sure about that?" Wyatt, grinning thinly, took a paper out of his pocket. "I expect it'll be a disappointment to you, but this is my appointment as a United States Marshal. Here, look it over."

Ike stood there stunned. The sheriff's jaw sagged.

Clanton came out of his confusion first. He backed off a step, cuffed some dust off his pants legs, and rasped the hand across his jowls. "Wait a minute," he growled. "Let's talk about this. I know we ain't often seen eye to eye, but I got nothin' ag'in' you, personal. I ain't lookin' for no fight, but Goddamit you got to stop crowdin' me. Why!" he said gruffly, "why don't we set a spell an' hash over this thing? I'll make you the best deal I know how. The best damn deal any star packer ever got dumped in his lap."

"The only deal," Wyatt said, "I'll ever make with you would be to run that herd straight back into Mexico." Shoving past the two frustrated, angry men, he got into his saddle and rode off up the lane. He should have been a little nervous; he had every right to be. If he had turned for one backward look his would have seen Clanton struggling to throw off the clamped grip with which Cotton Wilson was desperately combating every attempt the burly rancher made to bring his gun into line with the marshal's back.

* * *

WHEN THE NEW U.S. Marshal returned to the county seat, a reception committee composed of his brothers and J. P. Clum were anxiously standing before the door of the town Marshal's Office. Wyatt, pulling up before the hitch-rail, eyed them quizzically. "Where's the funeral?"

"By God, you had us worried," Virgil declared, letting out his breath.

"What happened out there?" Morgan asked.

Wyatt swung down, tossed his reins over the rail, ducked under it himself, and stepped up onto the porch. "Better get your men in, John," he said to Clum. "It looks like we got a war on our hands."

He entered the office, the rest of them following.

* * *

BACK AT THE CLANTON RANCH, Ike was furiously pacing the kitchen. Standing around the room were Ringo, Finn Clanton, and Tom and Frank McLowry. In the background Kate Fisher, hovering over the stove was brewing up a fresh pot of coffee. Neither Billy nor his mother were present at this conclave.

"What's keepin' that coffee?" Ringo growled.

"Be ready in a minute."

Cotton Wilson came in, mopping his face and puffing.

Ike jabbed at him with an angry finger. "You see the judge?"

Cotton jerked his head. "I seen him."

"Well, what the hell did he have to say?"

"No help there. Claims there ain't no legal way he kin keep a U. S. Marshal outa the county. He was packin' up to leave. Prob'ly more'n halfway to Utah by now. That town's really got the wind up. You never seen so many scairt fools in your life."

Ike slammed the table with a furious fist. Frank McLowry said nervous-like, "Mebbe it's time we was all packin' up." And Cotton Wilson grumbled, "It sure don't look good, don't look good at all, Ike. Before you know it that bunch will hev a whole army of gun throwers. They're swearin' in deputy U. S. Marshals fast as they kin write their names. You can't sell the herd an' you can't git a shippin' point."

"Ain't you the little ray of sunshine!" This from Kate, handing out mugs of coffee. "Why don't you dig a hole and crawl into it?"

Cotton glared.

Finn Clanton said, "Won't make no deal, eh?"

"Only deals bein' made is fer us to git planted."

"Shut up!" Ike roared and took a turn around the room. "One thing we can do, by God. We didn't have no trouble before them Earp's took over this country. Get rid of them Earp's an' the rest of that crowd'll cave like a bunch of pukin' pigeons!"

Tom McLowry said, "Mebbe we wouldn't hev to go that far. It's Wyatt thet's holdin' thet whole bunch t' taw. Git rid of him."

"We'll get rid of all of 'em," Ike snarled, banging his fists on the table.

"Makes sense to me," Ringo drunkenly offered. "Git rid of them Earp's an' we can take over everythin.'" He twisted his head to send a wink at Kate. "I'll take care of Doc Holliday myse'f."

"We'll ambush the bunch of them," Ike said.

"Shoot 'em into dollrags," Finn Clanton laughed. "Cut off their heads an' put 'em up on poles. That'll show 'em!"

The sheriff said, "It's Wyatt an' that sneerin' sonofa-bitchin' Doc."

"They've broke up," Kate said. "Doc's pulling out. Ringo made him look like a monkey. It did my poor heart good to see him crawl."

"You talkin' about *Doc Holliday?*" Finn looked at her skeptically, and Frank McLowry said, "That's a powerful lot to swaller, even if you seen it."

"Never mind," Ike growled. "We'll get them all."

"What about Cluni an' his Citizens' Committee?" the sheriff said. "What about them deputies Wyatt's swearin' in?"

"Cut off the head and the snake may wriggle but it sure as hell won't be doin' no bitin,'" Finn said. "Them boys got a lot of family pride. Comes right down to the pinch."

"Comes down to the pinch," Ike grinned, "they'll be standin' alone. Let's quit the yappin' an' get down to brass tacks."

He saw the sheriff sleeving off his face again.

"You scared of this, Cotton?"

"Well, Christ, I can't shoot another lawman." He swallowed uncomfortably. "I... I can't do you no good in a deal like that."

"You're in this up to your goddam neck! You're stayin' in, savvy?"

The sheriff's eyes squirmed away, and John Ringo's drunken laugh filled the room.

Ike finished his coffee. "We'll fix it up to get Wyatt when they make their last rounds. Tonight, I'm talkin' about."

"You better get all of them," Kate said vindictively.

"We'll get 'em," Ike said.

TWELVE

IT MAY STAGGER the contemporary reader to envisage a group homicide as cold-bloodedly conceived and entered upon as the bushwhacking planned for the Earp's by the Clanton's. But these people were feudists; with them, a grudge was a killing affair and Ike had never gotten over the gnawing suspicion that his father's death had been engineered by an Earp. And a lot of side issues were wrapped up in his decision. He was tied in with Curly Bill, self-styled leader of the local "cowboys," a confederacy of outlaws numbering over four hundred hard-riding men, and Ike was pretty certain the Earp's knew this. Pima County in those days was the wildest place in the American West, if not the wildest place the West has ever known. And Ike had told the whole truth when he said, "Get rid of them Earp's an' the rest of that crowd'll cave like a bunch of pukin' pigeons!" Get rid of the Earp's and they could plunder at will.

* * *

BACK IN TOWN that night it was getting along toward midnight when young Jimmy Earp came into the office with a jug of hot coffee. Wyatt, half across the desk with his face in his arms, looked up, fully roused, when the door swung open. Seeing his brother he sat up, stretched his arms to get the kinks from his back, and knuckled his eyes, managing a grin when he smelled the hot Java.

"Tired?" Jimmy asked.

"Yeah. Guess I must have been dozing. How's things outside, steaming up like usual?"

"Nothing new. Betty thought you might like something hot."

Jimmy poured the smoking liquid into a tin cup. Wyatt drank it and smacked his lips, afterward wiping the wet ends of his mustache. "Hits the spot, all right. Whew!"

Young Jimmy, at the window, was staring out at the town. "Seems powerful quiet, too quiet, Virg thinks. You reckon we'll have to fight it out with that bunch?"

"Wish I knew," Wyatt said reflectively. "Ike's in a bind. Those stolen cows have gobbled up all his graze. One way or another he's sure got to move 'em. He *might* just decide this deal is too rough and push them back into Mexico, but that wouldn't be like him. The McLowry's are in this, too, probably some more of that Curly Bill bunch. This no-gun edict has hit them all. They daren't come in here without their guns... When you look the facts of this straight in the face, they'd be ridin' high except for us Earp's."

He got up and stomped about. "There's another angle, too. There's a lot of counts piled up against Ike.

He's managed to get rid of most of the witnesses and he's likely wondering why I didn't fetch him in today. Time's runnin' out on him and don't think he doesn't know it."

Jimmy, slouched with a hip on a corner of the desk, looked as though his mind was miles and miles away. Wyatt, grinning, said, "Itchin' to get back to Californy?"

"I been thinkin' about it."

"Must be quite a girl."

"You ought to see her," Jimmy cried enthusiastically. "But I'm glad I came over here. It's the first time we've really been away from each other in the two years I've known her. It's made me see things clearer. It's like I'm all unstuck, only half a person. I'm glad I found this out before I..." He looked around at his brother guiltily. "I'm sorry, Wyatt."

"Hell don't mind me. I'm glad you found out, too, Jimmy. Best thing you can do is go back there and marry her. Leave star packin' to the fools like me." He picked up his hat. "Guess I better be makin' the rounds."

Jimmy said contritely, "Why don't you go in the back an' stretch out? I'll make the check. You look beat."

"Guess I could use a nap," Wyatt said through a yawn.

"Go ahead," the youngster urged. "I'll wake you up when I get back."

"You're a good kid, Jimmy Did I ever tell you that?"

The boy, grinning self-consciously, strapped on a shell belt, and stepped out on the street.

* * *

FROM THE MOUTH of the O. K. Corral, not too much of Fremont Street was in sight. The livery business was on the south side of the wide dirt road and the business establishments in this block were not of the character which sought night trade; only the O. K. Corral did a round-the-clock schedule.

It was crowding midnight when James Earp, moving along the north side checking doors, came past the dark front of the *Epitaph* office. The town's main drag was Allen Street, one block south. There were congregated the better hotels, saloons, and eating places, a good portion of the nightlife so frequently making the public prints.

The one hotel on Fremont, the Aztec House, was one block west. Jimmy could see its feeble lights, but these did nothing to dispel the roundabout blackness of deep-piled shadows. He didn't mind the dark; it was an old story with him and an adjunct he'd expected. But he didn't much care for the quality of the quiet that seemed to grow more solid, more uncannily stealthy, the nearer he came to the O. K. Corral. There were no bird or cricket sounds, only this vacuum of soundless hush through which his boot steps echoed hollowly. He could be heard even though he could not be seen well enough to be distinguished if there were anyone around.

He scoffed at himself but the tightness building inside him would neither go away nor loosen. He felt the probe of unseen eyes and told himself he was acting like a chicken-livered fool. Just the same, he wished now he had not volunteered to make this round.

He was directly across from the O. K. Corral when a horse whinnied sharply, breaking off in full voice. He thought to hear lesser sounds, perhaps a scuffle, the crack of leather. He crossed the dust of the road, eyes narrowed, cat footed, the gun half lifted in his hand as he tried to pierce the heavy blackness shrouding the livery's entrance.

As he drew nearer, Jimmy thought to pick out a vague blur of movement back where the night loomed inkiest. Stopped cold, he peered wide-eyed and had about convinced himself it was nothing but a figment of his imagination when flame and the lethal burst from six pistols blasted the silence into a cacophony of tumbling echoes.

Jimmy staggered, was whipped around in the slap of bullets, thrown against the scarred post of a hitching rail, down which he sagged into a motionless heap. His hat, fallen off, careened around in a circle and came to a wobbly stop about a foot away from his limp left hand.

A flurry of hoofbeats, thudding over the street, dimmed out in a diminishing whisper of sound.

* * *

THIS WAS OCTOBER OF 1881. Thus far, during his tenure of office as town marshal, Virgil Earp had little more to show for his efforts than his predecessor, Marshal Fred White, whom Curly Bill had shot down in his infamous demonstration of the "road agent's spin." Shootings continued unabated and, when nothing else could relieve their boredom, cowhands in from the roundabout ranches blew off excess steam in target matches that, as often as not, wound up in a gunfight. George Parsons, generally preoccupied with affairs of the soul, not long before had recorded in his diary: "Benson Corral man shot Calhoun but didn't hurt him much. Things continue lively." Several months back the Alhambra Saloon had been "treed" and taken over by Curly Bill's gang of roughneck cowboys who had then run everyone off the streets. And now James Earp lay dead in the dust. Lively times indeed!

* * *

WYATT, sitting bolt upright on his cot in the Marshal's Office, had no idea what had awakened him. But almost at once, he heard a dim outburst of shouts. Stamping into his boots he jumped up, flung his gun belt around him, and ran onto the street, the racket off yonder easily guiding him to the scene of his brother's murder.

A considerable crowd was standing around. He found Virgil's wife sitting on the ground with Jimmy's head in her lap. Lanterns showed her to stricken for tears. Morgan, kneeling nearby, had hold of one of the youngster's wrists. Virgil, back of Betty, had his hands on her shoulders. Morgan, dropping Jimmy's hand, rose to his feet just as Wyatt shoved through to them. "He's gone," Morgan said with his face hard as flint.

"Why," Virgil whispered, "did I send for him? Why?"

"You can't take the blame for this on yourself," Morgan growled." "It's bound to have been some of those goddam cowboys."

Wyatt strode off into the corral where he sagged against the rails trying to shut out the sight of his dead brother's body. A hand, reaching out of the shadows, gently squeezed Wyatt's shoulder.

Wyatt, recognizing Doc, said, "I thought you'd gone."

"Not yet. Not sure I will now. Things are shaping up pretty fast around here."

Wyatt rasped his jaw. "This is plain enough for me. Ike has called the play. Look around at those shells, a typical Clanton stunt by God. Well," he said, heading back toward the street, "he ain't goin' to get away with it."

Going back to the Cosmopolitan, the consumptive dentist-turned-gambler put down half a bottle of his "cough medicine," strapped on his gun rig, and returned to the street. A few minutes later Kate, in her boarding house, looked up from throwing things into a trunk to see the door burst open and her old wrestling partner, like a volcano about to erupt, standing there baleful as a scorpion with its tail up.

She stood petrified with fright as Doc, stepping into the room, cuffed the door shut behind him. "Taking a little trip?"

Kate thought her knees were going to come apart right under her. She'd had plenty of chance to know from firsthand experience just how mean a varmint he could be when he put his mind to it.

Watching him the way one snake will another, she commenced to edge away, trying to put the bed between them. Beneath his natty mustache, Doc's mouth writhed into a sneer. Step for step he moved inexorably after her, chuckling deep in his throat as her frantic eyes got bigger and brighter, her flaccid cheeks more pinched and chalky.

"No, Doc, no!"

"Start talking."

"I don't!"

"Never mind the lies. You been layin' with Ringo. He was in on it. Talk or by God, I'll twist it out of you."

She came up against the wall and there was no place else to go. She cringed and shook. Her hands came up as though by so frail a barrier she desperately thought to fend him away. "I.. you got to believe me! I didn't want that boy to get killed."

"Talk, you slut, before I cut the nose right out of that face."

"You know how it's been. I've messed everything up, but it's part your fault, too! You know how I am about you. I... I thought if Wyatt was out of the way you'd come

back, that things would be like they was before. I must have been out of my mind," she sobbed, but Doc's bleak face did not soften at all.

"Where, when did they hatch up this deal?"

"Today. Out at Ike's ranch."

"Who was there?"

She tried to hedge. "What do you want from me, Doc?"

"The names of every whippoorwill out there, every sonofabitch that pulled a trigger!"

"But it, they never knew it was James."

Doc started to reach, and she cried with her eyes rolling back like a bronc's, "It was Ike and Finn, Cotton Wilson, the McLowry's. "

"Wasn't Ringo there?"

She bobbed her head, speechless, then grabbed hold of new breath and said, "Wes Fuller, too."

There was a murderous rage in every inch of Doc's face, in the blazing eyes, the bared glint of his teeth.

Kate twisted away and tripped over a stool. A scream of sheer fright came wildly out of her as she scrabbled on hands and knees to get up. "Don't kill me, Doc, don't kill me!" she moaned.

She sprang up in a terrified lunge for the door, but he cut her off and she dived under the bed, crying, "No! No! No!" She came upon the far side and, hardly knowing what she did, rushed into a corner and found herself trapped. Her eyes bulged in horror as the gambler stalked after her, nastily grinning. Babbling, whimpering, clothes disheveled, cheeks pasty, she looked altogether crazy.

She had plenty of right to with Doc's strangling fingers reaching for her throat. "Doc! Don't!" she gasped, almost swooning with terror.

She closed her eyes to shut out the look of him and could still see, as against a pink fog, the kaleidoscopic whirl of light and shadow, but the hands never touched her. She heard his racking cough and she jerked open half-crazy eyes saw him reeling and gasping, clutching at his chest as he floundered blindly toward the bed.

Like a terrified rabbit, Katie jumped for the door.

But with her hand on the knob, she paused for a backward look to find him, still gagging and gasping, groveling on the bed in the frightful doubled over agony of the continuing paroxysm... saw him tangled in the bedspread, writhing off onto the floor.

She had the door open now. Shaking, uncontrollably whimpering, she stumbled into the hallway. But her legs would not take her farther. She stood mired in her own confusion, bound to the man as with ropes of steel. She peered again and was lost. "Doc! My God, oh, Doc!," she sobbed, and ran back, dropping onto the floor, frenziedly flinging her arms about him.

She got him onto his knees. The coughing stopped. Doc looked at her in wonder, then his glance fell away. He dragged a sleeve across his mouth and swore. Their cheeks came together, his arms locked tight around her. "Forgive me, Kate," he whispered into her hair.

She got one of his arms hooked over her shoulder and, someway, got him onto his feet. "It's goin' to be all right, honey. It will be all right. Put your weight on me. I'm going to take care of you."

* * *

PERHAPS A FEW MINUTES LATER, back at the Marshal's Office Wyatt, signing deeply, snuffed the lamp in the bracket above his desk and, clapping on his hat, stepped out onto the porch and locked the door.

He thrust the key in his pocket, bleakly eyeing the street, the shafts of light and deeper blackness, the three or four hipshot horses half asleep on tied reins in front of the Alhambra and the Occidental next door. Bob Hatch's, just east of the Alhambra, was dark and, as he stored with bitter thoughts, remembering the girl who would be waiting for Jimmy across the empty miles, a sudden stirring in the shadows dropped the spread of his hand to leather. The gun leaped free, and he whipped it up.

"Wyatt! Wyatt over here! It's me, Billy Clanton!"

Wyatt, gun leveled, walked into the pooled gloom of the arcade's overhang. "What are you doing here, Billy?"

The boy swallowed uncomfortably. "Ike told me to find you."

Wyatt pouched his gun. His left fist lashed out, meatily striking the boy in the face. Flung backward by the blow, he caromed off a hitching rail and fell into a water trough.

Gasping, teeth chattering and thoroughly soaked, he fished himself out and stood dripping and silent until Wyatt took hold of the front of his shirt. "I... I never had nothin' to do with that, with what happened to Jimmy. I never knew."

Wyatt drew back his fist with a snarl.

"You got to believe me!" Billy wailed. "You got to!"

The bunched shirt gradually slipped from Wyatt's loosening grip. "I'm sorry, son. I shouldn't of done that."

Just because your name is Clanton... I'm sorry, boy."

The marshal stepped back. "What was it you wanted to tell me?"

It was hard to make out the boy's face in these shadows.

"Ike... Ike wants to meet with you and your brothers. He wants to meet you man to man, he says, with no interference from Clum or his bunch."

Wyatt eyed the boy a long moment, wishing there might have been more light on him, or some other manner by which he could better gauge the sincerity of this message. "Where is Ike now?" he said finally.

"I don't know."

The marshal snorted. "Well, you can tell him I'll, sure enough, meet him. How many's he bringin'?"

"Finn, Ike himself, Ringo, and the McLowry's. Six of us."

"Where's this meetin' to be, and when?"

Billy hitched at his pants and said, "Sun-up. At the O. K. Corral."

"It would be there," Wyatt growled. "Who did he think he was shootin' tonight?"

"I don't know anything about that. I didn't even hear about it till it was over an' done with."

"I'll take your word for it. You said six of you. Who's the other one?"

The boy shifted his weight. "I'll be comin' with them."

"That all the sense you've got? Don't be a fool! Give yourself a chance, boy."

Billy said doggedly, "You can't make a silk purse out of a sow's ear. I've thought about this thing, real hard. But I'm in it. I'm a Clanton, too. How could I stay out of it? Ike an' Finn, they're my brothers, you know. Can't." He resumed desperately, "Can't you understand, Mr. Earp? Mebbe it ain't what I want, but they're my *brothers*."

Wyatt nodded. "I understand, son."

For a little longer the boy stood there, watching him. Then, whirling with a catch of breath he could not altogether hide, he disappeared into the deeper dark.

THIRTEEN

MORGAN, Wyatt and Virgin, half an hour later, sat grimly about the cleared table in the kitchen of Virgil's house at the western end of Fremont Street. Wyatt had just given the other the news. Betty Earp, one hand on her husband's shoulder, stood rigidly, palely, staring at Wyatt.

"How can you, *all of you*, sit there so calmly, and' discuss what amounts to cold-blooded murder! How *can* you?"

"It ain't easy," Wyatt said, "but it's sure got to be done."

And Morgan said, "Jimmy'll never rest easy until..."

"You make me tired, you men with your antiquated notions of 'honor.' How do *you* know," she stormed, "what Jimmy would have wanted? At least," she said bitterly, "you can take enough deputies along to make it even!"

Virgil shook his head. "Now, Sugar, it was just us Ike invited. He ruled out Clum, an' that's just the same as rulin' out deputies. It's us Earp's he aims to bust caps at."

"Arjd has taken good care to make sure he gets the job done. Six to three, you ought to have your heads looked at!"

"Well, it's done now," Morgan said. "Wyatt's give his word."

"To a bunch of bushwhackers who have just cut down his brother!"

Wyatt sighed.

Virgil said, "Betty, you don't understand. This is personal between us boys an' the Clanton's."

"But they've got the McLowry's and Ringo in on it. You're lawmen, all three of you! You've no business," she cried, "to put a personal issue above the safety of this town. Your duty is to the people, not to your stubborn pride."

When they refused to comment she seemed ready to hit them. "Oh, you proud, proud men, look at you!" Her scathing eyes raked the three impartially. "And what about me? And your children?" she lashed at Virgil. "Have you given us a thought? You're not humans! You're no better than animals!"

Virgil, scowling, got out of his chair. "That's enough!"

She whirled on Morgan. "Have you told your wife she'll be a widow tomorrow?"

Virgil roughly took hold of her shoulder. "I'd think you'd better leave the room."

She glared through red-rimmed eyes and stalked out. None of the brothers looked at each other. In that frozen silence they resembled effigies of men, plaster facsimiles, colored and clothed, but with no more warmth than you'd find in a bartender's heart.

Betty, cheeks tear-streaked, reappeared in the doorway. "Virgil, your son wants to kiss you goodnight."

Virgil, gritting his teeth, stamped out of the room. Morgan and Wyatt swapped uncomfortable glances. "Could we do it without him?"

"It's rough enough now, two to one, an' Ringo in it. Maybe," Morgan scowled, "you ought to of given us a little more leeway. Well, the hell with it. If we're going to cash in our chips, we'll cash 'em, I reckon. I know one thing: I'll take that bastardly Ike along with me!"

Wyatt sighed heavily. He pushed back from the table, got up, and put on his hat. "See you in the mornin.'"

Morgan nodded and followed him out.

Wyatt struck off through the dark, prowling aimlessly, morosely preoccupied with the things in his head. Not that he didn't have his guard up. He was always vigilant-it was the price he paid for continued existence, but he didn't in these few moments particularly care what happened to him. He was filled with a great and almighty weariness, a surfeit of gunplay. He would have liked to walk off and put it all behind.

In some ways Betty was right. Ike had tricked him. Trading on a man's pride, his vanity, Ike, in ruling Clum out, had played the three of them for suckers. He had gambled that Wyatt, all steamed up over Jimmy, would be too outraged and proud not to fall for this deal. Ike had them where he wanted them now.

Wyatt went down the middle of Fremont Street, walking east through the dust in a kind of numb shuffle. He stopped for some while when he came to the corral, just standing there, staring at it, cursing it finally before he moved on.

At the corner he turned into Fourth Street, passing the dark hulk of the Post Office, continuing south. There were still a couple of dim-lighted windows at the back of the Can-Can Restaurant on the northwest corner of Allen. He considered going in for a steak but finally plodded on, headed for his room at the Cosmopolitan. Old memories, old faces, tugged at him, taking his mind back to better times, days when he hadn't the woes of the world on his back.

He stepped up onto the porch and pulled open the door. In the dim hallway, still troubled, he paused in front of his door and stood a moment in meditation. Then he put out his hand and took hold of the knob, but he did not at once turn it. He stared over a shoulder at the door across the way. He chewed on his lip and frowning, wheeling, went over, brought up his hand, and gave an undecided knock.

"Come in," Doc growled. "And if it's trouble you're huntin,' come a-shootin.'"

Wyatt pushed open the door.

Doc lay sprawled on the bed, still with his clothes on, one arm, hanging over, almost touching the floor. On the boards, a little way from his fingers, Wyatt saw a tipped-over empty whiskey bottle. And he thought how like the skinny bastard this was.

"Oh, it's you," Doc muttered, bleary-eyed.

Stepping over to the bed Wyatt shook the gambler's shoulder. "Why the hell don't you go to bed proper? Sit up! I'll help you get out of those clothes. You smell like a calf in' pen!"

"Go away," Doc mumbled. "I'm sick. Leave me alone."

"You ought to be sick, swillin' that coffin varnish." Wyatt shook him again. Doc lay as limp as a bar rag. There appeared to be something folded into his left fist. Out of idle curiosity, Wyatt pried open the fingers. He found himself holding a broken watch. Engraved on the back was a minute inscription. *To our Beloved Son, Doctor John Holliday.*

Rolling Doc over onto his back Wyatt caught hold of him by the shoulders, trounced him around, and yelled, "Doc! Wake up! You hear me? Wake up!"

Doc groaned and coughed.

"Damn it," Wyatt snarled, "for Chrissake, wake up! You can't let me down now!"

"Take your hands off him," Kate said, coming out of a horsehair chair in the shadows. Stepping nearer she turned up the wick of the lamp. "Can't you see he's dying?"

The marshal stared in disbelief. His hands fell open, allowing Doc to drop back on the rumpled bed. Shaking his head, still with that baffled expression on his face, Wyatt backed over to the door and out into the hall.

Inside his own room Wyatt, slamming the door, strode over to a chest of drawers, yanked open the top one, hauled out a bottle, and stood impatiently picking and prying at the cork. In mounting exasperation, he broke off the neck of the bottle against the chest and upended it, downing a king-sized slug, nearly half of it trickling off his chin onto his shirtfront. "Whew!" he sighed on an outgoing breath and stood there scowling, trying to figure this, trying to get up Kate's words to the

facts as he knew them. It just didn't seem possible old
Doc could be actually on the way out. He was still
standing there when a quick tap of knuckles spun him
round to face the door. He let go of the bottle. His blur-
ring hand came up with a pistol. He went into a crouch
as the door cracked open.

His jaw sagged numbly when he found himself
peering unbelievingly at Laura. He couldn't seem to
collect his wits.

"I was in Tucson." She considered him gravely.
"Everyone's been talking about you and the Clanton's.
It's all over the country. Is it true what they're saying?"

Wyatt swallowed uncomfortably. "What are they
saying?"

"That you're going to shoot it out. It... it's just a
crazy rumor, isn't it?" She searched his face. Her shoulders appeared to sag a little. "It's true. You really
intend to."

"But!" He couldn't seem to find the things he had
any right to tell her. His face turned bleak. "They killed
Jimmy, Laura, bushwhacked him. Shot him down
without a chance."

The steadiness of her regard turned him restive. He
discovered he still held the pistol. He pouched it,
embarrassed, and stepped back a little, frowning. The
hopelessness that turned him inwardly hollow played
on his nerves and stirred up a gnawing feeling of guilt.
He lashed out at her angrily, "Can't you understand this
is something I have to do?"

"Yes. I can see that. You will always be confronted
with these things you have to do. I don't know why I
bothered to come here." She smiled wanly. "It was
pretty foolish of me, wasn't it?"

Her eyes watched him, still with the faint shine of hope; when that faded, when she would have left, he cried, "Laura!" and she turned back. He came toward her. "Laura, I'm scared," he said.

It was a strange admission for the Lion of Tombstone, the Iron Marshal. As though a dam somewhere inside had burst, he rushed on. "Someone told me, years ago, that this would happen. I couldn't believe it. I... I can't understand myself. Something's wrong with me. It's like everything inside had suddenly been ripped out of me. That's crazy, ain't it?"

She could only stand there dumbly.

He hauled her to him. His arms closed round her. He clutched her as though he would never let her go. "I need you, Laura!"

She could feel him shaking. She passed her stroking hands through his hair. "I've wanted so long, and so much, to hear that."

"You'll stay. You *will* stay, won't you?"

"Yes. I suppose I could stay, tonight, anyway, while you need me. But tomorrow...."

She closed the lids of her eyes against tears, "Tomorrow you'll be Wyatt Earp again, the stone-faced Marshal, the scourge of bandits. Tomorrow you'll be embarrassed to remember you could bring yourself to call for help. You'll be ashamed of it, Wyatt. Or you'll be dead."

"Just hold me," Wyatt said.

She put her arms around him and pressed his cheek against her breast.

FOURTEEN

THE FIRST CREEPING rays of the awakening sun touched a far hanging bank of clouds with pink, and a lot of folks saw this what would not normally have been up. Except for perhaps Doc Holliday, the whole town was aware that today was special, extra special because unless one side or the other begged off the Earp's and the Clanton's would meet for a shootout. Through the night this news had spread like wildfire and already the windows and doors of establishments overlooking the prospective site of the battle were crammed with avid, excited faces. Even the roofs were alive with people. Betting was rampant.

On the seat of a spring wagon bound for town, Mrs. Clanton sat hunched over the reins with her mouth tight locked and her eyes like agate. Ahead, the black rim of the mesa showed a capping of gold as, leaping to her feet, she began to whip up the team.

In Virgil's kitchen, Betty Earp stood peering with brimming eyes through the east window. She had young Tommy in her arms. Her husband's departing stride, the sudden slamming of the door, crashed against her ears with the numbing impact of a bullet.

The sun climbed with a poky, maddening indifference.

A cock crowed down in the bottoms somewhere and a wind sprang up and light rushed over the town in a golden floor, but no birds sang.

Inside Wyatt's room at the Cosmopolitan, Laura sat frozen as he buckled on his shell belts and checked the loads of his long-barreled pistols. He turned and for a moment looked mutely in her direction. Then he caught up a shotgun, pulled open the door, and went off down the hall, leaving Laura listening to the diminishing pound of his boots.

Somewhere another door slammed shut.

Where were the Clanton's?

Virgil and Morgan Earp were sighted walking slowly up Fourth between Allen and Fremont, both dressed in the black frock coats of gamblers. Then Wyatt was sighted cutting in from the left. His stride was brisk, his face expressionless. He carried a shotgun under one arm. The sun struck glints from the badge that now and again was uncovered by his open coat.

Doc, in his room, heard Wyatt stomp down the hall. He was awake and sober, but still, on his back, shoulders propped with pillows. He felt a vague curiosity as to what might have put Wyatt abroad so early. He told himself it was no skin off his nose, but he could not put his strange uneasiness aside.

Six riders cut darkly over the rim of the mesa and came on without talk up Allen and north on Third and around into Fremont, entering the corral, where they got off their horses and hitched them.

Ike spruced up in his cowboy best, stared around, looking over the situation. This O. K. Corral was a livery stable with open-air pens for the horses at the rear, that much of it extending no farther than an alley bisecting the block from east to west. North of the alley was an open yard. Fencing it across the Fourth Street end was the photoshop and studio of C. S. Fly. An assayer's office provided a wall on the Third Street side, and here for the moment both Clanton's, the two McLowry's and Claibourne were standing. Wes Fuller had stepped over to the alley to look about for the Earp's and make sure his friends were not surprised.

Meanwhile, on Fourth Street, Morgan and Virgil had been joined by Wyatt. Morgan, attempting to strike a lighter note, remarked. "You look like you've made up your mind to something. You're not aiming to call this deal off, I hope?"

"I guess," Virgil winked, "he's been wrasslin' with his conscience."

Wyatt, peering over at the assayer's office, seeming to be grimly studying the door, did not bother to answer this badinage. He did, indeed, have a rather determined expression on his face, eyes half shut, wholly absorbed in whatever had hold of him. It was here that Doc, hurrying north off Allen, caught up with them, breathing heavily.

When he got back enough of his wind to speak, he said rather testily, "A fine bunch you are, sneaking off with never a word. If Laura..."

"No sense," Wyatt growled, "you gettin' mixed up in a deal that was aimed primarily at me. Those rustlin' sons are after me, personal, an' after Virgil as chief upholder of the faw around here. It's got nothing to do with you, Doc."

"That's a hell of a thing for you to say to me!" Doc snarled, affronted.

He had some right to his outrage. Having spent most of the night sleeping off his jag, and no remembrance of Wyatt having come to his room, he would have remained totally unaware of what was impending if Laura hadn't burst into the room crying, "Doc! Get up! They're all fixed to slaughter each other over at the O. K. Corral!"

"Who? What?" Doc stumbled from the bed, fighting to hold his balance while the room spun around him, and trying to think what he had done with his pistol.

"The McLowry's, the Clanton's."

"Doc, you can't!" Kate said, coming out of her chair. "You can't hardly stand up!"

Doc squeezed his eyes shut, impatiently knuckling them. "Get out of my way, woman."

"No! I won't let you!" Glaring furiously at Laura, Kate cried, "Can't you see he's too weak, too sick to stand up? Ain't you got no decency in you at all? Doc, you get back in that bed."

He threw her hands off him. "Be still! You and I, we don't matter, never have an' never will. Wyatt's chewed off too big a chunk this time, and what happens to him could affect the whole country, set things back twenty years. He's got to have help, no two ways about it."

He got his gun rig buckled and shrugged into a gray coat, clapped on his hat, and went reeling through the door, leaving Kate fuming at Laura.

The crisp morning air, on top of the shock Laura's

words had given him, had by the time he reached Wyatt pretty well sobered him. Seeing him in that pearl gray suit and expensive headgear with a cane in his hand, you would hardly have guessed he'd just come off a bender. His color wasn't good, and bags sagged beneath his eyes. He hadn't stopped to shave but there was a deadly aura about him that turned Wyatt thoughtful. After all, this bunch was after Doc, too; about the only friends the gambler had in this town were the Earp's. He was not a man who made friends, not an easy man to know or like. But his word was good and if you had his allegiance you had it all the way.

"Get rid of that cane." Wyatt passed him the shotgun. "Stick this under your coat." He said to the others, remembering Laura, "We're going to do this different. Those boys are rustlers. Everybody knows it; there are enough counts against Ike to hang him twice over. There'll be no show of weapons. I intend to disarm and arrest the lot of them."

His brothers grunted in astonishment. Doc said, "You crazy?"

"Maybe. We'll pretty soon see."

"And what about Jimmy?" Virgil said. "You forgetting him?"

"I'm not forgetting a thing. We can't go after those boys on a personal basis. As officers, our first loyalty is to the people of Tombstone, to the law itself. It's *law* we're trying to establish in this town. If responsible people make every issue personal we'll never have anything around here but anarchy."

Morgan stared at Wyatt as though completely baffled. "But you told them we'd meet them."

"And so we will, but we'll do it as officers."

"They'll never give up their guns," Virgil said. "It's either wipe us out or they're done, and they know it. You're asking..."

"We've got to try," Wyatt said with finality.

"I've got a hunch," Doc grinned with a wink and a chuckle, "our righteous friend has been listening to a lady." He saw the angry glint coming into Wyatt's eyes and said quickly, getting down to cases, "That bunch, no matter what they proposed, ain't figuring to come out on the short end of this. They're going to have all the help they reckon to need."

Morgan nodded soberly. Wyatt said, "Let's get on with it."

Cotton Wilson, standing with Wes Fuller in the alley, came onto the street, intercepting them. Fuller, ducking back, went hurrying off. Wilson said, "You may have forgotten it, but I'm still sheriff and there's not going to be any gunplay while I'm able to prevent it."

"You figure you're able to, do you?" Wyatt looked him over, plainly skeptical. "I recollect asking for your cooperation. Seems you had a hands-off policy in anything like to advantage your friends."

"It's not a question of friendship."

"You been hobnobbing with 'em." Doc's cold eyes were as gray and hard as bullets. "You just come away from Ike, ain't even heeled, nor Tom McLowry. I've disarmed Wes Fuller."

"I been readin' 'em the riot act. They've seen the light. His shifting glance whipped to Wyatt. "You go starting a gunplay you're done around here." He said, red-faced, "I'll see you strung up!"

"Talk's cheap," Doc scoffed. "I've heard the wind blow before."

Cotton jerked away his angry eyes. "Wyatt, Ike wants to talk."

"Somebody sitting on his shirttail?"

"He'll do his talking over there. I can't blame him."

"Of course you can't, Cotton, not and pocket his money. All right, I'll step over."

"Don't be a fool!" Doc growled.

Morgan said with his face not over a foot from the sheriff: "Do you take us for suckers? We know what's back of this. This whole crummy deal was ribbed up by Ike. They laid for Wyatt last night and got Jimmy. Now they're fixin' to wipe out the rest of us."

"That's a goddam lie!" Wilson shouted.

Wyatt waved, Virgil back. "You've got a number of choices, Cotton. You can yank your iron now, or get on down there with your chums, or you can climb on a horse and start splittin' the breeze. And I'm telling you this in all kindness. The politics that's got you doubled over backward don't make no real never mind to me. What does matter to me is that this here locality has been under the Clanton heel long enough. We're arresting that bunch. Now get out of my way."

He shoved past the livid sheriff and struck off up the street, the others spreading out till their advance occupied the riffled dust from walk to walk, Doc flanking Wyatt.

"I never reckoned," Wyatt said, "you were going to be in on this. I'm not sure if I could have gone through with it without you."

Doc didn't answer, but under his breath, he began softly to whistle.

* * *

WES FULLER, back at the Corral, hurried into the wagon yard. "They're comin,' all four of 'em!" He showed a wolfish grin. "All three Earp's an' Doc!"

"Then we've got 'em where we want 'em. Get that wagon pushed over against the entrance."

He gestured at Ringo, Finn, the McLowry's, and young Billy, who was actually nineteen, not the sixteen Wyatt imagined. Behind his youth, he was as iron-nerved and reckless as the buck-toothed young hellion, Billy the Kid, whom he had adopted as his idol. He actually had more guts than the rest of this tribe all rolled into one. These five manhandled the wagon over to where Ike wanted it. As a matter of fact, this was a covered wagon, and it now pretty completely blocked the mouth of the Corral.

"Tom," Ike said, "you get inside of it. Take your rifle."

"Goddam," Tom growled, "that ain't much cover." And his brother, Frank, said, "I don't like it."

"Who's runnin' this deal?" Ike said.

Tom, still grumbling, got into the wagon. "That's our ace in the hole," Ike said to the others. "We'll draw their attention. All Tom's got to do is cut them sono-fabitches down."

Tom McLowry, then, behind his canvas, was the nearest man to the approaching officers.

Cotton Wilson, sprinting in from the alley, got Ike aside, unloaded his news, and ducked back toward Fremont. Ike and the rest of them deployed to take up positions with the adobe wall of the assayer's shack back of them. Now they could see the four approaching men fanned out across the street. Ringo said, "I'll take care of Doc, personal."

"You, Cotton," Ike growled, "git over there by them horses."

"Jesus Christ!" Cotton snarled, "I can't take part in this!"

"You'll take part. Git over there."

The Earp's and Doc were pretty close in, now, about twenty feet from the wagon-blocked entrance. They were now somewhat shadowed by those across the street buildings but, in all conscience, plain enough to be dropped by Tom McLowry where he hid inside the wagon.

All motion ceased. In this absolute quiet, Wyatt stepped into the full smash of the sun. "Ike," he shouted, "you and your outfit are under arrest for the murder of James Earp. Throw down your guns and walk out with your hands up."

A floorboard screaked inside the wagon. "Hit the dirt!" Doc yelled.

Wyatt was already dropping but the consumptive gambler, on the extreme outside edge, was unable to bring his Greener into play without being as likely to nick friend as foe. Behind his canvas-and-wood barricade, Tom McLowry's rifle sent the first report slam banging across that exploding quiet. The shot, with its ballooning burst of black power, gave away his hidey-hole. Virgil and Morgan, opening up with their six-shooters, splintered the wagon bed and gophered several holes through the rickety sideboards.

Wyatt, scrambling up, plunged over the dust. The Clanton's, ducking with his bullets whanging over them, allowed him to reach the corner of the assayer's shop. Morgan and Virgil, still in Doc's line of fire, prevented him from opening up with the shotgun. He was swearing like a muleskinner, cursing them and the Clanton's impartially. Finn, Billy Clanton, and Ringo made it too hot for Wyatt to quit his captured corner. Ringo, also furiously cursing, tried to get off a shot at Doc but was prevented by the squealing gyrations of the tied and frantic Clanton horses. Powder smoke swirled its stink over everything, reducing visibility, adding nothing at all to the belligerents' accuracy and doubtless, with the churned-up dust, delaying the bloody finish by several hectic seconds.

Cotton Wilson, not far from Wyatt but still in the open, stood shaking in his boots as the battle got underway. Stampeded into a sudden run, he got into the pitching Clanton horses, scrambled aboard one, and cut it loose. Ike Clanton, snarling, drove four shots into the sheriff's back. He might have wasted more if Ringo, furious, hadn't spun him around, pointing him at Doc's abruptly uncovered position.

It was easy, with that racket of shots bursting out, to imagine Virgil's wife Betty, left waiting and frightened in their home down the street, clutching their young son Tommy to her, perhaps lifting a tragic face in prayer.

Wyatt, pinned down behind his corner of the wall by the concentrated fire of Ringo, Billy, and the gaunt Finn Clanton, heard the thump and whine of the lead flying past him. Trying for a look at something to shoot at, he was nearly blinded by a spattering barrage of dust and adobe grit.

Doc saw him reel back. Saw Tom McLowry, abandoning both his cover and rifle, break from the sheeted wagon and, with a six-shooter shoved forgotten in the waistband of his pants, make a desperate dash for the terrified horses which had thus far kept Doc from flanking the main position. Morgan, attempting to do just that, raced into Fremont Street. Finn Clanton, diving forward, scuttled under the wagon, came upon one knee, and triggering furiously, cut Morgan down.

Both Wyatt and Virgil turned their guns on the now exposed Finn. Struck, arms flopping, Finn's hatless head went through the spokes of a wheel. His knees jerked up and then unfolded limply.

Billy Claibourne, sprinting out from his stance somewhat off to one side, started emptying his gun in the direction of Virgil, loosing three wild shots before, panicking, he dashed for the protection of Fly's photographic shop. Wyatt, Doc observed, was under fire from Billy Clanton and Frank McLowry. In the midst of this Wyatt, coming away from his wall in a zigzagging crouch, opened up with both pistols, doubling McLowry who clutched frantically at his belly and dived forward onto his face. Morgan Earp, though wounded and down in the dust, tried to drop Tom McLowry before Tom reached the horses.

Ike Clanton, a six-shooter hanging wholly useless from his fist, stood upright, staring glassy-eyed at the carnage round him until the vision of Claibourne's desertion and Frank McLowry's shriek of anguish as he grabbed both hands to his belly and fell unlocked him from his petrified stance. Pumping frozen legs into a spasm of activity big Ike, loudly yelling for mercy, charged toward Wyatt with both fists over his head.

"You sonofabitch!" Ringo snarled, jerking his gun up. Young Billy, slamming into the gunslinger's shoulder, upset his aim. Staggered by this deliberate collision Ringo was forced to forgo his intention, putting all his anger into keeping his feet.

Wyatt, in all the uproar and confusion, someway managed to keep his head and, with the yelling Ike boiling out of the powder fog practically upon him, almost running him down, had the astonishing forbearance not to put a slug through him. What he did as Ike grabbed hold of him, babbling hysterically not to be killed, was to shake the man off. "This fight's commenced," he snarled, livid with fury. "Get to fighting or get out of my way!"

Fly's studio wasn't ten jumps away and Ike barreled through the door Billy Claibourne shoved open for him.

But there was nothing of the coward about young Billy Clanton, already wounded and with blood running out of him. Nicked by Wyatt and with his right arm broken by a bullet from Virgil, he let go of his pistol, grabbed it into his left hand, and looked for somebody to use it on.

Meanwhile, Doc, in a cursing splutter of impatience at being so long compelled to the rôle of an observer, saw Tom McLowry, among the horses, commence to bang away at Wyatt. Wyatt creased one of the plunging animals; this and another snapped their reins and departed, leaving McLowry in the windy open.

Doc lost no time in throwing down on him. Swinging up his shotgun he emptied both barrels. For a moment it appeared that he had missed completely. McLowry, leaping past the corner of the corral, made off down Fremont at a skittering gallop. But on his seventh or eighth leap, he came apart in the middle and fell all spraddled out, dead enough to skin.

Billy Clanton, badly bleeding but upright and paying no attention to the bullets winging past him, with the gun in his left hand shot Town Marshal Virgil in the thigh, knocking him down. Before Billy could thumb back his hammer again Morgan, also bleeding from a bullet in his right shoulder, came out of the twists of dust and powder smoke and flung Billy back with a slug through the chest.

Doc, throwing his shotgun away, snatched out his nickel-plated Colt.45. Inside Fly's photoshop Claibourne and Ike now went into action, taking the officers from the rear. Morgan, whirling, was smashed back and down.

Doc drove two slugs through the nearest window. The rear door flew open and Ike, legs pistoning, came out with the gigantic jumps of a rabbit. Doc made two more tries but Ike, really heating his axles, loped off out of range and disappeared inside the barn. With but one bean left in the cylinder, Doc faced around and found young Clanton, still upright and dangerous, sidling along the wall toward the relative cover of the corner Wyatt, just moments ago, had abandoned. And Frank McLowry, incredibly up again after his collapse from Wyatt's belly shot, was moving with astounding fortitude and courage in the same direction, bare lipped and snarling, shooting as he went.

Wyatt put a slug through Billy's hips, nailing him in his tracks, but Frank was still on his way toward the street. His gun was up, and he was looking straight at Doc, grinning like a damned hyena.

"Gotcha this time!" he croaked with the blood frothing down his chin.

"All you've got is hell," Doc sneered and, twisting, drawing himself to the lanky full height of a dueler's stance, he squeezed off a shot at the same time Frank did. McLowry's slug scraped a streak of leather off Doc's holster, but the gambler's bullet, the last in his gun, went through Frank's heart. Almost simultaneously Morgan Earp, sprawled and bloody in the dust of the road, put a bullet through Frank's forehead. This time when he dropped, he stayed down, completely motionless.

Young Billy, with his chin on his chest and back, slumped now against the base of the wall, was still trying to get off another shot. Mumbling or muttering, some said later he was praying for just enough strength to do it, he kept desperately trying to bring his gun into line with Wyatt who, holding his fire, continued solemnly to watch him. Doc threw down on Billy Claibourne, now in full flight in the wake of Ike Clanton, but the hammer clicked emptily. Doc had no bullets left.

Billy Clanton finally toppled forward into the dust.

Witnesses have said that, from the time Tom McLowry got off the first shot until the gun dropped out of young Billy's lifeless hand, not over thirty seconds elapsed. The most conservative estimates place the duration of the battle at something under one minute.

Ike Clanton and Claibourne fled like the big-mouthed cowards they were. Both McLowry's, Billy Clanton and Cotton Wilson had gone to their rewards. The town came cautiously out of hiding and those who had been near enough to witness the action began to converge on the scene with diverse exclamations, more than a few of them shaking their heads and feeling inexpressibly thankful to be alive and no worse off than they were.

The power of the Clanton's was forever ended. Virgil, Doc, and Morgan were wounded. Doc had a bullet burn across his back. Morgan had a bullet hole through his right shoulder. Virgil, chief of the town's law enforcement officers, twice wounded, suffered most from the slug young Clanton had driven into his thigh. Only Doc and Wyatt, who had come through the fight unscathed, were able to carry on.

Fortunately, in addition to those coming to view the shambles, a number of Clum's vigilantes arrived to take over the policing of the town, fearing reprisals by others of the cow crowd. Announcing that Virgil and his deputies had their complete support, Clum's men mounted a twenty-four-hour guard to stand off any attempts against the wounded officers, who were promptly removed to Virgil's home.

With the gunshots from the battle crashing around their ears, Kate, and Laura, still in Doc's room at the Cosmopolitan, had been dying a dozen deaths of their own, Laura with her eyes shut, Kate with her head pushed against Laura's shoulder. The reports, though muffled by distance, were all too plain. At last, Kate jumped up. "I can't stand it!" she cried, beside herself, and rushed from the room, Laura hastening after her.

Doc, as he parted from Wyatt at the corner of Fourth, growled, "What in seven hells did you let Ike get away for?"

"He wouldn't draw," Wyatt said. "Did you think I would gun him down in cold blood?"

Right after Doc left him Wyatt heard the hoofbeats of a hard-running team arid saw the Clanton wagon coming. He stepped back on the walk but Mrs. Clanton, recognizing him, flung back on the reins and pulled the lathered broncs up. The old lady and the marshal exchanged a long look. Her eyes fell away from him. With an inarticulate cry, she snatched up the reins and drove on.

There was nothing Wyatt could have said to her, but he regretted it deeply. Too, he wanted to go over to Virgil's place and see how his brothers were getting along; indeed, he had been intending to do this when he'd taken leave of Doc. But it came over him now that his first duty, after all, was to the town and the law whose badge he wore. With a weary sigh, he reckoned he had better go back to the office.

* * *

DOC, almost immediately after leaving the marshal's company, encountered Kate and Laura hurrying toward the O. K. Corral. "Thank God!" Kate cried, trying to fling herself into his arms. The gambler caught her wrists and held her away from him. She started to fly into a rage and then, face went white, still and startled. She knew how intensely he disliked public displays, but she could not keep her concern from showing. "You've been shot!" she gasped. "My God, is it bad, Doc?"

"It's nothing but a scratch," he said, embarrassed and trying to edge around Laura. "If you've got to talk let's do it someplace else."

"Now you stand right there," Kate snapped, getting riled again. "If you're hurt, that's one thing. If you ain't."

Doc said to Laura, "Wyatt's all right. I think he's gone over to Virgil's. Virg and Morgan."

"You listen to me!" Kate shouted. "If you're able to stand here and gab, you can travel. You promised we were going to Bisbee today and I'm not forgettin' it. You go over to that saloon and get in some game we'll never get out of here! This town's...

Laura left them wrangling and moved on up the street. She felt sorry for Kate, but most of Kate's troubles came out of her own nature, her own impatience and foolishness, her own ungovernable rages. Doc wasn't a man who could be handled with belligerence.

She was tremendously relieved to learn that Wyatt had not been hurt. She loved him deeply, she guessed she always would, but she knew him as well as anyone could and was astute enough to see that he would not give up the star now. She tried to analyze her feelings, to study her needs, to discover if there were areas of common interest strong enough to bridge the disparity in their relations.

It was while she was doing this, searching her soul, that she rounded the corner and came abruptly upon him.

Wyatt's eyes lit up. "Laura! My dear!"

She gave him her hands. She saw his dismay when she refused to come into his arms, saw the bleakness enter his expression again, and turn his face unreadable.

"Don't," she whispered. "Don't say it, Wyatt. I'll always love you, but we've come as close to each other as we can. My things are packed, I'm leaving this noon."

* * *

DOC, when Wyatt reached the hotel, was standing by Wyatt's saddled horse, alone and not looking at all his usual immaculate and rather jaunty self.

Stepping over to his horse, Wyatt tightened the

cinches. The street seemed strangely deserted, strangely drab despite the bright sunlight and a freshening breeze.

"So you're finally making it to California," Doc said.

Wyatt frowned into space for a while. "No. I reckon not, Doc," He sighed. "I guess I'm just too set in my ways to get properly interested in a bunch of dumb cows." He laughed shortly, without mirth.

"You're staying here?"

"I'll stay till Virgil gets back on his feet. How about you?"

Doc stared out across the street. "Staying here, with me, is mostly a matter of pride, or maybe damn fool stubbornness. It might be that, like you, I've got into a rut, but it suits me. I'm comfortable." He looked very determined. Then he got to coughing.

Wyatt watched him cover his mouth with a handkerchief.

"You ought to go up to that hospital in Denver."

Doc glanced at the handkerchief and put it away. "And you ought to take Laura and head for California."

"It wouldn't work," Wyatt said. "We both know it."

Both men stood awkwardly silent for a space.

Then Doc, straightening his coat, said, "Let's go have a drink."

IF YOU LIKED THIS, YOU MAY ENJOY:
GUNSMOKE AND THE SHOOTIN' SHERIFF
BY NELSON C. NYE

**From Western Writers of America co-founder
and Spur Award-winning author Nelson C. Nye,
two classic action and adventure Western novels
packaged together for a thrilling read.**

In *Gunsmoke*, the town of Pecos had existed peacefully for
fourteen years, but that idyllic reverie wasn't meant to last.
Sheriff Lawler, a young no nonsense lawman, sees trouble
brewing on the horizon as strangers begin appearing in town.
Just as suddenly as they appear, each one turns up dead,
without rhyme or reason.

The only clue for Lawler to go on is a single-word cryptic
note found with each corpse: *Justice*. Will the sheriff catch
the killer before his warped sense of justice further damages
Pecos, or will he get away scot-free, leaving the terror he's
sown to linger and fester...

In *The Shootin' Sheriff*, sharp-dressed Wild Bill Dorne is
elected by the townsfolk of Spavined Nag, Arizona, and
tasked with cleaning up rustler Pecos Borst's outlaw's
paradise, which has been operating with impunity on the
edge of town for years.

Sharp dressed as he may be, Sheriff Dorne's shootin' is even
sharper, as Borst and his gang find out. They may have
underestimated the fiery red-headed lawman, but will his
skills with a six-shooter be enough to save the day, or will the
creeping tendrils of villainy continue to strangle the town...

**Nelson Nye's award-winning westerns: "Start at
top speed and keep going hell bent-for-leather
through to the smashing finish. The tempo of his**

stories is breakneck from start to finish. With climax piled atop climax." – *Tucson Daily Citizen*

AVAILABLE NOW

ABOUT THE AUTHOR

Nelson C. Nye (1907–1997) was an American author, editor, and reviewer of Western fiction, and wrote non-fiction books on quarter horses. He also wrote fiction using the pseudonyms Clem Colt and Drake C. Denver. Nye wrote over 125 books, won two Spur Awards: one for best Western reviewer and critic, and one for his novel *Long Run*, and in 1968 won the Saddleman Award for ""Outstanding Contributions to the American West."

Nelson Nye was born in Chicago, Illinois. Before becoming a ranch hand in 1935, he wrote publicity releases and book reviews for the Cincinnati Times-Star and the Buffalo Evening News. He published his first novel in 1936 and continued writing for 60 years. He served with the U.S. Army field artillery during World War II. He worked as the horse editor for Texas Livestock Journal from 1949–1952.

In 1953 Nye co-founded the Western Writers of America and served as its first president during 1953–1954. He was also the first editor of *ROUNDUP*, the WWA periodical that is still published today.